"You saw Izzy? Was she okay?"

Brayden hesitated, agitating her more. "Your nanny answered the door. She said Izzy was in bed, that she was sick."

Mila's pulse clamored. "But you didn't see her?"

He shook his head. "I'm afraid not."

Panic shot through her, and she dug her fingers into his arm. "I have to go to her, see her myself. Get her somewhere safe. Once DiSanti realizes what happened here today, he may hurt her or take her away somewhere."

Brayden nodded. "I'll tell Lucas where we're going."

"No," Mila cried. "Don't you understand? He has men at my house. They have guns. Izzy and I were video chatting when they burst in and took them hostage."

Brayden laid his hand over Mila's. The human contact felt comforting and made her want to spill everything to him.

But she still had secrets.

Secrets she had to keep to protect her daughter.

SHIELD AGAINST DANGER

USA TODAY Bestselling Author

RITA HERRON

Previously published as *Hideaway at Hawk's Landing*
and *Cold Case at Cobra Creek*

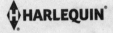

HARLEQUIN

ISBN-13: 978-1-335-42720-5

Shield Against Danger

Copyright © 2022 by Harlequin Books S.A.

Hideaway at Hawk's Landing
First published in 2018. This edition published in 2022.
Copyright © 2018 by Rita B. Herron

Cold Case at Cobra Creek
First published in 2014. This edition published in 2022.
Copyright © 2014 by Rita B. Herron

This edition published by arrangement with Harlequin Books S.A.

For questions and comments about the quality of this book, please contact us at CustomerService@Harlequin.com.

Harlequin Enterprises ULC
22 Adelaide St. West, 41st Floor
Toronto, Ontario M5H 4E3, Canada
www.Harlequin.com

Printed in U.S.A.

Recycling programs for this product may not exist in your area.

CONTENTS

USA TODAY bestselling author **Rita Herron** wrote her first book when she was twelve but didn't think real people grew up to be writers. Now she writes so she doesn't have to get a real job. A former kindergarten teacher and workshop leader, she traded storytelling to kids for writing romance, and now she writes romantic comedies and romantic suspense. Rita lives in Georgia with her family. She loves to hear from readers, so please visit her website, ritaherron.com.

Books by Rita Herron

Harlequin Intrigue

A Badge of Courage Novel

The Secret She Kept

A Badge of Honor Mystery

Mysterious Abduction
Left to Die
Protective Order
Suspicious Circumstances

Badge of Justice

Redemption at Hawk's Landing
Safe at Hawk's Landing
Hideaway at Hawk's Landing
Hostage at Hawk's Landing

Visit the Author Profile page
at Harlequin.com for more titles.

HIDEAWAY
AT HAWK'S LANDING

To my wonderful daughter, Elizabeth,
who helps real victims of domestic violence and
human trafficking every day—you are amazing!

Prologue

"Please, you have to take my baby." The young girl hid in the shadows of the awning, shivering as a dreary rain drizzled down, adding to the winter chill in the air.

Mila Manchester's heart ached for her. She knew her story. She was thirteen years old. Her name was Carina. Her mother had died in childbirth, and her father had abused her. Then he'd sold her to a man who used her as a sex slave.

Mila had helped Carina get to a shelter when she'd first escaped the monster.

Now Carina's slender pale face was shielded by a scarf, and her clothes were dark, allowing her to blend into the night.

A disguise.

She was terrified for her life.

The baby whimpered and Carina rocked her gently in her arms. "If he finds out little Isabella is his, he'll kill me and do God knows what with her."

Fear and grief laced the girl's voice. Carina was just a child herself. She should be in high school, hanging out with girlfriends, attending football games, shopping for dresses for the school dance.

Mila had wanted to report the situation to the police,

but the girl had begged her not to. She'd confided about her pregnancy and claimed that the man didn't know. If he found out, he'd never let her go.

And if she went to the police, he *would* find out.

"Please, you're the only person I trust, Dr. Manchester. Promise me you'll give her a good life," the girl cried.

"Of course I will," Mila said. How could she turn her away? "But what about you? Do you want to stay with me—"

The girl shook her head, her eyes wild with panic. "No, he'll find me and kill both of us."

Mila's heart pounded. Unfortunately, she was right. "What will you do then?"

"I talked to those women at the shelter like you suggested. They know somebody who'll give me a new identity. They've even found me a place to stay so I can go to school."

So, the underground team was still operating. They'd helped so many abused women and children that she'd been afraid the police would shut them down.

Emotions clogged Mila's throat. This girl needed a chance to have a life. And so did the baby.

A noise sounded from the street, and the girl glanced over her shoulder. "They're waiting. This might be my only chance." She kissed the baby on the cheek. "I don't want you to think I'm a terrible mother—"

"I don't," Mila said. "It's obvious you love her, or you wouldn't have come here." But how could she take care of the child when she was just finishing her medical residency herself?

The girl suddenly threw herself against Mila and broke into a sob. Mila wrapped her arms around her and the infant and soothed her. "It's okay, sweetie. What happened to you isn't fair or right. You deserve to go to school and make a life for yourself."

The girl nodded against Mila, but she was crying and trembling as she turned and fled toward the waiting car.

Mila blinked back tears. She could take the child to the authorities. They'd find her a home. One with two parents.

But then she'd never know what happened to her...

And what if Carina came back one day looking for her daughter?

She looked down into the baby's sweet face. Her big eyes were watching her. Then the baby curled a tiny hand against Mila's breast.

Mila's heart melted. This baby needed her. She'd raise her as her own.

And she'd do anything to protect her.

Chapter One

Three years later

Having Isabella, Izzy, had changed Dr. Mila Manchester's life forever. She would do anything for her little girl.

Time to check in.

Mila ducked into the break room at the clinic where she worked and dialed her home number. When she was working, she missed Izzy, but they FaceTimed at least three times a day. And Izzy loved her nanny, Roberta, who'd been a Godsend to them both.

Izzy smiled up at her with big brown eyes. "Mommy, Mommy, Mommy!" Izzy twirled around the kitchen, her sparkling tiara bobbing sideways on her head.

"Look, Mommy, I'm a princess today."

"You're my little princess every day," Mila said with a smile.

Izzy pointed to the sequins on the pink dress Roberta had made for her. "Look, they sparkle."

"I see. I bet when the lights are off, you'll glow in the dark." Mila's heart swelled with love.

Izzy bobbed her head up and down. "That's what Bertie says," Izzy said. She had a difficult time saying

Roberta's full name and had shortened it when she'd first started talking. Roberta didn't seem to mind.

Izzy raced over to the table and picked up a silver glittery wand. "Look, Bertie made this, too, so I can do magic."

"I can't wait to get home so you can show me your magic."

"Home?" Izzy ran around in circles. "Soon?"

"Mommy will be home in a little while." Mila's heart warmed at the sight of Roberta taking a pan of cookies from the oven. "Looks like you and Bertie are making yummy treats."

Roberta smiled from the bar, where she set the hot pan, and Izzy climbed up on the stool beside her. A bowl of chocolate frosting sat on the counter, and she jammed one finger in the bowl, scooped up a glob, then licked it off.

"Yummy!" Izzy squealed.

Mila rubbed her tummy with a grin. "Save me some, sweet girl."

Suddenly the back door into the kitchen at home flew open with a bang. Roberta startled and nearly dropped the second pan of cookies as two men in black stormed in, waving guns.

Mila clutched her phone, her heart pounding. "Roberta, Izzy—"

Roberta screamed and tucked Izzy close to her to protect her as one of the men aimed the semi at her. "Please, don't hurt us!" Roberta cried.

"Izzy, run!" Mila shouted.

But it was too late. Another bear of a man snatched Izzy.

"Put me down!" Izzy kicked and pounded the man's beefy arm with her fists.

He jerked her over his shoulder, then faced Mila. "Dr. Manchester, do what they tell you or you'll never see your daughter again."

They? What was he talking about?

Mila opened her mouth to plead with them, but a loud noise in the back of the clinic made her jump. She clutched her phone with clammy fingers and spun around as the door to the break room opened.

A man wearing all black stood in the doorway, a gun in his hand. "Get rid of the other people in the clinic and do it quietly."

She glanced at her screen again to see if Izzy was okay, but the call had ended. Panic shot through her. Battling the terror gripping her, she crossed her arms and struggled for calm. "You…have my daughter? Why?"

The man in black shrugged, thick brows puckering as he approached. "Do what we tell you and she won't get hurt."

Fear choked Mila. "What do you want?"

"You're going to give our leader a new face. Then we let your family go." He jerked her by the arm and shoved her toward the door. "Now, clear the clinic. The boss wants this done quickly and quietly."

"Who is your boss?"

"No names, Doc. It's better that way."

Mila sucked in a breath. "How do I know you'll keep your word and won't hurt Izzy?"

The man's cold eyes met hers. "You'll just have to trust us."

She didn't trust them at all.

He gestured toward the door, the gun aimed at her chest.

What else could she do? They had her daughter. She had no doubt they would hurt her if she didn't cooperate.

She stepped into the hallway and spotted one of her nurses frowning from the nurses' desk. She must have heard the noise.

"Unless you want her and your other staff to die, you'd better be quiet," the man growled behind her.

Mila nodded and stepped forward to get rid of her staff and the patients in the waiting room.

BRAYDEN HAWK WAS done with women. Especially with fix-ups.

His partner at the law firm, Conrad Barker, had told him Penny Lark was gorgeous. And she had been.

But he'd failed to point out that she had a hole in her head where her brain was supposed to be. That all she cared about was her beauty regime and money and being the focal point on the society page.

Of course, Conrad didn't care. He didn't date women for their brains or because he wanted a future with them. He simply wanted sex.

Tension eased from Brayden as he drove onto Hawk's Landing, the family ranch. The wind whistled through the windows of his SUV, trees swaying slightly in the late fall breeze.

At one time he'd been like Conrad. Not that he wanted a woman for her money, but he hadn't wanted a relationship either.

The last few months with his family had changed everything.

For nearly two decades, the ranch had been a sad, lonely reminder of his missing little sister, Chrissy. And also of the fact that his father had deserted them shortly after her disappearance.

Thankfully, Chrissy's murder had finally been solved and the family had closure.

Shortly after, his oldest brother, Harrison, the sheriff of Tumbleweed, had married Honey Granger.

And a few weeks ago, the next to the oldest brother, Lucas, an FBI agent, had married Charlotte Reacher, a victim in a shooting by a human trafficking ring Lucas was investigating.

On the heels of adding two wives to the family, his mother had opened the ranch to four foster girls, Charlotte's art students, who'd needed a home after Lucas had rescued them from the trafficking ring, an operation known as Shetland.

Unfortunately, the ringleader of the operation had escaped and was in the wind.

And now Honey was pregnant, due in just a few weeks, and the house was alive again with family, with talk of babies and the next generation of Hawks.

Odd how that conversation had sparked thoughts of settling down himself.

Brayden shook off the thought, climbed from the SUV, smiling at the sound of the horses galloping on the hill. Since the girls had moved in, they'd added more livestock, and he'd hired his friend Beau Fortner as foreman of the ranch operation.

His mother swept him into a hug as he entered the foyer. "So glad you made it to dinner, Brayden."

"I wouldn't miss it, Mom." The weekly family get-togethers had meant a lot to his mother during the lean years.

Truth be told, it had meant a lot to him, too. He'd harbored guilt over his sister's disappearance and had needed his family around him.

Charlotte and Honey and the girls were laying out a spread of food that would feed half of Texas while Lucas, Harrison and brother number three, Dexter, stood by the sideboard sipping scotch. Dexter handed him a highball glass, and Brayden inhaled the rich aroma before taking a sip.

"Thanks, I needed this."

"Bad day in court?" Lucas asked.

Brayden shrugged. He would have rather been in court than on that damn date. Thank God it had only been lunch.

His mother called them to the table, and they gathered for the blessing, then the meal. Excited talk of the nursery Honey was putting together for baby Hawk floated between the women while Dexter filled them in on the new horses he'd bought.

Lucas's phone buzzed with a text, earning a chiding look from his mother. She respected all their jobs but insisted they leave their phones and business at the door.

"Sorry, Mom," Lucas murmured. "It's about the Shetland operation."

The room grew quiet. Strained.

Lucas stood and walked to the foyer away from the table. Harrison followed. Tension stretched into a pained silence as they waited to find out if the Shetland ring had struck again.

MILA SWALLOWED BACK the terror clawing at her as she approached the head nurse in the clinic.

"Rhoda, will you please tell everyone to leave? I have to get home to Izzy. She's sick."

Rhoda gave her a worried look. "Is she okay?"

Mila fought a sob, then nodded. "She will be, but she needs her mommy. Just send the patients home and we'll reschedule." She squeezed Rhoda's arm. "You go home, too. I'll close up."

Rhoda was a single mother with a ten-year-old son at home, so she didn't mind an opportunity to take off early.

Mila felt the gunman's eyes piercing her as she watched Rhoda quickly clear the waiting room, then shut down the computer at the nurses' desk.

"Anything else I can do?" Rhoda called from the front.

"No, thanks for handling that. Have a good night with Trey."

Rhoda yelled good-night, then left through the front door.

The gunman motioned for her to lock up, and Mila rushed forward, locked the doors and closed all the blinds. Noises sounded from the back, and she walked toward the exam rooms on shaky legs.

"Why me? Why here?" Mila asked.

The gunman jabbed the gun into her back. "We know you helped some of our girls escape."

A cold chill washed over Mila. Some of their girls?

She had referred a few lost teens at the clinic to the women's shelter. And then there was Izzy's mother...

The back door burst open, and four more armed men strode in, their big bodies shielding another man in a suit who she assumed was the boss.

The guards scanned the interior, their posture braced to shoot. As they parted to search the clinic to make sure they were alone, she got her first real look at the man they called their leader.

Thick black hair framed an angular face that might be handsome if not for the scar running down the side of his cheek and the evil in his black eyes.

Eyes that looked familiar.

Pure panic robbed her breath.

She knew who he was. Arman DiSanti—the man who'd bought and used Izzy's mother as a sex slave.

Did he know that her daughter, Izzy, the little girl they'd taken hostage, was his birth child?

BRAYDEN TRIED TO keep everyone calm as they waited on Lucas to answer the phone call. When Lucas returned, he looked antsy.

"We have a lead on the ringleader of the Shetland operation. We think he's undergoing cosmetic surgery to change his identity." He pulled his keys from his pocket. "I have to go."

Harrison leaned over to give Honey a kiss. "I'm going with him."

As sheriff of Tumbleweed, Harrison had no jurisdiction outside their small town, but he'd caught the case when Charlotte had been shot during the abductions of four students from her art studio. Lucas had been called in then. At this point, the entire family and the girls were all invested in making sure the trafficking ring was shut down for good.

"Need backup?" Dexter asked.

Dex's PI skills had come in handy when they'd been tracking down the missing girls.

Lucas shook his head no. "This is an FBI operation, but thanks."

Charlotte stood and touched her husband's arm. "Where are you going?"

"A clinic outside Austin. Some plastic surgeon named Dr. Manchester is giving the bastard a new face."

Charlotte's eyes widened. "Dr. Manchester?"

Lucas nodded. "Mila Manchester. For all we know, she's on Shetland's payroll. Her volunteer work could be a cover to give her opportunities to do jobs like this."

Charlotte shook her head. "No, Lucas. Mila can't be involved."

Lucas narrowed his eyes at his wife. "You know Dr. Manchester?"

She nodded. "Her mother is the doctor who removed my port-wine birthmark when I was younger. I met Mila when I was at the clinic. And I've read about her volunteer work. She's a good person."

Lucas glanced at the table, where everyone was watching. Fear darkened the teens' faces while worry knitted his mother's brow.

"Maybe you think you know her," Lucas said. "But, Charlotte, these men could be paying her big money to help them."

Charlotte shook her head in denial again. "No, not Mila. She's kind and loving and giving just like her mother was."

Lucas looked torn but dropped a kiss on Charlotte's cheek. "I really have to go. We don't want this guy to get away."

"Be careful," Charlotte said, her voice strained. "And promise me you won't hurt Mila."

Lucas hugged her tightly. "Everything will be okay."

Brayden pushed back from the table and followed

Lucas and Harrison to the door. Dexter was right behind him.

Lucas stepped outside. "I'll call you when we have
him in custody."

Brayden nodded. "Just get the bastard."

Chapter Two

Mila typically took weeks to plan a facial reconstruction surgery. She had several consultations with the patient, conducted an analysis of problematic features needing correction, created computer sketches simulating what the finished product would look like and, if needed, arranged counseling with a professional. She'd also run blood work and tests to verify the patient was healthy enough for surgery.

Sometimes skin grafts were necessary. And sometimes multiple surgeries.

She had no time for any of that today.

DiSanti had shoved a photograph into her hands and told her exactly what he'd wanted. The changes would literally make him unrecognizable.

She'd been working for hours now. Her hand trembled as she finished the last of the sutures around his forehead. Perspiration trickled down the side of her face. Exhaustion bled through every cell in her body, adding to the tension thrumming through her. Her feet ached, her head throbbed and her eyes were blurring.

Twice his blood pressure had risen, and she'd thought she might lose him. That would be a blessing.

But the guards had warned her that if she made a mistake or if he died, she'd pay for it.

"How much longer?" the shortest of the guards asked.

"I'm almost finished. But he's going to need recovery time." She wanted to tell them they were fools to put him through so many alterations in one day. "I told you that I usually perform these procedures in steps."

"We don't have time for that," the bigger brute barked. "Just finish."

Images of Izzy and Roberta, terrified for their lives, taunted her with every minute she worked on the man. So far, she'd reshaped his nose, lifted his eyelids and added fillers to his cheeks and lips. His scar was history, as well.

He looked ten years younger and almost handsome.

But nothing could change the monster beneath that face.

The goons guarding the surgical room remained rigid, guns pointing at her.

Her finger slipped, and she bit her tongue as she dropped the instrument. The guard took a step forward, his glare a warning. If she lost DiSanti, she'd be dead in seconds.

She forced a breath to calm her nerves, then completed the row of stitches, dabbing away blood as she went.

Relieved to finally finish, she gestured toward her patient. "He's going to need rest, ice packs, pain medication. I'll send you with everything you need to take care of him."

A snide grin slid onto the brute's face. "We're not going to take care of him, Doc. You are."

Mila's pulse pounded. "Listen, I did everything you asked. Now let me go home to my little girl."

He shook his head. "Not happening yet. Not until he's healing and we know you didn't pull something on us."

The shorter man's phone buzzed. He stepped aside to answer, then spoke in a low hushed voice. Anger slashed his eyes as he hung up. "We have to move him now. The feds are on their way."

Mila gripped the steel counter where her instruments were spread out. If the feds were coming, maybe they'd save Izzy.

The men jumped into motion. Keeping the IV attached, they rolled the patient through the hallway and loaded him into the back of their van. The bigger guy jerked her arm. "Come on, Doc. Get whatever supplies you need to take care of him and let's go."

She dug her heels in. "Please let me go home to my daughter. I'll gather the supplies and you can take them with you."

He jammed the gun at her temple. "I said move it."

A siren wailed outside. One of the guards rushed in. "We have to go now. The damn feds are here!"

The man dragged her into the hall. She pulled back, desperate to escape. If they took her with them, they'd probably kill her and she'd never see Izzy again.

But the barrel of the gun pressed into her temple. "Fight and I'll kill you right here."

The siren wailed closer. No time to get supplies.

Mila fought a sob as the man dragged her out the back door.

Tires screeched. An SUV careened into the parking lot, a police car following. Blue lights twirled and flickered against the night sky.

Car doors opened, and a man shouted, "Stop, FBI!"

Two of the guards at the back of the van opened fire and men ducked for cover.

The man holding her arm lost his grip and fired back, then motioned for the two guards to get in the van. They jumped inside, while another one rushed into the driver's seat. The engine roared to life, then shouts and bullets flew.

The big guy shoved her toward the van, but she kicked him in the knee. He cursed and pushed her again, but she dived to the side and hit the concrete. Another round of bullets pinged around her, then the big guy jumped inside the vehicle.

Mila covered her head with her hands as the FBI fired at the van. Through the back window the guards unleashed another round.

She screamed as a bullet pinged onto the concrete by her face.

Tires peeled rubber as the van screeched away. Footsteps and shouts followed. The officers were leaving. She raised her head to look around, but a tall, dark-haired man stood over her, his gun aimed at her.

"Dr. Manchester?"

She nodded, her body trembling.

He hauled her to her feet. "You are under arrest."

She opened her mouth to protest. But he spun her around, yanked her arms behind her and snapped handcuffs around her wrists.

KEEPING THE HAWK women calm was an impossible job.

Brayden and Dexter tried everything from encouraging the girls to talk about riding to feigning interest in the plans for Honey's nursery.

The fact that Honey didn't want to talk about the baby's room was not a good sign.

Charlotte paced in front of the fireplace in the den, where they'd gathered to have coffee and the blueberry cobbler his mother had baked. But no one was hungry and everyone wanted drinks instead of coffee. Except for Honey, of course.

"I wish they'd call," Charlotte said as she made the turn at the corner of the fireplace for the dozenth time.

"Harrison has to come back okay." Honey rubbed her growing belly. "This little boy needs his daddy."

An awkward silence followed as her comment hit too close to home. He and his brothers had needed their father, but he'd left and never contacted them again.

"I'm sorry," Honey said. "That was insensitive."

"It's the truth." Their mother patted Honey's shoulder. "We are not keeping secrets or mincing words. Your baby needs Harrison, and he's coming back to you both."

Brayden's phone buzzed, and everyone startled.

"Is it Lucas?" Charlotte asked at the same time Honey asked if it was Harrison.

He checked the number. "Harrison." He quickly connected, then listened.

"I don't have much time. Arman DiSanti was at the clinic in Austin, but he escaped. Two FBI agents chased after him but lost him on the outskirts of Austin. We have an APB out for the van and have alerted all authorities."

The women were boring holes into him with their

anxious expressions. "Are you and Lucas all right?" Brayden asked.

"Yeah," Harrison said. "Lucas arrested Dr. Manchester. We're transporting her to the field office here in Austin for questioning. Tell Honey to go home and get some rest. I'll be home later."

Brayden frowned. "I will."

As soon as he hung up, Charlotte and Honey pounced on him. "What happened? Are they okay?"

"Lucas and Harrison are safe. Unfortunately, DiSanti escaped." Brayden glanced at Honey. "Harrison said for you to go home and rest."

Honey released a sigh of relief. "I know he loves what he does, but I can't help but worry."

Charlotte put her arm around Honey. "Me, too. Every time Lucas leaves the house, I say a prayer that he'll come back in one piece."

Mrs. Hawk clapped her hands. "Well, now that we know our men are safe, how about that pie?"

Honey rubbed her stomach again. "I don't think so, but thanks."

Dexter went for it, but Charlotte declined, then cornered him by the fireplace. "What happened with Mila?"

Brayden reached for the bottle of scotch to pour another drink. He'd held off while they waited, deciding he needed to remain sober in case there was an emergency. He'd only served on the police force a year before deciding on law school, but he knew how dangerous the streets were.

"Brayden, tell me," Charlotte said, an urgency to her voice that made him step away from the bar.

"Lucas arrested her. They're taking her to the field office in Austin for questioning."

Charlotte's face crumpled. "I'm going. I have to see her."

She rushed toward the coat rack in the foyer and retrieved her purse. Brayden hurried after her.

"Wait, Charlotte, I'm sure Lucas will call you."

"He arrested her," Charlotte said. "That's not right. I know Mila wouldn't help those men."

"Apparently, she did," Brayden said. "They were at her clinic."

Charlotte shook her head vigorously. "No. There's more to the story. And she's going to need a lawyer."

Brayden threw up his hands. He didn't want to get in the middle of an argument between Charlotte and his brother.

"Please," Charlotte said. "Go with me and listen to what she has to say."

Her pleading tone sucker punched him. He didn't know Mila Manchester. But he did know Charlotte, and his brother's wife was one of the most honest, caring women he'd ever met.

He tugged his keys from his pocket. "All right, I'll drive you. But I'm not promising anything."

He explained the situation to the family and agreed to keep them posted, then escorted Charlotte to his SUV. Her shaky breathing rattled in the SUV as he drove from the ranch onto the road through town, then to the highway leading to Austin.

"Tell me about this Dr. Manchester," he said as he sped around traffic.

She retrieved a photo of the doctor on her phone. His gut pinched.

Mila Manchester was a plastic surgeon—but she could have passed for a model. Well, maybe not a model. She wasn't rail thin or gaunt-looking or covered in layers of makeup.

Instead she was naturally beautiful. Huge dark eyes stood out against ivory skin and pale pink lips. Her hair was a fiery dark color with streaks of red.

There was also a softness about her that made her look wholesome.

He jerked his eyes back to the road. He couldn't get distracted by her good looks. Sometimes the lookers were shallow beneath.

Charlotte twisted her hands together. "I was born with a port-wine birthmark," Charlotte said. "No one wanted to adopt me because of it. Dr. Manchester, Mila's mother, did volunteer work and removed it for me at no cost." She paused, her voice warbling. "I met Mila the day before the surgery. She was about my age but wasn't turned off by the way I looked. I guess she'd seen worse at her mother's practice."

"Her mother sounds like a saint."

"She was," Charlotte said. "I owe so much to her. And Mila. She visited me every day at the clinic while I healed. She told me she wanted to be like her mother."

Her story was getting to Brayden. "And you think she is?"

Charlotte nodded. "I've read about her work. She's generous and caring and volunteers with Doctors Without Borders… There's no way she'd help the Shetland operation hurt innocent girls."

Brayden hoped she was right. Lucas's wife had been through enough without learning that her friend was a criminal.

They lapsed into silence until they reached Austin and the field office. As they parked and walked in, Charlotte grew more jittery.

Lucas was probably going to kill him for bringing her.

But her description of the doctor had piqued his curiosity.

Harrison met them at the front door.

"Lucas is about to question her," Harrison said.

"I'd like to observe," Brayden said.

Harrison frowned but glanced at Charlotte and seemed to realize Brayden was trying to appease Lucas's wife. He ushered them through security, then to a room with a viewing screen to watch the interrogation.

Brayden's gut tightened as Lucas appeared, his hand on Dr. Manchester's arm.

Damn. Even with her long dark hair tangled and escaping a haphazard ponytail, her clothes disheveled, and her face pale and exhausted-looking, she was stunning.

She heaved a weary breath and looked up at the camera in the corner as if she knew it was there. But she didn't make a move to fix her hair or put on pretenses.

Instead her big brown eyes were haunted and filled with fear.

Fear that made him want to find out the truth about what had happened today. Was she helping the Shetland operation?

Chapter Three

Mila fought tears, but they streamed down her face as Special Agent Lucas Hawk escorted her into an interrogation room.

He'd been careful to explain where they were and that she was in federal custody.

She didn't know what to do. Didn't know if Izzy and Roberta were dead or alive.

Pain mingled with panic at the thought.

If she talked, those terrible men would hurt Izzy.

Agent Hawk placed a bottle of water on the hard surface of the table in the room. She'd seen enough crime shows to know that she was being watched. That they'd record whatever she said. That they'd get her prints from the water bottle.

Sweat beaded on her upper lip and forehead, trickling into her hair.

It had been hours since she'd eaten or drunk anything. Hours since those men had broken in and threatened her. Hours since she'd started the surgeries that would enable that monster to escape.

Agent Hawk was watching her with steely eyes. Another agent named Hoover stood by the door, his arms folded, expression condescending as if he'd already tried and convicted her.

Agent Hawk's boots clicked on the hard floor as he crossed the room. He narrowed his eyes at her as if dissecting her, then removed a key from his pocket and uncuffed her hands.

She breathed out, grateful to be free of the heavy metal on her wrists so she could reach the water. Feeling dehydrated, she turned up the bottle and drank half of it in one long gulp.

Water trickled down her chin, and she wiped at it, then glanced at her fingers. Even though she'd worn gloves during the surgery, the stench of the ugly man's blood lingered.

"Dr. Manchester," Agent Hawk began. "You know the reason you're here?"

She nodded, then looked up at him, but she couldn't stand the accusations in his eyes, so she jerked her gaze back to her hands.

He slapped a photograph of Arman DiSanti onto the table. "You performed plastic surgery on this man today at your clinic?"

She chewed her bottom lip. He knew that or he wouldn't have arrested her.

"Answer me," he said, his tone cold.

She gave a slight nod. What good would a lie do when he'd practically caught her red-handed?

"Arman DiSanti is the man we suspect to be the ringleader of a human trafficking ring called the Shetland operation," Agent Hawk said bluntly. "This group has abducted dozens of teenage girls in Texas this past year."

She willed herself not to react. But Izzy's sweet face crying as that man snatched her taunted her. Where was her little girl now?

The agent paced in front of her, then spread several pictures on the table. "These are photographs of some of the teens abducted this year. At least these are the ones we rescued." He named each girl, then pinned her with an accusatory look as if she was responsible. "No telling how many more victims he's had kidnapped."

She swallowed back bile. She knew what a horrid man he was. That was the reason she'd taken Izzy from her mother to raise her.

The agent laid another photo on the table then another and another. The first one showed a dark building with a cage in it. Blood dotted the floor.

Another photo revealed pictures of chains attached to a pole. Then another yielded a close-up of the words *Help us* crudely etched into the wall.

"He chained them to the wall and locked them in a cage like they were animals." The next picture showed two young teens dressed skimpily as they stood in front of what appeared to be a camera. Both girls were glassy-eyed, drugged.

"Then he sells them at an auction like they're cattle. That's where he got the name Shetland for his operation." He tapped DiSanti's photograph. "This is the man you helped escape the law today, Dr. Manchester." He slapped one more picture on the table, this one of a dead girl, her skeletal figure decaying.

Mila bit back a gasp.

"This is a girl named Louise Summerton. She was murdered when she tried to escape the man who bought her."

Nausea welled in Mila's stomach.

She fought it, but her stomach heaved. Panicked, she covered her mouth, her chest convulsing. The agent at the door must have realized she was going to throw up because he grabbed a trash can and shoved it in front of her.

Emotions overcame her, and tears rained down her face as she retched into the trash can.

BRAYDEN BROKE OUT in a sweat as he watched Mila Manchester purge the contents of her stomach.

"Look at her," Charlotte cried. "Something's terribly wrong, Brayden. Tell Lucas to stop this right now. I want to see Mila."

Brayden gritted his teeth. Lucas was not going to allow that, not until he was satisfied he'd gleaned all the information from Dr. Manchester that he could. He'd been trained in interrogation techniques, taught not to allow emotions to interfere when questioning a suspect.

They'd both also been taught how to read body language. And this woman's body language screamed that she was frightened.

Charlotte reached for the doorknob, but Brayden placed a hand over hers. "Let me handle it."

Tears blurred Charlotte's eyes as she looked at him. "She didn't do this, Brayden. Tell Lucas I know she's innocent."

Except she had operated on the man. Had given him a new face.

She hadn't denied that.

Charlotte lifted her chin. "Tell Lucas I hired you to represent Mila."

Oh boy. That was not going to go over well.

"I don't want to come between you and Lucas—"

"You won't," Charlotte said. "But I have to do what's right. Mila and her mother helped so many people that it's time someone helped Mila."

Maybe she was right.

He stepped into the hallway. Harrison met him, his expression concerned. "Deputy outside Austin spotted the van, but men shot at him, and he lost them. Looks like they're headed west."

"Let's pray they catch them," Charlotte said from behind him.

Harrison nodded. "Did Dr. Manchester give Lucas any information?"

Brayden shook his head. "Not yet."

"I hired Brayden to represent her," Charlotte said in a tone that brooked no argument. "Maybe she'll confide in him."

Harrison's frown was exactly the reaction Brayden expected.

"Tell Lucas I want to talk to her," he said.

"Brayden—"

"Tell him," Charlotte said. "Or I'll go in there and tell him myself."

Brayden fought a tiny smile. Lucas said the woman had spunk. He was right.

Harrison grunted, then gestured for them to follow him, and a minute later, he knocked on the interrogation room, then poked his head in. "Lucas, a word please."

Lucas joined them in the hallway, took one look at Charlotte and grimaced. "You should have stayed home."

Charlotte folded her arms. "I couldn't. I know Mila, and she's innocent."

"We have proof," Lucas said.

Brayden cleared his throat. "Let me talk to her."

"This is an interrogation, Brayden. We're trying to find the man who runs the Shetland ring." He aimed a look at

Charlotte. "You do want him to be arrested, don't you? Because he will keep trafficking young girls unless we stop him."

"Of course I want him to be stopped," Charlotte said, her eyes widening in anger and surprise that Lucas would suggest she didn't.

"Maybe you should let Brayden try," Harrison said. "She might talk to him."

Lucas glared at Harrison. "If he speaks to her as her lawyer, he's bound by attorney-client privilege. What good will that do us?"

Brayden squared his shoulders. "Listen, Lucas, I'll find out the truth. If I think she intentionally helped the Shetland group, I won't represent her." He gestured toward the closed door. "But I was watching what happened in there. She looks terrified. She couldn't fake that kind of reaction when she saw those pictures."

Lucas stood ramrod straight. "Give me another minute. If she doesn't offer anything, then you can come in."

Brayden agreed, and Lucas disappeared inside again. He and Harrison and Charlotte returned to the room to watch the interview.

Mila was wiping her face with a paper towel. She looked pale and fatigued and on the verge of a breakdown.

"Dr. Manchester," Lucas said in a quiet but firm tone. "We know you performed plastic surgery on DiSanti. We just don't know why you helped him."

Mila rubbed her forehead, a sound of anguish coming from her, but she didn't reply.

"We understand that DiSanti will need time to recover from the surgery. He's well guarded by his pit bulls. Where were they taking him?"

Mila's lower lip quivered. "I don't know."

Lucas's jaw snapped tight. "If we don't stop him, he'll kidnap more young girls." Again, Lucas tapped the photos one by one, his tone full of disgust. "More innocent girls who will be turned into sex slaves to build his empire and pad his fortune."

Mila stared at the pictures, ashen faced.

"Where were they going?" Lucas pressed.

Misery darkened Mila's expression as she looked up at Lucas. "I don't know. I honestly don't."

Lucas stared at her for a long minute, then swiped the photographs into a stack, jammed them in an envelope and stalked from the room.

Brayden rushed to meet him in the hall, Harrison and Charlotte on his heels.

"All right, see what you can do," Lucas said. "Finding DiSanti is what matters. Tell her we'll offer her a deal if she talks."

Brayden reached for the door.

"I hope to hell you're right about her," he heard Lucas tell Charlotte just before he stepped inside the room.

One look into Mila's tormented eyes, and Brayden had to remind himself to be neutral. Beautiful women lied and deceived people all the time.

He had to convince her to tell him the truth. That was all that mattered. That and putting the Shetland ring out of business.

MILA TWISTED HER hands together, fighting another wave of nausea. More than anything, she wanted to tell Agent Hawk what was happening. To beg him to send someone to her house and check on Izzy and the nanny.

But if she did and DiSanti found out, they might hurt

Izzy. Her stomach knotted. What if they'd already taken her somewhere?

Panic clawed at her insides. The door opened again, and the agent appeared, but this time another man stood beside him. He was also tall, broad shouldered, muscular, with thick dark hair. They had the same dark brows.

"Dr. Manchester, this is Brayden Hawk. He's an attorney who my wife hired to represent you."

Mila stared at them in confusion. "Excuse me?"

"My wife is Charlotte Reacher," Agent Hawk said. "She's outside and insists you have counsel."

"Charlotte—is your wife?"

"Yes. We met when she was shot by DiSanti's men."

Oh God, that was right. She'd seen the news story. No wonder this man was out to get DiSanti. It was personal.

But he was allowing her an attorney...

Or was it a trap?

It struck her then—the attorney's last name was Hawk just as the agent's was. Were they related?

She scrutinized the men's features. Yes, they had to be brothers.

Agent Hawk gave his brother a dark look, then slipped from the room. Mila's head was spinning.

The lawyer cleared his throat. "Dr. Manchester, I know you've been through hell today. I'd like to hear your side of the story."

Mila's lungs squeezed for air. Was he really here to help her?

Could she trust him with the truth, or would telling him about her daughter being held hostage put Izzy in more danger?

Chapter Four

Brayden studied Mila as Lucas left the interrogation room. Some clients were desperate enough to pour out their story immediately.

Others took finessing. Especially if they were afraid.

And this woman was frightened of something…

Hoping to put her ease, he claimed the chair across from her and adopted a soothing voice. "Dr. Manchester, I agreed to talk to you because Charlotte is concerned about you." He softened his voice. "She believes in you, and Lucas and I both believe in Charlotte."

The woman's face twisted with emotions.

"Anything you tell me is confidential. But if I'm going to represent you, you need to explain your side of the story."

She rubbed her forehead, then looked down at her hands on the table.

"Please talk to me," Brayden said quietly.

Dr. Manchester sighed warily. "I already told you that I don't know where they were taking DiSanti."

Brayden let the silence stretch for a moment. "They didn't mention a city or town?"

She shook her head no. "I'm sorry. I…don't know what else to tell you."

"Stop giving me the runaround," Brayden said, his voice firmer. "Did you know who DiSanti was when you performed plastic surgery on him?"

Fear flashed in her eyes.

"You did," he said, reading her reaction. "But you helped him anyway."

She averted her gaze, then massaged her forehead again with a shaky hand.

"We know DiSanti has amassed a fortune," he continued. "Is that the reason you did it? For the money?"

Her troubled gaze jerked to his, but she bit her lip and didn't answer.

"Charlotte insists you do good work, that you donate your time and expertise to help people, especially children, in trouble." He raised a brow. "That description doesn't fit with you giving someone like DiSanti a new identity."

Dr. Manchester pressed a fist to her mouth and breathed heavily.

"Help me out here, Doc. I'm trying to understand."

"No one can understand," Dr. Manchester said, a warble to her voice.

"I might if you talk to me." Dammit, he wanted to believe her. Wanted her to be the person Charlotte described.

"Did he donate money to the clinic in exchange for a new face?"

She shook her head, misery darkening her eyes.

Brayden's patience was wearing thin. "Did you owe him for some reason?"

She twisted her hands together.

"Come on, Dr. Manchester, I can't help you if you

don't confide in me." He racked his brain for answers, then it hit him. "You're afraid. Did DiSanti and his people threaten you?"

MILA WANTED TO spill the entire story and assure him that she despised DiSanti and his men, that she'd never do anything to help them. That the entire time she'd been operating on him she'd felt sick to her stomach.

Most of all, she wanted to beg Brayden Hawk to check on her daughter.

But what if DiSanti's men were watching?

According to the news, the police suspected DiSanti had a local contact in Tumbleweed. Who knew how many he had in Austin?

Or who they were. He might have contacts right here in the FBI or at the local police department.

She didn't know whom to trust.

Brayden leaned across the table and pierced her with those blue eyes, eyes that were ice-cold. "Talk to me, Doc."

She chose her words carefully. "I wish I could tell you what you want to hear, Mr. Hawk, but I can't."

He cleared his throat. "Please call me Brayden. If you're concerned I'll tell the FBI, you don't have to be. As your attorney, I'm bound by attorney-client privilege."

Maybe she should talk to him. If he understood, he'd send someone to see if Izzy was okay. "He's your brother. How do I know this isn't a trap?"

The ice in his eyes hardened. "Because I'm a man of my word. I chose law to help people." He leaned closer. "And I think you're scared and that you need a friend right now."

Emotions swelled inside her at the compassion in his voice.

She opened her mouth to speak, but the door opened and Agent Hawk appeared again. This time another man in an expensive three-piece suit stood beside him. "Excuse me," Agent Hawk said, "but Mr. Polk, Dr. Manchester's attorney, is here."

The suited man strode into the room, his skin pale, his dark glare intimidating. "Dr. Manchester, don't say another word."

Mila bit her lip. Brayden Hawk frowned and glanced at the man, then back at her. Suspicion took root in his expression, then a flash of anger.

She gripped the chair edge with sweaty fingers.

"Dr. Manchester, is Mr. Polk your attorney?" Brayden asked.

Mila barely stifled a scream of protest. But the attorney shot her a warning look, and she refrained.

"Is he your attorney?" Agent Hawk asked.

She blinked back tears and nodded. But she couldn't look at Brayden. She had a bad feeling that Polk worked for DiSanti and Brayden knew it.

Worse, he hadn't come to help her. He'd come to make sure she kept her mouth shut about DiSanti.

BRAYDEN STOOD, SHOULDERS RIGID, debating how to handle the situation. Dammit, he'd been making headway with Mila Manchester until this lawyer showed up. He'd seen the agony on her face when she'd looked at those pictures and was inclined to believe Charlotte.

Dr. Manchester had been coerced into performing surgery on DiSanti. That was the only explanation that fit.

And he had no doubt that Polk had been sent by DiSanti to protect DiSanti's interests.

Mila looked terrified of the man.

He didn't want to leave her alone with him, but unless she spoke up, he'd have to.

Lucas cleared his throat. "We'll let you talk."

He opened the door and gestured for Brayden to leave.

"What the hell?" Brayden said as they walked down the hall.

Lucas ushered him into a small office next to the interrogation room.

"You know that man is not her attorney," Brayden said. "DiSanti sent him to keep her from talking."

Lucas ran a hand through his hair. "Probably so. But unless she orders him to get lost or decides to answer our questions, there's not a damn thing I can do about it."

He and his brother locked stubborn gazes. "Can't you charge Polk with being an accomplice or something?"

Lucas gave him a wry look. "Not without probable cause or evidence. And we have nothing on the man."

"Then find something," Brayden said. "Because you can't leave Mila alone with him or release her in his custody. He may be the one threatening her."

Lucas narrowed his eyes. "Did she tell you that she was threatened?"

Brayden clamped his mouth closed, frustrated. She hadn't actually said so, but he'd seen the fear in her eyes.

"You know I can't divulge anything she revealed to me in private."

"Right." Their gazes locked again, both at a standstill.

Brayden pasted on his poker face. If he wanted Mila to trust him, he had to prove he was trustworthy.

And that meant honoring Mila's confidence.

If he'd only had five more minutes with her...

"What are you going to do?" Brayden asked his brother.

Lucas scowled. "Find out everything I can on Polk before tomorrow."

"What about tonight?" Brayden asked.

"She'll have to spend the night locked up," Lucas said. "Maybe some time in a cell will persuade her to talk. If not, and Polk returns tomorrow to bail her out, I'll have to release her."

"She'll face charges?"

Lucas nodded. "Yes. It may be the only leverage we have."

God, he hated to see Mila Manchester spend the night in jail. But at least she'd be safe from that bastard DiSanti.

Meanwhile, maybe Lucas could dig up some dirt on Polk, hopefully enough to arrest him and keep him away from Mila.

MILA'S STOMACH KNOTTED as Polk settled into the chair across from her. His tight lips and beady eyes made her want to scream for help from Brayden Hawk.

At least she'd thought Brayden was sincere.

She'd promised to raise Izzy and keep her safe, but she couldn't do that in prison.

"You work for him, don't you?" she asked in a low whisper.

A sinister smile crept onto his face. "What did you tell them?"

She guessed that was her answer. "Nothing."

His thick brows shot up. "Nothing? Are you sure?"

"I'm sure," she said. "I have no idea how they learned he was at my clinic."

"You didn't tip off that nurse to call them?"

"No." Anger made her voice hard. "I did exactly what I was told. Now, where is my daughter? Is she safe?"

He made a low sound in his throat. "What did you think would happen to her when you tried to escape at the clinic?"

Her stomach roiled, tears choking her. She shook her head in denial. They couldn't have hurt her little girl; she had to be all right. Izzy was her whole life.

"Where is she?" she said through gritted teeth. "Did your people hurt her? Because if you did, what's to stop me from talking to the FBI?"

"Now, now, just calm down," the man said in a condescending tone. "Your daughter is safe. At least for now."

Her breath rushed out. She hated this man and DiSanti with every fiber of her being. "She's an innocent little girl," Mila whispered. "Please don't harm her. She has nothing to do with this."

"But she's important to you," Polk said sharply. "So, if you want her to celebrate her next birthday, then you'll cooperate."

"I already did," Mila said. "I performed the damn surgery. DiSanti has his new face, so leave me and my daughter alone."

"You said yourself that there's a risk of infection. Your services may be needed for recovery."

He stood, and ran his hand over his diamond-chip tie clip. "I will be back tomorrow to post bond. Meanwhile, you are not to tell anyone about our conversation. And you won't discuss DiSanti."

He strode to the door and turned back to face her, his look ominous. "Remember what I said. Your daughter has lovely eyes and hair, Dr. Manchester. And a perfect face for now. Wouldn't you hate for something to happen to change that?"

Cold terror shot through Mila. She pressed her hand over her mouth to stifle a scream as he walked out and shut the door behind him.

BRAYDEN DID NOT want to leave Mila locked up in that cell tonight. For all they knew, DiSanti had someone on the inside who might try to hurt her to keep her from talking.

Unless Polk had threatened her into silence.

"Let me talk to her one more time," he said to Lucas.

"She has an attorney," Lucas said tightly. "And you seem to be forgetting that she's a criminal."

"Not if she was coerced." Brayden gritted his teeth. "For God sakes, Lucas, don't be such a hard-ass. Your own wife asked me to represent her."

"I'm doing this for my wife and those girls at Mother's and all the other teens and women DiSanti has forced into sexual slavery."

Brayden silently counted to ten to gather his composure. On the surface, he knew Lucas was right.

But there were extenuating circumstances.

"She was on the verge of talking to me," Brayden said. "Give me one more shot."

A muscle ticked in his brother's jaw. "All right. Five minutes. But then I take her to a holding cell. Maybe a night in lockup will persuade her she needs to come clean."

Brayden agreed. What else could he do?

Lucas escorted him to the interrogation room, his expression grim. If she agreed to accept Polk's help as her attorney, his brother's hands were tied, too.

Brayden forced a neutral expression as he entered the room. The moment he saw the tears in Mila's eyes though, he nearly lost it.

Ever since he'd represented his friend, who'd been wrongly convicted, and gotten him off, he'd earned a reputation for fighting for the underdog.

Mila Manchester might be fooling him. Those tears could be due to the fact that she was upset about getting caught.

Or they were out of fear.

He crossed the room and claimed the chair across from her. "I don't think you wanted to perform plastic surgery on DiSanti, Dr. Manchester," he said quietly. "But I need you to tell me exactly what happened."

Emotions twisted her face, and she averted her gaze from his.

"If you're being coerced, I'll protect you."

She looked down at her hands, then lifted her head and her gaze met his. Emotions warred in her eyes. "Thank you, Mr. Hawk, but you can't help me. Mr. Polk is my attorney."

He studied her for a long minute, frustrated because he sensed she wanted his help, and that she needed it. But as Lucas said, their hands were tied.

He sighed, then stood. "All right. If you change your mind, let me know."

She stared at the card he laid on the table, but didn't

pick it up. He waited another minute, hoping she'd change her mind, but she dropped her gaze to her hands again and remained silent.

Those hands had given DiSanti a new face so he could escape and continue spearheading the Shetland operation.

The man was despicable and needed to be put away.

If he was wrong about Dr. Manchester, she deserved to be prosecuted, as well.

Still, his gut churned as he left the room.

Chapter Five

Frustration filled Brayden as he watched Lucas lock Mila Manchester in a holding cell.

He thought she was terrified and had been coerced. But what if her teary eyes and trembling hands were part of a well-orchestrated act?

Lessons learned in the past taunted him.

He'd been fooled once by a client's lies. A pretty young woman who'd batted innocent-looking eyes at him and cried on his shoulder. A woman who'd used him to put her boyfriend away for a crime that she'd committed. He'd gotten her off, then realized that she was a manipulative user.

Thankfully, she'd tried her scam on another guy and been caught red-handed.

But he'd walked away feeling like a fool and had vowed never to fall for another pretty face again.

Still, the sight of the doctor's forlorn expression as she sank onto that dingy narrow cot made his gut tighten.

He turned away and noticed the same frustration in Lucas's scowl.

"Charlotte's going to be angry," Lucas said between gritted teeth.

Sympathy for Lucas swelled inside him. Charlotte had gone through hell because of the Shetland ring. She'd been injured, had lost her vision for some time and had been sick with worry about her students who'd been kidnapped. She had good reason to want DiSanti locked away.

The fact that she praised the doctor's humanitarianism spoke volumes on Dr. Manchester's behalf.

"What are you going to do?" he asked Lucas.

"Check out that lawyer," Lucas said. "Maybe we can find something to charge him with and force Dr. Manchester's hand."

"I could talk to her coworkers," Brayden offered.

Lucas shrugged. "You aren't her lawyer, Brayden."

Brayden walked beside Lucas until they reached the front door of the field office. "I know. But I might find out something to explain why Dr. Manchester performed surgery on that monster. It just doesn't feel right."

Lucas nodded. "I agree. I'll get our analyst to pull up everything she can find on Polk as well as the doctor."

"There has to be something DiSanti's people used to force her to work for them," Brayden said. "Maybe an indiscretion in the past."

"Or maybe she met him when she was volunteering abroad," Lucas suggested. "Seeing the vast needs and poverty in the underprivileged areas she visited may have driven her to accept money to fund her clinic."

True. For Charlotte's sake, he hoped not.

"You want me to drive Charlotte home?" Brayden asked.

Lucas shook his head. "I need to talk to her myself."

He didn't envy that conversation between his brother and Charlotte.

Meanwhile, he'd talk to Dexter. His PI skills could be helpful in finding information on the doctor's clinic and her coworkers.

Talking to them might provide insight into what had driven Mila Manchester to break the law.

MILA DROPPED HER face into her hands, her body shaking with worry and fear. Where was Izzy now?

Was she safe? Was the nanny still with her? Or had the men taken Izzy somewhere else so the police couldn't find her in case a neighbor reported a disturbance at the house?

She rose and paced the cell, her agitation mounting. The image of that man holding a gun to Roberta and Izzy taunted her. Izzy must be terrified.

She was only three. A tiny little pip-squeak of a girl with big dark eyes and an infectious laugh and an obsession with playing dress up. She loved dolls and pretending she was a princess with a tiara and poufy skirt.

But other times she liked to dig in the earth and play with worms and kick the soccer ball in the backyard.

Izzy had started a campaign to convince Santa to bring her a puppy for Christmas and had drawn pictures and cards of how she'd take care of the animal.

She liked strawberry ice cream with sprinkles and brownies and loved mac and cheese. She enjoyed making her own pizza and PB&J sandwiches. She snacked on carrots and cheese, and apples with peanut butter and wanted b-b's, blueberries, for breakfast with her pancakes.

She hated tuna fish, turned her nose up at broccoli and stirred her green peas around on the plate to make it look like she'd eaten some when she hadn't put a single pea in her mouth.

She was stubborn and loud and messy and got up way too early on the weekends, but Mila loved her with all her heart.

Another wave of fear washed over her.

Even if she did exactly what DiSanti's men instructed her to do, how could she trust that they'd let her go and release Izzy and Roberta?

What if she did everything they demanded, but they killed her when they were finished?

What would happen to her daughter?

She heaved a breath, her lungs aching for air as panic seized her.

Would DiSanti keep her hostage or sell her into his sex slavery business when Izzy got older?

The thought made her so sick inside that she sank onto that thin mattress, then dropped her head down between her knees to keep from passing out.

BRAYDEN TRIED TO stay out of the way as Lucas explained the situation to his wife.

Charlotte burst into tears. "You can't do this, Lucas," Charlotte cried.

Lucas rubbed his wife's arms. "Brayden offered to represent her, but this other lawyer showed up, and she deferred to him."

"There has to be an explanation," Charlotte said.

"If there is, we'll get to the bottom of it." Lucas wrapped his arms around Charlotte and hugged her, the bond between them so strong it made Brayden envious. When they pulled apart, he stroked her arms. "I'll check out this lawyer tonight and see what I can find on him."

He glanced at Brayden as if he needed backup, and

Brayden fought a chuckle. Nothing scared Lucas more than failing his wife.

"Hang in there, Charlotte. I'm going to look into Dr. Manchester's coworkers and see if they know what's going on," Brayden said.

She still looked worried, but she nodded and thanked him.

Brayden said good-night to them then hurried out to his SUV. As soon as he got inside, he phoned Dexter and explained the situation.

"I'll see what I can dig up on her and her staff," Dexter said.

"Let's examine her financials," Brayden said. "If DiSanti paid her, the money should show up somewhere."

"I'm on it," Dexter agreed.

"We need all the information we can gather before Dr. Manchester bonds out," Brayden said. "DiSanti has long-reaching tentacles across the world. If Polk takes her out of the country, we may never see her again."

MILA FINALLY LAY back on the cot. She doubted she could sleep, but she was so exhausted from the grueling hours of surgery and from worrying about her daughter that she practically collapsed.

She closed her eyes and said a prayer that Izzy and Roberta were all right. Roberta loved Izzy and would protect her if she could.

The fact that she might not be able to frightened her the most.

Polk said Izzy was all right. For now.

She had to do whatever they said. She'd give her life to save Izzy.

Carina's young face flashed in her mind. Izzy looked a little like Carina. She just hoped DiSanti didn't see himself in Izzy's eyes.

She hadn't heard from Carina since the night she'd fled in terror. Not that she expected to. But she couldn't help but wonder if the girl was still in school, if she'd found friends or a family where she fit in.

She'd suffered so much abuse at such a young age. That kind of trauma affected most people for life. Add to that trauma the fact that she'd given birth to a baby alone, a baby born from a rape. And then she'd given that child away.

A certain amount of guilt might plague her for that decision, although she had no reason to feel guilty. She'd made the most unselfish choice she could make—she'd put her baby's future before her own.

Had Carina been able to overcome the emotional trauma and focus on making a future for herself?

Unable to keep her eyes open any longer, she finally fell into a deep sleep, a sleep filled with nightmares that made her wrestle with the hard pillow on the cot.

She and Izzy were at the beach. The warm sunshine played off her daughter's dark hair as she raced along the edge of the water. Mila chased after her, laughing as Izzy darted back and forth to dodge the waves. She loved the water and the sand and the creatures they found on the beach.

They watched a baby crab disappear into his home underground, then used plastic sand toys to dig and create a castle complete with a moat. Izzy laughed as she spilled water from the bucket all over her feet, then squealed when Mila picked her up and swung her around.

She dropped her onto the middle of a whale-shaped float, and Izzy laughed in delight as she bounced on a wave.

The next minute, Izzy was screaming in terror. The sun and ocean had disappeared, and a big man was hauling her daughter from their house. Izzy kicked and cried, but the man clamped his hand over her mouth, then tossed her in the back of a van.

Tires squealed and the van screeched away.

A gunshot sounded and Roberta ran after the van. Then Roberta was gone, and the van lurched to a stop at a dark, rotting shed somewhere in the desert. It had to be a million degrees during the day.

And frigid at night.

Desperate to find her daughter, Mila combed the desert, walking miles and miles until she fell face-first into the scorching sand. A storm surfaced, and sand swirled and swirled around her in a blur. She couldn't see anything, not even her own hand in front of her.

Another scream. Izzy. She was lost out there in the sandstorm.

Izzy screamed again, and Mila pushed herself to her hands and knees and crawled forward.

What was that man doing to her daughter?

She had to get to her, to save her...

She was walking again, then running, her feet miring down into the sand...

Then Izzy was in front of her, her little body unmoving, the sand covering her as it raged through the air. She dug with her hands, determined to reach her, but the sand was burying her like quicksand...

Mila jerked awake, shaking and crying, her heart sinking as Izzy disappeared into the ground.

BRAYDEN LOVED THE RANCH, but he and his brothers needed privacy now they were older and busy. Still, his mother had kept rooms for them to use when they visited. Recently, Harrison and Lucas had both built houses on Hawk's Landing for them and their wives.

Brayden and Dex also had offices in Austin. Brayden had rented an apartment above his law office, and Dex found a cabin on the edge of town that he could work out of, as well.

Brayden drove to Dexter's, knowing he couldn't go home and sleep right away, not when Mila Manchester's sad eyes haunted him.

Dexter greeted him with a cold beer. His brother had a state-of-the-art computer system and was a whiz at finding information on the web. Sometimes he sensed Dex didn't follow the rules; then again, that was the reason he'd formed his own PI agency instead of studying law.

If he crossed the line, Brayden didn't want to know about it. So far, Lucas and Harrison hadn't asked questions either. As sheriff, Harrison had called on Dex for help a few times. He was pretty sure Lucas had, too, but Lucas only shared information on a need-to-know basis.

Dex pressed a few keys and a photo of the doctor appeared along with articles on her services for the needy.

"Look at this," Dexter said. "Judging from the awards and press Mila's received, she's everything Charlotte claims. She practically runs her own clinic and offers services pro bono for families and children in need across the country. Hell, across the world."

Brayden's gaze skated over the dozens of articles featuring Mila's mother, Andrea Manchester, and had to agree.

"She's following in her mother's footsteps." Dexter

accessed a photo of Mila's mother receiving an award for her Doctors Without Borders work, just a month before she died in a shooting in Syria. She'd operated on a child born with a cleft lip and cleft palate.

"I suppose it's possible Mila became overwhelmed with the vast needs for her services and the cost, and accepted money to fund her efforts," Dexter said. "But my preliminary search into her financials didn't reveal anything suspicious. No large deposits, no offshore accounts." He gestured toward another computer screen showing the doctor's personal account then her business one. "There is an account for donations that has around a hundred grand, but it'll take me time to sort through the ins and outs of the accounting to see if all the donations are legit."

Brayden scrubbed a hand through his hair. Money could be one motive. But if she'd been coerced, there had to be a more personal reason. "How about family? Does she have parents, a sister or brother, anyone DiSanti might threaten to persuade her to do his dirty work?"

"Wait, this is interesting," Dexter said.

Brayden shifted, hoping his brother had found something he could use to convince Mila to talk to him. "What?"

"Mila was adopted, although both of her adopted parents have passed," Dexter said.

Brayden's brows shot up. "Any information on her birth mother or father?"

Dexter shook his head. "Apparently she was abandoned as a baby. No father listed anywhere. Dr. Andrea Manchester was working at the hospital where Mila was brought in by paramedics. She and her husband adopted Mila."

No wonder she'd wanted to follow in her mother's footsteps. "Anything on her coworkers?" Brayden asked.

Dexter shrugged. "The head nurse is a single mother named Rhoda Zimmerman. She has a ten-year-old son and lives close to the clinic." He pressed the print button and the printer spit out a page of names and addresses. "Other employees include a receptionist, another nurse and a PA."

Brayden checked his watch. "It's too late tonight to talk to any of them. But first thing in the morning, I'll get on it."

"It'll go faster if we divide the list," Dexter said.

"Thanks. I'll take the head nurse and receptionist."

"I'll talk to the others," Dexter offered.

Brayden noticed a file on the desk, one that was labeled Hawk. His gaze shot to his brother, then he gestured to the folder. "What's that about?"

A wary look flashed across Dexter's chiseled face. "A file on Chrissy."

"You were looking for her all these years?"

Dex nodded. "Glad that's settled."

Unfortunately, she was dead and had been since the day she'd gone missing.

"Guess I can put it away now." His brother swept the folder off the desk and jammed it in the drawer.

Something about how quickly he removed it made Brayden suspicious. He could usually read his brother like a book. But not tonight.

Was Dexter keeping something from him?

Chapter Six

Mila jerked awake from her nightmares, only to realize that she was living a real one. The dark holding cell was cold and lonely, and felt a million miles away from home and her daughter.

She scrubbed her hands over her eyes, wiping away more tears. If she lost Izzy, she didn't know what she'd do.

Desperate to keep it together until she was released so she could find her little girl, she forced her mind to her work.

Images of former patients, children in need, their parents' gratitude that she'd given their children a chance at a normal life, flashed behind her eyes.

Little Robin, who had a scar from falling through a window. Seven-year-old Jacob, who'd suffered abuse at his father's hands—she'd repaired the damage to his face, although the sweet child would never get his vision back in his left eye. Tiny Sariana, whose leg had been burned in a car accident. Baby Jane Doe, who'd been left for dead in the woods and mauled by an animal.

There were other children and families out there who needed her.

But what would they think if they discovered she'd given a new face to a human trafficker so he could escape?

Carina had borne the brunt of his vile ways and barely survived.

Mila had promised to protect her baby. But she'd failed. Now Izzy was in the hands of DiSanti's goons.

We know you helped some of our girls escape, the man who'd stormed into her clinic had said.

She massaged her temple. How had they known?

Had they been watching her? Or had they found one of the girls and forced her to talk? Maybe they'd discovered the underground ring that helped women and children and young girls escape abuse to find a better life?

Carina… Was she safe and still in hiding?

BRAYDEN WOKE TO a text from Lucas.

Bond hearing for Dr. Manchester at ten a.m.

Brayden took a quick shower, then dressed and rushed out the door. He drove to the diner near him, picked up coffee and a sausage biscuit and wolfed it down as he drove to Dr. Manchester's clinic.

It normally opened at eight. A truck and sedan sat in the parking lot while an SUV was parked in the employees' spaces. He spotted a woman in a nurse's uniform at the door with an older lady holding a baby, and a thirtyish woman with a teenage boy.

"I'm sorry, folks, the clinic is closed today," the nurse said. "Dr. Manchester won't be here."

Brayden hung back and listened to see if she offered more of an explanation, but she didn't.

"We'll reschedule as soon as I hear from her and we adjust our schedule," the nurse said.

The lady with the baby walked toward the sedan and the young woman and teenager climbed in the truck.

Brayden approached the nurse cautiously. If she conspired to help DiSanti, he'd find out.

The nurse tacked a sign saying Closed on the door, then retrieved keys from her purse.

"Excuse me, Miss Zimmerman?"

Her eyes widened as she looked up at him. "Yes?"

"The clinic is closed?"

"I'm afraid so. Did you have an appointment?"

He shook his head.

"Well, if you need one, call back and leave your number, and I'll have our receptionist get back to you."

"I'm not a patient," Brayden said, then introduced himself. "Were you aware that Dr. Manchester was operating on a wanted fugitive yesterday?"

The nurse gasped. "What? My God, that's not true."

"I'm afraid it is." He showed her a picture of DiSanti. "Do you recognize this man?"

The shock on her face looked real. "No, I've never seen him before. Why do you think he was here?"

"We know he was here," Brayden said matter-of-factly. "You didn't see him yesterday?"

She shook her head again. "No. And Dr. Manchester would never help a criminal, not if she knew who he was. She devotes her time to families, especially children in need."

That was what everyone kept saying. "Maybe so, but she performed plastic surgery on him yesterday."

A tense second passed. She shifted, then glanced through the glass door with a frown.

"What is it? You know something," Brayden said. "Were you working yesterday?"

She nodded, her eyes dark with emotions he couldn't quite define. "I did, but Dr. Manchester asked me to clear out the waiting room and sent me home early. She said her daughter was sick and she had to leave."

"Her daughter?" That was news. "I didn't realize she had a child."

The nurse's expression softened. "Her name is Izzy. Dr. Manchester loves that little girl like crazy."

"Did she seem upset? Afraid?"

Her brows furrowed. "Come to think of it, she did seem a little nervous. But I just thought she was worried about Izzy."

"Did you see anyone else here? Maybe a car in the parking lot?"

"I didn't really notice. There could have been, but I went out the front door." Worry deepened the grooves beside her eyes. "Why? What's going on?"

"That's what I'm trying to figure out," Brayden said. "Sometime after you left work yesterday, the FBI discovered that DiSanti and his crew were here and stormed the clinic. Dr. Manchester was arrested."

The nurse gasped. "My God, that's not right. Mila would never—"

"She did," Brayden said. "And I think she may have been threatened."

The woman clamped her lips together, then fumbled with her keys. "I don't know what to tell you. But I'm going to stop by her house and check on Izzy and the nanny."

Brayden put his hand over hers. "No, I'll go by and check on them."

If something was wrong with Izzy and the nanny, it might be dangerous.

He thanked her, then phoned Dexter on his way to Dr. Manchester's home address and filled him in. "She has a daughter?" Dex asked.

"According to her head nurse, yes. Her name is Izzy."

"That's odd. There's no mention of them in anything I've found about her. Dr. Manchester must keep her personal life very private."

He supposed he could understand that. But usually when people kept secrets, it meant they were hiding something.

"How about the father?" Dex asked.

"No information on him." Brayden pulled a hand down his chin. "Is there any record that she was married?"

"I didn't see one," Dexter said.

So who was the little girl's father? "I'm driving by her house to check on the child and nanny, then to the field office for the bond hearing."

"I put calls in to the other staff. I'll let you know if they add anything to what you've already learned."

Brayden thanked him, then hung up and veered toward Dr. Manchester's. She lived in a small neighborhood outside Austin, only a few miles from her clinic. He searched the area as he drove down the street. Most of the houses were renovated ranches and bungalows. Judging from the children's bikes and toys dotting the yards, the neighborhood catered to young families. The yards were well kept, complete with fall decorations and pumpkins.

Dr. Manchester lived in a Craftsman-style house at the end of the street. Her backyard jutted up to woods and land that hadn't yet been developed, offering privacy and a yard for her little girl to run and play.

Everything he'd learned indicated the plastic surgeon was the admirable selfless doctor that Charlotte, the nurse and the media claimed her to be.

But an uneasy feeling tightened his gut as he parked and walked up the drive. A dark green sedan sat in front of the garage, the only car on the premises. The nanny's? Two drives down, he noted a white van, and across the street, a black Cadillac. The neighbors'?

He scanned the front porch and windows, but the blinds were closed, and he couldn't see inside. Nothing outside looked amiss though. And he didn't hear signs that anyone was inside.

He punched the doorbell and tapped his foot as he waited. A minute later, he raised his fist and knocked. If he didn't get an answer, he was going to check around back, see if a window was open.

Footsteps shuffled inside. A low voice. Female?

He straightened and pasted on a smile as the door opened slightly. A short dark-haired woman peered up at him.

"My name is Brayden Hawk," he said. "I'm a friend of Dr. Manchester's. I stopped by the clinic to see her, but the clinic was closed today so I thought she might be home."

"I'm afraid not. I can tell her you stopped by." She started to close the door, but Brayden caught it with his hand.

He studied her, searching for signs she was upset or being coerced somehow. "The nurse said the doctor's daughter was sick. Is she here?"

The woman's eyes darted to the side, then she nodded. "In bed. She has a fever and needs rest."

He slipped his business card into her hand. "I hope it's nothing serious," he said. "If you need anything, call me."

The woman's hand trembled as she jammed the business card in her apron pocket. "I'm sorry, mister. I need to go take care of her." She didn't wait for a response. She closed the door in his face.

MILA CLASPED HER clammy hands together as she waited on the lawyer to meet her before the bond hearing. Nerves bunched in her stomach, and her head throbbed from lack of sleep.

The door to the interrogation room creaked open, and Agent Hawk appeared with Polk. His beady eyes skated over her, threatening and unrelenting.

"You have five minutes," Agent Hawk said as he glanced between the two of them. "Then it's time to see the judge."

"It will only take two," Polk said curtly.

Fluorescent light accentuated Polk's bald head. He strode toward her, then claimed the chair across from her, his lips set in a firm line.

"Is my daughter all right?" Mila asked in a low whisper.

His thick brows furrowed together into a unibrow. "As I said last night, she will be fine as long as you do what you're told."

"Please let me go home to her," Mila said. "I promise not to tell anyone about yesterday. I've been here all night and I didn't say a word."

"*He* had a rough night," Polk said, as if he didn't intend to incriminate himself by saying DiSanti's name aloud. "Once he's on his way to recovery, you and your daughter will be reunited."

Would she?

"How do I know you're not lying, that you haven't killed her already?" Mila crossed her arms. "I want proof that she's safe, then I'll do whatever you ask."

Polk cursed, then pulled his phone from his pocket and accessed a photograph.

Tears choked Mila's throat. It was Izzy in her room. The princess clock on her nightstand read 7:00 a.m. Not long ago.

Izzy was curled in bed with her pink blanket and baby doll clutched to her. Relief made her shoulders sag.

But it was temporary.

DiSanti never left a witness behind. When he'd kidnapped Charlotte's students, his men had shot Charlotte and left her for dead. In fact, she was the only one who'd survived his men.

If they killed her when she finished nursing that monster DiSanti back to health, who would raise Izzy?

Chapter Seven

Brayden shared what he'd learned about Mila with Lucas as they entered the courtroom.

"I know you want her to be innocent and so does Charlotte," Lucas said. "And you may be right. But unless she speaks up, my hands are tied."

The court was called to order, and Lucas quieted as the judge heard two cases, then Mila's. It took no time for the judge to grant Mila's bond. Her lawyer kept a tight rein on her, his shoulder touching hers as they exited as if he needed to keep her close. Mila remained silent, her hands knotted, body tense.

Her gaze darted to him as they reached the exit, then Polk took her arm and ushered her outside.

He and Lucas followed. Brayden's instincts screamed that something was wrong. Maybe the nanny had lied to him. Maybe Izzy wasn't sick, but someone had been in that house holding a gun on her.

Or maybe his imagination was running wild. Maybe he was projecting what he wanted to be true onto Mila.

Just like he had that other woman. He'd long ago stopped using her name. It hurt too much to think what a fool he'd been.

He wouldn't repeat the same mistake.

Morning sunshine shimmered off the autumn leaves as they exited the courtroom and made their way to the steps of the courthouse. Traffic slogged by, pedestrians hurrying to breakfast and work, mingling with joggers and parents pushing baby strollers toward the park two blocks down.

Mila tucked her head down as they descended the steps. Polk kept a firm grip on Mila's arm as if he expected her to bolt any minute, then steered her to the right toward a parking deck.

"I don't like this," Brayden said.

"Neither do I." Lucas quickened his pace to keep Polk and Mila in sight, and Brayden kept up with him. Polk guided her across the busy street to the exit of the parking deck, one hand shoved in his jacket pocket.

"He's got a gun." Lucas darted across the street and Brayden sprinted after him, dodging a car that screeched to a stop barely an inch from him.

Brayden threw up a hand to apologize, but didn't have time to slow down. Mila's terrified gaze met his, making his heart skip a beat.

"Wait!" Lucas shouted as he jogged toward Polk.

A dark van pulled up beside Polk, and Polk reached for the door handle.

"Stop, Polk!" Lucas shouted again.

But the man spun around and fired at Lucas and then at Brayden. Brayden jumped to the side, and Lucas ducked behind the rear of the van for cover. People shouted and ran from the street into the parking deck, coffee shop and neighboring stores. Police officers raced from the courthouse outside to clear the streets and provide backup.

Lucas inched toward the side of the van and fired at

Polk. He retaliated by opening fire and shoving Mila toward the van. She screamed, stumbling, then hit the ground on her hands and knees. A short robust beefy guy jumped out and grabbed Mila.

"Let her go!" Brayden yelled.

Lucas fired at Polk again, and this time Lucas's bullet hit home. The man's body bounced back as the bullet penetrated his chest, then he staggered and collapsed.

Brayden lunged toward Mila, but the gunman put his weapon to her head. Brayden froze, cold terror slamming into him.

Lucas took cover at the edge of the vehicle, his gaze meeting Brayden's. Brayden understood. He needed to create a distraction.

Brayden held up his hands in surrender mode. "You don't want to do this, buddy. Just release the doctor and no one else gets hurt."

The beefy guy shook his head and pushed Mila toward the van. She cried out and slammed into the side of it.

Lucas inched up behind the bastard and jammed his gun in the man's back. "Drop it. Now."

The bastard spun around and swung the butt of his gun toward Lucas's head. Lucas knocked it away and they fought, then Lucas sent the man's gun sailing to the ground.

Mila darted away from the gunman and hit the ground a few feet away.

The brute lurched for his weapon, but Lucas fired, hitting the man in the chest. Blood spattered, and Lucas ran to him, then kicked the man's gun into the shrubs.

Brayden rushed forward and helped Mila to stand.

She was shaken and in shock, her body trembling as she collapsed against him.

Shouts erupted, and several officers jogged toward them to assist. Lucas gestured for Brayden to get Mila inside. He wrapped his arm around her waist and coaxed her back into the building in case more of DiSanti's men were watching.

An officer rushed toward Brayden as they stood in the corner in the lobby of the courthouse. "Anyone hurt? Do you need medical assistance?"

Brayden tilted Mila's face up so he could examine her for injuries, then checked her clothes for blood. "Are you hurt, Mila?"

She shook her head, but terror glazed her eyes.

He pulled her to him and rubbed her back to calm her. "Can you take us to a room where we can wait on Agent Hawk?"

"Of course." The officer led the way down a hall then into a conference room. "I'll get some water."

Brayden nodded and ushered Mila toward one of the sofas. Instead of sitting down though, she grabbed his shirt lapel. "You shouldn't have stopped him! You should have let me go!" Tears rained down her face as she pummeled him with her fists. "Why didn't you just let me handle the situation!"

"Because you were in trouble."

"I had it under control," Mila cried.

Brayden swallowed hard, then forced a calm voice. "Lucas saw Polk's gun. He thought he was going to hurt you."

"You don't know what you've done! You...you should have let me go." Sobs racked her body, and he grabbed her fists in his hands and held them to his chest.

"I know you're upset, but Polk was dangerous and so was the bastard who shot at us."

She gave up the fight and sagged against him. He held her and stroked her back to calm her, murmuring low, soothing words. "It's going to be all right, Mila. I promise."

She pushed back, anger slashing her eyes as she swiped at her tears. "No, it's not. You don't know what you're talking about."

"Then tell me what's going on," he said. "Why you helped DiSanti. Why you were willing to go with a man who had a gun on you and probably planned to kill you when he got you away from here."

A helpless look passed through her eyes, followed by fear and panic. She choked on another cry, then dropped her head into her hands. Her body shook again, more tears falling.

His mind raced with possible scenarios, all of which he didn't like. All of which involved her safety or the safety of her nanny and little girl.

He gave her a few minutes, took the water from the officer who entered with it, then slipped the bottle into her hand.

"Drink."

She twisted the cap, but her hand shook so badly that she dropped it onto the floor. She guzzled half the bottle before setting it on the coffee table in front of her.

When she looked at him, despair seemed to weigh her down.

He retrieved the bottle cap and set it on the table. "Mila, I know that you're a good person. Charlotte vouched for you. I saw your awards, and talked to your head nurse. I also know you have a daughter."

Her lower lip quivered.

"If you tell me the truth, I promise I'll help you."

Her face crumpled. "They have her," she said in a haunted whisper. "They threatened her if I didn't cooperate." Anger hardened her voice. "Do you know what that means?"

Her tormented gaze met his, his heart pounding.

"It means you and your brother may have just gotten my little girl killed."

MILA BIT HER tongue to keep from confiding the rest of the story to Brayden. But she'd sworn not to reveal the truth about Izzy's mother or father to anyone, and she had to keep that promise.

It was the only way to keep her daughter safe.

Her heart pounded. She shouldn't have told him anything.

But what choice did she have?

"Let me get Lucas. He can help—"

"No." Mila grabbed his hand. "You said whatever I told you was in confidence."

Brayden shifted, his eyes assessing her. "If you want me as your lawyer, yes, everything you tell me is private."

She released a sigh of relief. "Agent Hawk is your brother though—"

"It doesn't matter," Brayden said. "We're both professionals. He knew when he allowed me to talk to you that I was bound by attorney-client privilege."

Mila wanted to believe him. She had to trust someone. And he seemed sincere.

Brayden made a low sound in his throat. "I'm sorry, Mila. I can call you that, can't I?"

"I don't care what you call me," Mila said. "All I want is to protect my daughter."

Brayden nodded. "Yesterday when I talked to you, I suspected something was off, so I did some digging. You didn't ask to call anyone when Lucas brought you in, which was odd. When I learned about your daughter, I put two and two together. I went by this morning to check out the situation."

Mila's eyes widened. "You saw Izzy? Was she okay?"

Brayden hesitated, agitating her more. "Your nanny answered the door. She said Izzy was in bed, that she was sick."

Mila's pulse clamored. "But you didn't see her?"

He shook his head. "I'm afraid not."

Panic shot through her, and she dug her fingers into his arm. "I have to go to her, see her myself. Get her somewhere safe. Once DiSanti realizes what happened here today, he may hurt her or take her away somewhere."

Brayden nodded. "I'll tell Lucas where we're going."

"No," Mila cried. "Don't you understand? He has men at my house. They have guns. Izzy and I were FaceTiming when they burst in and took them hostage."

Brayden laid his hand over Mila's. The human contact felt comforting and made her want to spill everything to him.

But she still had secrets.

Secrets she had to keep to protect her daughter.

BRAYDEN STUDIED MILA AGAIN, grateful she'd finally come clean. Lucas wouldn't like being left in the dark, but Brayden was bound by confidentiality, and he would honor it.

Although it wouldn't take Lucas long to figure out what was going on himself.

He'd researched the lawyer. No doubt the FBI already knew about Mila's daughter.

"Please," Mila said. "I need to see Izzy."

He nodded. "You said men with guns were at the house. It's too dangerous."

Mila shot up. "I don't care. She's my little girl, and she needs me. Now either take me to her or let me go."

"We'll talk to my brother. He can send the FBI there to rescue her," Brayden said.

She shook her head no. "They will kill her if they see the feds or cops."

He touched her arm again. The simple contact sent a tingle of awareness through him that he had no business feeling for a client, much less a woman in trouble with both the law and a man liked DiSanti.

But being with her was the only way to keep her from getting hurt and to learn the truth—if she was lying about her part in DiSanti's surgery.

"I'll drive you, but you have to do as I say and stay in the car."

Her gaze locked with his for a brief moment. Finally she gave a nod.

"I'll tell Lucas that you're upset, that I'm taking you someplace so we can talk."

Indecision warred in her eyes. "That's *all* you'll tell him."

He nodded. "Trust me, Mila."

But the odd flicker in her eyes indicated she didn't trust anyone. He wondered who'd betrayed her to the point that she felt that way.

None of your business. A little girl's life might be at stake.

He had to do his job.

Then again, she might be right not to trust. DiSanti had people everywhere. For all he knew, the man might own a judge or a cop or even a fed...

He stepped to the door to text Lucas. His brother was in the hall, so he joined him.

"How is she?" Lucas asked.

"Shaken, but physically all right."

"We need to convince her to tell us more about DiSanti."

"I'm aware of that." Brayden held up a hand. "But she's scared, Lucas."

Lucas studied him for a minute, obviously torn. "You think she was coerced, don't you?"

Brayden pasted on his poker face but gave a slight nod. "Release her into my custody, Lucas. I'll get to the bottom of this. I promise."

Lucas studied him for a long moment. "All right. But don't let her get away. She's the only lead we have to DiSanti."

He knew that. But he was more worried about her child at the moment than catching that monster.

"I'll have an officer escort you to your SUV just in case DiSanti's men are watching."

He thanked his brother, then ducked back into the room and told Mila he'd cleared her to leave with him. When they exited the room, the officer was waiting.

Brayden took Mila's arm, and the guard led them from the building to his SUV.

"I've got it from here." Brayden dismissed the guard,

and the officer turned and walked back to the court-house.

"I'm going to call my brother Dexter to meet us at the house. He's a PI."

"You promised that everything I told you was confidential," Mila said sharply.

He angled himself toward her. "It is. But I'm not a fool either, Mila. These men are dangerous. We'd be crazy to go there without backup."

"But he might call Lucas—"

Brayden shook his head. "Dex likes to bend the rules. We've kept more than one secret from Lucas and Harrison, our other brother who's sheriff of Tumbleweed." He paused, teeth gritted. "If there's anyone I trust to keep your secret, it's Dex."

A world of doubt settled in her eyes, but she must have realized that she didn't have much choice and agreed. He phoned Dexter, gave him a brief rundown and asked him to meet them at Mila's.

When he hung up, he started the engine and pulled into traffic. A strained silence stretched between him and Mila as he drove.

When he neared her house, he slowed and waited five doors down until Dex arrived. Dex climbed in the back seat and he made quick introductions, then coasted past Mila's to survey the house and property.

Everything looked quiet.

Mila leaned forward, searching, worry creating lines around her mouth and eyes.

He turned around at the end of the street, then drove two houses away and parked on the street. "Stay here, Mila. Dex and I will find Izzy."

She clenched her hands in terror, but gave a small

nod. Dammit, he hated to leave her in the car. What if DiSanti's men were watching and grabbed her from his SUV?

"You can stay with her," Dex said as if he read Brayden's mind.

"No," Mila said. "I'll be fine. It'll take both of you to handle the men."

"She's right," Brayden said. "If you can stave off the goons, I'll get Izzy and the nanny outside."

He gave Mila's hand a quick squeeze, retrieved his gun from the dash, then he and Dexter slipped from the car. They ducked through the neighbor's backyard, staying low in the bushes as they approached the back deck of Mila's house.

He just prayed the nanny and Izzy were still here, and that he and Dexter could get them out alive.

Chapter Eight

Brayden gestured for Dexter to check the door while he crept up to the back window and peered inside.

The interior was dark and quiet. He didn't see movement, but the hallway offered no view of the interior of the rooms.

He mouthed to Dex that he didn't see anyone, then kept watch while his brother climbed the steps to the deck and inched to the door. His brother held his gun at the ready and checked the doorknob.

The door screeched open.

Not a good sign.

Dex gave him a questioning look, and Brayden joined him, careful not to make a sound.

Senses alert, Brayden peered inside the doorway.

No movement. Except for the low hum of the furnace, no sound came from the house.

Odd.

The hair on the back of Brayden's neck prickled. This morning the nanny had been here.

Now the place felt eerily empty.

Did DiSanti's men know about the shooting at the courthouse? Had they left with Mila's daughter?

That wouldn't be good…

Dexter headed down the hall, and Brayden followed close behind. They passed a powder room, which was empty, then two bedrooms, one on the left, the other on the right.

Brayden eased into the one on the right. Mila's. A white iron bed covered in a blue quilt, dresser on one wall, a walk-in closet and bath.

Dex checked the second room, then shook his head indicating no one was there.

Antsy now, Brayden pushed a third bedroom door open. Dex stood behind him, gun aimed in case an ambush awaited.

A white four-poster twin bed was covered in a pink comforter with dozens of dolls and stuffed animals scattered on top of it. A dollhouse occupied one corner. Blocks, puzzles and a pink baseball glove filled bookshelves in the corner. A pink sneaker lay on the floor by the dollhouse, missing its mate, and a board game looked as if someone had stepped on it. Maybe one of the goons?

The bed was unmade, closet empty. The space beneath the bed held a box of clothing and several mismatched socks.

No little girl here.

His gut tightened, and he gestured to Dexter that they should check the living room. Although at this point, it appeared no one was here.

Dex led the way with his gun still drawn. An acrid odor hit Brayden as they neared the front of the house.

The kitchen-living room was to the right, dining area on the left. A lamp had been overturned, magazines strewn on the floor, a muddy boot print left on the entrance by the door.

No sign of the nanny or Mila's little girl.

An open carton of milk sat on the kitchen counter along with boxes of crackers and snacks. The farmhouse table held a pizza box along with an empty Scotch bottle that he had a feeling didn't belong to Mila.

Dexter crossed to the table in search of something that might indicate where the men would have taken the nanny and Izzy.

The rancid odor hit Brayden again, and Brayden's stomach jolted as he spotted drops of blood spatter on the floor in the kitchen.

Nerves raw, he eased toward it, then peered around the edge of the counter, praying that Izzy wasn't there.

And that the blood didn't belong to her.

MILA WAS BARELY holding on by a thread.

She stared at the clock on the dashboard, counting the minutes and seconds as Brayden and his brother Dexter went inside her house. If they could just find Izzy and get her away from DiSanti's men, she would tell the Hawks everything.

Her mind turned to the Hawk men. Brayden looked to be in his early thirties, was tall and broad shouldered with dark, neatly trimmed hair. He was handsome and imposing in his suit like the lawyer he purported to be. But those boots hinted at a tough cowboy beneath. And so did those intense eyes.

How many Hawk men were there? Were they all in law enforcement?

What did it matter? As long as he saved her little girl. Then she could worry about the charges against her. She hoped, if she gave the police a description of DiSanti, maybe worked with a sketch artist to convey an image of his new features, they'd drop the charges. She had been forced to perform surgery at gunpoint, her family threatened.

She twisted sideways and scanned the street. She'd bought this house because it was in a safe neighborhood. Because other families and children lived and played here. Because it was close to her work, and she could run home for lunch. Sometimes Roberta strolled Izzy up to the clinic when it was sunny, and they had a picnic in the park across the street.

The streets were empty now. Kids at school. Parents at work. Except for the mother of twins in the first house on the block. She'd seen the four-year-old little boys playing on the swing set in the backyard and kicking a ball around.

Mila raked a hand through her tangled hair, well aware she needed a shower and some clean clothes. She reeked of sweat and blood from the grueling hours on her feet the day before.

When this was over, maybe she should take some time off. Stay at home with Izzy for a while.

Sometimes she missed dinner and got home too late to put Izzy to bed. Moments like giggling at the table and reading bedtime stories meant everything to her now, even more than her work, which had driven her for as long as she could remember.

Although she'd wanted to be a role model for Izzy the way her adopted mother had been for her. Her adopted parents had taken Mila in when she was just a newborn, because her birth mother had abandoned her in a junkyard. A body shop repair mechanic searching for a fender to replace the one he'd torn off when he'd crashed into a tree had found her in a beat-up old Chevy.

If he hadn't been looking for that fender that day, she might not have survived.

She'd wanted to give Izzy the same chance at life that her adopted mother had given her.

She closed her eyes, bowed her head and prayed that she got the chance.

BLOOD SPATTERED THE FLOOR, cabinets and wall of the kitchen.

Brayden cursed, although relief mixed with anger. Not Izzy, thank God. But the nanny was dead.

She lay on her back, one arm above her head, the other on her chest, fingers curled toward her palms. She'd probably thrown her hands up to protect her face.

It hadn't done any good. The bullet pierced her forehead between her eyes. Blood dotted her forehead and cheeks and pooled beneath her head.

A professional hit.

Of course it would be. DiSanti's goons had no qualms about killing a woman. Rape and trafficking, selling young girls into sex slavery, was just a business to them. Bastards.

"No one's here," Dexter called from the living room.

Brayden motioned for him to come over. "They killed the nanny," Brayden said. "Gunshot to the head."

"Damn." Dexter appeared behind him, but both held back. The last thing they wanted was to contaminate the crime scene.

"It's my fault," Brayden said. "My visit this morning probably spooked them. So they killed her and took off with Izzy."

"Don't blame yourself. They probably got word of what happened at the courthouse," Dex said.

Brayden's lungs squeezed for air. "Mila warned me that if I interfered, I'd get her daughter killed."

Dex laid a hand on Brayden's back. "Stop. Izzy may still be all right. We'll find her."

But would they find her in time?

They needed a description of DiSanti's new face. But he understood Mila's reluctance. She was terrified and had a right to be. DiSanti was ruthless.

Other than the people who worked for him, Mila was the only person in the world who would recognize him now.

Which meant he would come after her. And he'd kill her so she wouldn't identify him.

"Call Lucas and get a crime scene unit out here," Brayden said. "I'm going to check on Mila."

He hurried to the door, then jogged outside toward his SUV.

MILA STARTLED WHEN Brayden knocked on the window. His grim expression as he unlocked the door and slid into the driver's seat made her stomach knot.

"What? Oh God, not Izzy—"

"No, Izzy wasn't there."

She bit back a cry, but was afraid to ask more.

"They must have taken off with her," he said softly. "She's the only leverage they have to keep you quiet, and they know it, Mila."

Mila nodded, grasping onto hope that his logic was right.

Brayden cleared his throat. "I'm sorry to have to tell you this, Mila. But they killed your nanny."

She shook her head in denial. Roberta was gone.

Poor, sweet Roberta. Izzy loved her like a second

mother. She'd met the woman at a shelter because she was homeless. Twenty years in an abusive relationship had taken its toll. Her husband, the man who'd beaten her too many times to count, had been shot by a gang member. His death meant her escape, except that she'd been destitute and determined not to fall into the trap of working for drug runners.

Mila had wanted to help her. It had been a blessing for all of them that Roberta had agreed to be a live-in nanny.

Now, because of her, Roberta was dead.

"Listen to me, Mila." Brayden gripped her arms and shook her gently to make her look at him. "I can see the wheels turning in your head. This was not your fault."

Mila fought tears, but they trickled down her cheeks anyway. "She wouldn't have been killed if she hadn't been working for me."

"Where would she have been, Mila?"

She jerked her gaze to his.

"I don't know much about her, but you obviously cared about her," Brayden said softly. "Did she have any other family?"

She shook her head. "No, her husband died because of gang activity. She was homeless and alone…"

"And you took her in and gave her a family," Brayden said, his voice tender.

She nodded. "She loved Izzy so much, and Izzy adored her."

Brayden cupped her face between his hands. "She knew that you loved her, and she died protecting the little girl she loved."

Mila clutched his arms, her heart aching. "Izzy must

be so devastated. What if she witnessed them kill Roberta? She'll be traumatized and—"

"Shh," Brayden said softly. "One step at a time, Doc. I understand you're upset about your nanny, but right now we have to focus on finding Izzy."

He was right. But once she got Izzy back, she'd give Roberta the memorial service she deserved. She'd died protecting Izzy—she was a true hero.

"Focus on the fact that Izzy is all right. And remember, for now DiSanti needs you. He won't hurt Izzy, because he needs her as leverage."

"You can't tell your brother about what happened here," Mila insisted. "It's too dangerous for Izzy."

Brayden's expression looked torn. "I'm sorry, Mila. But there was a murder at your house. We have to report it. We can't leave Roberta lying there in the house for days."

Mila struggled with right and wrong, with grief and anger, with fear that no matter what she did, she might never see her little girl again.

"You can trust Lucas," Brayden said. "He may be a federal agent, but he's a good guy. He'll protect Izzy and you."

It was still dangerous. And there was no way she could confide the truth about Izzy's father. No one could know.

"Mila?"

She clutched his arms, her mind racing. "Then you have to make sure that DiSanti knows that I haven't talked."

"We will," Brayden said. "I'll arrange for Lucas to make a statement to the press that you aren't cooperating with the FBI. All right?"

She bit her lower lip, but agreed. "What can we do to get my daughter back?"

Brayden stroked her arms. "First a crime team will process your house for forensics. Maybe the men who killed Roberta and took Izzy left evidence behind."

"Does it matter who they are?" Mila asked. "We know they work for that monster DiSanti."

"Identifying any one member of his group might lead us to some clue about DiSanti's plans or location. Lucas's people are analyzing Polk's and the gunman's phones, contact information and correspondence for any clue as to where DiSanti is hiding."

Mila's stomach churned, but she lifted her chin defiantly. "We have to do more. Give him some way to contact me." She'd even use herself as a pawn if she had to.

Chapter Nine

Emotions warred inside Brayden. It was beyond reprehensible that DiSanti would hurt a little girl.

Then again, they knew for a fact that he had hurt countless women and young girls, some as young as age twelve. To DiSanti and his people, the female population was put on earth to exploit. He did that for money without batting an eye.

Brayden couldn't help but wonder what had made the man so cold. Maybe his upbringing?

Not that it mattered. There was no excuse or justification.

He wanted the bastard to pay now more than ever.

But first, they had to get Izzy back safely.

Mila still looked uncertain about the plan. But what else could they do?

If he didn't work with Lucas, Dexter could try to track down DiSanti. But the FBI had resources that Dexter didn't.

Brayden believed in the law. But he wasn't stupid either. He'd learned to shoot a rifle when he was a teenager. His experience on the force had taught him how to handle a weapon, about apprehending a suspect, about when to shoot and not shoot.

Most of all, it had taught him that nothing could combat a bullet except one in return. Not a pretty lesson, but being street-smart meant surviving.

He didn't intend to die at the hands of DiSanti and allow him to continue his reign of terror.

"I need my cell phone," Mila said. "DiSanti's people might contact me through it."

"Good point."

"I probably should go back to the clinic," Mila suggested. "They might show up there."

"I don't think so. They know we'll be watching it," Brayden said.

The sound of an engine made them both jerk their heads around. Lucas.

Mila twisted her hands in her lap, fear returning to her eyes. "What if I'm doing the wrong thing? What if calling your brother gets Izzy killed?"

Brayden frowned, his pulse hammering. "Mila, I think we both know that you're in over your head. There's no way DiSanti will let you live, not when you're the only person outside his people who can identify him."

Her face turned ashen, but she didn't argue.

MILA RECOGNIZED THE truth in Brayden's words. But she didn't like it, and it scared the hell out of her to involve the FBI.

If they discovered Izzy wasn't her biological child and that DiSanti was Izzy's father, she might lose Izzy to him because of legality issues.

She'd have to watch every word she said to Brayden's brother. Only tell him what was necessary to find her daughter.

Agent Hawk slowed as he approached them, then pulled over and parked behind Brayden. Brayden climbed out to talk to his brother, and she studied the two, praying she hadn't made a mistake in trusting Brayden.

But Charlotte had married Lucas, so he must be an okay guy. When she'd first seen the news story on the shooting that had rendered Charlotte temporarily blind, she'd wanted to reach out to Charlotte, but she'd held back because of Izzy. She'd hated DiSanti and hoped the feds would find him and put him away for life.

She'd never imagined that she'd be the one to help him escape.

For a moment, Lucas and Brayden appeared to be in a heated argument. Brayden gestured toward her and her house. Finally, they both walked back to the car, and Brayden opened the passenger door.

"Lucas insists on speaking to you, Mila."

Her heart pounded, but she inhaled a deep breath. She'd do anything to protect her little girl, even lie to the FBI.

She slowly climbed from the vehicle, desperately wishing she'd had a shower. Maybe once they processed her house, they'd let her inside to gather some clothes.

"Dr. Manchester, Brayden explained the situation. I'm sorry that your nanny was killed. And most of all, sorry that your daughter is missing." His gaze seemed to be scrutinizing her as he spoke.

Mila cleared her throat. "He'll kill her if he thinks I talked to you."

Lucas nodded. "I understand your fear. And I promise that I'll do everything I can to bring your daughter home."

"Then you have to let him know that I haven't told you anything." She lifted her chin. "If it means locking me back up, then do it."

BRAYDEN GLANCED AT LUCAS, ready to argue if his brother agreed to put Mila back in a cell. She didn't belong there, not after all she'd suffered in the last twenty-four hours.

But a mother's love was so strong that he realized she'd do anything for her child, just as his mother would do anything for him and his brothers. She'd been devastated when their little sister had gone missing. They all had.

He'd blamed himself. So had his brothers.

And their father had just skipped out.

"I don't think that'll be necessary," Lucas said to Mila. "In fact, if DiSanti sent Polk after you, he'll send someone else."

Mila shivered. And this time she might not survive.

"I want to place you in protective custody until we catch DiSanti." Lucas speared Brayden with a questioning look. "Agreed?"

Brayden nodded. "I could drive her back to the ranch."

Mila twisted her hands together. "How will DiSanti contact me about Izzy?"

"She needs her phone," Brayden told Lucas.

Lucas nodded. "I can arrange that. Meanwhile, I'd like for you to work with a sketch artist."

Mila clamped her teeth over her bottom lip. "If you air a picture of his new face on the news, he'll know I talked."

"We won't release it to the public," Lucas said.

Mila folded her arms across her chest. "But what if someone in the police department or the FBI is working with DiSanti?"

Silence stretched between them, fraught with tension.

"She's right," Brayden said. "DiSanti may have people in his pocket that we don't know about."

Frustration darkened Lucas's eyes. "I promise you that I'll be discreet. I'll only share with people I trust. Once you make contact, and we get your daughter back, we'll go wide and launch a full-fledged hunt for the bastard."

A white crime scene van rolled up and slowed as it passed them.

"I need to meet them at the house," Lucas said.

Mila heaved a wary breath. "Would it be possible for me to go inside and get some clothes?"

Lucas and Brayden exchanged a look. "You don't need to see your nanny like she is now," Brayden said softly. "I can collect some things from inside for you if you want."

Lucas shrugged. "That would work. Give us time to process the house first." He narrowed his eyes at Brayden. "You didn't touch anything inside, did you?"

Brayden shook his head no. "Dex and I just searched the house. We found the nanny in the kitchen."

Mila clenched her hands together as if struggling to maintain control.

"I'll let you know when you can come in," Lucas said.

Lucas got back in his car and drove two houses down to Mila's.

Despair and worry knitted Mila's brow, making

Brayden want to pull her into his arms and comfort her. To assure her that everything would be all right.

But he couldn't do that. Not when he had no idea where DiSanti's men had taken Izzy.

MILA WATCHED LUCAS and the crime team park in her driveway with a sense of trepidation.

That little bungalow was her home. She'd bought it with high hopes of settling there forever and giving Izzy a happy childhood full of sweet memories.

But Roberta was dead inside. And her daughter was a victim of a kidnapping...

Worse, Izzy might have witnessed her nanny's murder. Mila hoped not. But still, the trauma of those men holding her and Roberta at gunpoint could damage Izzy for a long time.

The images from that FaceTime call haunted her and always would. She could see the men bursting through the door. The guns aimed at Roberta and Izzy. Izzy screaming as that brute snatched her.

Once she got Izzy back, could they return to the house they'd once called home?

She didn't know...

"Mila, I realize this is a terrifying situation, but try to stay positive. DiSanti wants you, not Izzy."

Her breath grew painful in her chest. If DiSanti knew Izzy was his daughter, he would want Izzy.

And he'd kill Mila for keeping Izzy from him for the past three years. But Izzy would never have a normal life if DiSanti discovered the connection between them.

He'd probably hunt down Carina like a dog, too. Mila couldn't allow that to happen.

"I promise to do whatever is necessary to help apprehend him once we save Izzy," Mila said.

A long silence stretched between them as they both watched her house. Another van passed them and pulled into her drive.

"Who is that?" Mila asked.

"The ME. They'll transport Roberta's body to the morgue for an autopsy."

Her heart squeezed. The world had been a better place with Roberta's warm smile and love of life. Even if she and Izzy survived this, they would forever have a hole in their hearts where Roberta belonged.

"A crime scene crew can clean up after the investigators are finished," Brayden said.

"That would be nice." She was accustomed to the sight of blood from performing surgeries. But seeing Roberta's spilled from being murdered was different. Personal.

Brayden turned to face her. "Mila, I have to ask you something else."

She tensed at the grave sound of his voice.

"It's personal, but the reason I'm asking is that it might have some bearing on finding your daughter."

She inhaled a deep breath. "All right."

His blue eyes softened. "Is Izzy's father in her life?"

Oh God... She forced herself to remain calm. "Why do you want to know about him?"

He shrugged. "We know DiSanti orchestrated this situation, but should we contact Izzy's father?"

"He's not in her life and never has been." At least that was true.

Another pause. "Is it possible then that he might have taken a payoff to help DiSanti get to you?"

Mila understood his question now. Oftentimes in kidnappings, a parent was involved.

That was certainly true in her case. But not for the reasons that Brayden thought.

She faced him with an earnest expression, hoping to end this line of questioning once and for all.

"That's not possible. Izzy's father is dead," Mila said.

Chapter Ten

Mila was so antsy she thought she would come out of her skin as she waited on the crime scene team to finish with her house.

All she could think about was where they'd taken Izzy. What was happening to her? Was she hurt?

Izzy didn't like scary movies or TV shows. Izzy insisted Mila and Roberta check the closets and under the beds for monsters at bedtime. She slept with a nightlight on and had never had a sleepover away from home.

She had to be terrified out of her mind.

"We'll find her," Brayden said softly.

She wanted to believe him. She had to.

Needing a distraction, she asked Brayden about his family. "How many brothers do you have?"

"There's four of us," Brayden said. "Harrison is the oldest and sheriff of Tumbleweed. Lucas is second in line. Then Dex, then me." He hesitated, his eyes darkening. "We had a little sister named Chrissy, but lost her when she was ten."

Mila frowned. "What happened? Or do you not want to talk about it?"

He shrugged, but averted his gaze and looked out

the window. A fall breeze stirred the trees, sending an array of colorful leaves to the ground. Yet dark clouds hovered, adding a dismal gray cast to the sky.

"I'm surprised you didn't see the news story about it. She disappeared one night when our parents were gone. For years, we had no idea what had happened. But a few months ago, we discovered the truth." He paused. "Unfortunately, she was dead and had been since the day she'd gone missing."

"I'm so sorry," Mila said. "That must have been difficult on you and your family."

"It was," Brayden admitted in a low voice. "My brothers and I all blamed ourselves because we were supposed to watch Chrissy that night. My mother went into a depression after she disappeared, but never gave up hope that we'd find her." His voice cracked. "Then my father just up and left."

"He abandoned your family?" Mila asked.

Brayden nodded. "We haven't heard from him in years."

How could a man desert his sons and wife, especially when they needed him?

"What about your family?" Brayden asked. "Any siblings?"

Mila's stomach twisted as she saw the ME and a crime worker carry Roberta out on a stretcher. Because Roberta was enclosed in a body bag, Mila couldn't see the physical damage done to her friend, but her experience filled in the blanks.

Thankfully, no neighbors were home to see what was going on, and the media hadn't shown up.

"Mila?"

She dragged her gaze from the van as the ME closed the back door.

"No. I was adopted but lost both of my adopted parents a while back."

"Charlotte mentioned a little about your past. I'm sorry about your birth mother," Brayden said.

She shook off his concern. "I was lucky to have the two parents I had. My mother traveled to foreign countries to help children in need. I wanted to follow in her footsteps, and I did." Another reason she'd had to take Izzy from Carina—she wanted to give Izzy the same chance that her adopted parents had given her.

Lucas appeared outside her house, then drove back to them.

She tensed as he got out and approached them. Brayden opened the door and stepped out. Mila wanted to know what was going on, so she joined them.

"Are you ready to talk to that sketch artist?" Lucas asked.

Mila's stomach knotted. She still didn't trust anyone. "I was thinking that perhaps I could work with Charlotte, that way we don't have to involve anyone else."

A muscle ticked in Lucas's jaw. "I suppose we could do that."

"About my clothes?" Mila asked.

"Tell me what you'll want and I'll go in," Brayden offered.

Mila squared her shoulders. "I'll get them. I'm a doctor, I've seen blood before."

"This is different," Lucas said.

"I'll be fine," Mila said sharply. "It won't take long."

"I'll go with her," Brayden said.

Lucas nodded. "I'll stand guard outside the house."

BRAYDEN ESCORTED MILA INSIDE. "There's probably fin-gerprint dust all over everything. Just ignore it, and we'll have a cleanup crew in here ASAP."

Mila gripped her hands together. "She was in the kitchen?"

Brayden nodded. "Your room and Izzy's are blood free."

Unease flittered through Mila's eyes. No matter what he'd said, she probably felt responsible for the nanny's death and would carry guilt with her for a long time.

He understood that himself. Even after they'd found Chrissy's body a few months ago, he couldn't shake the fact that if he hadn't encouraged her to sneak out with him and go to that swimming hole where Lucas and the other teens were celebrating the end of the school year, she'd still be alive.

He was eleven at the time and wanted to explore the caves at the edge of the mountain. He fell and hurt his ankle, and lost sight of Chrissy. Later he rode his bike home thinking she'd be there, but she hadn't shown up.

Instead...

He couldn't go back to the past.

Mila needed him to focus now. He hadn't been able to save his little sister. He had to save Mila's daughter.

He opened the door for her, and they walked in-side. The scent of blood and death filled the air. He'd seen crime scenes before, but this one felt more per-sonal because he knew a child had been kidnapped in the process.

Mila might be accustomed to blood and gore in the hospital and operating room, but a crime scene was different—violence at its worst. And this one involved her little girl.

She exhaled and walked quickly past the kitchen, then hurried to her bedroom. He followed but remained at the door to keep watch, offering her privacy to absorb the shock and gather her thoughts.

Her experience in crisis situations was evident as she lifted her chin and went straight to work. She pulled an overnight bag from the closet and threw in a couple of pairs of jeans, shirts and a sweater. She opened her dresser drawer, and he noticed pajamas and underwear, so he turned to face the wall.

He didn't need to see or even think about what kind of underwear the pretty doctor wore. But his imagination took him there anyway, and he pictured her curves encased in thin black lace.

His body hardened at the image in his mind. Dammit, he could not fantasize about her. Not when finding her child took priority.

He scrubbed his hand over his eyes to clear his mind. Footsteps sounded behind him, then her voice.

"I'm ready."

He turned toward her and took the overnight bag from her. "I need my phone."

"Your phone is still being held in evidence, but we'll get you another one and set it up with the same number."

She glanced inside Izzy's room. Her composure slipped slightly at the disarray.

"She always sleeps with her stuffed monkey. She named him Brownie," Mila said. "She cries without him."

His chest clenched. "I know this is difficult," Brayden said. "But you have to stay strong, Mila. She'll need you when we bring her home."

MILA DUCKED INSIDE Izzy's room to retrieve the monkey, but she couldn't find it. Maybe she had it with her. At least the stuffed animal would give her comfort.

The sight of her daughter's empty, unmade bed tore her heart in two. Thoughts of what DiSanti did to young girls threatened, but she staunchly pushed them away. Izzy was only three. He wouldn't touch her that way.

At least not now. When she was a teenager though...

No, they'd get Izzy back.

She hung on to that thought, grabbed the pink blanket Izzy slept with, then some extra clothes and one of her dolls and stuffed them in the overnight bag.

She crossed back to the door where Brayden was waiting. They walked through the house in silence and met Lucas at the door.

"Do you want me to follow you to the ranch?" Lucas asked.

Brayden shook his head. "I'll take her from here. Just get her a phone in case DiSanti's men try to reach her."

Mila hesitated. In spite of the fact that Lucas had arrested her, the Hawk family seemed caring and determined to do the right thing. Even Lucas wasn't bad—he'd saved those teenagers and married Charlotte. He'd even arrested her to stop DiSanti once and for all. How could she fault him for that?

"Get me the phone, then take me to a hotel, Brayden," Mila said. "I don't want to put your family in danger."

The Hawk men exchanged a look, then Lucas spoke. "Let us worry about the family," Lucas said. "Harrison can arrange extra protection for the ranch."

"But what if DiSanti discovers I'm there?" Mila asked.

Brayden took her arm. "Trust me, no one will know."

There was that word again. *Trust.*

She climbed into Brayden's SUV and looked out the window as he drove. Once they left the outskirts of Austin, the city gave way to beautiful countryside. Farms and ranches and wide-open spaces.

All places Izzy would love.

Tears pricked her eyes, but she blinked them away and grappled for courage.

Once Izzy was safe, she'd see that DiSanti paid.

Exhaustion and stress wore her down, and she closed her eyes. The next time she opened them, Brayden was crossing under a sign for Hawk's Landing.

She blinked in awe at the acres and acres of beautiful land. Barns and stables dotted the hills, and horses galloped across open pastures. In the distance, she spotted a big rambling farmhouse with a huge wraparound porch, then a couple of rustic cabins nearby.

"This is where you grew up?" she asked.

Brayden smiled. "Yeah, except for losing my sister, it was pretty great."

She imagined it was. "Do you and your brothers all ride and work the ranch?"

"We all ride. As teenagers, my brothers and I worked the ranch. Dexter has a place in Austin for his PI business, but he also handles the equine operation and has added horses this last year since Charlotte's students came to live with my mom." He gestured toward a dirt road that led to acreage lush with more pastures. "My brother Harrison and his wife live up there." He pointed the opposite direction toward more land that stretched far and wide. "Lucas and Charlotte live over there. Harrison's wife, Honey, owns a renovation business. She remodeled the cabin they moved into as well as the one Lucas and Charlotte chose."

"And yours?"

He shrugged. "Maybe someday. For now, it's just me, so no need for fuss."

"The ranch is amazing," Mila said, and meant it.

The smile that lit Brayden's eyes was so sincere that it warmed her inside.

"Like Dex, I have a place in the city, too. But I keep a cabin on the ranch for when I'm home." He slowed as they neared the turnoff for the main farmhouse. "Do you want to meet my mother and the girls?"

She shook her head. "I don't want to involve them in any of this. I'd never forgive myself if one of them were hurt because of me."

"Mila," Brayden said in a husky voice. "My mother is housing four girls who were kidnapped by DiSanti. My family is as invested in seeing DiSanti brought down as anyone."

"I appreciate you saying that," Mila said. "But I spent the night in a jail cell last night. I need to clean up."

"Of course. I'm sorry. I'm not trying to pressure you." He veered down another dirt road, the SUV bouncing over ruts as he passed a pond and headed up a hill. To the right, she spotted a cowboy riding across the pasture, corralling some horses toward the barn. Instantly her nerves went on edge.

"Who is that?"

Brayden laid his hand over hers. "Relax, Mila. That's our foreman. He's the reason I went into law."

Mila narrowed her eyes. "What happened?"

"He was framed," Brayden said. "I was a cop at the

time and realized the injustice, so I decided to study law to help him. I did, and now he works here."

Mila licked her suddenly dry lips. Brayden was definitely one of the good guys. A rancher at heart, a lawyer who represented the underdog.

She'd accept his help, then she'd get out of his life so she wouldn't cause him or his family any more trouble than she already had.

Then and only then would her secret about Izzy be safe.

JADE KRAMER WRAPPED the little girl Izzy in a soft blanket, then cradled her close and rocked her to sleep.

The poor little angel had cried so much her eyelids were swollen and red and she'd finally exhausted herself into sleep.

She wanted her mommy. Who could blame her?

She'd wanted her own mother when DiSanti had first brought her here, and she'd been fourteen years old.

That was over a year ago, and she still missed her family. She couldn't make herself believe that her father had sold her to DiSanti as he said.

Sure, she'd believed him at first.

But living on his compound and being bartered like cattle had taught her a lot.

DiSanti was a liar and a bastard, and he didn't care who he hurt as long as he made money.

The little girl stirred again, her tiny body trembling as she fought in her sleep.

She rocked her back and forth and stroked her hair away from her forehead, then kissed her cheek and began to sing her a lullaby. It was one her mama used to sing to help her fall asleep at night.

God, she missed her mama. Wished she could go back to being an innocent kid again. But those days were long gone.

Izzy whimpered and clawed at her arm, but Jade held her close and whispered sweet nothings in the child's ear.

She had to keep her quiet. DiSanti didn't like anyone to mess up his plans. She'd seen what he could do when he was angry.

It wouldn't matter that Izzy was just a tiny, innocent baby.

He'd give orders to get rid of her without blinking an eye.

Hot tears burned Jade's eyes. She'd long ago stopped crying for herself and for what the men had done to her. Her life no longer mattered.

But this little girl's did.

She'd do anything to keep her alive.

Chapter Eleven

Brayden considered putting Mila in one of the guest cabins, but he didn't want to leave her alone, so he took her to his place. She was so independent and frightened for her daughter that if she heard from DiSanti, she might attempt to face him by herself.

And that would be dangerous for her and Izzy. DiSanti was going to kill both of them anyway.

Unless they stopped him.

"This is nice," she said as he showed her through the kitchen/living room/dining area, then to the guest bedroom and bath. "Take your time. I'll run up to the house and see if Mother made dinner and grab us a plate."

She rolled her shoulders, obviously exhausted and worried. He waited until she ducked into the bathroom, then he locked up and drove to the farmhouse.

He spotted the teens outside with the foreman brushing down the horses, then found his mother cleaning up in the kitchen. The scent of homemade soup and corn bread lingered.

"Lucas called and explained that you have a guest." His mother's concerned gaze penetrated his. "Is there anything I can do to help?"

Brayden offered his mother a smile.

"If you have leftovers, we could use some. We haven't eaten all day."

A smile brightened his mother's face. They could always count on Ava Hawk for a good meal. "I'll pack up some soup and corn bread. And I have a fresh pumpkin pie."

His stomach growled. "Sounds wonderful."

She bustled around scooping soup into a container, then wrapped up two big chunks of corn bread, covered half a pie with foil and placed everything in an insulated bag for him to carry home.

He gave her a kiss on the cheek. "Thanks, Mom."

She hugged him tight. "Take care and be safe, son. And save that doctor's little girl."

"We're going to," he said, praying he didn't let Mila down.

His phone was buzzing with a text as he got back in his SUV. Lucas.

Charlotte and I are on our way. Bringing a phone for Mila.

He texted okay, then sped back toward his place. Hopefully, Mila's description of DiSanti's new face would enable them to track down the bastard and put him away.

MILA SHOWERED QUICKLY, grateful to finally clean the stench of DiSanti's blood from her skin. But she couldn't wash away the vile odor of what he was.

She quickly threw on a pair of sweats and towel dried her hair. By the time she emerged, she heard the door opening and Brayden calling her name.

She met him in the kitchen, where he was ladling vegetable soup into two bowls.

"My mom sent this and some corn bread and pie. I hope you like soup."

"It smells heavenly," Mila said. She couldn't remember when she'd last eaten. A breakfast bar the morning before she went to the clinic, then she'd skipped lunch while she was working on DiSanti. They'd offered her food in that cell, but she'd been too sick to her stomach to keep anything down.

They carried the bowls and corn bread to the farm table, and he returned with silverware and napkins.

"Would you like a drink? I have beer and bourbon, and I might have a bottle of wine left from Charlotte and Lucas's wedding."

"Water is good," Mila said. She had to keep her wits about her.

He poured them both glasses of ice water and sat down across from her at the table.

She was so hungry that she practically inhaled the meal. He was quiet, too, as they ate.

Then he dished them slices of pumpkin pie that made her mouth water. "Your mother is a good cook."

"She loves it. We used to grow our own vegetables when I was young, before we lost Chrissy." He shrugged. "She's talking about having a garden next summer since she'll have the girls to help."

"Giving those girls a home is admirable."

"Yeah, my mom is something else. Strong…like you."

Their gazes locked, tension simmering between them. She'd thought she was strong until she saw that gun at Izzy's head. Then she'd wanted to crumble.

"Charlotte and Lucas are on their way," Brayden said as he brewed a pot of coffee.

Fatigue knotted her shoulders, but she knew she had to face them.

If she could help find DiSanti, it would lead to Izzy.

A knock sounded on the door and Brayden rushed to get it. Lucas entered, then Charlotte.

Although Mila hadn't seen her friend in years, the connection they shared was still there. Charlotte raced over to her, and they hugged.

"God, Mila, I'm glad you're okay, but I know you're worried sick about your daughter."

Mila leaned into her friend and accepted her comfort, although the sincere worry in Charlotte's tone brought fresh tears to her eyes.

When they finally pulled apart, Charlotte cradled Mila's hands in hers. "I understand you're scared, but Lucas and the Hawk men are the best there is. They'll find your little girl."

Mila offered Charlotte a sympathetic smile. "I heard about what happened to you and your students. I'm so sorry for what you went through."

Charlotte squeezed her hands. "It was difficult, but I survived. The girls are happy now that they have a home at Hawk's Landing. Ava has given them love and emotional support." She glanced at Lucas with a smile. "I also met my husband from the ordeal. He's been amazing."

"I'm so glad you found happiness," Mila said sincerely. Charlotte had suffered ridicule as a child because of her port-wine birthmark. Mila's adopted mother had removed the birthmark, the first step in helping Charlotte recover her self-esteem.

"So," Charlotte said. "I understand that we need to sketch what that horrible DiSanti looks like now."

"Yes, we might as well get started."

Brayden offered coffee, but Charlotte declined, and so did Mila. She was already shaky. Caffeine would only make it worse.

Charlotte removed a large sketch pad and arranged her supplies on the coffee table between the two wing chairs facing the fireplace.

Lucas gave her a phone. "You have the same number as before, so if DiSanti calls, he won't realize the difference. We placed a trace on the phone. Keep him on the line as long as possible so we can get a location."

She nodded that she understood, then joined Charlotte.

Charlotte gestured toward a photo of DiSanti. "I thought the picture would be a good starting point. Then you can tell me how you altered features and I can draw them in for a composite."

WHILE MILA AND CHARLOTTE collaborated on the sketch of DiSanti, Brayden and Lucas convened at the kitchen table.

Lucas spread out a map, then removed three photographs of different men from a folder and laid them in a row.

"Right now we have made connections from DiSanti to each of these men, although we don't have enough evidence to make arrests."

He tapped the first picture, a dark-haired, dark-skinned man in a slick suit with a mole beside his upper lip. "This is Juan Andres. We believe he's the major connection in Colombia and is also part of the drug cartel. So far though, no one has or will speak out against him. The two people who tried are dead. Tortured and butchered and left hanging in their village to make a statement to anyone else who contemplated turning to the authorities. Another problem is corrupt law officials who turn a blind eye for money."

Disgusting.

Lucas continued, all business. "Next is a man named Lem Corley. He owns a ranch between here and Austin. Corley's operation has grown by leaps and bounds the past five years."

"Have you questioned him?"

"Not yet, I'm working on obtaining enough information for warrants. Corley also owns a second property near Juarez. We suspect he's taking payoffs for smuggling the girls through an underground tunnel across the border from the US to Mexico. From there, it's easier to send them wherever they want."

Brayden silently cursed.

"The third is a shocker because it's close to home."

Brayden's pulse jumped. "Isn't that Jameson Beck, the candidate for mayor?"

"Exactly. We've suspected he was corrupt as a councilman, but he has money and charm and has fooled people into voting for him. If he wins this bid as mayor, there's no telling how much damage he'll do."

Brayden's mind raced. Even when they found Izzy, Lucas still had his work cut out to make DiSanti's empire fall apart.

Charlotte and Mila stood and walked outside on the back deck.

Lucas poured himself more coffee and Brayden followed.

As usual, Lucas's eyes assessed him. His brother had an intimidating air, which worked well with felons and the evil dregs that he hunted down.

But he hated it when Lucas aimed those suspicious eyes toward him.

"Do you think Mila has told you everything?" Lucas asked.

Did he?

Brayden grabbed his coffee mug from the counter and blew into the steaming brew. "Yes."

Was Lucas going to remind him of the time when he fell for a client's innocent act?

"She's never married?" Lucas asked.

Irritation knifed through him. "It's not uncommon for women to have children without marriage, Lucas."

His brother sighed. "I know that. But what about the little girl's father? Did she tell you who he is?"

Brayden shook his head no. "He's dead."

A tense silence stretched between them. "And you believe her?"

"I have no reason not to. Now let's look at the facts. A dead man has nothing to do with Izzy now."

"What if she's lying?" Lucas said.

Brayden didn't want to believe that Mila would lie to him. But he'd been fooled before by another woman.

"Hell, Brayden," Lucas said. "Use your charms—do whatever it takes to find out his name. For all we know, he could be working with DiSanti."

MILA FROZE AT the sound of Lucas's question. Brayden told Lucas exactly what she'd said.

But Lucas wanted more.

He would probably keep digging away until he discovered the truth.

She couldn't let that happen.

"Mila, are you all right?" Charlotte asked.

She jerked her attention back to Charlotte and nodded. "Just thinking about Izzy. Wondering if she's hungry or if she slept last night. If she thinks I've forgotten her or knows that I'm looking."

Charlotte stroked Mila's shoulder. "Izzy knows you love her. She'll hang on to that." Charlotte glanced at the Hawk men, a tenderness in her eyes that Mila envied.

The Hawks had a close-knit, loving family here. They'd endured hard times and pulled through them together. And this ranch—it was spectacular. It offered a child a great place to grow up and a safe haven from the dangers of the world.

Not that her childhood had been bad. Her parents had helped save the world. But they'd moved and traveled so much that she'd never called a place home.

She wanted that for Izzy.

Even if she had to forgo her trips abroad, she'd give Izzy that sense of stability and home.

Charlotte took the sketch to Lucas. Both men studied it as if memorizing every detail.

"Basically, I removed his scar, then gave him cheek implants, lip fillers, a nose job and eyelid lifts," Mila said. "It'll take time for the swelling to go down and the redness to fade, but he'll be handsome and charming, and no one will know there's a monster lurking beneath that slick face."

The fact that she'd helped him achieve that made bile rise to her throat.

"Thank you for the description," Lucas said.

Mila folded her arms. "Are you going to keep your promise about airing it?"

Lucas gave a clipped nod, then flipped on the TV. "I gave an interview before I came here. It should be airing any minute."

They grew quiet as a young brunette anchorwoman spoke into the mike. "Last night the FBI and local police arrested Austin plastic surgeon Dr. Mila Manchester for allegedly helping a wanted felon Arman DiSanti escape. Authorities have been searching for DiSanti for months in relation to a sex trafficking ring called the Shetland operation." She gestured toward a screen. "I spoke with Special Agent Lucas Hawk earlier today regarding the arrest. Here's what he had to say."

The camera focused on Lucas. "While it is true, we arrested Dr. Manchester for allegedly conspiring to help DiSanti escape authorities, Dr. Manchester has refused to cooperate with us or reveal anything about DiSanti and his operation. Nor did she divulge the man's whereabouts, his plans or his new face."

Mila clenched her hands by her side. Lucas had kept his promise, at least regarding the media.

She just hoped DiSanti bought the story. And that his men took the bait and gave her a call.

Chapter Twelve

Mila had to keep her secrets safe. If Brayden and Lucas knew the truth about Izzy being DiSanti's daughter, Lucas might lock her up. They might even accuse her of kidnapping, and then she might go to prison.

Lucas approached her, his look suspicious. "Dr. Manchester—"

"Please call me Mila."

Charlotte's presence comforted her in the face of Lucas's distrust.

"All right, Mila," Lucas said. "Tell me why DiSanti came to you for help."

She chewed the inside of her cheek. "Because I'm a plastic surgeon," she said, stating the obvious.

Irritation lined Lucas's face. "But why *you*? There are other plastic surgeons who could have performed the surgery."

She shrugged. "I don't know. Maybe he, or one of his people, read about me in an article featuring my work with needy children."

Lucas arched a brow. "Had you met DiSanti before? Or done work on him prior to this?"

"No, we'd never met." That part was true.

"DiSanti is from Colombia," Lucas pointed out. "You've traveled there to perform surgeries?"

Mila couldn't lie when he could easily check her schedule. "Twice. My mother also worked at a free clinic in Colombia at one time."

Maybe that would distract him from thinking about her, and Izzy's father.

Lucas narrowed his eyes. "Did you go with her?"

She nodded. "She was the reason I chose plastic surgery and work with Doctors Without Borders."

Charlotte rubbed Mila's arm. "She was a hero to me, that's for sure."

Lucas hesitated, his gaze softening as he looked at his wife.

Then he turned back to Mila. "Was it possible that DiSanti knew your mother?"

"She never mentioned his name to me. And if she'd known what kind of man he was, she certainly wouldn't have helped him. Her work focused on children and teenagers." Although it was possible that DiSanti had heard of her mother, and that he linked her to Mila.

"Let me ask you something else," Lucas said. "When you and your mother were in Colombia, did you hear about DiSanti and what he was doing? Was there talk or rumors about sex trafficking?"

Mila strained to remember. "I suppose, but I was only twelve at the time and didn't fully comprehend the details. I do recall that guards watched the clinic, and I was warned to stay close." A shudder coursed up her spine. "A couple of times, rape victims were brought in. Those frightened me because the girls were so young and traumatized."

Lucas studied her for a long moment, then seemed

to accept what she said. At least for the moment. "Let me see the sketch again," Lucas said.

Charlotte handed the drawing to him, and Lucas scrutinized the features. "Did DiSanti or his men say anything while they were in your clinic?"

"Other than threatening my daughter?" Mila asked with a hint of sarcasm to her voice.

"I know that was harrowing," Lucas said. "But think about it? Maybe you overheard them discuss where they were going to take DiSanti to recover."

"If I knew where he was, I'd tell you." Mila rubbed her temple in thought. "All I remember is being so terrified that they'd hurt Izzy that I just did what they said. I cautioned them that I usually performed extensive plastic surgery in steps, but they insisted everything had to be completed that day."

Lucas removed a manila envelope from inside his jacket, and then took out a picture. "We took this from your house. Is this one of the latest pictures of your daughter?"

Mila traced a shaky finger over Izzy's innocent face. Her heart squeezed at the picture of Izzy sitting atop that pony. She'd been so excited about her first horseback riding lesson. "That was in the summer. I took Izzy camping, and we made s'mores over the campfire, and slept under the stars." She bit her lip. "She was so happy that day."

"I'd like to issue an Amber Alert for her," Lucas said. "That is, if you agree."

Mila looked at Charlotte for advice. Yet the threat to her daughter rang in her ears. If they released a photograph, DiSanti and his men would know that she'd talked.

She shook her head. "Not yet."

Lucas sighed. "But if we don't hear from DiSanti's men by tomorrow, we should release it to the public. I probably don't have to tell you that with every hour and every day that a child is missing, the chances of recovering them grow slimmer."

Mila swallowed hard.

Charlotte tugged at Lucas's arm. "Why don't we let Mila get some sleep? Maybe she'll remember more once she's rested."

"If anything comes to mind, call me." He squeezed her arm. "Hang in there, Mila. We'll find your daughter."

His tender encouragement made emotions well in her throat.

Lucas and Charlotte left, and Mila went to look out the window. It was dark again. Nighttime.

No word about her daughter or where she was. Or even if she was safe.

She gripped the phone Lucas had left for her, walked outside onto the porch, sank into one of the porch rockers and willed it to ring.

BRAYDEN CLEANED UP the kitchen, tension lingering. Mila pushed the porch swing back and forth, her hand clutching that cell phone.

She'd spent last night in jail without Izzy. Tonight, she'd spend it alone again.

Something about his brother's conversation with Mila troubled him. He sensed she was holding something back.

But what? Everything she'd told them about her mother was inspiring. And easy to check.

DiSanti was a good fifteen years older than Mila. He could have easily met her mother when she traveled to Colombia. He could also have seen Mila and read about her in the news. It made sense.

Lucas wanted him to find out about Izzy's father.

Frustrated, he settled in front of his laptop and sent Dexter an email giving him the names of the three men the FBI suspected to be involved with DiSanti's operation.

He asked Dex to send him everything he had on all three men.

He'd crossed paths with Jameson Beck before on the job. He'd heard rumors that the man was corrupt. That he had huge financial support from an unknown source.

Beck was slick, charming and made promises left and right to the public to win their votes.

Brayden didn't know the rancher Corley personally, but he and Dex could check him out together.

Beck was all his though.

Brayden accessed his personal number from his contact list, so he called it. The phone rang four times then went to voice mail. He left a message saying it was urgent, and that he needed to speak to him right away.

He hung up, hoping Beck would return his call tonight.

The next two hours crawled by. He researched everything he could find on persons of interest in the sex trafficking trade. Two arrests caught his attention, and he texted Harrison and asked him to go to the prison and question the inmates. They might be able to offer a lead as to where DiSanti and his men were hiding out.

Or if DiSanti had another connection in the States.

Antsy that he couldn't take action tonight, he walked

outside to join Mila. He was frustrated—she must be going out of her mind.

She gave him a brief glance, then returned to staring out at the ranch. Normally he'd be bragging about their operation and how far they'd come this past year in updating the ranching side of the business.

But tonight, all he could think about was Mila and the sadness and fear in her eyes.

SOMETIME IN THE wee hours of the morning, Mila finally fell into an exhausted sleep.

She dreamed about the surgery.

She was on her feet for hours. Long stressful hours when she could barely focus for worrying about what Izzy was going through.

Her head throbbed and her feet ached. Sweat poured down the side of her face. She was so thirsty she had to pause for a quick sip of water.

"What are you doing?" one of the men barked.

"I need water," she said, then grabbed a bottle from the side table.

He kept his gun aimed at her. "Get back to it, Doc. If you try to pull anything or if the cops show up, you'll never see your kid again."

Rage heated her blood. She wanted to throw something at him, take that gun and turn it on him.

But she was a doctor, not a killer.

Although if they hurt Izzy, she might forget her oath.

She guzzled half the water bottle, then wiped her forehead with a cloth and returned to work. With every maneuver of the scalpel to alter his looks so he could walk away free, she imagined digging the blade into his cold, cold heart.

Voices echoed from the side. Concern flickered in one of the men's eyes as he answered a phone call. He motioned to the other man, and they surrounded her.

"Hurry up, we need to move."

"I need more time," Mila said. "What you're putting him through is dangerous."

"His choice," the brute said with a wave of his gun.

"I can't in good conscience finish if his blood pressure drops again."

"Just do your job. We have a place set up for his recovery."

"I can't work 24/7," Mila protested. "My hands aren't steady when I haven't slept."

"You'll have help and supplies where we're going," the man snapped.

"He's not up for travel," Mila argued.

The men conversed in Spanish for several seconds. Short, clipped angry words. She'd picked up a few phrases but wasn't fluent.

But she thought they said something about a medical facility close by.

Another clinic? A hospital?

The man with the radio jammed the gun at her chest. "Finish and do it now. We have to go."

Mila jerked awake, her heart racing. For a moment, she was so disoriented she thought she was back in the clinic operating room. But the curtain in the room was flapping, the soft whir of the furnace rumbling.

She glanced around, clutched the bedding in her clammy hands and blinked to focus. No, not in the clinic or her house.

At Hawk's Landing. Brayden's cabin.

She pushed the covers aside, then padded to the door.

A dim light burned from the desk in the corner of the den. Brayden was slumped over the desk snoring lightly.

She tiptoed into the room, which was bathed in early morning sunlight shimmering through the French doors leading to the porch. Dawn was just breaking the sky.

Wrapping her arms around herself, she padded over to him and laid her hand on his shoulder.

"Brayden?" she whispered.

He startled, then jerked his head and looked up at her. "Yeah?"

"I remembered something. They said they had a place with medical supplies set up for DiSanti to recover. I think it was close to the clinic."

Chapter Thirteen

Brayden sat upright and rubbed his hand over his eyes. "Did they say where it was?"

Mila ran a hand through her tangled hair. Flannel pajamas be damned. Sleepy eyed with those unruly strands draping her shoulders, she looked young and sexy.

Not a good thought, man.

"Not specifically," Mila said, her voice riddled with frustration. "They were speaking in Spanish. I'm not fluent, but I understand a few phrases and words from our trips abroad."

Needing a distraction from his earlier thoughts, he stood, walked over to the kitchen and started a pot of coffee.

"Did they mention a direction they were going? A landmark?"

Mila pinched the bridge of her nose. "It sounded like they said something about a corral."

Brayden frowned. They were in Texas, a land rich with ranches, farmland and corrals.

He poured her a cup of coffee and himself a mug, then offered cream and sugar.

"Black," she said, and thanked him.

He carried his coffee to his desk, then checked his

phone for messages. Beck still hadn't returned his call. He checked his email next and had one from Dexter listing a property that Jameson Beck owned that he thought they should search.

He sent his brother a text asking him to look for locations that might involve a medical setting, old doctor's office, abandoned hospital or lab, using the word *corral*.

Dex sent him a quick response that he was on it.

"Hopefully, Dex will get back to us about the corral. I'm going to talk to Jameson Beck."

Mila sipped her coffee. "What does he have to do with this?"

"He may be involved with DiSanti's operation," Brayden said.

Mila looked perplexed. "Jameson Beck is supposed to be helping citizens, not exploiting them."

"If we prove he's involved," Brayden said, "everyone will know exactly what he's done. Not only will his political career be over, but he'll serve time."

"I'm going with you," Mila said.

Brayden hesitated. "I'm not sure that's a good idea. I haven't told Lucas—"

"I don't care," Mila said. "DiSanti's people still haven't contacted me. If Beck is involved and knows what's happening with my daughter, then he should have to face me."

She had a point. It might be easier for Beck to blow him off, but not so easy when Mila made the situation personal.

"All right," Brayden said. "But let me do the talking."

Mila agreed, although determination flared in her eyes. "I'll get dressed."

He rushed to shower himself. Jameson Beck could

be an imposing man. He wanted to present himself as an equal.

But if he had anything to do with Mila's daughter being taken, those kid gloves would come off.

MILA STUDIED JAMESON BECK with a skeptical eye. She'd always considered him a slick, cunning politician. He was impeccably dressed, hair groomed, teeth postcard white. He said the correct things and smoothed ruffled feathers with locals over unemployment, issues facing the ranchers and taxes.

He pretended to be an advocate for the lower income although he sported an expensive foreign car and the cost of his Italian loafers would go a long way toward feeding the impoverished.

Nerves pricked Mila's spine. Beck shook both their hands, invited them into his office and offered coffee. But her stomach was twisted so tightly she could barely swallow water.

She certainly didn't intend to swallow his lies if he dodged their questions.

And what if he was conspiring with DiSanti and tipped him off that she was cooperating with the police?

"I received your message late last night," Beck commented. "You said it was urgent."

"It is. I'm assuming you saw the news story about Dr. Manchester's arrest," Brayden said. "I'm representing her."

Beck's gray eyes showed no reaction. "I'm afraid I didn't see the story," Beck said. "I was out of pocket all day yesterday and didn't get in until late last night."

Mila didn't believe him. In his position, he had people who kept him informed of what was happening in his city. With the upcoming election, he could pounce on anything juicy or topical and bend it to impress his constituents.

"Dr. Manchester was forced at gunpoint to perform surgery on DiSanti, a man suspected of spearheading the Shetland operation. You are familiar with that, aren't you?"

Brayden's biting tone seemed to raise Beck's hackles, but he quickly masked a reaction.

Beck rolled an expensive pen between his fingers. "Of course. I believe your brother made some arrests a few months ago and recovered four missing girls who'd been abducted by that group."

"That's correct." Brayden used a calm voice. "We need your help. If you know anything about DiSanti and his whereabouts, it's important that you tell us."

Beck leaned back in his desk chair, a picture of calm. "I wish I could help you, but I'm afraid I can't."

"Can't or won't?" Brayden asked, his voice challenging.

Beck clicked the pen. "I represent the people, Mr. Hawk. I would never associate with someone involved in illegal activities."

Brayden stood and leaned his hands on Beck's desk. "We both know that's a lie. Now, listen to me. I'm not after you. All I want is information about DiSanti and where he's hiding."

Anger slashed Beck's eyes. "I told you that I'm not involved with him."

"Maybe not," Brayden barked. "But if you're connected with someone who is, then tell me what you do know."

Beck buttoned his suit jacket. "I've asked and answered your question. Now it's time for you to leave."

Mila couldn't stand it any longer. She lurched up from her chair. "Mr. Beck, this man not only abducts and sells young women as sex slaves, but his people kidnapped my three-year-old little girl." Her voice broke. She snatched a picture from her wallet, a candid of Izzy at Christmas holding her baby doll. "Her name is Izzy," Mila said. "She's three, and she's afraid of the dark, and she likes macaroni and cheese and rainbows and ice cream."

A vein throbbed in his neck.

Mila gave him an imploring look. "If you know where he's holding her, please tell me."

His gaze met hers. His was full of steel, although a twinge of something akin to worry flickered in his eyes. Worry for himself or for her daughter?

He exhaled. "I'm sorry, Dr. Manchester. I hope you find her."

The calmness in his tone infuriated her even more. He was lying. She sensed it and refused to let him off the hook.

She snatched him by the collar and jerked his face toward hers. She expected Brayden to yank her away, but he didn't.

"If he hurts her, and I find out you knew where she was and didn't help me," she said through gritted teeth, "worrying about winning the election won't be an issue."

His gaze shot to Brayden. "You need to calm your client, Mr. Hawk."

Mila shook him. "This is calm, Mr. Beck." Venom laced her tone. "I promise you that if I don't get my daughter back safe and sound, jail will be the least of your problems."

"You heard her threaten me," Beck said to Brayden.

Brayden shrugged. "I didn't hear anything of the sort."

Mila straightened and reluctantly released Beck.

Beck cleared his throat, his nostrils flaring. "The next time you want to talk to me, go through my attorney."

Brayden shot him a cynical smile. "Fine. I'm sure the residents of Austin will be interested in knowing that instead of helping us find a known sex trafficker and a missing child, that you lawyered up to protect your own ass."

Brayden didn't wait for a response. He took Mila's arm and they left the room.

Her heart hammered in her chest. Brayden Hawk was a formidable man and lawyer.

He was also one of the good guys, not like Beck, who was all show with a selfish, greedy side lurking beneath.

BRAYDEN'S PHONE BUZZED as he and Mila climbed back into his SUV. Dex.

He quickly connected. "I'm just leaving Beck's office. That bastard knows something, but he sure as hell isn't talking."

"I'll keep digging," Dex said. "I did find something though—at least I think I did. You said Mila mentioned something about a corral?"

"Like I said, they were speaking in Spanish, so she wasn't sure of the translation."

"I found an abandoned hospital in a small hole-in-the-wall town called O'Kade Corral," Dex said.

Brayden's pulse jumped. "Where is it?"

"Sending the address to your phone now," Dex said. "The town was built around some old mines, which was the reason for the hospital. But the mines yielded nothing, so the workers moved on and the town crumbled."

But it would provide a hiding spot for DiSanti during his recuperation.

Dex agreed to meet him there, and Brayden hung up, then glanced at the address Dex had sent. Mila was checking her own phone, willing it to ring again, he guessed.

Disappointment lined her face as she laid it back in her lap. "What's going on?"

Brayden explained about Dex's call. "The town isn't far from here."

Mila fastened her seat belt. "Let's go."

Brayden fastened his own seat belt, started the engine and veered into traffic. He wove through the downtown streets of Austin, then onto the highway leading out of the city.

Mila twisted her phone between her hands, constantly checking it as he raced down the highway. He considered calling Lucas, but he didn't want to waste Lucas's time if this was a wild-goose chase.

The city landscape gave way to farmland and ranches, then he veered onto a narrow road that wove through miles and miles of nothing. The road was bumpy and filled with potholes, another sign that the area was deserted.

He maneuvered a turn, then spotted several small buildings in the distance. The town looked like a ghost town—a small building that had once been a mercantile, a bank, a diner and honky-tonk. All deserted, the buildings weathered, paint fading.

He scanned the streets and surrounding land for cars or signs indicating someone was here. A few pieces of rusted mining equipment had been left near the overgrown trails leading to the mines.

"It looks vacant," Mila said, disappointment tingeing her voice.

In the distance sat a larger building that could be the old hospital. A white van and an ambulance were parked near the building, half hidden by weeds and patchy shrubs.

Mila clutched his arm. "They were driving a van the night they brought DiSanti to the clinic."

Brayden pulled over between a clump of trees to wait on Dexter. The last thing he wanted was to alert DiSanti's men they were here before backup arrived.

If he got himself and Mila killed, he couldn't save Izzy.

He texted Dex to tell him to approach with caution and pull off where he'd parked. The air in the car felt charged with tension as they waited, Mila's anxiety palpable.

Five minutes passed, then Dex coasted up in his black pickup. He slowed and veered into the space beside Brayden and parked. Brayden removed his handgun from the locked dash and checked the magazine.

Both he and his brother eased their doors open and slid out, carefully closing them so they didn't make noise. Mila joined them, but Dexter and he exchanged understanding looks.

"Stay here while we take a look around," Brayden said.

"But if Izzy's there, she'll be scared and need me," Mila whispered.

Brayden gently touched her arm. "It's too dangerous, Mila. Once we scout out the hospital, we'll let you know if it appears anyone is there. If DiSanti's here, we'll call Lucas for backup."

"But if Izzy's in there—"

"Rushing inside without a plan could work against us," Brayden said. "We have to play it smart. The most important thing is to get Izzy out safely."

Mila sighed and gripped the edge of the SUV. "Please find her, Brayden."

His heart stuttered. Dex's face twisted with emotions, as well.

"We'll do our best," Brayden said. "But I need you to stay in the SUV, lock the doors and keep down. If DiSanti has men watching or riding the property, we don't want them to see you."

Mila agreed, and he waited until she was locked inside the vehicle, then he and Dexter headed through the woods toward the building.

Dex pulled binoculars from his pocket and focused on the van and ambulance first, then across the property.

He shook his head, indicating he didn't see movement.

Brayden gripped his gun at the ready, and they crossed behind some trees, taking cover as they moved toward the building.

Dex motioned that he'd check the side windows, while Brayden veered around the right to the back window near the parked ambulance.

Just as he grew close, something caught his eye.

A small stuffed monkey. It looked well-worn and loved, its ears frayed.

His throat closed. If it belonged to Izzy, she might be here.

Chapter Fourteen

Brayden stooped down, picked up the stuffed monkey, his heart clenching at the tattered ears. Izzy, or some child, had loved this little toy. It had probably given comfort.

He stuffed it inside his pocket and inched forward until he reached the back door, a metal one with a window covered to offer privacy to patients it had once served—or to hide whoever was inside.

Dex gave a low whistle from the side of the building and gestured that he couldn't see inside.

In fact, all the windows were covered.

Suspicious.

Brayden crept forward and gently turned the doorknob. Locked.

Dex appeared a second later. Brayden ignored the fact that his brother carried a lock-picking tool and that they had no warrant. If he had to, he'd say they thought they heard a child crying inside.

Dex picked the lock and turned the knob, pushing it open an inch at a time. Brayden peered through the opening. The interior was dark. Quiet.

His heart hammered.

Dex motioned for them to go inside, and Brayden

slipped into the doorway. Dex kept his gun at the ready and went right, and they both paused to listen. A rattling sound. Wind whistling through the cracks in the windows.

No voices. No lights.

Still, they moved with caution in case DiSanti's men had been here and left a lookout guy to ambush them. He followed his brother down the hall, each checking rooms on the side of the hall. Exam rooms, a surgical wing, a pharmacy with glass cabinets that had once held drugs, a recovery room, then several patient rooms, two of which still housed hospital beds.

All empty.

Dex motioned to another room at the end, and he inched along behind Dex, both treading quietly until they reached the room. Brayden peered through the window of the door. Empty.

But it looked as if someone had been there recently.

He pushed open the door and stepped inside, waving Dexter to join him. The lights were off, so he pulled his flashlight from his pocket and shone it around the room.

Alcohol, blood stoppers and medical supplies filled a metal side table. Bloody clothes were stuffed into a bin next to a hospital bed that appeared to have recently been slept in. A sheet and blanket stained with blood were rumpled on top of the mattress, and a used syringe lay on another steel table.

"They're gone," Dexter said. "Do you think they knew we were coming?"

"I don't know how they could," Brayden said. "You only discovered this place today."

"Maybe one of them figured out that Mila overheard their conversation."

"I guess that's possible." Brayden's hand rubbed the stuffed monkey in his pocket, and he showed it to his brother. "Let's search the cabinets and closets in case Izzy was here."

Dex traded a worried look with him. If she was, and they thought Mila had ratted them out, they might have ditched her.

He prayed that wasn't the case, but DiSanti was the most ruthless man he'd ever encountered.

WHAT WAS TAKING so long?

Mila remained hidden, but the minutes dragged by, intensifying her anxiety. Had the Hawk men found something inside?

She turned and scanned the property for vehicles, but the place appeared deserted. Fresh tire marks marred the dirt leading up to the hospital, another set leading past the hospital to the opposite side.

Someone had been here recently, and they were gone. But where? What lay to the south?

She reached for the doorknob to go and look in that van herself, then remembered Brayden's warning.

Still jittery, she checked her phone. No text or phone call.

She logged in to her work email and checked messages at the clinic. Not that DiSanti would send her a message there. It would be too easy for the police to check.

Why hadn't they called? Lucas had announced that she wasn't cooperating.

Maybe she should ask Brayden and Lucas to set up a TV interview where she could make a public plea for her daughter's return. By now, DiSanti and his men could be hundreds of miles away.

If they had Izzy with them, she might never see her little girl again.

Panic robbed her breath. She reached for the door handle once more, but saw movement ahead.

Brayden and his brother Dexter exiting the building.

Disappointment swelled inside her. Izzy wasn't with them. They were no closer to getting her back than they had been before.

Lucas's statement taunted her. She'd read the statistics, too. Every minute, every hour, every day that they didn't find Mila's daughter diminished her chances of finding her alive.

Brayden halted by the van, opened the door and climbed inside while his brother searched the back of the ambulance. She held her breath as she waited, her patience waning when they finished and walked toward her.

She slipped from the SUV. "Did you find anything inside?"

Brayden's dark expression made her stomach knot. "They were here," he said. "There were bloody cloths and medical supplies spread out, but they're gone."

Mila gestured toward the tire tracks. "It looks like a vehicle left that way," she said.

Dex shone his light on the tracks to examine them.

Mila rocked back on the balls of her feet. "Brayden, was there any sign of Izzy?"

Brayden removed something from his jacket pocket and handed it toward her. "Is this hers?"

Mila nodded, then took the tiny monkey and pressed it to her chest.

BRAYDEN'S PHONE BUZZED. LUCAS.

"Was there any clue where?" Mila asked.

"I'm afraid not," Brayden said. "But DiSanti's men could have taken her to another location, maybe where they're holding other victims."

They'd kept Charlotte's students at an abandoned ranch off the grid. If Izzy was with other girls, she wouldn't be quite so terrified. Except they usually kept those girls drugged and incoherent.

There hadn't been reports of any abductions near Tumbleweed or Austin in the past few weeks, but DiSanti's people might be moving victims from other states through. Or they could be playing it more low-key, taking one victim at a time, choosing from runaways or girls without families who no one would report missing.

His phone buzzed again. "It's Lucas. I need to get this."

Mila leaned against the car while he walked a few feet away for privacy.

"Where are you?" Lucas asked.

Brayden braced himself for one of Lucas's big-brother lectures. But if they wanted to find DiSanti and Izzy, they had to work together, so he explained.

"Dammit, Brayden, why didn't you call me?" Lucas asked.

Because he didn't want to get his brother in trouble in case Dex and he straddled the law. "There wasn't time," Brayden said. "Besides, I didn't know if it would lead to anything. I want you working your end."

"I am," Lucas said. "But I can't do that if I have to worry about you going off on your own."

"I'm not alone," Brayden said.

Lucas exploded with a string of expletives. "Dex is with you?"

"Yes, but we haven't broken any laws, Lucas. Dex and I just checked out an abandoned hospital. DiSanti was here, but he's gone."

Lucas hissed between his teeth. "Any sign where they went from there?"

"No, but I found a stuffed toy indicating Mila's daughter was here."

"Dammit." Lucas paused, breath wheezing out. "I heard that you paid Jameson Beck a visit."

Brayden clenched his jaw. "Yeah, but he's not talking."

"I didn't expect him to. But our analyst traced one of his phone calls to an old inn in a small town about thirty miles south of Austin."

The tire tracks leading away from the hospital were headed south.

"Send me the address."

"Brayden, let me do this."

"Let's meet, Lucas. If Izzy's there, she'll need Mila." He lowered his voice so she couldn't hear. "And if Izzy's hurt or if there are other hostages, they might need medical attention."

A strained heartbeat passed. "I don't like it, but you're right."

He ended the call then went to tell Dexter and Mila the plan.

MILA TWISTED THE monkey in her hands as Brayden drove toward Cactus Grove, a small town south of Austin that drew tourists for its desertlike garden, variety of cacti and sagebrush. A local museum showcased the history of the wagon trains that used to travel through the town to Austin, and the town still boasted a working train station.

"Is Dexter coming?" Mila asked.

Brayden shook his head. "He's going to check with one of his CIs. Maybe he'll have information that can help."

"Does Lucas think DiSanti's in this town?" Mila asked.

Brayden shrugged. "It's possible. He traced a call from Beck to Cactus Grove. If DiSanti's operation is using the town as a holding place for trafficking and we can connect it to Beck, then we can use it as leverage to force Beck to talk."

Mila fidgeted with her phone. "Why haven't they called me, Brayden?"

Brayden clenched his jaw. "Maybe they're just regrouping."

Or maybe they'd left the country and taken Izzy with them.

The countryside flew past as Brayden sped down the road to Cactus Grove. The wind stirred the pines and sagebrush, flinging dust across the road in a brown fog.

As they approached the small town, traffic built slightly, although compared to Austin they were in the wilderness. They passed the train station and museum, then a newer inn in town that was decked out for Thanksgiving. At the end of the square, an old-fashioned diner and a Western saloon invited customers to enjoy a taste of days gone by. Brayden parked in front of the town stage.

"What are you doing?" Mila asked.

"Waiting on Lucas."

Mila studied the wooden platform in front of them. "What is this place?"

"Every year the town performs a reenactment of a historical gunfight that occurred in the town a hundred years ago."

She tapped her foot, impatient as they waited on Lucas to arrive. A black sedan crawled by and slowed as if looking at them, then a dark gray Cadillac.

Lucas pulled up and motioned for them to join him in his sedan. When they climbed in, Lucas gave them both stern looks.

"I'm in charge here, so you two need to do as I say."

"Yes, sir," Brayden said with a tinge of irritation.

"I mean it, Brayden. I know you have experience, but I don't want either of you getting hurt."

"I don't give a damn about getting hurt," Mila said. "All I want is my daughter back."

"That's exactly what worries me," Lucas said with a frown.

Brayden raked a hand through his hair. "He's right, Mila. When we get there, you have to stay inside the car and remain hidden. If we find something, we'll come and get you. I promise."

Mila bit down on her lower lip and nodded. She'd been held at gunpoint by DiSanti's men. She knew what it was like to be powerless. The last thing she wanted was to get her daughter hurt or to die and leave Izzy without a mother.

Lucas started the engine, then turned onto a narrow road leading toward more farmland.

"There's an inn out here?" Mila asked.

Brayden nodded. "It was the original one and catered not only to tourists, but miners who still thought they might find gold in the mines. They abandoned the inn a couple of years ago when they built the new one by the train station. Made it easier for people to walk the town."

They passed several abandoned small cabins and a building that had probably once been used to store mining supplies, then she spotted the inn, an antebellum house with a big porch that looked homey and quaint.

Those abandoned buildings could be used to hold trafficking victims.

A black van was parked in back of the inn, an old pickup near the warehouse.

"We'll check the inn first, then those buildings," Lucas said.

Brayden gave Mila a pointed look. "I meant what I said. Stay put."

"I will," she said, her hand stroking the monkey's ears.

"If you see something, text me," Brayden said. He shocked her by slipping a small .22 into her hand.

She looked at the gun, not sure if she could use it. But an image of Izzy being held by that monster taunted her, and she knew she could shoot if it meant saving her daughter's life.

Lucas took the lead as the men climbed from the car and inched toward the inn.

She held her breath, praying for their safety and that they found Izzy before it was too late.

Time seemed to stand still. The tension thrumming through her made her feel sick inside.

Suddenly her phone buzzed. She startled, then glanced down at it. Brayden?

No.

A text. She opened it and gasped. A picture of her little girl huddled in a dark corner, teary eyed and terrified.

Then a message.

If you want to see your daughter again, ditch the cops. Will contact again with instructions.

Chapter Fifteen

Brayden approached the inn, his senses alert. Lucas motioned to let him take the lead, and Brayden did. Entering an unknown situation that could be an ambush was never his favorite part of police work.

He'd gotten spoiled by dealing with trouble and crime in the courtroom instead of on the front line. Although the law could be frustrating at times, too.

Seeing a guilty criminal released without being punished was infuriating and happened too often, while watching an innocent person go to prison was intolerable.

Lucas paused to listen at the door, his brows furrowed. When he looked back at Brayden, his brother gestured that he heard something.

Maybe someone was inside?

He eased open the door, gun at the ready, and inched inside. Brayden peeked past him. The interior was dark and appeared deserted. At one time, this place housed tourists and travelers driving from Austin toward Mexico. It had drawn miners but also catered to cattle ranchers and horse lovers.

Paintings of wild mustangs hung in the entryway,

where the wallpaper was fading, the curtains a dull pale gray.

Lucas swung left and Brayden went right. He scanned the dining room while his brother ducked into a formal living room/parlor that had probably once hosted afternoon tea for guests.

The room was empty, but led to a large kitchen with a giant oak table. A case of bottled water sat on a grimy counter. Loaves of bread, canned beans and cans of soup filled a box indicating a recent shopping trip.

Someone had been here.

A noise sounded from upstairs, and he froze. Maybe someone was still here.

Lucas's footsteps echoed from the front. He must be going up the staircase. A back stairwell caught Brayden's eye, and he headed toward it. He forced his footfalls to remain light, although the old wooden floors squeaked as he climbed them.

He stopped on the landing and noted a large room to the right. The hall led to other rooms that had once been rented to guests.

Lucas appeared at the opposite end, then ducked into one of the bedrooms. Brayden veered into the larger room, which must have been used as a suite. The front area held a love seat, chair and coffee table. He crept toward the inner door and thought he heard a noise coming from behind it.

He hesitated, listening for voices, determined not to walk into a trap. No male voices. Maybe someone crying?

His pulse jumped. Was it Izzy?

Body coiled with tension, he eased open the door,

keeping his gun braced in case one of DiSanti's men lay waiting on the other side. Another sound. A moan.

Crying. Definitely crying.

Anger forced him forward, his temper rising even more when he spotted three cots in the room. Cots where three young girls lay.

In one quick glance, he realized they'd been drugged. Two of them were either asleep or unconscious while the third, a scrawny brunette who was probably about thirteen, lay huddled with her knees up, sobbing into her hands.

He took a deep breath, then slowly approached her. His foot made the floor creak, and she startled and jerked her head up, her eyes wide with terror.

"Shh, it's okay," he murmured. "I'm here to help you."

She scooted as far as possible against the wall, body trembling, eyes red and swollen from crying. He took a step closer, wanting to check the other girls' pulses, but she shrieked and shook her head wildly, causing him to stop.

He held up his hand in a sign that he wouldn't hurt them. "You're okay now. I'm going to get help."

She stared at him wide-eyed, and he backed toward the door. He ran into Lucas in the hall.

"There are three girls in there," he told his brother.

"Two more in the other room," Lucas said gruffly. "Both drugged and unconscious." He removed his phone from his pocket. "I'll call an ambulance."

Brayden nodded. "I'll get Mila."

"Good idea." Lucas walked to the door to peek in on the three girls Brayden had found, his expression grim.

They still needed to check the outbuildings, but he'd get Mila first.

MILA CHECKED HER phone a dozen times, hoping for another message, but nothing yet.

She had to do whatever DiSanti's men said. But separating herself from Brayden and Lucas would be difficult. And how would she rescue Izzy on her own?

If she went with them, they still might kill her and Izzy...

A movement on the hill startled her. Brayden exited the inn. His face looked stony as he scanned the property and exterior of the outbuildings. Then he hurried toward the woods where they'd parked.

She'd hoped he'd find Izzy, but that text had killed her hopes. If there was nothing here, maybe Brayden was ready to go. She'd have him drive her back to her place or the clinic, somewhere she'd have access to a car.

He tapped on the window, and she unlocked the door and opened it with a shaky hand.

"We found some girls inside," Brayden said. "They've been drugged. We need you."

Her medical training kicked in, and she scrambled out of the car.

"I don't have a medical bag with me," she said, frustrated. She always carried one in her car. She might need one when she found her daughter.

"It's okay. Lucas called an ambulance so help should be here soon. One girl is conscious and terrified of me. Maybe you can calm her until the medics arrive."

"Of course." Mila raced beside him as they climbed the hill. "Any sign of DiSanti or his men?"

"Just some cans of food and water, but no evidence of DiSanti or medical supplies." His breath heaved out as they made it to the door. "No telling how long the girls have been here. This is probably a holding spot until they can move or sell them."

Lucas met them at the bottom of the stairs. "Two in the room on the end. Both have pulses, but they're weak. I was afraid to get too close to the others and spook the one who's conscious. Ambulance should be here in ten."

"No sign of Izzy?" Mila asked.

Lucas shook his head. "Perhaps the girl who's conscious can tell us something about where they were going."

Mila latched onto that hope as she followed Brayden up the stairs. The dust, cobwebs, fading wallpaper and scratched floors were a sign that the inn hadn't been used in at least a decade.

DiSanti had taken advantage of that just like he took advantage of everything else.

"Brace yourself," Brayden said in a low voice. "It's not pretty."

"I've seen a lot of bad things in my field," Mila said, although the inhumane treatment people inflicted on others never ceased to amaze—and disgust—her.

Brayden opened the door, but she motioned for him to let her enter first. The lighting was dim, the smell of sweat and urine strong. Someone had also been sick.

She breathed out, emotions welling inside her at the sight of the two unconscious girls on the cots. Both wore dresses way too short for them, which had ridden up their legs as they lay sprawled on the beds.

The third girl was shaking and crying, her arms wrapped around her knees, her fear a palpable force in the room.

"Hi," she said in a soft tone as she slowly walked toward the teens. "My name is Dr. Mila Manchester."

She offered the frightened girl a warm smile. "My friend Brayden works with the police. We're here to rescue you." The crying girl sniffed and clenched her legs tighter.

"I promise, we won't hurt you. We know some bad men brought you here, and we're going to take you to the hospital for treatment, then make sure you're safe."

The girl's face crumpled, and a wail escaped her. Mila was afraid she'd said the wrong thing, but she didn't have time to second-guess herself. No telling what DiSanti's cronies had done to the young girl.

She approached the cots where the two unconscious girls lay, hair spilled on the pillows, bodies limp. At first glance, they didn't appear to be breathing. She stooped between the two cots and gently pressed her hand to the first girl's cheek, a sandy-blonde girl with pale skin and freckles. Her skin felt cold and clammy, and she didn't respond. Mila checked for a pulse and was relieved to find one, although, as Lucas reported on the other two teens, it was weak.

She gave Brayden a quick nod to indicate the girl was alive, then turned to the other, an auburn-haired girl. Bruises darkened the pale skin beneath her eyes and covered her legs. One arm dangled from the side of the bed, while the other hand clutched the sheet to her as if she was fighting to cover herself and preserve her dignity.

Mila checked for a pulse, then breathed a sigh of relief that she had one. Gently, she stroked the girl's cold cheek with the back of her hand. "Hang in there, sweetheart. You're going to be okay."

Anger churned in her belly at what these girls had endured. They had to survive.

All the more reason to save Izzy. If not, and DiSanti killed her and kept Izzy alive, she might end up like these teenagers. That was not going to happen to her daughter, no matter what she had to do.

Satisfied the girls were breathing, she turned her attention to the brunette staring at her with terror-glazed eyes.

"Hey, sweetie, I told you my name is Dr. Manchester, but you can call me Mila."

The girl clamped her teeth over her lower lip and simply stared at her with distrust.

Who could blame her? She had reason not to trust.

Mila offered her a sympathetic smile. "Your friends, the other girls here, they're alive, and I'm going to make sure they receive medical treatment." And psychiatric help if needed.

"I understand that you're scared," Mila said, inching closer. "But everything's going to be all right. You're never going to have to see those bad men again."

The girl's breath hitched.

Mila offered her another smile. "What's your name, sweetie?"

The girl gave a wary nod, then whispered, "Keenan."

"Hi, Keenan, it's nice to meet you. Like I said, my name is Mila. I'm a doctor. Can you tell me how you ended up here?"

The girl whimpered. "They took me…from the shelter," she said in a raw whisper.

"I'm so sorry, honey." She patted the girl's thin hand. "Do you have some family I can call? A mother? Father? Grandparent?"

Keenan shook her head no. "My grandma took me

to the shelter when we got evicted, but she was sick…
and she didn't make it."

"Do you remember the name of the shelter?"

The girl rubbed her forehead, then shook her head.
"No, it was late, and I was so upset over Granny that I
didn't pay attention."

"Shh, it's all right now. I promise I'll take care of
you." She reached out and patted Keenan's thin shoulder, relieved when the young girl didn't jerk away. "I
think you were drugged. Am I right?"

Another nod.

"Do you have any idea what they gave you?"

Keenan shook her head no.

"Was it in your food? Or did they inject you?"

The girl held out her arm. Mila gritted her teeth at the
sight of the needle marks. Fury mushroomed inside her.

The sound of a siren wailed from outside, and
Brayden stepped back into the room and motioned that
the ambulance had arrived.

"The paramedics are going to transport you and the
other girls to the hospital," Mila said.

Fear flashed in Keenan's eyes, and she clutched Mila's hand, her ragged nails digging into Mila's palms.

Mila's heart ached for her. "I'll go with you," Mila
promised. "And I'll stay with you every step of the way."

The girl nodded vigorously, tears trickling down her
cheek. Fear streaked her face as she glanced at the door.
"They're coming back for us," she said on a sob.

Mila glanced at Brayden, then squeezed the girl's
hand. "They won't find you, I promise. Brayden's
brother is with the FBI."

Brayden murmured that it would be okay, too. "We'll

post someone here and catch them when they return," Brayden assured her.

Mila inhaled a deep breath. "Keenan, the men who brought you here and drugged you work for another man named DiSanti. Does that name sound familiar?"

Keenan gave a small shrug. "Maybe."

Mila patted her arm. "I need to ask you one more question." She removed her phone and showed her a picture of Izzy. "I think those same men kidnapped my little girl. She's only three and her name is Izzy."

The girl's eyes widened, and she gasped for a breath, as if she was having a panic attack.

Panic clawed at Mila. "Did you see Izzy? Was she here?"

Chapter Sixteen

Mila felt as if her heart stopped beating. "Keenan, have you seen this little girl?"

The young girl wiped at her tears with the back of a bruised hand and gave a little nod.

Mila's pulse jumped. "Was she here?"

The girl nodded again.

Mila swallowed back a sob. "Was she okay? Was she hurt?"

Keenan's look softened. "She was scared, but Jade took care of her."

"Jade?"

"She was one of us," Keenan said. "She kept the little girl close to her, and told the men to leave them alone."

Relief lightened Mila's fear for a millisecond. At least they hadn't hurt Izzy. Not yet.

But Lucas was searching the outbuildings now.

She held Keenan's hand again, warming it between her own. "When did they leave you here?"

"This morning."

Damn. If they'd only gotten here sooner…

She straightened. She had to focus. "Was Jade with Izzy when they left?"

Keenan nodded. "The little girl was clinging to her."

Emotions throbbed inside Mila's chest. "Did the men say where they were going?"

The young girl rubbed her forehead again, her eyes crinkling. "No...at least I didn't hear them."

Footsteps sounded in the hall, then Brayden appeared with two medics.

Mila patted Keenan's hand and stood. "It's going to be okay now. Hang in there, sweetie."

Mila hurried to meet the medics and watched as they began taking vitals.

"Let's get them to the hospital stat," Mila said. "I want a full blood panel to identify the drugs they were given, also rape kits and full body workups."

The next few minutes were hectic as the medics carried the teens to the ambulance. Keenan was weak, but seemed to be stronger now that she realized she could trust Mila, and insisted she could walk. Mila helped her down the steps and outside.

Lucas and Brayden met them at the ambulance.

"Nothing in the outbuildings," Lucas said.

Brayden touched her elbow. "Did the girl tell you anything?"

Mila whispered to Keenan to climb in the ambulance and assured her she'd ride with her. But first she had to talk to Brayden. "Keenan said Izzy was here. A girl named Jade was taking care of her, protecting her from DiSanti's men."

"Any idea where they went?" Brayden asked.

"I'm afraid not. But they just left this morning so maybe they haven't gotten too far," Mila said.

Brayden stepped to the back of the ambulance. "Keenan, did you see what kind of vehicle the men were driving when they left?"

The girl shook her head. "They put us in a white van."

They'd used white vans before. So generic, dammit. "I'll ask Lucas to have their analyst check traffic cams on the highways near here."

Mila checked her phone again.

Still nothing.

Frustration knotted her stomach, but she climbed in the back of the ambulance.

She'd help Keenan and the others while Lucas searched for the van.

Lucas called a crime scene team to process the house and property, then Brayden and his brother followed the ambulances to the hospital.

The staff rushed the girls to the ER, and Lucas spoke with the doctor on call to request rape kits for the victims, although the doctor reported that Mila had already requested the exams be done. Keenan became upset at the idea, but Mila soothed her and promised to stay with her every step of the way.

The next hour dragged by as they waited on tests and for the girls to regain consciousness. Lucas checked in constantly with his people, hoping for word on the van or DiSanti.

Brayden phoned Dexter to relay the latest events.

"I've been digging into locals who might be involved in this trafficking unit. Lem Corley is on Lucas's short list," Dexter said. "Word is that he's retired and hired a cowboy out of El Paso to run the cattle ranching business. He's also bought up property near the Mexican border in Juarez."

"We know that. Do you have anything new?" Brayden asked. "What about his financials?"

"Corley has a hefty savings, but he could argue that he's built that from the cattle operation." Dexter paused. "I found an offshore account with a couple million in it. There's no indication that his business pulled in that kind of money."

Brayden chewed the inside of his cheek. "That is suspicious."

"Could be drugs," Dexter said.

"Or he could be shuffling young women across the border for DiSanti." Brayden glanced at Lucas, who was talking to one of the nurses. "Send me the address for the ranch near Austin. We'll talk to Corley once we finish here."

"Copy that. I'll keep digging and see if I can find out more on that property in Juarez."

Brayden thanked him, then hung up and joined Lucas.

"The girls are traumatized," the doctor said. "Two of them regained consciousness, but they're terrified and not talking. I've requested a psych exam and counselor."

"Let me call my wife, Charlotte," Lucas said. "You may remember her from a few months ago when her art therapy studio was invaded and four of her students were abducted."

The doctor nodded. "Yes, I was glad to hear that they were all found alive and safe."

"We think the man who orchestrated their abduction spearheaded the Shetland operation," Lucas said. "We also believe he's behind the trafficking ring that was holding the five victims here hostage. It's imperative I speak with them when they regain consciousness. They might be able to give us a lead as to where the ringleader went."

"I understand, but as I said before, these patients are severely traumatized. They need rest, medical treatment and therapy."

"My wife, Charlotte, can help," Lucas insisted. "She's an art therapist and has experience with DiSanti's victims. These girls might feel comfortable with her and open up."

"Excellent," the doctor said. "The other girls are stable, but were heavily medicated, so it may be hours before they become lucid."

"When they do, I want Charlotte to talk to them," Lucas said. "A little girl is missing and is in the hands of the leader of the trafficking ring."

The doctor wiped perspiration from his brow. "Of course."

Lucas thanked him, then stepped aside to call Charlotte. Mila appeared at the entry to the waiting room, looking worried and exhausted.

Brayden rushed toward her. He wanted to hold her, to promise her everything would be all right.

"Keenan is finally calmer and sleeping," Mila said.

"Was she able to tell you anything else?" Brayden asked.

Mila shook her head. "I'm afraid not. Unfortunately she was pretty incoherent when the men were around."

Brayden's heart went out to the girl and to Mila. She was a gutsy, strong woman. Even though she was terrified for her daughter, she had compassion for these victims.

"The doctor said two of the girls have regained consciousness. Maybe they can help."

Mila's eyes darkened with concern. "I hope so."

Brayden couldn't resist. He pulled her up against him and wrapped his arms around her. "It's going to be okay, Mila. We'll find her."

Her heavy breathing punctuated the air. He thought she might pull away, but she laid her head against his chest and seemed to give in to her own needs for a moment. He rubbed her back, rocking her gently in his arms. When she lifted her head and looked into his eyes, the agony in hers nearly sent him to his knees.

"Keenan is so lost," Mila said. "I don't know if she'll ever truly recover. Or the others."

He offered a smile of encouragement. "It may seem like that now, but I've seen the progress Charlotte's students have made these last few months. It's amazing. With her help and my mother's love, they feel secure now and are moving on, even looking forward to the future. They have a family, even if it's not the one they were born to."

Mila bit down on her lip, then pulled away.

"Did I say something wrong? You don't think that my mother could love them like they're her own?"

Mila stiffened. "Of course I believe that. I was adopted myself." She thumbed a strand of hair away from her cheek. "You said two of the girls are awake now. I'd like to talk to them."

"I know. So would I, but the doctor asked us to wait. Lucas is calling Charlotte to come and counsel the girls. Maybe you and Charlotte can talk with them together."

Mila nodded. "Yes, I'm sure they need a counselor after what they've been through. And I promise not to push them too hard. I want what's best for the girls, too."

She was the most unselfish woman Brayden had ever met. He was falling for her.

That thought should have shaken him up.

But for some reason, in the midst of the ugliness surrounding him, it felt right.

"Charlotte is on her way." Lucas's commanding voice forced Brayden to put his personal thoughts on hold. He jerked his mind back to the case.

"Dexter sent me GPS coordinates for Lem Corley's ranch. He checked Corley's financials and found an off shore account with a hefty amount in it. He's also looking into his property in Juarez."

"It's near the border," Lucas said. "We have an agent investigating it."

"He could be helping DiSanti move victims across the border into Mexico."

A muscle ticked in Lucas's jaw. "I'm going to talk to him now."

Brayden cleared his throat. "I'll go with you." He glanced at Mila. "That is, if you'll be okay here for a while."

Mila clasped her hands together. "I'll be fine. I want to stay with the girls until they're out of the woods."

MILA MEANT WHAT she'd told Brayden. But even as she'd assured Keenan she was safe, all she could think about was Izzy and what was happening to her.

If DiSanti could possibly have figured out that she was his child.

She prayed not, that her secret was safe.

She'd die before she'd let that bastard know he had a precious little girl. Izzy belonged to her.

She went to the vending machines, bought a cup of

coffee and carried it back to the waiting room. Charlotte was just coming in the door when she arrived. She made a beeline toward Mila, then embraced her.

They were both a little teary when they pulled away.

"Lucas said that one of the girls saw Izzy. That's good news, Mila."

Mila forced a smile, although her heart wasn't in it. "That's been hours though." It had been hours since that text message too and still no word of what she should do.

DiSanti wanted her to lose the feds. Did that mean he was watching her to see if she complied?

She glanced around the hospital, suddenly suspicious that one of the staff or maybe one of the people in the waiting room—there was a big guy in a hoodie—might be on DiSanti's payroll. He could have planted someone to follow her.

The doctor on call, a man named Dr. Hembry, approached her. "Dr. Manchester, I came to give you an update. The two girls who regained consciousness are physically going to be fine. But they're scared to death."

Mila gestured toward Charlotte. "This is Charlotte Reacher Hawk, the wife of the federal agent you were talking to. He told you she could help."

"That's right, you're the therapist." He shook Charlotte's hand. "At this point, having a kind face, especially a woman's, will go a long way."

"Then I can see them?" Charlotte asked.

Dr. Hembry nodded. "We thought it might help if we put the girls in the same room," Dr. Hembry said.

He led the two of them to an ER room, and they slipped inside.

Mila took one look at the two young girls, and hated

DiSanti more than ever. The battered teens looked lost and terrified and small in the hospital beds.

She and Charlotte approached slowly, and Mila explained that she was with the federal agent who'd rescued them.

Charlotte introduced herself, then Mila did the same.

She offered them a sympathetic smile. "I understand you've both been through a frightening ordeal, and we want to help you."

Charlotte scooted a chair between the beds, so she could face both girls. "I'm here for whatever you need," she said softly. "I know some other girls who were abducted by the same man who took you. We rescued them last year, and they're safe now. So are you."

The girls traded wary looks, both limp from the drugs and their ordeal.

"You can start by telling us your names," Charlotte said. "Also, tell us if you have family or a friend that you want us to call."

Unfortunately, the girls had no one to call just as Keenan hadn't. Perfect targets for DiSanti's people.

She and Charlotte spent the next hour soothing the girls and coaxing them to open up. Anita Robinson was fourteen, from El Paso and had run away from home after her mother died. Left with a stepfather who abused her, she took to the streets. She had no idea how long she'd been held hostage and had no family to call. But she'd ended up at a group home called Happy Trails.

Frannie Fenter was thirteen. She was kidnapped outside the group home where she was living. The same group home, Happy Trails, a ranch that supposedly helped orphans as the Hawks were doing.

Was the home legit or part of the Shetland operation?

Izzy CURLED UP with the raggedy blanket the big girl had given her. She was cold, hungry and scared. She wanted her mommy bad.

Tears ran down her face, but she pressed her fist to her mouth so she wouldn't cry out loud.

Jade, the girl who'd let her sleep with her the night before, rubbed her arm and shushed her.

She tried not to cry. But she couldn't help it. She wanted her mommy. She missed her and Roberta and Brownie and her pretty bed with the pink quilt. She wanted to run and play in her backyard and dig up worms and climb on her jungle gym. There were bird's eggs in a nest, too. Had the babies hatched already?

"I wanna go home," she whimpered. "I want Mama."

Jade wrapped the blanket around her tighter and pulled her up against her. "I know, sweetie. I know."

Jade looked sad, too. She said she hadn't seen her mother in years.

That made Izzy even more scared that she'd never see her mama again.

Chapter Seventeen

Mila stewed over what the girls had revealed so far. None of them had families, making them easy targets for DiSanti's men. Without family to report them missing, it might take months before anyone realized they were gone.

Except the head of the group home would have known.

Mila wanted to know more, but first, she had to ask them about her daughter. She showed them Izzy's photo. "This is my little girl. She's only three. Keenan said that she was at the house where you were. Do either of you recall seeing her?"

Frannie nodded, but Anita shook her head.

"I'm sorry. I don't remember much," Anita said.

"Did the men say anything about where they were going when they left?" Mila asked.

Frannie's lower lip quivered. "I heard one of them say they had to move us again, but they needed to take care of something first."

"Do you know what that something was?" Mila asked.

She shook her head. "It seemed important though. He shouted at the other man."

Charlotte stroked Frannie's arm. "You're doing great, sweetie. Did he mention a name? Or a place?"

Frannie's face paled. "I'm sorry. I wish I could help, but…he saw me watching, and gave me more drugs."

"Did they mention where they were taking Izzy?" Mila asked. "A town or another state? Or out of the country?"

"I…don't know…" Frannie grew agitated, and Anita wiped at more tears. Mila knew she was pushing hard, but her daughter's life was at stake.

"Tell us about the group home where you were living," Mila said gently.

"It was called Happy Trails," Frannie said. "We were supposed to work with the horses and learn to ride. But it didn't turn out that way at all."

"What happened?" Charlotte asked.

She cast her eyes downward, fear flashing across her face.

"Listen to me," Charlotte said in a tender but firm voice. "You're not in trouble, and you haven't done anything wrong."

"She's right," Mila said softly.

Charlotte cleared her throat. "You can tell us anything, no matter how bad you think it might sound, and we promise not to judge. We're here to help, and will do whatever necessary to make sure you're safe."

Frannie and Anita exchanged looks, then Frannie cleared her throat. "It wasn't a horse ranch at all. At first, they made us do chores and work outside on the farm. But then…"

Mila's stomach knotted. "Then what?"

"They brought men in," Anita cried. "They made us dress up in skimpy party dresses, then took pictures of us. I think they put them on the internet."

Mila forced herself not to react, but she was seething

inside. DiSanti's men would use the photos as advertisements to sell the girls to the highest bidder.

"YOU TOLD HARRISON where we're going?" Brayden asked Lucas as they drove to Corley's ranch.

"Yeah. I would have asked him to meet us, but Corley's ranch is out of his jurisdiction. Harrison assigned a couple of deputies to watch Hawk's Landing in case DiSanti's men traced Mila there."

"Good. We want Mom and the other girls safe." Brayden paused. "And Honey, too. That baby means everything to Harrison."

"He is excited about being a daddy," Lucas said with a twitch to his mouth.

"How about you and Charlotte? Any talk of kids?"

Lucas cut his eyes sideways. "She went through a lot this last year. We're taking our time, but maybe soon."

Envy stirred inside Brayden.

"Has Mila said anything else about Izzy's father?" Lucas asked.

Brayden clenched his jaw. He hadn't exactly pushed her for information the way Lucas had suggested. "I told you he's dead, so I don't see how he'd have anything to do with this."

Lucas veered down the long drive to the Corley ranch, which consisted of acres and acres of pastures for his cattle. The barns and stables looked weathered as if they were in disrepair. Odd since his financials indicated that he had money to invest back into the place.

Late-afternoon shadows darkened the tree-lined drive. A couple of pickup trucks were parked by one of the outbuildings.

Lucas barreled over the ruts in the road and came to

a stop at a farmhouse that looked as if it had been built a hundred years ago.

"He sure as hell hasn't put his money into fixing up his place," Brayden commented.

"I spoke to the deputy director earlier. He sent two agents to investigate Corley's property near Juarez."

Brayden's stomach tightened. "We can't let DiSanti's men take Izzy across the border."

"I've alerted the border patrol along with the airports and train stations to be on the lookout for Izzy," Lucas said.

Brayden had mixed feelings about that. He wanted a damn Amber Alert issued across the country. But doing so might spook DiSanti into carrying out his threats.

He couldn't live with that.

"I requested a warrant for Corley's computers, finances and electronic transmissions," Lucas said as he parked. "But the judge denied it. Said we didn't have probable cause."

Brayden silently cursed, Sometimes the law worked for them and sometimes against them. The reason Dexter did things his way.

"A missing child sounds like probable cause to me."

"I'm still working on it. Our analyst is looking for connections." Lucas checked his gun, then opened his car door and slid out. Brayden followed, his gaze scanning the property for signs of trouble. No gunmen in sight.

That didn't mean they weren't hiding in the shadows though.

He and Lucas walked up the graveled drive to the sagging porch and climbed the steps. A beagle lay snoring near a rusted porch swing.

Lucas knocked, and a minute later, a short robust woman wearing an apron answered the door. Lucas flashed his ID and introduced them, then asked her name.

"Harriet," she said.

"Have you worked here long?" Lucas asked.

"A few months," Harriet said. "I do the cooking and cleaning for the hands."

"We need to speak to Lem Corley," Lucas said. "Is he here?"

She gestured for them to come in. "In the back. He was just about to head back out. I'll go get him."

"Wait," Lucas said. "Can we ask you something first?"

A wary look crossed her face, and she wiped her hands on her apron. "I suppose. What's going on?"

Lucas showed her a picture of Izzy. "We're looking for this little girl. She's missing."

She narrowed her eyes as she studied the picture. "Haven't seen a child around this place, not since I've been here." She looked back up at Lucas. "What makes you think she'd be here?"

Lucas removed another photo from his pocket. DiSanti. "This man is wanted for human trafficking. We believe he and his men kidnapped the little girl. Have you seen him before?"

"I don't believe so. It's pretty quiet around here. Mostly the ranch hands. Occasionally Mr. Corley has one of his friends from the Cattleman's club out to talk business, but they hole up in his study so I don't really know any of them." She folded her arms across her ample stomach. "Why would you think Mr. Corley knows this man?"

Lucas maintained a poker face. "We're talking to anyone who owns large plots of land where DiSanti's men could hide the girls they abduct before trafficking them to buyers. Corley has property here and near Juarez, so his name cropped up."

She looked relieved. "I see. Well, I've never been to his Juarez place, but I can tell you that I haven't seen or heard of any girls being brought here."

Dammit. The property was large enough for the men to hide away from the house. But he and Lucas needed a warrant to search the land.

"What in the hell are you telling my cook?" a man's deep voice bellowed.

Harriet startled and pressed one hand over her mouth as Corley stomped toward her.

"Harriet?"

"I'm sorry, Mr. Corley," Harriet said. "These men are looking for a missing child, and were just asking some questions."

Corley pushed past her and confronted them, eyes blazing with anger. "I don't know why in the hell you'd think I'd know anything about a missing kid. I run cattle here."

"We're aware of that," Lucas said. "But you have a big spread, and it's possible that the men who abducted her could be hiding out on your property without your knowledge."

Corley scrubbed a hand over his balding head. He looked confused by Lucas's statement. Brayden admired his brother's tactic.

"The men who kidnapped her are extremely dangerous, Mr. Corley," Lucas said. "You wouldn't want to endanger your hands or Harriet, would you?"

"Uh…of course not," Corley stammered.

"Then you won't mind showing us around your property," Lucas said, his voice calm, nonjudgmental.

Corley shifted. "Do you have a warrant?"

Lucas's brow lifted in a challenge. "If you don't have anything to hide, then why would I need one?"

Corley inched backward as if to argue, but then seemed to think better of it. "All right. I'll show you around, then you can get off my property and leave me alone."

"Thanks for your cooperation," Lucas said.

Brayden followed them outside to Corley's truck.

Lucas gestured toward the vehicle. "It's a tight fit. Why don't you wait here, Brayden?"

Brayden jammed his hands in the pockets of his jacket and watched Corley and Lucas drive away.

Lucas had just given him a chance to dig around. He'd talk to Harriet again, then slip out to the stables and barn and talk to Corley's hands without Corley breathing down his neck.

MILA PATTED FRANNIE'S HAND. "Can you tell us how to get to Happy Trails?"

The girl shrugged. "Not really. The social worker from the shelter drove us there."

"From the shelter?" Mila asked.

Frannie nodded. "That's where I met Keenan."

Keenan had mentioned a shelter where her grandmother had taken her.

"What was the name of this social worker?" Charlotte asked.

Anita piped up. "Valeria. She was nice until she took us to that ranch. When I told her I didn't want to stay, she got mad and said I had no place to go, that I had to earn my keep."

"She told me the same thing," Frannie said.

Mila gritted her teeth. "Do you remember Valeria's last name?"

Both girls shook their heads.

"How about an agency she worked with?"

Again, neither knew the answer to that question. Which meant she might not have worked with an agency at all.

"Maybe Lucas can find out her name," Charlotte said.

"We need to locate this place, Happy Trails," Mila said. "Izzy might be there."

Charlotte clenched her hand. "We'll let Lucas and Brayden know. If she's there, they'll get her back."

Charlotte's trust and confidence in the Hawk men was rubbing off on Mila. She couldn't give up.

Her daughter needed her.

Charlotte retrieved her sketch pad. "Girls, let's see if you can describe the social worker who dropped you at Happy Trails."

"We'll try," Frannie said.

Anita spoke up. "She was tall, thin and had dark hair pulled back in a tight bun."

Charlotte quickly drew the image.

"Her features were sharp," Frannie said. "She had high cheekbones. Plump lips. And thick eyebrows."

Charlotte finished detailing the features.

"Was there anyone else with you at the ranch?" Mila asked.

Anita glanced down at her bruised knuckles. "Another lady. She was older, and she seemed afraid of the men."

"What was her name?" Mila asked.

"They called her Shanika," Frannie said.

Charlotte settled her sketch pad on her lap and removed her pencils.

Mila gripped her phone in her hand. "I'm going to call Brayden and tell him what we learned."

Charlotte nodded, and Mila left the room.

Her pulse hammered as she checked her phone for messages. Still no word about what DiSanti wanted her to do.

BRAYDEN GAVE HARRIET his business card. "This little girl's life is in danger. If you hear something that can help, please call me." He touched her arm gently. "I'm a lawyer. I can protect you."

She gave him a wary look, but nodded that she would. Brayden walked out to the barn and approached one of the hands, a tall dark-haired Hispanic cowboy. He was cleaning one of the stalls.

The cowboy jerked his head up at the sight of Brayden, then started to run. Brayden jogged after him and snatched him before he could exit the barn. He jerked the man around to face him and pushed him against the stall.

"You know the reason I'm here?" Brayden asked.

The man frowned. "I…heard you with Mr. Corley."

"What's your name?"

The man's gaze darted sideways.

"I'm not playing around here," Brayden said in a low growl. "What is your name?"

"Jorge."

Brayden clenched Jorge by the collar. "Is Corley working with DiSanti, helping traffic women and girls?"

The man shrugged. "I don't know anything about it. I'm just supposed to clean stalls and repair fences."

"Tell me what you do know," Brayden said.

"I told you I don't know anything." Fear vibrated in Jorge's voice.

Brayden arched his brows. "Then why run?"

Jorge lowered his gaze toward the ground, and the truth hit Brayden. "Because you're in the country illegally, aren't you?"

Shame and fear darted into the man's eyes as he glanced up at Brayden. "He said he knew somebody. That I could earn my freedom."

Anger radiated through Brayden. So Corley, or DiSanti, or both, had used Jorge's status as an immigrant to coerce him into doing their dirty work.

His gaze met Jorge's. "Just what did you have to do to earn it?"

Chapter Eighteen

Indecision played across the ranch hand's face. Jorge was definitely scared. Of being deported? Or maybe his family had been threatened as Mila's had?

The sound of an engine roaring closer made panic streak Jorge's face. Corley and Lucas returning. Dammit.

"I told you I know nothing," the cowboy said. "I just do my job."

"Does that job entail holding innocent girls hostage?"

A muscle ticked in the young man's jaw as he looked down at his shovel.

"We think that's what Corley is into," Brayden said. "Do you really want to live off money made that way? Is your freedom worth the life of a little three-year-old girl?"

Jorge winced.

"Think about it," Brayden said as Corley approached. "Do you have a sister or friend with a sister? Would you want her sold as a sex slave?"

The man looked up at him as if he was going to say something, but Corley's truck roared to a stop in front of them, gravel spewing, and Jorge clammed up.

Brayden slipped a business card from his pocket and pushed it into Jorge's hand. "Call me if you can help. If they take this little girl out of the country, her mother may never see her again."

The truck door slammed, and Corley climbed out, looking pissed. Lucas followed, his expression indicating he hadn't found anything helpful.

Brayden's cell phone buzzed. Mila.

He quickly connected. "Yeah?"

"Did you find her?" Mila asked, her voice quivering.

God, he hated to tell her no. "Not at Corley's. Hopefully one of the ranch hands or the cook will talk. We'll see."

A tense heartbeat passed. "Charlotte and I have been talking to the girls who regained consciousness. They're frightened, but they said that they were taken from a group home called Happy Trails. It was supposed to be a ranch for girls, but men were brought there for them to entertain. They were also dressed up and photographed."

"For potential clients," Brayden guessed.

"I think so."

"Where is this place?" Brayden asked.

"Neither girl knew the location. I was hoping you could find out."

"I'll talk to Lucas. Anything else?"

"A social worker named Valeria took them to the home. She might be in on the Shetland operation."

Hard to believe another woman would be involved, but it happened.

"A woman named Shanika was also at the ranch," Mila said. "Izzy could be there, Brayden."

"Lucas and I will get right on it. Hang in there."

"I could go with you," Mila said.

Brayden hesitated. If Happy Trails was a holding ground for the Shetland operation, it would be dangerous.

"I think you're better off there," Brayden said. "You and Charlotte did good today. See what else you can learn from the victims."

Silence stretched between them for a long moment. "Mila?"

"I'm here," she said. "Just find her, Brayden. I can't let her end up like these girls."

He wouldn't let that happen either. "I promise, we'll bring her back to you."

Damn, even as he made the promise, he knew he shouldn't, that he might not be able to deliver on it.

Then Mila would hate him.

That bothered him more than he wanted to admit.

He wanted to be her hero. Save her daughter.

Be the man she could turn to and trust.

Disappointing her would crush him.

THE AFTERNOON DRAGGED into evening as Mila and Charlotte sat with the girls. They moved Keenan in with Frannie and Anita and encouraged them to rest.

Mila checked her phone a dozen times, but still no word. She paced the waiting room while Charlotte went to check on the other two girls.

Why had DiSanti's men sent her that message and not followed through?

Her anxiety rose with every passing second. Did they know she'd turned to the Hawks for help? Had they discovered that Lucas and Brayden had rescued these girls?

Would they punish her daughter because they'd foiled DiSanti's plans?

Charlotte appeared with coffee in hand. "Unfortunately, the other girls couldn't offer anything more. Except that one of them confirmed that a girl named Jade was with Izzy and that she was taking care of her."

That was a small relief, but Mila latched onto it as they walked back to say good-night to the girls.

Lucas had arranged for guards to watch the girls' rooms, and the doctor agreed to keep her updated. Charlotte planned to coordinate with the Department of Family and Protective Services regarding the teens.

Charlotte hugged each of them and promised to visit the next day.

"What's going to happen to us?" Keenan asked.

Charlotte stroked Keenan's hand. "We'll find you a safe place to live, someone who'll care for you and help you get back on your feet, and back in school. Everything's going to be all right."

Mila hugged her, as well. "She's right, Keenan. Charlotte and I are on your side. You're not alone now."

Keenan didn't look completely convinced, but her eyes were closing, fatigue weighing on her, and she drifted to sleep.

"Come on," Charlotte said. "Ava has dinner waiting for us."

"Ava?"

"Lucas's mother," Charlotte said. "She's amazing. Honey and Harrison will be there, too."

Mila hesitated, willing a message to appear on her phone. But she checked it. Nothing.

"I don't want to endanger the Hawks," Mila said.

Charlotte grabbed her hand. "We all have a vested interest in seeing that DiSanti is stopped once and for all. You'll understand when you meet the girls the Hawks took in." A twinkle flickered in Charlotte's eye. "Besides, we have to talk to Ava and see if she has room in her heart for a few more young women in need."

IT TOOK A while to locate Happy Trails. Brayden would have thought it would have been well-known, at least on the internet, but it wasn't.

A sign of what it had been used for and by whom. DiSanti's group had wanted to keep it under the radar.

Damn him.

Charlotte had faxed sketches of Valeria and Shanika to Lucas to forward to the FBI field office in Austin. Their analyst forwarded them to law enforcement agencies and alerted airports, train and bus stations, and the border patrol to be on the lookout for the women, especially if they were traveling with a little girl.

Izzy had been gone too damn long for comfort. For all they knew, DiSanti's people could have carried her halfway across the world by now.

Or killed her and dumped her little body someplace where they might never find her.

No. He couldn't let himself think about the worst case. And he certainly couldn't divulge those concerns to Mila.

He and his family understood how painful it was to live year after year with no word of where your loved one was, or if they were dead or alive.

First his little sister, Chrissy. Then his father.

Lucas's phone buzzed, and he hit Connect. "Yeah. Okay. See you there."

"That was Charlotte," he said when he hung up.

"She's driving Mila to the ranch. Mom has dinner. I told her we'd meet them there."

Brayden nodded. His mother would love Mila.

He liked her. A lot. Maybe more than like. He wanted to be with her and rescue her daughter more than he'd ever wanted anything in his life.

Lucas steered the vehicle down the road leading to Happy Trails. Brayden spotted smoke in the distance.

"Look," he said, pointing toward the east. "There's a fire."

Lucas hit the gas and sped up. "That's the ranch," he said through gritted teeth.

Brayden gripped the seat edge as Lucas raced toward the smoke. Gravel spewed from their tires, gears grinding as he maneuvered a pothole and flew over a small hill. The smoke was growing thicker, curling up into the sky.

As soon as they dipped downhill, Brayden spotted flames. They engulfed the main house and two buildings to the side.

"Call the fire department," Lucas said as he took the curve on two wheels.

Brayden punched 9-1-1 and gripped the seat edge as Lucas swung the vehicle near a cluster of live oaks and careened to a stop. Flames shot into the sky, lighting up the darkness. Suddenly a black pickup darted from behind the burning building and roared past them.

Brayden threw the car door open and jumped out. "Go after him! I'll see if anyone's inside!"

Lucas hesitated for a second, but Brayden waved at him to go. If the person in the car knew where Izzy was, he was getting away.

Lucas sped after the vehicle, and Brayden ran to-

ward the burning farmhouse. Flames shot from the roof
and back of the house, and smoke billowed upward in
a thick fog.

Brayden yanked a bandanna from inside his jacket
and tied it around his mouth, then darted through the
front door. Smoke seeped through the entry, but the
blaze hadn't yet reached the doorway.

He conducted a quick survey of the house. All one
floor. Rooms to the right, a hall to the left that probably led to bedrooms.

"Is anyone here?" he shouted as he glanced down
the hall.

Wood crackled and popped in the blaze, but he didn't
hear voices. Still, he shouted again and again as he
raced down the hall to the bedrooms. He jumped over
wood that had splintered down from the ceiling, dodging flames as the fire crawled along the doorways eating the rotting wood.

Two rooms held a series of single beds that resembled
a dorm. He counted a dozen, although fire was spreading quickly. He dodged flames as he checked the closets
to make sure no one was hiding or had been left inside.

Flames rippled up the wall, catching the curtains
on fire and crawling toward the beds. He raced to the
next room, dodging falling debris, and wove between
patches of burning embers to check those beds and the
closet. Clothes inside the closet were aflame, but no
one was inside.

Relieved, he headed back to the front then into the
hall toward the kitchen. Already fire blazed a trail along
the back wall. He coughed, but had to check the storage closet.

Smoke created a thick fog, but he dived through

it, calling out as he went. Surely DiSanti's goonies wouldn't have left anyone inside, especially Izzy.

He reached out to touch the doorknob of the pantry, but it was hot, so he searched the kitchen for some cloths, grabbed one, wrapped it around his hand and opened the door.

His gut tightened at the sight of a woman inside the closet. Dammit. Too late. She was dead. A gunshot wound to the front of her head.

He stooped to check for a pulse anyway, but knew she was gone. Judging from the sketch Charlotte had sent, this was Shanika, the woman from Happy Trails.

THE HOMEY SCENTS of apple pie and beef stew wafted through the Hawks' main house, stirring memories of Mila's own family when she was little. Granted, they hadn't stayed in one place long, but they had shared meals as often as possible.

Mrs. Hawk took her hands and pulled her into the kitchen. "I'm so sorry for what you're going through, dear, but my boys will find your daughter. I have faith."

She wanted to have faith, too, but she was struggling. "Thank you for having me here tonight, Mrs. Hawk."

"Please call me Ava," the woman said. "We're all family."

Four teenagers were chatting and laughing as they set the table. Charlotte pulled her toward the doorway. "Mila, this is Mae Lynn, Evie, Adrian and Agnes."

The girls piped up with hellos and how much they loved the ranch.

Mila's adopted mother would have loved Ava. She'd opened her home to four teenagers in need and treated them like her own children.

The girls helped carry platters of food to the table, then the door opened and Ava greeted her oldest son, Harrison. Amazing how much the men resembled one another, but each was distinct.

"I'm Honey," a perky, very pregnant blonde said as she gave Ava a hug.

Mila exchanged greetings with the couple, her heart squeezing at the sight of Honey's blossoming belly. She hadn't gotten to carry Izzy herself, but she loved that child as if she had.

"My grandson will be here soon," Ava said with a beaming smile for Honey. "It'll be pure joy to have a baby around the house again."

Izzy's little face taunted Mila. Her arms felt empty, and she ached to hug her daughter. Never again would she take it for granted when she sang Izzy a lullaby or tucked her in bed or read her a good-night story, even if she read the same story a dozen times.

She barely managed to keep her emotions at bay during the meal. Thankfully the girls filled the silence with talk of Christmas shopping and the gifts they were making for the children's hospital. Ava was teaching them to piece quilts, and they were making blankets for the kids to snuggle with and take home when they were released.

After dessert, the teenagers retreated to the arts and craft room Ava had set up for them to work on the Christmas projects.

Harrison cleared his throat and stood. "Mom, thanks for dinner. I'm going to get Honey home. The baby's been keeping her up at night."

"It's only the beginning," Ava said with a laugh.

Mila watched as Harrison helped Honey stand. He

was sweet and protective and loving just as Lucas was to Charlotte.

"I hope everything goes well during delivery," Mila said.

Honey gave Mila a sympathetic smile. "Thanks. I can't imagine what you're going through. I'll say a prayer that Lucas and Brayden find your daughter soon."

Mila thanked her, then they said good-night. "You have a beautiful family, Ava," Mila told Brayden's mother.

"I'm blessed, for sure," Ava said. "My boys, and now their wives, and now Mae Lynn and Evie and Adrian and Agnes." She pressed her hand over her chest. "My heart is bursting with love."

"I'm so proud of those girls," Charlotte said. "You've made such a difference in their lives, Ava. They're blossoming under your care."

A broad smile curved Ava Hawk's face. "They've given me just as much as I've given them." She clasped Charlotte's hand. "Tell me about the ones you rescued today."

Mila listened quietly while Charlotte filled her in. But worry and fatigue weighed on her, and finally she stood. "If it's all right, I'm going to the cabin to get some rest." Maybe if she was alone for a while, DiSanti would finally get back in touch.

Concern darkened Charlotte's eyes. "I'll drive you over."

She didn't have time to respond. Footsteps sounded from the front. Then Lucas's and Brayden's voices.

Mila hurried to meet them, hoping they had good

news. But the moment she saw their grim expressions and smelled the smoke on Brayden, her hopes died.

Charlotte and Ava joined them, and Ava gasped when she saw Brayden's soot-streaked face. "Son, what happened? Are you all right?"

"I'm fine," Brayden said. "When we reached the house at Happy Trails, it was on fire. I ran in to make sure no one was inside."

Lucas relayed how he'd chased the man who'd set the fire. "I tried to catch him, but he crashed into a ravine and died instantly."

Brayden gave Mila's arm a soft squeeze. "Izzy wasn't in the house or outbuildings, Mila. I searched every nook and corner." He sighed. "Unfortunately, we found that woman Shanika."

"Did she tell you anything?" Mila asked.

Brayden's eyes darkened. "I'm afraid not. She was dead."

Fear clogged Mila's throat, despair threatening. DiSanti's men killed the woman who'd helped them at Happy Trails.

What did that mean for Izzy?

Chapter Nineteen

Brayden sensed despair in Mila's body language.

She had been taking care of DiSanti's victims, he reminded himself. That alone would weigh on anyone with a heart. And Mila had plenty of heart.

"Would you like to go back to the cabin?" he asked.

Mila nodded and looked down at the floor. "You're probably hungry though. Your mother made a delicious dinner."

"I'll pack him a plate to go," Ava said.

"Thanks, Mom, but Lucas and I grabbed something earlier."

Hugs went all the way around as Lucas gathered Charlotte, and he escorted Mila out to his SUV.

"Did you really eat?" Mila asked as Brayden drove her back to his cabin.

"We grabbed a burger while we were waiting on the location of Happy Trails."

He parked in front of the cabin and they went inside. "Do you mind if I take a shower?" Mila asked.

A shower was nothing. He wished he could offer her more. "Of course not. It's been a long day."

"The longest," she said in a weary voice.

He swallowed hard as he watched her duck into his

guest bedroom, then the shower kicked on, and he decided to clean up himself. He smelled like smoke and soot and sweat.

The hot water felt heavenly, although thoughts of Mila in his other bathroom naked and wet ignited a different kind of tension, one that made his body harden with desire.

Dammit, Brayden. The last thing Mila needs is you coming on to her.

He toweled off, shrugged on clean jeans and a T-shirt and strode into the den. But the sound of Mila crying echoed from the bedroom and tied him in knots.

He moved to the door, his heart aching as he listened to her sob. He wanted to go to her, pull her into his arms, comfort her, assuage the agony she was feeling.

He ordered himself to walk away instead.

But her crying grew louder, and he lost his restraint.

He pushed open the door and slipped inside. She stood at the window, her hair damp, her body trembling.

He closed his arms around her and pulled her against him, then held her tight.

MILA SANK AGAINST BRAYDEN, soaking in his warmth and strength. His arms felt like a safe haven, one she desperately needed at the moment.

Images of Izzy, terrified and crying for her, bombarded her, making her feel weak and helpless, chiseling away at her hope.

Brayden murmured soft, comforting words, his calm, gruff voice full of understanding.

She purged her emotions until she was exhausted with the tears. God, she'd never been a crier, had always been tough and took charge of things like her mother.

Struggling for control, she wiped at the moisture on her cheek, then lifted her head and looked into Brayden's eyes. She expected pity, but saw compassion.

She ordered herself to pull away. But she wanted so much more.

Selfish as it was, for just a brief moment, she wanted to feel his lips against hers. Anything to drive away the pain and worry.

His eyes flickered with something dark. Sexy.

A passion that lay beneath.

His chest rose and fell against hers, and she stroked her hand over it, absorbing the solid strength in his embrace. He thumbed a strand of hair from her cheek, then heaved a breath and started to pull away.

She caught his arm and drew him back to her. Their gazes locked, heat flaring between them. He'd run into a flaming building tonight to search for her daughter, had risked his life.

Brayden Hawk was honorable and caring and a damn good man, just like his brothers. The Hawks were the most loving family she'd ever known.

Hunger blossomed inside her, and she lifted her hand and placed it against Brayden's cheek. He sucked in a harsh breath.

"Mila, you should go to bed," he said in a gruff voice.

The need in that voice and in his eyes mirrored her own. She couldn't resist. She rose on her tiptoes and pressed her lips to his, melding their mouths in a sensual kiss.

Sex appeal oozed in his touch. He was a cowboy— rugged, tough, a fighter. A man who loved the land.

He ran his hands up her back and tangled them in

her hair, moving his lips across hers. First gently. Then desire spiraled, and he deepened the kiss.

She welcomed his tongue and teased him with her own.

Passion spiked inside her, and she moaned, then pushed at his T-shirt, desperate to feel his hot, bare skin against hers.

Suddenly he wrenched away. His breathing was erratic, his eyes hot with passion. "Mila, we can't." He rubbed her arms. "I don't want to take advantage of you."

He spun away from her, then walked outside onto his deck.

Tears of humiliation burned the backs of her eyelids, then she realized what he'd said. Not that he didn't want her.

He didn't want to take advantage of her.

Even in the face of her throwing herself at him, Brayden Hawk was doing the honorable thing.

His honorable intentions made her want him even more.

She inhaled a deep breath, then joined him on the deck. "It's not taking advantage of me if I want it."

BRAYDEN'S HEART POUNDED. More than anything he wanted to turn around, drag Mila into his arms, carry her to bed and make love to her.

But he forced himself to remain still. If he looked out at the ranch long enough maybe he'd forget the desire he'd seen in her eyes.

He'd tried to do the right thing. He cared too much about Mila to hurt her or take advantage of the moment.

But it was damn hard to deny that he wanted her.

"You're vulnerable now," he said, forcing out the words. "What kind of man would I be to ignore that?"

Her footsteps sounded behind him, then she eased around to face him. Anger flared in her expressive eyes. "Either you're trying to be chivalrous, which isn't necessary since I'm a grown woman and can make decisions for myself, or you really just don't want me."

He released a pent-up breath. Then he made the mistake of looking into her eyes. Raw need darkened the depths, triggering his own hunger to override his reservations.

She parted her lips, then traced her finger over his lips, and resistance fled.

"You're sure?" he growled as he yanked her to him.

A seductive smile tilted her mouth, and he kissed her again, this time with all the need he'd tried so hard to squash earlier.

She slid her arms around his neck, and teased him with her tongue again, driving him mad with hunger. Taking her cue, he traced her lips with his own tongue, then delved inside.

She tasted like sweetness and desire and raw need all at the same time. Her hands pushed at his T-shirt, and cool air brushed his belly. Realizing they were still outside, he broke the kiss long enough to coax her inside, then swept her into another embrace.

Their hands grew frantic, pushing and tearing at each other's clothes. Lips and tongues melded and danced in a sensual rhythm that ignited a burning fire in his belly. He wanted her naked, her skin sliding against his.

He wanted her in his bed.

She shoved his T-shirt over his head and tossed it onto the couch, and he grabbed her hand and tugged her to his bedroom. She pulled at his belt, and he ripped it off, then slowed her by slipping a finger beneath the hem of her shirt.

She made a soft sound in her throat, then removed her shirt and threw it to the floor. Heat darkened her expression as he gazed at her beautiful breasts spilling over tiny scraps of black lace.

Black lace—just as he'd fantasized.

Her lustrous hair dangled over bare shoulders, inviting his touch, and he threaded his fingers through the silky strands and yanked her to him once more. She moaned as he kissed her again, then raked his tongue and teeth along her ear and down her throat.

He backed her to the bed, and they fell on it in a tangle of arms and legs and frenzied passion. Her jeans came next, then his. He groaned at the sight of that thin strip of lace covering her femininity.

Another deep kiss, then he trailed his mouth down her throat again to her breasts. He tugged the lace aside with his teeth, then closed his mouth over one turgid nipple. She moaned and moved against him, drawing him into the V of her thighs. His sex hardened, his body pulsing with sensations as he stroked her heat with his erection.

He teased one breast, then the other, suckling her until her body quivered against him, then he dipped lower to lick and kiss her belly. His fingers toyed with the edge of her panties, his mouth watering for a taste.

She threw her head back in abandon, offering herself, and he tugged her panties off, parted her legs and dived into her honeyed sweetness with his tongue.

Passion overcame him as she fisted her hands into his

hair, and he teased and tormented her with his tongue until she cried out in pleasure with her orgasm.

A SHIVER RIPPLED through Mila as erotic sensations engulfed her. Her body tingled all over, the connection so intense that she clawed at his back to keep him from leaving her.

She wanted more.

She wanted Brayden.

He started to move off her, but she grabbed his arms and flipped him to his back. Surprise lit his eyes, and he traced a line down her throat to her breasts. Her nipples hardened to buds, begging for his mouth.

But it was time to give him pleasure.

She kissed him again, then lowered her body on top of him and stroked his thick length against her warm center. She wanted him inside her.

He kissed her deeply, then gently pushed her away.

"Brayden?"

He held up a finger, then reached into his nightstand and snagged a condom. Relieved he wasn't ending their lovemaking, she snatched the foil packet, ripped it open and rolled it over his rigid length. He grew harder, thicker, and a low growl escaped him as she finished.

"You're torturing me," he said in a husky whisper.

She climbed on top of him, angled her head for another kiss, then impaled herself. Inch by inch, he filled her, stirring her arousal again. He traced a finger over her nipples, then ran his hands over her hips and yanked her harder on top of him.

Passion flared, and a frenzy of need overwhelmed her as they increased the tempo. Skin against skin, lips against lips, bodies dancing in rhythm together... Titillating sensations built within her until they erupted in a firestorm of colors.

Brayden groaned her name, then rolled her to her back and plunged inside her, over and over until he called her name as his own release overcame him.

Mindless with pleasure, they rocked back and forth until the sensations ebbed and slowly subsided. Even then, he wrapped his arms around her and held her so close she could feel his heart beating.

When their breathing steadied, he slipped into the bathroom. A minute later, when he returned he dragged her into his arms again. She curled next to him, taking solace in his strength.

Thoughts of DiSanti threatened, and she kissed him once more, then crawled down his body to take his length into her mouth. Brayden groaned and protested, but she brought him to arousal again, then he rolled her to the side and made love to her.

This time when she came, emotions and exhaustion mingled, and she collapsed against him.

As long as she closed her eyes and felt him next to her, she could convince herself that everything would be all right.

Eventually, she fell asleep, a deep sleep where she dreamed that Izzy was home and that Brayden was in their lives and they were a family.

BRAYDEN LISTENED TO Mila's labored breathing for a long time. She had to be exhausted from the emotional strain of the last couple of days. Making love to her had been mind-blowing.

He cradled her closer, willing her to rest. And for tomorrow to bring them good news about her daughter.

God knows he'd wished this same thing for years where Chrissy was concerned. He prayed for a better outcome with Izzy.

Then what? Mila would return to her life with her daughter. And he would go back to his life. Alone.

Except the thought of that disturbed him.

He liked Mila. He wanted her to have her daughter. But he wanted to be in their lives, as well.

Would she have room for him once Izzy was returned?

And what if he couldn't deliver on his promise to bring Izzy home safely?

He had to...

For hours, he lay in bed contemplating what he should be doing differently on the case. How he could find DiSanti.

Hours later, he drifted to sleep, but a loud knock jerked him awake. He blinked, confused for a moment, then saw Mila asleep in his bed, and memories of the night before returned. Sweet, blissful, erotic memories of lovemaking that he wanted to repeat.

The pounding sounded again.

Mila stirred, but he pulled the covers over her, and crawled from bed. He yanked on jeans and a T-shirt, then padded into the den. Another knock and he swung open the door.

Lucas.

He looked angry.

"What's going on?" Brayden asked as Lucas stormed past him.

Lucas spun around, arms folded, dark intimidating eyes filled with suspicion. "You tell me."

Brayden scratched his head. His eyes were blurry from lack of sleep.

"Mila has been lying to us," Lucas said through gritted teeth.

Brayden glanced at the closed bedroom door, where Mila was still warming his bed. "What are you talking about?"

"The analyst at the Bureau can't find any record of Izzy's birth or of Mila having a child," Lucas said with a dark scowl.

"What? There has to be a mistake," Brayden said.

"Yeah. The mistake is in believing Mila. She's been playing you, Brayden," Lucas said grimly. "Mila isn't just afraid of DiSanti because he threatened her. I think the bastard is Izzy's father."

Chapter Twenty

Brayden stared at his bedroom door, his stomach knotting as Lucas's statement echoed in his head. "What makes you think he's the father?"

"When I saw Izzy's picture," Lucas said, "the similarities struck me. I can't believe you didn't notice."

Because he'd been blinded by Mila.

"So I had my analyst start digging for information. Mila was actually volunteering in Colombia at the same time DiSanti was there four years ago."

Brayden's mind raced, putting the pieces together. If DiSanti was Izzy's father, then Mila had had a relationship with the man.

Had slept with him.

The idea of that monster's hands touching her made him want to punch a wall.

Had she crawled in bed with *him* last night as a distraction to keep him from discovering the truth?

She'd said Izzy's father was dead—which had obviously been a lie. No wonder she'd been secretive and uncooperative when Lucas had arrested her.

Had DiSanti known all along that Izzy was his daughter and taken her because she belonged to him?

Had Mila lied about being coerced to perform the

surgery, too? Had she helped DiSanti escape because they had a child together?

A sense of betrayal cut thought Brayden like a sharp knife. He was a fool. Had done the very thing he knew not to do—he'd fallen for a client and been used again.

Brayden made the mistake of glancing at his closed bedroom door, and Lucas paced in front of the fireplace. "Good God, don't tell me you slept with her. What the hell were you thinking, Brayden?"

That I wanted her and admired her and thought we might have something special.

Idiot.

The door to his bedroom squeaked open, and Mila appeared, her hair tousled. She had dressed in jeans and a flannel shirt, and dammit, she looked beautiful.

But her wary gaze met his. Had she heard their conversation?

"Dr. Manchester," Lucas said, eyebrows arched in question. "Maybe you should join us."

Mila gave a little nod and entered the room, her expression wary. "Did you find Izzy?"

Lucas shook his head no. "But I did learn some interesting information about your daughter's father."

Brayden held his breath, hoping Lucas was wrong. That there was another explanation other than Mila being with DiSanti.

But she heaved a breath and averted her gaze for a brief second, and he had his answer.

"You…and DiSanti," Brayden said, the harsh words erupting. "You lied to me, used me."

Mila shook her head and walked toward him, but he threw up a hand, warning her to stop. She halted, then lifted her chin. "It's not what you think."

"What I think is that you had a relationship with that bastard, then helped him escape to protect your little girl's father." Disappointment mushroomed inside him. "How did you meet and get involved? Did you know who he was and what he was doing when you were together?"

Mila glared at him and then Lucas, then folded her arms. "You have it all wrong. I wasn't involved with DiSanti."

Brayden simply waited. "But you—"

"I told you it's not what you think," Mila said flatly.

He and Lucas exchanged confused looks. Then a sickening thought occurred to Brayden. "Mila...he didn't... force you, did he?"

Mila's face turned ashen, and she walked to the French doors and looked out at the back deck. Brayden's heart hammered. Lucas stood still, his body tense as they waited.

Brayden crossed the room to Mila, took a deep breath and gently turned her to face him. He braced himself for the gory details. "Tell me the truth. What happened?"

"It wasn't me," Mila said in a low voice.

He narrowed his eyes. "What do you mean, it wasn't you?"

"DiSanti didn't rape *me*," she said, emphasizing the word *me*.

"I don't understand," Brayden said.

"Just tell us the truth this time," Lucas interjected. "We've wasted enough time on your lies."

Mila swayed backward as if she'd been punched. Brayden was angry, too, but he gave his brother a warning look. Mila might have lied to them, but the terror in her expression was real. "Please, Mila, I told you that you could trust me, and you can."

Indecision warred in her eyes. "It's complicated."

"Is DiSanti Izzy's father?" he asked through gritted teeth.

Mila closed her eyes as if pained, then opened them and gave a wary nod. "Yes, but I'm not her birth mother."

Shock slammed into Brayden. That was the last thing he'd expected to hear.

And it complicated everything. If Mila wasn't Izzy's mother, then who was? Worse, DiSanti had kidnapped his own child, meaning they had no legal recourse to take her from the man.

MILA'S HEART ACHED at the look of betrayal on Brayden's face. She'd never wanted to lie to him, but she had to protect her daughter at all costs.

But now her secret was out.

What would Lucas and Brayden do with it?

Brayden suddenly swung away from her, disappointment and anger radiating from him. "I need caffeine."

Lucas remained pensive as Brayden started a pot of coffee, making her even more antsy. She had no idea what was going on in that head of his.

Brayden poured coffee in mugs, then brought Lucas and her one. She sank onto the sofa and cradled the cup between her hands to warm herself as she struggled to find a way to begin.

Brayden returned for a mug for himself, then joined them, the tension thick.

"Tell us what happened," Lucas said. "You took DiSanti's baby?"

Mila sipped her coffee, then decided to tell him everything. She might be in trouble, but the most important thing was saving Izzy from that horrible man. "You asked if I was raped and I told you no. But Izzy's birth mother was one of DiSanti's victims."

Brayden hissed between his teeth at the image she painted.

"Go on," Lucas said.

The memory of Carina coming to her that rainy night flashed back, stirring pain and fear. "The girl's name was Carina," Mila said. "I met her at the clinic after she escaped DiSanti. She was pregnant and alone and terrified. She had no place to go, so I arranged for her to stay in a shelter."

"She could have come to us," Lucas said. "If she'd testified, we could have protected her."

Mila swallowed back disgust. "You don't understand how terrified and traumatized she was. She was a little girl herself. She'd been drugged and forced to entertain men. Then DiSanti decided he wanted her for himself." She sipped her coffee again, the chill inside her growing more intense at the memory. "He locked her in his private lair and raped her repeatedly."

Silence, thick and filled with the horror of her words, stretched between them for several seconds.

Lucas cleared his throat. "How did she get away from DiSanti?"

Mila traced a finger around the rim of her mug. "She said the minute she realized she was pregnant, that she decided she had to leave. She didn't want him to know about the baby." She paused, thinking about how frightened Carina must have been. And how brave.

"DiSanti traveled a lot," she continued. "One night when he was gone, she sneaked out the window. She said she ran for miles and miles. His men came after her, but she hid in a drainpipe, then an abandoned mine for days with no food. She drank water from a nearby creek at night when she thought no one was looking for her."

Emotions twisted Brayden's face, but he didn't comment.

"Then what?" Lucas asked.

"One night she hitched a ride to Austin. By then, she was feverish and dehydrated. A woman picked her up and brought her to my clinic. She was terrified and so alone, but eventually she told me her story."

"You knew who DiSanti was?" Lucas asked.

Mila nodded. "I'd heard his name floating around in relation to human trafficking." Mila released a pent-up breath. "When she was feeling better, I helped Carina move into a shelter. In the past three years, two more girls escaped DiSanti and showed up at the clinic. I helped them find a safe place, as well."

Brayden finally spoke. "Good God, Mila, does DiSanti know all this?"

"When he showed up at my clinic for the surgery, he said I'd taken girls away from him and that I owed him."

"That's the reason he chose you for the cosmetic surgery," Brayden said, as if it made sense now.

"Did DiSanti know about Izzy?" Lucas asked.

She shook her head. "I don't think so. At least, he didn't mention her or her mother."

"No doubt he would have if he'd known," Lucas said.

Mila nodded. "He would probably have killed me right after I finished the surgery."

A strained silence fell between them, mired in the truth of her statement.

Brayden shifted. "So how did you come to have Izzy?"

Mila rubbed her temple where a headache was staring

to pulse. "One rainy night shortly after Izzy was born, Carina showed up at my door. She said the people at the shelter found a home where she could live and attend school. She knew she was too young to raise a child on her own and wanted to make a future for herself. Then she begged me to take Izzy and raise her." Her voice cracked. "What was I supposed to do?" she said in a raw whisper. "I couldn't turn her away or let that little baby go into the system. And I sure as hell couldn't let DiSanti have her."

Only now he did.

"Do you know where DiSanti is or where he was going?" Brayden asked.

Mila gaped at him. "Of course not. If I did, I would have told you."

"Did Carina sign Izzy over to you? Did you file adoption papers?" Brayden asked.

Mila chewed the inside of her cheek. There was no use lying. He would find out that there was no official adoption. "No, she was scared and in a hurry when she left. I was afraid if I filed for adoption, that DiSanti would discover the truth and come after Izzy."

Brayden cursed, then stood and walked to the French doors. She wanted to join him, to ask him to forgive her for keeping secrets.

But he obviously didn't want to hear it.

Lucas cleared his throat. "Have you been in touch with him since we left the FBI field office?"

Mila glanced down at her hands again. She wanted to trust them, to tell them about the text.

But DiSanti had her little girl. And she couldn't do anything to jeopardize Izzy's life.

So she shook her head no.

BRAYDEN NEEDED TIME to assimilate everything Mila had confessed.

Faced with the fact that she'd lied to him, he didn't know whether to trust her now. She'd bent the truth to help Izzy and her young mother, or at least that's what she wanted them to believe.

The Mila he thought he knew would have done that.

But for some reason, he sensed she was still holding back.

Not to mention she'd broken the law. Technically DiSanti had legal rights to his daughter whereas Mila could be charged with kidnapping.

He believed in upholding the law, but this time there were grays. Mila's daughter was an innocent, trusting little girl.

How could he put her back in the hands of the monster who sold and traded young girls and women?

Lucas's phone buzzed, and he stepped aside to answer it.

"I'm sorry, Brayden," Mila said. "I wanted to tell you everything that day at the FBI office, but I was afraid."

"Afraid you'd go to jail for kidnapping?" Brayden asked, his voice harsher than he'd intended.

Hurt flashed across Mila's face. "No, afraid DiSanti would learn about Izzy. If you'd seen this thirteen-year-old girl, beaten and bruised and terrified of DiSanti, you'd understand."

He had seen Evie, Mae Lynn, Adrian and Agnes. "You should have trusted me to understand."

Mila shrugged. "All I wanted to do was help Carina recover and have a future. That's what she wanted for her baby, too." She touched his arm. "What else could I have done?"

A muscle ticked in Brayden's jaw. Before he could

respond, Lucas stepped back inside. "I have to go. Charlotte is on her way to pick you up, Mila. One of the girls at the hospital wants to talk to you."

"Does she have information?" Brayden asked.

"I don't know," Lucas said, "but they opened up to Charlotte and Mila yesterday. Maybe one of them remembered something helpful." He gestured to his phone. "Meanwhile, forensics identified a print from Dr. Manchester's house. Belongs to a man associated with Jameson Beck. I'm going to question him."

Brayden couldn't just sit around. He wanted to do something.

And he needed space from Mila. Although he understood her reasons for keeping secrets, it hurt that she hadn't trusted him.

Especially after the night before.

A knock sounded, and Brayden let Charlotte in. She took one look across the room and must have felt the tension. "Should I come back?"

Mila shook her head no. "Let me freshen up. I'll be right back." She ducked into the guest room and the shower water kicked on.

"What's going on?" Charlotte asked.

Lucas explained the situation while Brayden cleaned up in his bathroom. Ten minutes later, he was ready. Mila emerged about the same time. She'd pulled her hair back into a low ponytail, and looked young and vulnerable, and so damn sad that he wanted to draw her in his arms again and make love to her until they both forgot the obstacles between them.

But he was done playing the fool.

As soon as they got Izzy back, figured out what to do with her and captured DiSanti, she'd be out of his life.

Chapter Twenty-One

Mila's nerves were on edge as Charlotte drove toward the hospital. Her friend turned into the parking lot of a small diner before they arrived and cut the engine.

"Come on, we're stopping for a hot breakfast," Charlotte said. "You look like you need it."

Mila swallowed the lump in her throat. She needed her daughter back. "I'm really not hungry."

Charlotte touched her arm and offered her a stern look. "You may not be, but you need to eat and keep up your strength."

Tears blurred Mila's eyes. "I can't believe you're being so nice to me. Aren't you angry like Lucas and Brayden?"

Charlotte's heartfelt sigh mirrored the tender understanding in her eyes. "How can I be mad at you for protecting your child?"

Mila bit her lip. "Didn't Lucas tell you the rest?"

Charlotte squeezed Mila's hand between her own. "What? That DiSanti is her father?"

Mila nodded miserably. "Her mother—"

"Was a terrified young girl who was raped," Charlotte said. "For that alone, DiSanti needs to go to prison. And then there's all his other crimes. When I think of what he did to Evie and Mae Lynn and Adrian and Agnes, I get riled up all over again."

"She was so scared when she came to me," Mila said softly.

"And brave," Charlotte said. "She escaped him, and she did the most unselfish thing anyone can do. She must have loved the baby to give her up."

"She wanted her to have a better life," Mila said. "And I wanted that for both of them."

"I know you did," Charlotte said softly. "And I promise that we'll find Izzy, and she'll have a future with you."

"But Brayden looked so hurt, and they're both furious that I didn't tell them the truth sooner." Mila gulped. "And technically Izzy isn't mine. What if I get her back and they take her away from me?"

Charlotte hissed between her teeth. "Don't worry about that. The Hawk men may be miffed now, but they're the most protective bunch of males I've ever met. They won't let DiSanti keep Izzy. And they'd never let anyone take a baby out of her mama's arms."

She released her hand. "Except legally I'm not her mama."

"You are in every way that counts," Charlotte assured her. "The rest is paperwork. And Brayden is excellent at cutting through red tape." She opened her car door and motioned for Mila to follow. "Now, let's grab some breakfast before we visit the girls. It's going to be another long day."

Mila checked her phone as she got out and said a prayer that she'd hear something today.

She didn't know how much more waiting she could take.

BRAYDEN'S EMOTIONS BOOMERANGED all over the place. Dammit, he still wanted to help Mila. And he sure as hell wanted to save Izzy from DiSanti.

"I know you're upset, brother," Lucas said. "I didn't realize you and the doctor had gotten…chummy."

Brayden silently cursed. "It just happened. She was upset, worried. I wanted to comfort her."

Lucas pulled down a side street. "You sleep with all your clients to comfort them?"

Anger flared inside Brayden. "That's not fair, man. You slept with Charlotte."

Lucas grimaced. "For the record, I'm not proud of the fact that I was on the job." A smile tugged at his mouth. "That said, I'm not sorry it happened though. She's the best thing that ever happened to me."

That was true.

For a second last night, Brayden had entertained the idea that Mila was his Charlotte.

Fool.

Brayden scanned the parking lot of the feed store where this guy Theo was supposed to be working. "Once we catch DiSanti and rescue Izzy, what's going to happen to Izzy?"

Lucas shifted the vehicle into Park and cut the engine. "Let's just get him and save Izzy. Then we'll discuss where to go from there."

What more could Brayden ask for?

For Lucas not to arrest Mila for kidnapping? Technically she hadn't… In her situation, he would have done the same thing. And no way would Lucas have let that baby be carted off by DiSanti.

Lucas climbed out, and Brayden followed him up to the door of the feed store. The store looked empty, a truck parked to the side by a loading dock. Brayden took a few steps and noticed more trucks in the back at the loading dock. Voices echoed from the dock, and cigarette smoke curled into the air near the rear door.

He motioned to Lucas that he was heading that way while his brother strode inside the store. He dug his hands into the pockets of his jacket and adjusted his Stetson, glad he'd worn jeans and a T-shirt and cowboy boots. Sometimes the suit was intimidating.

Two men looked up and went still, their conversation quieting.

A big burly guy in a jean jacket and battered boots sauntered toward him, his posture defensive. Brayden wasn't a small guy, but this man probably outweighed him by fifty pounds and carried himself like a street fighter. "What can we do for you, mister?"

Brayden tilted his hat to the side. "Looking for Theo Reeves? Is that you?"

The guy's brows pinched together. "Who's asking?"

It was Reeves. Damn. Brayden had to stall. He might need backup. He moved forward, lifting his chin. "I'm looking for a missing kid. A three-year-old little girl named Izzy Manchester. I think you know where she is."

Panic flashed across the brawny man's face. "Don't know what the hell you're talking about."

"Really?" Lucas appeared from the back door. "Because your print showed up at her house. The very house where she was abducted at gunpoint."

The man's gaze shot from Lucas to him, then he growled and broke into a run. Lucas raised his gun and shouted for the man to stop, but Reeves dived into the driver's side of a feed truck.

Brayden was closer and jogged after him, then yanked at the door as the man started the engine. The engine fired up, and Theo started to back away.

Lucas fired a shot at the tires. Brayden yanked at the car door and pulled it open. Theo punched him in the face, and Brayden's head jerked backward. Dammit, he didn't intend to let this bastard get the best of him.

Mila and Izzy needed him.

He clutched the door and grabbed Theo's beefy arm. But Theo lifted his free hand and raised a gun with it, pointing it straight at Brayden.

Brayden cursed and reached for his own, but the man pushed the gun at Brayden's temple, and he froze.

A second later, a bullet whizzed by his head. Theo's body bounced backward, and blood spurted from his forehead where Lucas's bullet had hit its mark.

MILA HADN'T THOUGHT she could eat, but she felt marginally better after a hearty breakfast and coffee. Still, the uncertainty of where Izzy was and what Brayden and Lucas planned needled her.

When they arrived at the hospital, she checked on Keenan and Anita and Frannie while Charlotte went to visit the two other victims.

Keenan was sitting up and looked more rested and focused, as if the last of the drugs had been flushed from her system.

"Did you find Izzy?" Keenan asked.

Mila shook her head. "Not yet."

Keenan twisted the sheets between her fingers. "I remembered something else. I don't know if it's important or not."

Mila stroked the girl's shoulder. "Even the smallest detail might help, sweetie."

"I heard them talking about a plane."

"You mean a flight they were going to catch?"

Keenan shook her head. "I think it was a small plane. A private one."

Mila sucked in a sharp breath. Of course, DiSanti had the money for a private jet. It also made it easier for him to escape.

"Did they mention where they were flying?"

Keenan shook her head. "They said they had to wait until he was feeling better."

"He?"

"They didn't use his name. But I knew who they were talking about."

Mila's phone vibrated in her pocket. She grabbed it and checked the screen.

You aren't listening, Dr. Manchester. I thought you wanted to see your daughter again.

Fear caught in her throat. She told Keenan she'd be right back. She walked down the hall to the vending machine then sent a return text to DiSanti, but the text immediately bounced back.

She made a pained sound, barely stifling a scream. A footstep sounded behind her. She started to spin around to see who was there, but something sharp jabbed her in the back.

Then a man's low growl in her ear, "If you scream or try to alert someone, the kid is dead."

Mila went perfectly still. "I'll do whatever you say, just don't hurt my daughter."

"Then walk."

Mila forced a breath in and out, then did as he ordered. She passed two nurses she recognized from the night before, then ducked into the elevator. The man holding the gun on her remained close behind her, the barrel of his gun digging into her back.

Her heart pounded when a janitor and a young couple with a baby entered the elevator. The baby in the pink blanket reminded her of her daughter.

The janitor narrowed his eyes at her as if he recognized her, maybe from the night before, but she simply smiled at him, then pretended interest in her phone.

The doors whooshed open on the second floor, and the janitor exited. The couple followed, and she was left alone with the man and his gun. He ordered her toward an exit, and she walked on unsteady legs to the door.

Outside, the skies had turned a dark gray, and the wind had picked up as if a storm was brewing. Mila stumbled as he pushed her forward, then caught herself and walked on.

A white van pulled up in front of the emergency room door, and the man shoved her toward it. A second later, the side door opened and he pushed her inside. As soon as she fell onto the floor, someone dragged a bag over her head.

Then she felt a hard whack to the back of her skull, and the world went black.

LUCAS STAYED WITH Reeves's body until the ME arrived while Brayden checked in with Dexter. Nothing new. Dammit.

Lucas's cell phone buzzed. "Charlotte," he said, then connected the call.

Maybe one of the girls at the hospital had offered some new information.

Lucas scowled, then cursed. "All right. I'll see if we can trace her phone."

A bad feeling shot through Brayden.

"Call me if you hear anything." Lucas hung up, his expression grave.

"What's going on?" Brayden asked.

"Mila's gone."

Brayden's lungs tightened. "What do you mean *gone*?"

"She and Charlotte had breakfast on the way to the hospital, then split up to talk to the girls," Lucas said. "When Charlotte went to find Mila, she saw her at the end of the hall leaving with a man."

Fear robbed Brayden's response.

"Charlotte called security, but by the time they showed up, Mila was outside. The guard saw a man push Mila into the back of a van."

Brayden released a string of expletives. "Did security get the license plate?"

Lucas shook his head. "Apparently there wasn't one."

Brayden pinched the bridge of his nose. This couldn't be happening. He'd promised Mila he'd protect her and bring Izzy back to her, but now DiSanti's men had them both.

"What now?" Brayden said. "We've exhausted our leads."

Lucas gave him a big brother look. "Don't give up. I'll call our analyst and see if she can trace Mila's phone. Charlotte said Keenan mentioned hearing the men talk about a private airplane. I'll get our people looking into that."

"Don't you think it's time to go wide with the media

on this?" Brayden said. "We kept quiet because of Mila. But we need any lead we can get."

"That would help," Lucas said. "Or it could spook DiSanti into killing Mila."

Emotions crowded Brayden's chest. "We both know he's probably going to kill Mila anyway. If DiSanti knows Izzy is his child, he's probably furious and out for blood."

Lucas nodded. "You're right. I'll issue an Amber Alert for Izzy and send her picture and Mila's out to the media and all the authorities."

Desperation made sweat break out on Brayden's neck. They had to find Mila and Izzy before it was too late.

MILA'S HEAD THROBBED as she roused from unconsciousness. She rolled to her side and realized she was still in the back of the van, the hood over her head.

The van bounced over potholes and tossed her against the side of the vehicle. The floor was cold, hard.

She forced herself to listen for sounds that might indicate where they were taking her. A bus? Train? Traffic? Planes?

Nothing but dead quiet and the chug of the engine.

Fear mingled with relief that she would at least get to see Izzy again. But what would happen then?

Her phone vibrated in her pocket, but her hands were bound, and she couldn't get to it. Had Charlotte realized she was gone by now? Was Brayden looking for her?

The van rolled to a stop, brakes squealing, then the door screeched open. Cold hard hands grabbed her and she fought, but he dug in her pocket, grabbed her phone, then slammed the door again.

Tears pricked her eyes. Brayden and Lucas could have traced her with the phone, but the brute had probably tossed it.

The engine started up again and roared away, throwing her across the back of the van. They rode for what seemed like forever before tires ground on the graveled road, and the van bounced to a stop.

She waited on it to start up again, but it didn't. Instead, the van door screeched open, and the brute yanked her from the back of the vehicle. She stumbled, willing him to remove the hood, but he dragged her forward, keeping her in the dark.

Thunder rumbled, then another male voice echoed in the distance.

She struggled to remain upright, her feet slipping and clawing at the rough gravel as they climbed a hill. A minute later, she heard another door open, then the man pushed her forward. The ground turned to a wooden floor, and they were walking. A hall?

Another male voice echoed in the distance, but her abductor yanked her arm again. Her feet grappled for control as she struggled to keep up with him.

A door creaked open, then he pushed her again, this time so hard that she stumbled. With her hands tied and face covered, she lost her balance and completely collapsed onto the floor.

The door slammed shut.

She cried out in frustration, but a low whisper rose from the corner. She went still.

Then shuffling and someone was lifting the hood from her head. She blinked into the darkness, disoriented, heaving a breath.

The person who'd removed her hood slowly slipped into focus.

"Dr. Manchester," the girl whispered.

Shock hit her like a fist in the gut. "Carina?"

Tears trickled from the young girl's terrified eyes. She was bruised and battered, but she was here.

"How? Why?"

"He found me," she said on a ragged whisper. "He knows everything."

Chapter Twenty-Two

Mila tried not to react, but then she saw Izzy curled in the corner, trembling, curled in a fetal position, and her composure crumbled.

"Untie me," Mila cried. "I have to get to Izzy."

Carina moved behind Mila and worked the knots in the rope.

"Are you hurt?" Mila asked. "Did they hurt Izzy?"

"We're both okay," Carina said softly. "They didn't hurt her. She's just scared and misses you."

The tenderness in the girl's eyes made Mila's heart ache. Carina had probably earned those bruises protecting Izzy.

"She's beautiful," Carina said as she finished untying Mila.

Mila shook the feeling back into her fingers and hugged Carina. "Yes, she is. Now we have to get her away from DiSanti and his men."

How she was going to do that she didn't know.

She crawled toward her daughter, her heart racing. "Izzy, it's Mommy," she whispered. "I'm here."

She gently stroked Izzy's soft hair away from her face, and Izzy lifted her head. When she saw Mila, her eyes widened, and she threw her arms around Mila, her little body shaking.

Mila cradled her daughter against her, then rocked her while she cried. Her own tears blended with Izzy's, then Carina was beside them, and she pulled the young mother up against them.

"WE HAVE AN ADDRESS," Lucas said as he and Brayden sped down the road. "Mila must have left her phone on so we could trace it."

Thank God she was smart. He just hoped she was still alive.

He said prayer after prayer as Lucas careened around a corner and sped onto a graveled road.

Brayden's phone buzzed. He checked it, hoping for a miracle. Not Mila though. A number he didn't recognize.

He pressed Connect. "Brayden Hawk."

Silence. Breathing.

"Hello? Who is this?"

"Mr. Hawk?"

Brayden stilled. The voice sounded familiar. "Yes."

"It's Jorge."

The ranch hand that worked for Corley. "I'm really busy, Jorge, so unless you called to help—"

"I did," Jorge said in a muffled voice as if he didn't want anyone to hear him. "Did you mean what you said about helping my family?"

Lucas glanced over at him with a raised brow, then slowed as they neared an abandoned stretch of land. Boulders created a natural landmark where the road forked.

"Yes, I meant it. I'll do whatever I can to make sure your family is safe and you're with them," Brayden said.

"I saw the news. Is it true that this man DiSanti kidnapped Dr. Manchester?"

"It's true. She and her daughter are both in danger. Now, tell me what you know."

Jorge cleared his throat. "I heard Mr. Corley talking on the phone. He said they needed to move the merchandise, to get the contacts in Juarez ready."

So Corley was involved. "Did he say where the merchandise is being held?"

"No. But Mr. Corley told him to take care of his problem before he flew out."

Keenan had mentioned a private plane. "Anything else?"

"He said he didn't want the feds breathing down his neck." Jorge paused again, static on the line as if he was muffling his voice. "He's back. I have to go."

"Thanks, Jorge. I'll be in touch about your family."

The phone clicked silent.

Lucas screeched to a stop at the group of boulders, then climbed out.

"What are we doing?" Brayden asked as he joined his brother.

Lucas's dark scowl tracked the area as if searching for something. "This is where the trace ended."

Brayden's heart clamored. Either Mila's phone had been tossed here... Or her body had.

MILA WIPED AWAY Izzy's tears. "I'm here now, honey. I've been looking for you, and I'm going to find a way to take us home."

Carina was watching Izzy with a mixture of love and sadness in her eyes.

"All of us," Mila said, knowing she couldn't abandon the girl who'd given birth to Izzy.

The door suddenly opened, and a big barrel of a man with black hair and black eyes strode into the room. He was heavily armed.

Without a word, he jerked Mila to a standing position. "DiSanti needs you, Dr. Manchester."

Mila fought a cry of terror. Was he going to kill her now? If so, what would happen to Izzy?

She and Carina traded an understanding look—they would both protect Izzy with their lives.

She held up a finger to the man. "Just one second." She jerked away, then stooped and gave Izzy another hug and a kiss. "I love you, sweetie. You and Carina hang tight while I take care of my patient." She squeezed Carina's hand, déjà vu taking her back to the night Carina brought Izzy to her door.

If she died, Lucas and Brayden would keep looking for Izzy. Maybe they could help Carina, too.

The man grunted, then motioned it was time for her to go. She grappled for courage, then stood and followed him out the door on wobbly legs.

Without the bag over her head, she took inventory of her surroundings as they walked down the hall. The house was an older ranch, wood floors, rooms on both sides of a kitchen in the center. Through the windows, she spotted acres and acres of farmland.

They were in the middle of nowhere.

How would Lucas and Brayden ever find them?

A noise sounded, and she hesitated, then realized it was the sound of a small airplane. DiSanti's private jet.

The brute with the gun gestured for her to walk down the hall, and she entered a large room with a king-size bed. The double window offered a view of a landing strip.

Against the wall stood a steel table with medical supplies and bandages. A woman dressed in a nurse's uniform was jotting notes on a clipboard. She must have been caring for DiSanti. But the bed was empty.

Then Mila saw DiSanti. He was sitting in a chair in the corner, hidden in the shadows. His face still looked puffy and slightly red, but she had to admit that he was some of her best work. If she didn't know who he was, she wouldn't have recognized him.

DiSanti looked up at her with cold, rage-filled eyes, then stood and walked toward her, his shoulders rigid. "You stole my daughter," he said. "Now you know what that feels like."

Mila inhaled a fortifying breath. "Her mother wanted her to have a future, to be raised in a normal, safe environment."

The man raised his hand and slapped her across the face. She stumbled backward.

"She's mine and she belongs with me," he growled.

"Why?" Mila asked sharply. "So you can sell her or turn her into a sex slave for a monster like yourself?"

Another blow, this one so sharp and hard that her face stung, and she tasted blood. Then another one and another until Mila fell to her knees, the world spinning.

BRAYDEN RELAYED HIS conversation with Jorge to Lucas, and Lucas phoned his analyst at the FBI to search for a location that might house a private runway. While he spoke with her, Brayden began to search the area for Mila's phone, praying she was still alive.

The land was parched, although gray skies above threatened a downpour. He had to hurry before the clouds unloaded.

Tumbleweed blew across the terrain, miles and miles of desolate land stretching before them. He checked around the boulders, but didn't find a phone or any signs of Mila. No footprints either, meaning the men hadn't gotten out of the vehicle.

Of course, they could have simply slowed and pushed her body out of the van, but why would they do it in an open area? Granted, this property was off the grid, but DiSanti's men would most likely have found a ravine or wooded area, someplace not easily detectable.

God... He had to stop thinking like that. Mila was not dead. She couldn't be.

He loved her too much to lose her.

Love?

He kicked gravel from his boot. He had no time to think about love when Mila's and Izzy's lives hung in the balance.

He walked along the edge of the road, searching the bushes and weeds and the ditch, then crossed the road to the opposite side. About six feet down, something shiny glinted against the dirt.

He jogged toward it, then knelt and dug the phone from the foliage. A quick examination confirmed it was Mila's.

He brushed it off and yelled to Lucas that he'd found the phone as he headed back toward his brother.

Lucas nodded. "I don't think Mila's here. They probably just dumped her phone to throw us off." His phone buzzed and Lucas skimmed a text, then motioned for Brayden to get in the car. "Let's go. I have the location of an abandoned ranch equipped with its own runway. It's not far from here."

Brayden's pulse hammered as he buckled up, and Lucas sped away. Gravel spewed behind them as Lucas careened down the road. The scenery whisked by in a blur.

Minutes dragged into half an hour, making Brayden's nerves more frazzled. He thought they'd never get there, but finally the property appeared in the distance. The ranch was enormous, with acres and acres of unused land. Wild mustangs galloped on a hill in the distance, the land beginning to roll into hills as it stretched for miles.

Lucas slowed as he turned down the drive, he and Brayden alert in case DiSanti's men were watching.

A mile onto the property, and someone shot at the car. Lucas swerved to the right, and Brayden rolled down his window and fired. One shot, two. He hit the bastard who was perched on the back of a flatbed truck.

Anger coiled inside him, and Lucas was stone-faced, his hands clenching the steering wheel in a white-knuckled grip. Another mile and Brayden spotted the farmhouse, a giant rambling structure that had seen better days.

Set back here in the middle of nowhere, it was the perfect place to hide. Another reason DiSanti had chosen Texas. Its vastness alone offered a multitude of remote locations, undeveloped properties and abandoned farms.

Lucas parked a half mile from the house, and the two of them got out, both armed and alert.

A gunshot blasted the air, and Brayden ducked. Lucas spun to the left and fired, nailing the shooter, who'd been hiding in a thicket of trees.

They crept closer, weaving between the bushes bordering the drive, then slipped up to the house.

More gunshots. Two men firing from the barn by the house. Lucas fired back and had to roll in the dirt to dodge a bullet.

An engine sounded from the back of the house. The plane.

Dammit.

Lucas shook his head, warning Brayden to stay put, but Brayden ignored him and raced around the side of the house. Lucas was right on his tail, and they made it to the back just as three big gunmen emerged, guarding DiSanti.

Brayden wanted to shoot him then, but they had to find Mila.

The back door opened, and two men hurried out, dragging someone with them.

Dear God. Mila. She was beaten and limp, her hair tangled around her bloody face.

Behind them another man hauled a too-thin teenage girl beside him. She looked frail and frightened but clutched a little girl—Izzy, it had to be—in her arms. Izzy had her head buried against the teen, obviously terrified.

If DiSanti had hurt Izzy, Brayden would kill him with his bare hands.

Lucas motioned for Brayden to follow his lead, then Lucas identified himself and ordered the men to halt or he'd shoot.

They didn't listen. They opened fire, and all hell

broke loose. Lucas took cover behind a bush and fired at the men while Brayden aimed his gun at the man holding the teenage girl and Izzy.

He didn't take time to analyze what he was doing. He was going to save that kid.

He fired at the bastard and nailed him in the head. The big man's body bounced back with a grunt, then he dropped to the ground like a rock.

Brayden motioned for the girl and Izzy to run. Just as they did, Lucas fired at the men holding Mila, but the men dodged the bullet and dragged Mila toward the plane.

Two more shooters fired from behind barrels stacked next to the hangar, forcing Brayden and Lucas to duck to avoid being hit.

Another shot from the right, and Brayden swung around and fired, hitting the shooter and taking him out.

Lucas caught the big guy in the shoulder, and Mila suddenly shoved the other man to the ground and ran toward her daughter and the teen.

The bastard rolled on the ground and lifted his weapon again. Brayden fired, but the man managed to get off a round first.

At the same time, Izzy started running toward Mila. Panic seared Brayden. No… Izzy was in the line of fire.

The teen suddenly threw herself in front of Izzy. The bullet hit her in the back, and she collapsed to the ground, shielding Izzy with her body. Brayden nailed him, but the damage was done.

Mila screamed and dived for Izzy and the girl while Lucas raced toward the plane.

The door to the plane closed, the engine roared and the plane sped down the runway.

Lucas chased the plane, shooting at it, but the plane soared into the sky. Brayden ran to Mila. She was sobbing and lifting the limp teenager away from Izzy.

Brayden knelt and helped her roll the girl off Izzy, and Mila pulled Izzy into her arms, frantically checking her for injuries.

Izzy was wide-eyed in shock, still clinging to the young teen. Mila dragged the girl into her lap so she could hold both her and Izzy.

Then the girl's eyes fluttered open and she looked up at Mila.

"Take care of our little girl," Carina whispered.

Mila sobbed the girl's name and promised that she would.

Chapter Twenty-Three

Brayden held Mila and Izzy while they waited for an ambulance. Mila was devastated over Carina's death. What a senseless loss.

Even after all she'd suffered, Carina had loved that child.

And he had overheard Carina ask Mila to take care of her daughter. He'd use that in court as leverage to file adoption papers. Although getting DiSanti to release his rights would be difficult—maybe impossible.

He would figure out the details later. For now, he was grateful Mila and Izzy had survived.

Although seeing Mila battered and beaten tore him in knots. Lucas called reinforcements to take care of the bodies and his people were working on tracking DiSanti's plane.

But he might be long gone.

Mila and Izzy wouldn't be safe until he was locked away—or dead.

Brayden would prefer the latter. In fact, he'd like to be the one to put a bullet in DiSanti's head.

When the ambulance arrived, Brayden stepped aside while they examined Izzy and Mila. True to her nature, Mila was more worried about her daughter than herself.

Lucas approached him, expression stony. "I'll stay here and tie things up at this place if you want to go with Mila and the little girl to the hospital."

Brayden murmured agreement. His emotions were wreaking havoc with his nerves.

"Who was the teenager?" Lucas asked. "One of DiSanti's victims?"

He nodded. "Izzy's birth mother." That touching exchange had cemented his drive to make sure Mila kept Izzy. "Just before she died, she asked Mila to take care of their little girl."

Lucas raised a brow. "So Mila was telling the truth about the girl giving her Izzy?"

Brayden nodded. "It won't be easy, but I have to figure out a way to make sure Mila is granted legal custody."

A tense silence stretched between them as the medics helped Mila and Izzy into the ambulance and the crime workers arrived to process the scene.

"You know he'll come back for them, Brayden? They won't be safe until we find him."

"I know." Brayden raked a hand through his hair. "We have to protect them, Lucas."

"We will," Lucas assured him.

But Brayden's heart was heavy as he went to join Mila and Izzy.

MILA WAS AN emotional basket case. Carina had died protecting her baby girl.

It wasn't fair.

At the hospital, she assured the staff that she was okay. Bruises would heal. She was far more concerned about the emotional and psychological trauma to Izzy.

At least physically, Izzy was unharmed. Mila cradled her close in the back seat as Brayden drove them to Hawk's Landing. Fearing the house where she'd been abducted might trigger traumatic memories for her daughter, Mila agreed to stay at Brayden's with Izzy, at least for the night.

DiSanti had escaped. Again.

She squeezed Izzy tighter. She couldn't think about that right now. Izzy needed to be comforted and to feel safe.

Carina's face flashed in her mind, and a wave of grief washed over her. One day, she'd tell Izzy the truth about her birth mother, about the selfless, brave love Carina had for her.

Not tonight though.

Brayden steered the SUV down the drive to the ranch, and Izzy clutched Mila's arm. "Where are we going, Mama?"

Mila soothed her with a kiss and stroked her hair. "Brayden is a nice man, honey. He helped me find you. And he's going to let us stay at his ranch for a few days so we can rest."

Fear flickered in Izzy's eyes. "Are the bad men coming back?"

Mila hugged Izzy tighter. "Not tonight, sweetie. We'll be safe at Brayden's ranch."

Izzy stared at her wide-eyed for a moment, then bobbed her head up and down.

"Do they gots horses at the ranch?" Izzy asked.

Mila smiled, grateful that children were resilient. "Yes, they do. Tomorrow we'll ask Brayden if we can see them." She stroked Izzy's hair again. "But tonight we're going to soak in a warm bubble bath and get a good night's sleep." Izzy probably hadn't really slept since she'd been abducted. At least, the doctor confirmed that she hadn't been drugged or molested.

Izzy spied a horse galloping in the pasture nearest the road and squealed in delight.

Mila took it as a good sign that her daughter would be all right, but she would watch for nightmares and signs of anxiety. Brayden had been quiet the entire ride, leaving her wondering what he was thinking.

He'd risked his life to save her and Izzy. His face was bruised, although she had no idea how he'd earned it. She looked worse, but she didn't care.

Tonight Izzy would sleep beside her safe and sound. That was all that mattered.

BRAYDEN COULD BARELY control his rage over the bruises on Mila's face and arms. He wanted to make DiSanti suffer for hurting her.

But she and Izzy had seen enough violence. He inhaled a deep breath as he parked to rein in his temper.

Still, he'd make it his mission to find the bastard and keep him from abusing another girl, woman or child.

He opened the back door for Mila and helped her out of the car, his jaw clenching at the dried blood on her lower lip.

"Do you want me to carry Izzy?" he asked gruffly.

She shook her head no. "Thanks, but I think she needs some alone time with me right now."

That was probably true. But he felt like Mila was shutting him out.

He closed the door after her and hurried to steady her as she climbed the steps with Izzy in her arms.

Izzy looked up at him with wary, big dark eyes as he unlocked the door.

"I heard you like horses," he said with a smile.

Her eyes crinkled with childlike excitement as she bobbed her head up and down.

"Tomorrow I'll take you and your mom around the ranch. You can even pick out one to ride."

"Really?" she asked in such a sweet, innocent voice that she instantly snagged a piece of his heart.

"Really." Mila gave him a grateful smile as they entered.

"Let me know what you need," he said as she carried Izzy toward the bedroom.

"We're going to soak in a nice bath." She looked at her daughter. "Do you want something to eat, sweetie?"

Izzy gave a little nod.

"I don't have much," Brayden said, "except for some frozen mac and cheese."

"I love mac and cheese," Izzy squealed.

"Then mac and cheese it is," he said with a wink.

Mila laughed, and Brayden thought what a beautiful sound. A sound he wanted to hear more often.

Every day.

Deciding Izzy had probably seen enough blood and bruises in her lifetime, he washed up in his bathroom, then took the box of mac and cheese from the freezer and followed the directions to heat it. He also had a frozen pizza so he stuck it in the oven.

Not a gourmet meal, but he had a feeling food wasn't as important tonight as mother and daughter simply being together.

That was what family was about.

Damn. He wanted that family for himself.

Shaken, he stepped onto the back deck for some air.

It was a good half hour before Mila and Izzy emerged from the guest room. Izzy was cocooned in a pair of pink flannel pj's with kitty cats on them, and Mila had dragged on a pair of sweatpants and a long-sleeved T-shirt. Her hair lay in damp strands over her shoulders. She'd dabbed on a little powder to help camouflage the bruises on her face, most likely an effort to spare Izzy.

He lit a fire in the fireplace and made coffee, then set out his brown whiskey and the wine he'd offered Mila before.

They gathered at the farmhouse table by the fire to eat. Izzy looked brighter and surprised him by wolfing down the mac and cheese and a slice of pizza.

Mila laughed as the little girl inhaled a glass of milk on top of it. He had some chocolate chip cookies his mother and the girls at the house had made, and she snatched two of them with a giggle.

Mila sipped a glass of wine after eating, the love in her eyes for her daughter so intense it humbled Brayden and made him forget his anger over the information she'd withheld from him.

But hurt still needled him that she hadn't trusted him.

Izzy yawned, and Mila started to clean up, but he caught her hand and took the plate from her. "I'll handle this. Just enjoy your time with Izzy tonight."

She gave him another grateful look, then scooped Izzy into her arms and carried her to the bedroom. When the door closed behind them, Brayden had a feeling he wouldn't see either one of them until morning.

He cleaned the table and plates, then checked outside to make certain it was quiet. Satisfied DiSanti and his men hadn't had time to track Mila and Izzy to Hawk's Landing, he poured himself a shot of whiskey and carried it to the recliner by the fire.

He stared into the burning embers, his mind contemplating the last few days and all that had happened.

Last night he and Mila had shared the hottest, most mind-boggling sex he'd ever experienced. But it was more than just sex.

He was in love with her.

He had no idea what he was going to do about it though.

Chapter Twenty-Four

Mila savored the next three days at Hawk's Landing. She made arrangements for Roberta and Carina to have proper memorial services and for another doctor to assume her responsibilities at the clinic for a while. She wanted to focus all her energy on being with Izzy.

Her little girl blossomed at the ranch. True to his word, Brayden gave them a ranch tour and helped Izzy choose the tamest riding horse they had for lessons.

Izzy had asked about Roberta and Carina, and about some girl named Jade, who stayed with her when she was abducted.

Brayden and Lucas added Jade to their list of missing girls. Mrs. Hawk also found room for the girls at the hospital to move onto the ranch temporarily. One of her friends had agreed to open her home to them but needed renovations done to make room. Honey volunteered to oversee the project.

The Hawks were amazing people. She understood now why Charlotte had fallen fast and hard for Lucas. And why she loved his family so much.

She watched as Brayden rode Izzy around the riding pen. He was patient and kind and funny. Izzy adored him.

And she was in love with him.

Lucas approached her, his look solemn. Her stomach knotted. She'd hoped every day that he'd find DiSanti so she and Izzy could live free of fear.

He anticipated her question and shook his head no.

She tamped down her sigh of frustration. He was doing everything possible to find the bastard.

But with every passing day, the chances of DiSanti's men finding her at Hawk's Landing increased.

"I appreciate all you and your family have done for me and Izzy," Mila said. "But Izzy and I can't stay here forever."

"You don't like the ranch?" Lucas asked.

Mila sighed. "I love it here, and so does Izzy, but we're imposing on your family." And Brayden. The longer she stayed, the more she didn't want to leave. It was starting to feel like a home, the one she'd always wanted.

"I know you're anxious," Lucas said. "But it's not safe for you to go home yet or back to work."

"As much as I don't like it, I agree." Mila leaned on the rail, soaking in the sight of Izzy with Brayden. The little girl's father was a terrible man and didn't deserve to have a child.

On the other hand, Brayden would make a wonderful father.

She glanced back at the farmhouse and saw Honey in the porch swing chatting with Ava. Evie, Mae Lynn, Adrian and Agnes were showing the new girls their favorite places on the ranch.

Hawk's Landing had become a safe haven for the lost.

But she couldn't stay here forever.

"I have to leave," Mila said. "It's too dangerous for your family for me to stay here."

Indecision and regret played across Lucas's face. Charlotte was walking toward them with Mae Lynn, her cheeks rosy with the cold.

The day before Charlotte confided to Mila that she was pregnant. After all she'd been through, she deserved to have her baby and a life with Lucas in peace.

"We don't want you to go," Lucas said.

Mila's heart squeezed. "I appreciate that, Lucas. Your family is the most generous, loving one I've ever known. But that's the reason I *have* to go. DiSanti will use anyone I care about to get to me and Izzy. I won't do that, not to you and Charlotte, or Brayden, or Honey and Harrison or your mother and the girls who escaped him."

Lucas's gaze met hers for a tension-filled moment. Izzy squealed as Brayden swung her down from the palomino he'd chosen for her. Izzy loved that horse and had already started calling the animal hers.

She couldn't allow her daughter to become more attached to this place and these people, then yank her away from this family.

"Will you arrange for us to go into WITSEC?" Mila asked.

Lucas nodded. "I can do that. But you know if you join WITSEC, none of us, including Brayden, can know where you and Izzy are. You'll have to sever all contact with him, and you and Izzy will change your names and go wherever the US Marshals place you. And Mila—" he hesitated "—you won't be able to practice medicine or do any related kind of work. DiSanti and his men could use that to find you."

Pain washed through Mila, but she murmured that she understood. She'd do whatever necessary to protect Izzy and this family that she'd grown to love.

Even if it meant she couldn't be with them.

Three days later

"MILA, DON'T GO," Brayden said as Mila stood by the car that Lucas had arranged to take her and Izzy away. "I'll do whatever I can to protect you and Izzy."

Mila pressed a hand to Brayden's cheek. "I know you will. That's one reason we have to leave. I won't endanger you and your family."

Emotions darkened Brayden's eyes. "But I love you," he said, his heart pounding with fear. He was losing her, had been arguing with her about this ever since she'd told him her plan.

He had a bone to pick with Lucas, too. His brother had made arrangements with WITSEC without including him in the decision-making process.

"I could go with you," Brayden said. "Then you and Izzy won't be alone."

Mila shook her head. "No. I have to do this by myself, Brayden. Izzy is my family, not yours."

Dammit. Her dig hit home.

He'd professed his love, but she hadn't reciprocated. Because she didn't love him.

That hurt the most.

After all she'd been through, he couldn't force himself on her and her daughter. They needed to be free, even if it meant they needed freedom from him.

He was the fool for falling in love with her.

Emotions clogged his throat. "Will you let me know if you're all right?"

"You know I can't do that," Mila said. "When we leave, it's a clean slate for all of us."

As much as he didn't like it, she was right. Talking to him would only put her in danger. By now, DiSanti and his men might have discovered that he and his family had helped her and given Izzy a home.

He had to let her go to keep her safe.

He opened the car door, where Izzy sat in her car seat, clutching her stuffed animals and pink blanket to her chest. Tears pooled in her big dark eyes.

"I'm going to miss you, sweet pea," he said, then gave her a hug.

She wrapped her arms around him and held him tight, a sob escaping her little body. The precious little girl had definitely stolen his heart.

"I love you," she choked out. "I don't want to leave Blondie." The palomino.

"I love you, too," he murmured, then he pressed a kiss to her hair. "And Blondie will be waiting when you and your mommy can come back."

Mila gave him a warning look as he pulled away.

He didn't know how Mila had survived when Izzy had been in that monster's hands. His heart felt like it was literally breaking into pieces.

Mila gave him a quick kiss on the cheek, then ducked into the car, and the driver sped off.

He watched to see if she looked back at him. But Mila didn't look at him once.

THREE WEEKS LATER, Mila was still crying into her pillow at night.

She didn't dare show her feelings to Izzy, who talked

about Brayden and Blondie and the ranch and the Hawk family every single day.

The apartment the US Marshals had put them in was in the middle of this small town in Colorado, far away from Hawk's Landing and the people she loved.

Brayden's face haunted her. She wanted to see him, talk to him, be with him. Every day she relived the sound of his voice telling her that he loved her.

She hadn't said it back. If she'd admitted her feelings out loud, she wouldn't have been able to leave him.

And how could she have asked him to abandon the job and ranch and family that he loved for her? Not when being with her might get him or his mother or family members killed. Ava had lost one child. Mila refused to take away another.

Izzy finished drawing another sketch of Hawk's Landing and the horse she'd ridden. "I miss Blondie, Mommy."

Mila nodded, vying for patience. It wasn't Izzy's fault they were in this mess.

"Do you think Santa will find us here?" Izzy asked in a tiny voice.

Mila pulled Izzy into her lap. "Of course he will, sweetie."

"Will he bring me a puppy?"

Mila hesitated. She hated for Izzy to get attached to anything else, and then possibly lose it, but she'd be damned if her child would have to sacrifice owning a pet. They couldn't have a horse here, but maybe a puppy...

"Santa knows you're the best girl in the world and he'll remember you on Christmas Eve."

Izzy laid her head back against Mila. "I asked him for something else, too."

Mila closed her eyes and rocked Izzy in her arms. "What was that, sweetie?"

Izzy shrugged. "If I tell you, it won't come true."

Mila kissed her forehead and ran her fingers through her daughter's hair in a loving, soothing gesture. In time, they'd both adjust and accept their new life.

She just wished Brayden was in it.

THANKSGIVING CAME AND WENT. Now it was five days until Christmas. Brayden was miserable.

His family had gathered for their weekly dinner. Lights and decorations adorned the tree. The scent of cinnamon apples and pine filled the air.

Harrison and Honey were cuddled on the couch laughing as they discussed baby names.

Charlotte and Lucas were almost as obnoxious. With Charlotte's announcement about her pregnancy, Lucas would barely let her out of his sight.

Dexter piled another log on the fire to keep it going, while the girls who'd taken refuge at Hawk's Landing decorated cookies in the kitchen.

But someone was missing.

Two people—Mila and Izzy.

His mother pushed a coffee in his hands. "I know it's difficult, son. You love her, don't you?"

Apparently his poker face only worked in the court-room. He was as transparent as glass around his family.

"It doesn't matter. She doesn't love me."

His mother made a low sound in her throat. "Don't tell me you believe that."

He shrugged. "I told her how I felt and she said nothing. No, wait, she did. She left."

"She left to protect her little girl."

"I know that, and I love Izzy, too. I could have protected them both."

"Men." His mother rolled her eyes. "Mila left *because* she loves you."

"What?" That made no sense.

"Mila is loving and kind and donates her time to help kids and families. Do you think she would have stayed if being here endangered our family or you?"

Brayden rubbed a hand over his eyes. "No, but—"

"Go after her," his mother said. "She wanted to protect you and us. I heard her talking to Charlotte before she left."

Emotions welled in his throat. Was she right? Did Mila love him?

"But, Mom, I can't leave my job and you. I know how hard it was when you lost Chrissy and then Dad—"

His mother gripped his hands and turned him to look at her. "We all had a difficult time. But one thing I learned from all of it is that when you love someone, you have to show them. You have to treasure every moment you have with them." She kissed his cheek. "You and your brothers are awesome men, Brayden. I'm so proud of you I could burst. That means I want you to be happy."

Brayden swallowed hard.

"Mila and Izzy need you." She gestured toward the kitchen, where the girls had burst into Christmas carols. "I'll be fine. And one day when the danger is over, you'll all come back to us."

Brayden sucked in a breath. "I love you, Mom." He kissed her on the cheek, then gave her a heartfelt hug.

He headed toward Lucas to tell him to arrange for him to join Mila and Izzy.

He just hoped his mother was right and that Mila wanted him.

He motioned to Lucas that they needed to talk. Dexter and Harrison followed them onto the deck with tumblers of whiskey.

Then Brayden explained his decision.

Lucas shook his head. "We can't let you do that," Lucas said.

"Do you know where she is?" Brayden asked.

"No." Lucas sighed.

"Then find out," Brayden said. "You never should have talked her into this without consulting with me."

"It was Mila's choice," Lucas said. "She came to me, Brayden."

"Because she wanted to protect us," Brayden said. "But she's dealing with all this alone, and that's not right."

Lucas offered him an understanding smile, then held up a warning hand. "Listen. We have a lead on DiSanti. I got a call last night. I'm heading out to track him down."

"I'm going with you," Brayden said.

Harrison squared his shoulders. "He messed with my town. I'm in, too."

Dexter shrugged. "Might as well make it four."

Lucas hesitated, then nodded.

Brayden's heart raced. The Hawk men always stuck together. If anyone could stop DiSanti, once and for all, it was them.

Chapter Twenty-Five

Brayden was anxious to get DiSanti.

Harrison met with Jorge to offer protection and arrange for him to be reunited with his family. With Lucas's connections, they'd already struck a deal to help the man get citizenship.

Brayden and Lucas traveled to the property Corley owned in Juarez. Internet chatter revealed that a large merchandise shipment was about to be transported across the border, confirming the information Jorge had supplied. Dexter was headed to a second location they suspected was used to house more victims.

Lucas called for backup when they arrived in Juarez, and they met two teams of agents on the outskirts of the compound.

"I wish you'd stay back," Lucas told Brayden. "Let us handle this, brother."

Normally, Brayden would do exactly that. But this time, he had a personal stake in the case. And he wanted to have his brother's back. After all, Lucas was going to be a father.

And he wanted to see DiSanti locked up, or dead, himself. It was the only way to free Mila and Izzy so they could come out of hiding and have a normal life.

If they failed today though, he would join her in WITSEC. He hadn't slept a single night for wondering where she was, if she and Izzy were okay, if DiSanti might have found them. The only way he'd know she was safe was to be with her. They'd face the danger and uncertainty together.

Lucas parked a mile from the compound, a large ranch fenced with barbed wire and only a couple of miles from the border. Armed and ready, they hiked on foot until they reached the property. He and Lucas went one direction while Harrison and Dexter joined another team. They split up to approach from different angles.

Gunshots came out of nowhere, and Lucas and Brayden returned fire, taking two guards out. They slipped past the dead guards, snatching their semiautomatic weapons to use if they ran out of ammunition.

The next half hour all hell broke loose. Brayden and Lucas and the teams charged the compound. A helicopter dropped in reinforcements, and they stormed the property.

A bullet clipped his arm as he inched down a long corridor inside the main structure, but he shook off the sting and ducked into a room. Empty.

Lucas's voice echoed from the mike. "Team A located the merchandise. A storage container on the property. Ten girls. Jade was one of them. They were about to be forced through an underground tunnel that crosses into Mexico."

"Any sign of DiSanti?"

Static echoed back. Then gunfire.

Brayden's heart pounded. "Lucas?"

Silence.

Dammit, had Lucas been shot?

"Talk to me, man."

More gunfire. Shouts. Then a low grunt.

Brayden took off running. He couldn't lose his brother.

MILA SMILED AS Izzy added sprinkles to the cookies they'd just baked. A dollop of icing dotted her cheek, and she reached up and wiped it away with one finger.

"I think you have as much on you as you have on the cookies," she said with a laugh.

Izzy licked a gob of sprinkles and icing from her hand. "Yummy!"

Mila laughed and set the second tray in front of her daughter. They had enough cookies for a party.

But it was just the two of them.

"Can we get a tree, Mommy?" Izzy asked.

Mila glanced at the tiny house they'd rented. It was satisfactory, but nothing about it spelled home. They hadn't brought anything with them except clothes and a few of Izzy's toys.

A Christmas tree would at least make the house feel festive. "Of course we'll get a tree. I saw a tree farm in town. We'll go pick out one later and buy some decorations."

"Yippee!" Izzy bounced up and down, and Mila hugged her.

Izzy deserved a happy holiday with Christmas cookies and decorations and Santa Claus.

"Mommy?"

"What, sweetie?"

"Is Santa going to bring me that puppy?"

"We'll see." Maybe they'd visit a rescue shelter later, too, and Izzy could pick out a dog. A pet would be good company for both of them.

Mila looked out the window again at the fresh falling snow. It was beautiful, but she missed Texas and her work.

Most of all, she missed Brayden.

BRAYDEN RACED THROUGH the compound, dodging bullets from two more goons. He found Lucas outside at the back of the compound near a hangar, where he spotted DiSanti's private plane.

Lucas stood, hands raised in surrender as two men pointed guns at him. One of them was DiSanti.

"I'll find her," DiSanti said. "And I'll get my child back."

"Why?" Lucas barked. "So you can sell her like you do other people's children?"

DiSanti motioned to one of his goons, the one with the gun on Lucas. "Kill him, and let's get out of here."

Brayden went cold inside. He refused to lose his brother to this monster. DiSanti had already destroyed too many lives.

He moved slightly so Lucas could see him, then held up three fingers, counting down.

When he reached zero, he aimed a shot at DiSanti's head. Lucas whipped around and punched the goon with the gun, and they fought.

Brayden's bullet hit its mark, the center of DiSanti's forehead. Blood and brains splattered as the bastard collapsed to the ground.

A gunshot blasted the air, and he jerked his head back to Lucas and the man on the ground. His heart raced. Lucas?

His brother rolled off the shooter, checked the man's pulse, then looked over his shoulder at Brayden.

Thank God. Lucas wasn't hit.

Lucas shoved the man's gun aside, then stood and walked over to DiSanti.

Brayden breathed a sigh of relief when Lucas gave him a smile of approval.

DiSanti was finally dead.

He could go after Mila and bring her home.

MILA DRAGGED IN the Christmas tree, shaking snow from her boots. Colorado was beautiful but cold.

Izzy's teeth chattered.

"I'll make us some hot chocolate," Mila said. Although first she wanted to make certain they hadn't been followed. All day she'd had the strangest feeling that someone was watching her. She'd especially sensed it at the Christmas tree lot.

Izzy ran in, yanking off her gloves, hat and coat, then raced toward the bag of decorations they'd picked up at the thrift store.

Mila hurried back to the door to close it. A dark SUV pulled into the drive, sending fear through her.

Had DiSanti found her?

She started to scream at Izzy to run and hide, but the driver's door opened, and a man emerged. Not DiSanti.

A tall dark-haired cowboy in a Stetson, boots and jeans and a long Western duster coat.

Her heart flip-flopped in her chest.

Brayden.

But fear followed. Was he here to tell her that she and Izzy had to move again?

She opened the door, soaking in the sight of him as he climbed the steps.

A slow smile curved his mouth as his gaze met hers.

"Brayden?"

"He's dead."

Relief nearly knocked her off her feet. "When? What happened?" Heart racing, she stepped onto the porch. "Never mind. I don't care. I'm just glad you're here." She couldn't help herself. She'd missed him so much, she threw her arms around him.

He swept her into a hug and growled in her ear. "I love you, Mila. I want you and Izzy to come home with me."

Love swelled inside her, and she lifted her head to look into his eyes. "I love you, too, Brayden."

"You do?"

Her pulse hammered. "I do."

"Then you'll marry me?" The tentative look in his eyes warmed her heart even more. Did he really expect her to say no?

She slid her arms under his and wrapped them around him. "Yes, I would love to marry you," she whispered.

They both laughed, then their lips fused for a tender, passionate kiss. Seconds later, Izzy squealed and joined them. She wiggled in between them, and they all hugged, then Brayden scooped her up.

"Izzy, I want to marry your mommy, is that okay?"

She bobbed her head up and down, her eyes bright with laughter.

"That means that you'll live with me," Brayden said. "I'd like to be your daddy, too."

"Yes, yes, I want you as my daddy!" She giggled and wrapped her little arms around his neck. When she finally pulled away, she looked over at Mila.

"Santa came early, Mommy."

Mila rubbed her daughter's back. "What do you mean?"

"I tolded you I asked Santa for something else."

Mila smiled. "Yes?"

"I asked him to bring me a daddy of my own!" Izzy squealed. "And he did!"

Tears pricked the back of Mila's eyelids. Izzy and she would have a family now with Brayden at Hawk's Landing.

Santa would also make all of Izzy's wishes come true. Not only would she get a puppy, but she'd get a pony. Blondie would be hers forever.

* * * * *

COLD CASE AT COBRA CREEK

To all the Harlequin Intrigue fans—
thanks for reading me all these years!

Prologue

Sage Freeport vowed never to trust a man again.

Not after the way Trace Lanier had treated her. Promises of love and happily ever after—until she'd gotten pregnant.

Then those promises had evaporated, like rain on a strip of scorching-hot pavement.

Her three-year-old Benji had never met his father. She'd worried about him not having a man in his life and done her best to be two parents in one. Still, she couldn't throw a softball worth a darn, and baiting her own hook to go fishing at the pond literally made her feel faint.

Then Ron Lewis had come along a few months ago and swept her off her feet with his kindness and intelligence—and treated Benji like his own son.

Her gaze strayed to the tabletop tree she and Benji had decorated just yesterday. Together they'd made ornaments to hang on the tree, and when he was asleep last night, she'd wrapped his gift. He was going to be ecstatic on Christmas morning to find the softball and glove he'd asked for.

She pulled a pan of homemade cinnamon rolls from the oven to let them cool before her guests at the B and

B she owned surfaced for breakfast, then went upstairs to check on her son.

Benji was normally up by now, underfoot in the kitchen when she was cooking—chatting and asking questions and sneaking bacon as soon as she took it off the pan.

But when she opened Benji's door, he wasn't in bed. A few toys were scattered around the floor, a sign he'd gotten up to play after she'd tucked him in the night before.

Figuring he was playing some imaginary game, she darted into his bathroom.

But he wasn't there, either.

She checked under his bed and frowned. "Benji? Where are you, honey?"

No answer.

Her heartbeat stuttered for a moment, but she told herself not to panic. The inn was a big house. The B and B held eight rooms, although most of them were empty at the time. With the holidays approaching, most people were staying home, going to visit family or flying to some exotic location for a winter vacation, not visiting small-town Texas.

She peeked inside Benji's closet but didn't see him. Yet the dresser drawer stood open, and his clothes looked as if he'd pawed through them.

Probably to dress himself. He was three and starting to vie for independence that way. She just had to teach him how to match colors now.

Then she noticed his backpack was missing.

Her heart suddenly racing, she turned and looked at his room again. The big bear he normally slept with wasn't in his bed. Not on the floor or in the room at all. Neither was the whistle he liked or his favorite red hat.

But his blanket was there. He'd never go anywhere without that blue blanket.

Fear seized her, but she fought it off.

Surely Benji was just pretending he was on a camping trip. He and Ron had been talking about hiking the other night. Ron had even asked Benji which one of his special friends/toys he would carry with him if he was going on a long trip.

The bear, whistle and red cap were on his list.

Her hands shaking as other scenarios taunted her, she raced down the hall to the empty rooms and searched inside. No Benji.

Hating to disturb the two guests she did have but panicked now, she knocked on the door to the Ellises', an elderly couple on an anniversary trip. The gray-haired man opened the door dressed in a robe. "Yeah?"

"I'm sorry, Mr. Ellis, but have you seen my son, Benji?"

"No, ma'am. Me and Henrietta been sleeping."

"Would you mind checking your room in case he snuck in? He's only three and mischievous at times."

He scratched his head, sending his wiry hair askew. "Sure." He left the door open, and Sage watched as he checked under the bed, the closet and adjoining bathroom. "Sorry, Ms. Freeport, he's not in here."

Sage's stomach knotted. If—no, *when*—she found Benji, she would explain that hiding from her was not okay.

She climbed the steps to the third-floor attic room. A woman named Elvira had chosen it, saying she needed solace and to be alone. The poor woman had lost a child, and Sage had given her privacy to mourn.

But Elvira didn't answer. Sage let herself in and found a note from the lady saying she'd decided to leave early and didn't want to disturb Sage.

Benji liked this room because the window offered a view of the creek behind the house.

But the room was empty.

Nerves on edge, she ran downstairs, once again checking each room and shouting Benji's name. She rushed outside, wind beating at her as she searched the yard, the garden out back, the swing set, the fort and the tree house.

Benji was nowhere to be found.

Terrified, she ran back inside to call the sheriff. But the phone was ringing as she entered the kitchen. Maybe a neighbor had found Benji.

She grabbed the phone, determined to get rid of the caller so she could phone the sheriff. But his voice echoed back.

"Ms. Freeport, it's Sheriff Gandt."

Her stomach pitched. "Yes, I was just about to call you. My little boy, Benji… He's gone."

"I was afraid of that," Sheriff Gandt muttered.

Icy fear seized Sage.

"I think you'd better come down to River Road Crossing at Cobra Creek."

"Why?" She had to swallow to make her voice work. "Is Benji there?"

"Just meet me there."

He hung up, and Sage's knees buckled. She grabbed the kitchen counter to keep from hitting the floor.

No… Benji was fine. He had to be…

She grabbed her keys and ran outside. The minivan took three tries to crank, but she threw it in gear and tore down the road toward the river crossing.

As soon as she rounded the bend, she spotted flames shooting into the air. Smoke curled upward, clogging the sky in a thick, gray blanket.

Tires squealed as she swung the van to the shoulder of the road, jumped out and ran toward the burning car.

Sheriff Gandt stood by while firemen worked to extinguish the blaze. But even with the flames and smoke, she could tell that the car was a black Jeep.

Ron drove a black Jeep.

"Do you recognize this vehicle?" the sheriff asked.

A cold sweat broke out on Sage's body. "It's Ron's. My fiancé."

Sheriff Gandt's expression looked harsh in the morning light. Then she saw what he was holding in his hands.

Benji's teddy bear and red hat.

No… Dear God. Had Benji been in the car with Ron when it crashed and caught on fire?

Chapter One

Two years later

Dugan Graystone did not trust Sheriff Billy Gandt worth
a damn.

Gandt thought he owned the town and the people
in it and made no bones about the fact that men like
Dugan, men who weren't white, weren't fit for office
and should stay out of his way.

Gandt had even tried to stop Dugan from taking on
this search-and-rescue mission, saying he could use his
own men. But the families of the two lost hikers had
heard about Dugan's reputation as an expert tracker and
insisted he spearhead the efforts to find the young men.

Dugan rode his stallion across the wilderness, scrutinizing every bush and tree, along with the soil, for
footprints and other signs that someone had come this
way. A team of searchers had spread across the miles
of forests looking for the missing men, but Dugan had
a sixth sense, and it had led him over to Cobra Creek,
miles from where Gandt had set up base camp for the
volunteer workers involved in the search.

Dammit, he hated Gandt. He'd run against him for
sheriff and lost—mainly because Gandt bought votes.

But one day he'd put the bastard in his place and prove that beneath that good-old-boy act, Gandt was nothing but a lying, cheating coward.

Born on the reservation near Cobra Creek, Dugan had Native American blood running through his veins. Dugan fought for what was right.

And nothing about Gandt was right.

Money, power and women were Gandt's for the taking. And crime—if it benefited Billy—could be overlooked for a price.

Though Dugan owned his own spread, on the side, he worked as a P.I. His friend, Texas Ranger Jaxon Ward, was looking into Gandt's financials, determined to catch the man at his own game.

The recent flooding of the creek had uprooted bushes and trees, and washed up debris from the river that connected to the creek. Dugan noted an area that looked trampled, as if a path had been cut through the woods.

He guided his horse to a tree and dismounted, then knelt to examine the still-damp earth. A footprint in the mud?

Was it recent?

He noticed another, then some brush flattened, leading toward the creek. Dugan's instincts kicked in, and he shone his flashlight on the ground and followed the indentations.

Several feet away, he saw another area of ground that looked disturbed. Mud and sticks and…something else.

Bones.

Maybe an animal's?

He hurried over to examine them, his pulse pounding. No…that was a human femur. And a finger.

Human bones.

And judging from the decomp, they had been there

too long to belong to one of the two teenagers who'd gone missing.

The radio at his belt buzzed and crackled, and he hit the button to connect.

"We found the boys," Jaxon said. "A little dehydrated, but they're fine."

Dugan removed his Stetson and wiped sweat from his forehead. "Good. But I need the coroner over here at Cobra Creek."

"What?"

"I found bones," Dugan said. "Looks like they've been here a couple of years."

A foreboding washed over Dugan. Two years ago, a man named Ron Lewis had supposedly died in a car crash near here. Sage Freeport's son had been with him at the time.

The man's body and her son's had never been found.

Could these bones belong to Ron Lewis, the man who'd taken her son?

SAGE SET A PLACE at the breakfast bar for Benji, then slid a pancake onto the plate and doused it with powdered sugar, just the way her son liked it. His chocolate milk came next.

The tabletop Christmas tree she kept year-round still held the tiny ornaments Benji had made and hung on it. And the present she'd had for him the year he'd gone missing still sat wrapped, waiting for his small hands to tear it open.

It was a glove and ball, something Benji had asked Santa for that year.

Would the glove still fit when she finally found him and he came home?

Two of her guests, a couple named Dannon, who'd come to Cobra Creek to celebrate their twentieth anniversary, gave her pitying looks, but she ignored them.

She knew people thought she was crazy. Mrs. Krandall, the owner of the diner in town, had even warned her that perpetuating the fantasy that her son was still alive by keeping a place set for him was dangerous for her and downright creepy.

She also suggested that it would hurt Sage's business.

A business Sage needed to pay the bills—and to keep her sanity.

But she couldn't accept that her son was dead.

Not without answers as to why Ron had taken Benji from the house and where they'd been headed.

Not without definite proof that he wasn't alive out there somewhere, needing her.

Of course, Benji's hat and bear had been found at the scene, but his bones had never been recovered.

Sheriff Gandt theorized that Lewis and Benji probably had been injured and tried to escape the fire by going into the creek. But storms created a strong current that night, and their bodies must have washed downstream, then into the river where they'd never be found.

She should never have trusted Ron with her son. It was her fault he was gone....

She refused to believe that he wouldn't be back. She had to cling to hope.

Without it, the guilt would eat her alive.

DUGAN GRITTED HIS TEETH as Sheriff Gandt studied the bones.

"Could have been a stranger wandering through," Gandt said. "Miles of wilderness out here. I'll check the databases for wanted men. Criminals have been known to hide out here off the grid."

The medical examiner, Dr. Liam Longmire, narrowed his eyes as he examined the body they unearthed when they'd swept the debris from the bones. Most of the skeleton was intact. Of course, the bones had decayed and been mauled by animals, but there were enough that they'd be able to identify him. That is, if they had medical records to compare to.

"What about Ron Lewis?" Dugan asked. "It could be him."

Sheriff Gandt adjusted the waistband of his uniform pants and chewed on a blade of grass, his silence surprising. The man usually had an answer for everything.

Dr. Longmire looked up at Dugan, then Gandt. "I can't say who he is yet, but this man didn't die from a fire or from the elements."

"What was the cause of death?" Dugan asked.

Longmire pointed to the rib cage and thoracic cavity. "See the markings of a bullet? It shattered one of his ribs. I can tell more when I get him on the table, but judging from the angle, it appears the bullet probably pierced his heart."

Dugan glanced at Gandt, who made a harrumph sound.

"Guess you've got a murder to investigate, Sheriff," Dugan said.

Gandt met his gaze with stone-cold, gray eyes, then glanced at the M.E. "How long has he been dead?"

"My guess is a couple of years." Dr. Longmire paused. "That'd be about the time that Lewis man ran off with Sage Freeport's kid."

Gandt nodded, his mouth still working that blade of

grass. But his grim expression told Dugan this body was more of a nuisance than a case he wanted to work.

"I'll request Lewis's dental records," Dr. Longmire said. "If they match, we'll know who our victim is."

Gandt started to walk away, but Dugan cleared his throat. "Sheriff, aren't you going to get a crime unit to comb the area and look for evidence?"

"Don't see no reason for that," Gandt muttered. "If the man's been dead two years, probably ain't nothin' to find. Besides, the flood last week would have washed away any evidence." He gestured to the south. "That said, Lewis's car was found farther downstream. If his body got in the water, it would have floated further downstream, not up here."

"Not if his body was dumped in a different place from where he died."

"You're grasping at straws." Gandt directed his comment to the M.E. "ID him and then we'll go from there."

The sheriff could be right. The victim could have been a drifter. Or a man from another town. Hell, he could have been one of the two prisoners who'd escaped jail a couple years back, ones who'd never been caught.

But the sheriff should at least be looking for evidence near where the body was found.

Gandt strode toward his squad car, and Dugan used his phone to take photographs of the bones. Dr. Longmire offered a commentary on other injuries he noted the body had sustained, and Dugan made a note of them.

Then Longmire directed the medics to load the body into the van to transport to the morgue, making sure they were careful to keep the skeleton intact and preserve any forensic evidence on the bones.

Dugan combed the area, scrutinizing the grass and

embankment near where the bones had washed up. He also searched the brush for clues. He plucked a small scrap of fabric from a briar and found a metal button in the mud a few feet from the place where he'd first discovered the bones. He bagged the items for the lab to analyze, then conducted another sweep of the property, spanning out a half mile in both directions.

Unfortunately, Gandt was right. With time, weather and the animals foraging in the wilderness, he couldn't pinpoint if the body had gone into the river here or some other point.

Frustrated, he finally packed up and headed back to town.

But a bad feeling tightened his gut. Gandt had closed the case involving Sage Freeport's missing son and Lewis too quickly for his taste.

How would he handle this one?

By late afternoon, news of the bones found at Cobra Creek reached Sage through the grapevine in the small Texas town. She was gathering groceries to bake her famous coconut cream pie when she overheard two women talking about the hikers that had been recovered safely.

The checkout lady, Lorraine Hersher, the cousin of the M.E., broke in. "A body was found out at the creek. Nothing but the bones left."

Sage inched her way up near the register.

"Who was it?" one of the women asked.

"Don't think they know yet. Liam said he was checking dental records. But he said the man had been dead about two years."

Sage's stomach clenched. Two years? About the time Ron's car had crashed.

Could it possibly be…?

Desperate for answers, she pushed her cart to the side, leaving her groceries inside it, then hurried toward the door. The sheriff's office was across the square, and she tugged her jacket around her, battling a stiff breeze as she crossed the street.

Sheriff Gandt had been less than helpful when Benji had gone missing. He wouldn't want her bugging him now.

But she'd long ago decided she didn't care what he thought.

She charged inside the office, surprised to see Dugan Graystone standing inside at the front desk. She'd seen the big man in town a few times, but he kept to himself. With his intense, dark brown eyes and brooding manner, some said he was a loner but that he was the best tracker in Texas. Tall, broad shoulders, sharp cheekbones—the package was handsome. Half the women in town thought he was sexy, while the other half were afraid of him.

Dr. Longmire stood next to him, the sheriff on the opposite side of the desk.

All three men turned to look at her as she entered, looking like they'd been caught doing something wrong.

Sage lifted her chin in a show of bravado. "I heard about the body you found at Cobra Creek."

Dugan's brown eyes met hers, turmoil darkening the depths, while Gandt shot her one of his condescending looks. She couldn't believe the man had ever been married and understood why he wasn't anymore.

She had heard that he'd taken in his ailing mother,

that the elderly woman was wheelchair-bound, difficult and demanding. Even though she disliked Gandt, she had to admit his loyalty to his mother was admirable.

"Who was it?" Sage asked.

Dr. Longmire adjusted his hat, acknowledging her with a politeness bred from a different era. "The body belonged to Ron Lewis."

Sage gasped. "You're sure?"

"Dental and medical records confirm it," the M.E. said.

Sage's legs threatened to give way. She caught herself by dropping onto a chair across from the desk. Tears clogged her throat as panic and fear seized her.

But she'd been in the dark for two years, and she had to know the truth.

Even if it killed her.

"Was Benji with him?"

Chapter Two

Sage held her breath. "Sheriff, did you find Benji?"

Sheriff Gandt shook his head. "No. Just Lewis's body."

Relief spilled through Sage. "Then my son... He may still be out there. He may be alive."

Dugan and the medical examiner traded questioning looks, but the sheriff's frown made her flinch. Did he know something he wasn't telling her? Was that the reason he'd closed the case so quickly after Benji disappeared?

"Ms. Freeport," Sheriff Gandt said in a tone he might use with a child, "Dr. Longmire believes Ron Lewis has been dead since the day of that crash. That means that your son has been, too. We just haven't found his body yet. Probably because of the elements—"

"That's enough, Sheriff," Dugan said sharply.

Sheriff Gandt shot Dugan an irritated look. "I believe your part is done here, Graystone."

Sage gripped the edge of the desk. "How did Ron die, Sheriff?"

"Ms. Freeport, why don't you go home and calm down—"

"He died of a gunshot wound," Dugan said, cutting off the sheriff.

Sage barely stifled a gasp. "Then the car crash...? That didn't kill him."

"No," Dr. Longmire said, "he most likely bled out."

Sage's mind raced. Who had shot Ron? And why? "The shot caused the crash," she said, piecing together a scenario in her head.

"That would be my guess," Dr. Longmire said.

"Was there a bullet hole in the car?" Dugan asked Gandt.

Sheriff Gandt shrugged. "I don't know. The fire destroyed most of it."

Sage folded her arms and stared at the sheriff. "But that bullet proves Ron Lewis's death was no accident. He was murdered."

DUGAN WORKED TO rein in his anger toward Gandt. The weasel should be comforting Sage and reassuring her he'd do everything humanly possible to find the truth about what happened to her son.

That was what he'd do if he was sheriff.

But he lacked the power and money the Gandts had, and in this small town, that seemed to mean everything.

"It appears that way," Sheriff Gandt told Sage. "And I will be investigating the matter. But—" he lifted a warning hand to Sage "—if your son had survived, we would have found him by now, Ms. Freeport. Odds are that the shooter fired at Lewis, he crashed and managed to get out of the car and fled. Maybe your son was with him, maybe not. But if he made it to the water with Lewis, he couldn't have survived the frigid temperature or the current. He would have been swept downstream and drowned."

"Sheriff," Dugan snarled, hating the man's cold bluntness.

The M.E. gave Sage a sympathetic look, then excused himself and hurried out the door.

Sheriff Gandt tugged at his pants. Damn man needed a belt to keep the things up. That or lose thirty pounds around his belly so he didn't have to wear them so low.

"I know you want me to sugarcoat things, Graystone, but I'm the sheriff, not a damn counselor. I tell it like it is. Good or bad."

Still, he could consider Sage's feelings. She'd lost a child. "Part of your job is to protect innocent citizens and to find out the truth when something happens to one of them. Benji Freeport was three. He was certainly innocent." Dugan squared off with the sheriff. "But you haven't done a damn thing to give his mother closure or find the answers she needs."

"You think bringing her a mangled bunch of bones is going to make her feel better?" Sheriff Gandt said.

"That would hurt, but at least I'd know the truth," Sage said. "And now that we know Ron was murdered, there is a chance that whoever shot him took Benji." Sage's voice cracked. "That means that Benji may be out there, alone, in trouble, needing me. That he's been waiting for us to find him all this time."

Dugan's chest tightened at the emotions in her voice. Emotions she had every right to feel, because she'd spoken the truth.

Sheriff Gandt swung a crooked finger toward the door. "I don't need either of you telling me how to do my job. Now, leave so I can get to it."

"Then let me know what you find." Sage clutched her shoulder bag, turned and walked out the door.

Dugan stared at the sheriff. "She deserves to know what happened to her son. And if he's alive, she deserves to bring him home."

"She's deluding herself if she thinks she'll find him alive," Sheriff Gandt said. "She needs to accept that he's gone and move on with her life."

Dugan had never had a child, but if he did and that child disappeared, he'd move heaven and earth to find him. "You are going to investigate Lewis's murder, aren't you? After all, you owe it to the people in the town to make sure that his killer isn't still among them."

Gandt tapped his badge. "In case you've forgotten, Graystone, the people elected me, so they obviously have confidence in my abilities. Now, get out of my office."

Dugan shot him a go-to-hell look, turned and stormed out the door. The man might make a token gesture to solve Lewis's murder.

But he doubted he would put forth any effort to hunt for Benji Freeport.

Dugan spotted Sage sitting on a park bench in the square, her face buried in her hands, her body trembling.

He headed across the square to join her. If Gandt wouldn't find Sage's son for her, he would.

SAGE WAS SO ANGRY she was shaking all over. Sheriff Gandt had stonewalled her before.

But how could he dismiss her so easily now that they knew that Ron Lewis had been murdered?

Ron's face flashed in her mind, and her stomach revolted. She'd been such a fool to trust him. Why had he taken her son with him that day? Where was he going?

And who had killed him?

The questions ate at her. None of it made sense.

Ron had waltzed into her life and charmed her with his good looks, his business sense and his talk of giving the town a face-lift and bringing in tourism. Tourists would have greatly impacted her income, so she'd been on board from the beginning.

Maybe that was the one reason he'd warmed up to her. Had he thought she could influence the town council with his plans for putting Cobra Creek on the map?

Footsteps crunched on gravel, and she suddenly felt someone beside her. A hand on her shoulder.

She jerked her head up, wiping at the tears streaming down her face, and stared into Dugan Graystone's dark eyes. The man was a rebel of sorts and was the only person she'd ever known to go up against the sheriff.

High cheekbones sculpted an angular face, evidence of his Native American roots. His chiseled face was bronzed from work on the ranch, his hands were broad and strong looking, his big body made for ranching and working the land.

Or for a woman.

She silently chided herself. Just because she felt vulnerable and needy, and Dugan was strong and powerful looking, didn't mean she'd fall prey to his charms.

No man would ever get close to her again.

"What do you want?" Sage asked, a little more harshly than she'd intended.

Dugan's eyes flared at her tone. "Gandt is a first-class jerk."

His comment deflated her anger, and a nervous laugh escaped her. "Yes, he is."

"He said he'd look into Lewis's murder."

"Sure he will." Sage brushed her hands together. "Like he looked into the crash two years ago."

Dugan sank his big body onto the bench beside her. "I know you were engaged to Lewis and want answers about who killed him."

Anger shot through Sage. "We may have been engaged, but that was obviously a mistake. The minute he took my son from my house without my permission, any feelings I had for him died." She swallowed the lump in her throat. "I don't care why he was murdered. In fact, I would have killed him myself for taking Benji if I'd found him."

A tense second passed. "I understand," Dugan said in a gruff voice.

"Do you? That man took everything from me."

The anguish in her tone made his chest squeeze. "I'll help you," he said. "I'll find out why Lewis was murdered."

Sage studied his face. He seemed so sincere. Earnest. As if he actually cared.

But she wouldn't buy in to that, not ever again.

On the other hand, Dugan had run for sheriff and Gandt had beaten him, so he probably had his own personal agenda. He wanted to show Gandt up and prove to the town that they'd elected the wrong man.

She really didn't care about his motive. "All right. But understand this—the only reason I want to know who killed Ron is that it might lead me to my son. Whatever dirt you dig up on Ron is fine with me. I don't care about his reputation or even my own, for that matter."

Dugan studied her in silence for a few minutes. Sage felt the wind ruffle her hair, felt the heat from his body, felt the silence thick with the unknown.

"I'll do everything I can to help you," Dugan said gruffly. "But I may not find the answers you want."

Sage understood the implications of his statement. "I know that." She gripped her hands together. "All I want is the truth...no matter what it is."

"Even if it's not pretty?"

Sage nodded. "The truth can't be any worse than what I've already imagined."

DUGAN HOPED THAT was true. But there was the possibility that they'd find out her little boy had been burned in the fire. Or that he'd been kidnapped by a cold-blooded murderer.

The scenarios that came to mind sent a shot of fear through him. For all they knew, the shooter could have abducted Benji and sold him or handed him off to a group trafficking kids. Hell, he could have been a pedophile.

In fact, kidnapping the boy could have been the endgame all along.

Someone could have hired Lewis to get the boy.

But if so, why?

He had to ask questions, questions Sage might not like.

"You've done investigative work before?" Sage asked.

Dugan nodded. "I've been called in as a consultant on some cold cases. I have a friend, Texas Ranger Jaxon Ward, who I work with."

"How do you know him?"

"We go way back," Dugan said, remembering the foster home where they'd met.

Sage arched an eyebrow in question, but Dugan let the moment pass. They weren't here to talk about him and his shady upbringing. "In light of the fact that Lewis's body has been found, I'm going to enter your son's picture into the system for missing children."

Emotions darkened Sage's soft green eyes, but she nodded. "Of course. I tried to get Sheriff Gandt to do that two years ago, but he was certain Benji died in the crash or drowned, and said it was a waste of time."

That sounded like shoddy police work to him.

"If you want to stop by the inn, I can give you one of the latest pictures I took."

"I'll walk with you over there now."

Sage stood, one hand clutching her shoulder bag. "Why don't you meet me there in half an hour? I have an errand to run first."

"Half an hour," Dugan agreed.

Sage hesitated a moment, her breath shaky in the heartbeat of silence that stretched between them. "Thank you, Dugan. I can't tell you what it means to have someone listen to me. I...know some people think I'm nuts. That I just can't let go."

He had heard rumors that she set the table for her son at every meal, as if he was coming home for dinner. Hell, was that crazy, or was she simply trying to keep hope alive?

"I don't blame you for not giving up," Dugan said gruffly. "At least not without the facts or proof that your son is really gone."

He let the words linger between them, well aware she

understood the meaning underscoring his comment. If he found proof Benji was dead, she'd have to accept that.

But if there was a chance the boy was out there somewhere, he'd find him and bring him back to her where he belonged.

SAGE UNLOADED THE GROCERIES, grateful the couple staying at the inn had taken a day trip and wouldn't be back until bedtime. Breakfast came with the room rental, but lunch and dinner were optional. In addition, she provided coffee and tea and snacks midmorning and afternoon, including fruit, cookies and an assortment of freshly baked pastries and desserts. She usually conferred with the guests on check-in and planned accordingly.

The doorbell rang; then the front bell tinkled that someone had entered. She rushed to the entryway and found Dugan standing beneath the chandelier, studying the rustic farm tools and pictures of horses on the wall.

People who visited Texas wanted rustic charm, and she tried to give it to them.

"I came for that picture." Dugan tipped his Stetson out of politeness, his rugged features stark in the evening light.

"Come this way." She led him through the swinging double doors to the kitchen. His gaze caught on the tabletop Christmas tree, and she bit back a comment, refusing to explain herself.

Maybe Benji would never come back.

But if he did, his present would be waiting. And they would celebrate all the days and holidays they'd missed spending together the past two years.

Chapter Three

Sage opened a photo album on the breakfast bar and began to flip through it. Dugan watched pain etch itself on her face as she stared at the pictures chronicling Benji's young life.

A baby picture of him swaddled in a blue blanket while he lay nestled in Sage's arms. A photo of the little boy sleeping in a crib, another of him as an infant in the bathtub playing with a rubber ducky, pictures of him learning to crawl, then walk.

Photos of Benji tearing open presents at his first birthday party, riding a rocking horse at Christmas, playing in the sprinkler out back, cuddled on the couch in monster pajamas and cradling his blanket.

Sage paused to trace her finger over a small envelope. "I kept a lock of Benji's hair from his first haircut."

Dugan offered a smile, tolerating her trip down memory lane because he understood her emotions played into this case and he couldn't ignore them.

He shifted uncomfortably. He had a hard time relating to family; he had never been part of one and didn't know how families worked. At least, not normal, loving ones. If they existed.

He'd grown up between foster care and the rez, never really wanted in either place.

She brushed at a tear, then removed a picture of Benji posed by the Christmas tree. "I took that the day before he went missing."

Dugan glanced at the tabletop tree and realized the same present still lay beneath the tree's base. Dammit. She'd kept the tree up all this time waiting on her son to return to open it.

"Can I get the photograph back?" Sage asked. "As you can see, this is all I have left...."

The crack in her voice tore at him. "Of course. I'll take good care of it, Sage." And maybe he'd bring back the real thing instead of just a picture.

But he refrained from making that promise.

"Sage, before I get started, we need to talk. There are some questions I need you to answer."

Sage closed the photo album and laid a hand on top of it. He noticed her nails were short, slightly jagged, as if she'd been biting them.

"What do you want to know?"

"Do you have any idea why Ron Lewis had Benji in the car with him that day?"

"No." Sage threaded her fingers through the long, tangled tresses of her hair, hair that was streaked with red, brown and gold. "Sheriff Gandt suggested that he was taking Benji Christmas shopping to buy me a present."

A possibility. "What do you think?"

"Ron knew how protective I was of my son. I don't understand why he would have left without telling me or leaving me a note. He knew that Benji was all I had, and that I would panic when I woke up and discovered they were gone."

"What about other family?" Dugan asked.

Sage sighed wearily. "I never knew my father. My mother died the year before I had Benji. A car accident."

He knew this could get touchy. "And Benji's father?"

Resignation settled in her eyes. "Trace Lanier. I met him right after my mother died." She traced a finger along the edge of the photo album. "I was grieving and vulnerable. Not that that's an excuse, but we dated a few times. When I discovered the pregnancy, he bailed."

"Where is he now?"

"I have no clue. He worked the rodeos, traveling town to town."

"Did he express any interest in seeing his son?"

Sage laughed, a bitter sound. "No. He didn't even want to acknowledge that Benji was his. In fact, he accused me of lying, of coming after him for money."

Dugan waited, his pulse hammering. Sage didn't strike him as that type at all.

"I was furious," Sage said. "I told him that my mother was a single mother and that she'd raised me on her own, and that I would do the same. I didn't want his money. And I didn't care if I ever saw him again or if he ever met his son."

"And that was that?"

Sage brushed her hands together. "That was that. I never heard from him again."

Dugan contemplated her story. "Do you think that he might have changed his mind and decided he wanted to see Benji?"

Sage shook her head. "No. I think he's doing pretty well in the rodeo circuit now. Making a name bronco riding. That brings the rodeo groupies. The last thing he'd want is to have a child get in the way of that."

Dugan had never met the bastard, but he didn't like him.

Still, he'd verify that information. Perhaps Lanier's manager had suggested that having a little boy could improve his popularity. It was a long shot, but Dugan didn't intend to ignore any possibility.

SAGE HATED ADMITTING that she had fallen for Trace Lanier's sexy rodeo looks, but she had. Even worse, she'd believed Ron Lewis was different.

Could he have simply been taking Benji Christmas shopping and gotten killed before he could bring her son back?

And why would someone kill Ron?

Or had Ron taken Benji for another reason?

But why? She didn't have money to pay a ransom....

"Do you want coffee?" Sage asked.

Dugan nodded, and she poured them both a mug, then placed a slice of homemade pound cake on a plate in front of him. "It's fresh. I baked it last night."

A small smile curved his mouth. "I've heard you're a good cook."

"Really?" Sage blushed. What else had he heard?

"Yes, I'm sure it helps with your business."

"I suppose so," Sage said. "I used to stay with my grandma when I was little, and she taught me everything she knew."

He sipped his coffee. "Tell me about Ron Lewis. How did you two meet?"

"Actually he stayed here when he came to town on business," Sage said. "He was a real estate developer. He wanted to convince the town council to go forward on a new development that would enrich the town, create jobs and tourism and bring us out of the Dark Ages."

"I remember hearing something about that project," Dugan said, although he hadn't exactly been for the development. The group handling it wanted to buy up ranches and farms in the neighboring area, and turn Cobra Creek into a tourist trap with outlet malls, fast-food chains and a dude ranch.

"So you struck up a friendship?"

Sage nodded. "I was reluctant at first, but he was persistent. And he took an interest in Benji."

"Benji liked him?"

"Yes."

"He would have gone with him, without being afraid?"

"Yes," Sage said, her voice cracking. "Ron stayed in Cobra Creek most of that summer, so we went on several family outings together." She'd thought she'd finally found a man who loved her and her son.

Fool.

Dugan broke off a chunk of cake and put it in his mouth. Sage watched a smile flicker in his eyes, one that pleased her more than it should.

"Did the town council approve his plans?"

Sage gave a noncommittal shrug. "They were going back and forth on things, discussing it." She frowned at Dugan. "Do you think his murder had something to do with the development?"

"I don't know," Dugan said. "But it's worth looking into."

Sage contemplated his suggestion. She should have asked more questions about Ron's business, about the investors he said he had lined up, about *him.*

And now it was too late. If something had gone wrong with his business, something that had gotten him killed, he might have taken that secret with him to the grave.

DUGAN NEEDED TO ask around, find out more about how the locals felt about Lewis's proposal. What had happened to the development after his death? Had anyone profited?

But Sage's comment about Ron's interest in Benji made him pause. "You said he showed an interest in Benji?"

Sage stirred sweetener in her coffee. "Yes, some men don't like kids. Others don't know how to talk to them, but Ron seemed…comfortable with Benji."

"Hmm," Dugan mumbled. "Did he come from a big family?"

Sage frowned. "No, I asked him that. And he actually looked kind of sad. He said he was an only child and lost his parents when he was young."

"Was he married before? Maybe he had a child."

"No, at least he said he'd never married," Sage said. "But at this point, I don't know what to believe. Everything he told me could have been a lie."

True. In fact, he could have planned to kidnap Benji all along. He'd warmed up to the boy so he'd go with him willingly.

But why?

For money? Maybe someone had paid him to take Benji, then killed Ron Lewis to get rid of any witnesses.

But why would anyone want to kidnap Benji?

Sage wasn't wealthy, and she had no family that could offer a big reward. Kidnappers had been known to abduct a child to force a parent into doing something for them, but if swaying the town council to vote for the development had been the issue, it wouldn't have worked. Sage had no power or influence in the town.

Then again, Dugan had no proof that Ron Lewis

had done anything wrong. That the man hadn't been sincerely in love with Sage, that he hadn't come to the town to help it prosper, that he was an innocent who had been shot to death for some reason.

And that he might have died trying to save Sage's son.

"DID LEWIS LEAVE anything of his here at the inn? A calendar? Computer?"

"No, I don't think so," Sage said.

"I know it's been two years, but what room did he stay in?"

"The Cross-ties Room."

He arched an eyebrow.

"I named each room based on a theme. People who come to Cobra Creek want the atmosphere, the feel of the quaint western town."

"Can I see that room, or is someone staying in it?"

"You can see it," Sage said. "I have only one couple staying here now. They're in the Water Tower Room."

Sage led Dugan up the stairs to the second floor. She unlocked the room, then stood back and watched as he studied the room.

"Have you rented this room since he was here?"

"Yes, a couple of times," she said. "I was full capacity during the art festival both years."

He walked over and looked inside the dresser, checking each drawer, but they were empty. Next he searched the drawers in the oak desk in the corner. Again, nothing.

"What are you looking for?" Sage asked.

Dugan shrugged. "If Lewis was killed because he was into something illegal, there might be evidence he left behind." He opened the closet door and looked inside. "Did he take everything with him that day when he left?"

Sage nodded. "His suitcase and computer were gone. That was what freaked me out."

"If he'd simply been taking Benji shopping, he wouldn't have taken those things with him."

"Exactly." Sage's heart stuttered as she remembered the blind panic that had assaulted her.

"Did he mention that he was leaving town to you?" Dugan asked.

"The day before, he said he might have to go away for a business meeting, but that he'd be back before Christmas."

"Did he say where the meeting was?"

Sage pushed a strand of hair away from her face. "No…but then, I didn't bother to ask." Guilt hit her again. "I was so distracted, so caught up in the holidays, in making a stupid grocery list for Christmas dinner and finishing my shopping, that I didn't pay much attention." Her voice broke. "If I had, maybe I would have picked up on something."

Dugan's boots clicked on the floor as he strode over to the doorway, where she stood. "Sage, this is not your fault."

"Yes, it is," Sage said, her heart breaking all over again. "I was Benji's mother. I was supposed to protect him."

"You did everything you could."

"Then, why is he missing?" Sage asked. "Why isn't he here with me this year, wrapping presents and making sugar cookies?"

"I don't know," Dugan said in a low voice. "But I promise you that I'll find out."

Sage latched on to the hope Dugan offered. But the same terrifying images that haunted her at night flashed behind her eyes now.

If the person who'd shot Ron had abducted Benji, what had he done with him? Where was he? And what had happened to him over the past two years?

Was he taken care of or had he been abused? Was he hungry? Alone?

Would he remember her when they found him?

"They found Lewis's body."

"Dammit. How did that happen?"

"Floods washed the body up. That Indian uncovered his bones in the bushes when he was looking for those hikers that got lost."

"After two years, they identified Lewis?"

"Yes. Damn dental records. I should have extracted all his teeth."

A tense second passed. "Hell, you should have burned the bastard's body in that car."

"I thought it was taken care of."

"Yeah, well, it wasn't. And Sage Freeport is asking questions again. Knowing her, she'll be pushing to get the case reopened. She's like a bloodhound."

"If she doesn't settle down, I'll take care of her."

"This time make sure nothing can come back to haunt us."

"No problem. When she disappears, it'll be for good."

Chapter Four

"Did Lewis always stay in this same room?" Dugan asked.

"Yes."

"How long was he here?"

Sage rubbed her temple. "The first time he came, he stayed a couple of weeks. Then he left for a month. When he returned, he stayed about six months."

"Where did he go when he left?"

"He was traveling around Texas. Said he worked with this company that looked for property across the state, small towns that were in need of rebuilding. Part of his job was to scout out the country and make suggestions to them."

"Where was his home?"

Sage straightened a pillow on top of the homemade quilt, which had imprints of horses on the squares. "He said he was from South Texas, I think. That he grew up in a little town not too far from Laredo."

Dugan made a mental note to check out his story. Maybe someone in that town knew more about Lewis.

He walked through the room again, the boards creaking beneath his boots as he stepped inside the closet.

His toe caught on something and when he looked down, he realized a plank was loose.

He knelt and ran his finger along the wooden slat, his senses prickling. Was something beneath the board?

He yanked at it several times, and it finally gave way. He pulled it free, laid it to the side and felt the one next to it. It was loose, too, so he tugged it free, as well.

His curiosity spiking, he peered beneath the flooring. Something yellow caught his eye. He slid his hand below and felt inside the hole. His fingers connected with a small manila envelope.

"What are you doing?" Sage asked over his shoulder.

"Something's under here." He wiggled his fingers until he snagged the envelope, then removed it from the hole.

"What is that?" Sage asked.

"I don't know, but we'll find out." Dugan felt again just to make sure there wasn't anything else lodged beneath the floor, but the space was empty. Standing, he walked back to the corner desk, opened the envelope and dumped it upside down.

Sage gasped as the contents spilled out. "What in the world?"

Dugan picked up a driver's license and flipped it open. A picture of Ron Lewis stared back at him.

But the name on the license read Mike Martin.

"That's a fake driver's license," Sage said.

Dugan raked his hand over the lot of them, spreading a half dozen different licenses across the bed. "Each one of these has a different name."

"My God, Dugan," Sage whispered. "Ron Lewis wasn't his real name."

"No." Dugan met her gaze. Aliases indicated the man

might have been a professional con man. "And if he lied about who he was, no telling what else he lied about."

SAGE SANK ONTO the bed, in shock. "I can't believe he lied to me, that he had all these other identities." She felt like such a fool. "Why would he do that, Dugan? Why come here and make me think he was someone else? Just to make me fall for him?"

Dugan's mouth flattened. "Do you have a lot of money, Sage?"

"No." She gestured around the room. "I put everything into remodeling this house as a bed and breakfast."

"You don't have a trust fund somewhere?"

"God, no," Sage said, embarrassed to admit the truth, "I'm in debt up to my eyeballs."

"Then he didn't fabricate his lies to swindle you out of money," Dugan said. "My guess is that this business of a land development was some kind of sham. You just happened to get caught in the middle."

"So, he never really cared for me," Sage said. She'd asked herself that a thousand times the past two years, but facing the truth was humiliating. It also meant she'd endangered her son by falling for Ron Lewis's lies.

Dugan's apologetic look made her feel even more like an idiot.

"Even if he was running a con, maybe he really did fall in love with you and Benji," Dugan suggested.

"Yeah," Sage said wryly. "Maybe he was going to change for me." She picked up one of the fake IDs, read the name, then threw it against the wall. "More like, he took me for a moron and used me." She studied another name, her mind racing. "But why take Benji that day?"

"I don't know." Dugan shrugged. "Did he know about your debt?"

Sage nodded. "He told me not to worry, that when this deal came through, my B and B would be overflowing with business and we'd make a fortune."

"Maybe he meant that," Dugan said. "Maybe he really wanted to make things better for you and your son."

Sage made a sound of disgust. "Like you said before, Dugan, he lied about his name. What else was he lying about?" She scattered the IDs around, trying to recall if he'd mentioned any of the other names he'd used. "I can't believe I fell for everything he said." Because she'd been lonely. Vulnerable.

Had liked the idea of having a father for her son.

Never again would she let down her guard.

Not for any man, no matter what.

DUGAN GATHERED THE fake IDs to investigate them. As much as he wanted to assure her that Lewis had been sincere about his intentions with her, the phony IDs said otherwise.

A liar was a liar, and Dugan hadn't found just one alias. The man had a string of them.

Meaning he probably had a rap sheet, as well, and maybe had committed numerous crimes.

It also opened up a Pandora's box. Any one of the persons he'd conned or lied to might have wanted revenge against him.

The fact that he'd lied to Sage suggested he might have lied to other women. Hell, he might have a slew of girlfriends or wives scattered across Texas. Maybe one in each city where he'd worked or visited.

All with motive, as well.

"Do you know who Lewis met with in town about the new development?"

"George Bates, from the bank," Sage said. "He also met with the town council and talked to several landowners, but I'm not certain which ones or how far he got with them."

"I'll start with Bates." Dugan stuck the envelope of IDs inside his rawhide jacket.

Sage followed him to the door. "Are you going to the sheriff with this?"

Dugan shook his head. "I don't think he'd like me nosing into this, and I don't trust him to find the truth."

"I agree." Sage rubbed her hands up and down her arms, as if to warm herself. The temptation to comfort her pulled at Dugan.

God, she was beautiful. He'd admired her from afar ever since the first time he laid eyes on her. But he'd known then that she was too good for a jaded man like him. She and her little boy deserved a good man who'd take care of them.

And that man wasn't him.

But just because he couldn't have her for himself didn't mean that he wouldn't do right by her. He would take this case.

Because there was the possibility that Benji was alive.

Dugan wouldn't rest until he found him and Sage knew the truth about what had happened two years ago.

Sage caught his arm as he started to leave the room. "Dugan, promise me one thing."

He studied her solemn face. Hated the pain in her eyes. "What?"

"That you won't keep things from me. No matter

what you find, I want—I need—to know the truth. I've been lied to too many times already."

He cradled her hand in his and squeezed it, ignoring the heat that shot through him at her touch. "I promise, Sage."

Hell, he wanted to promise more.

But he hurried down the steps to keep himself from becoming like Lewis and telling her what she wanted to hear instead of the truth.

Because the truth was that he had no idea what answers he would find.

SAGE WATCHED DUGAN LEAVE, a sense of trepidation filling her.

At least he was willing to help her look for the answers. But the phony drivers' licenses had shocked her to the core.

How could she have been so gullible when Ron was obviously a professional liar? And now that she knew Ron Lewis wasn't his real name, who was he?

Had he planned to marry her and take care of her and Benji?

No…everything about the man was probably false. He'd obviously fabricated a story to fit his agenda.

But why use her? To worm his way into the town and make residents believe he cared about them, that he was part of them?

Devious. But it made sense in a twisted kind of way.

She straightened the flooring in the closet, then went to Benji's room. Benji had loved jungle animals, so she'd painted a mural of a jungle scene on one wall and painted the other walls a bright blue. She walked over to the shelf above his bed and ran her finger over each of his stuffed animals. *His friends,* he'd called them.

At night he'd pile them all in bed around him, so she could barely find him when she went to tuck him in. His blankie, the one she'd crocheted before he was born, was folded neatly on his pillow, still waiting for his return.

Where was her son? If he'd survived, was he being taken care of? Had someone given him a blanket to sleep with at night and animal *friends* to comfort him in bed?

She thought she'd cried all her tears, but more slipped down her cheeks, her emotions as raw as they were the day she'd discovered that Benji was gone.

The news usually ran stories about missing children. For a few weeks after the car crash, they carried the story about Ron and her son. Although the implication was that both had died in the fire, a request had been made for any information regarding the accident. They'd hoped to find a witness who'd seen the wreck, someone who could tell them if another car had been involved.

But no word had come and eventually other stories had replaced Benji's on the front page. With this new development, maybe she could arouse the media's interest again.

She hurried downstairs to the kitchen and retrieved the scrapbook with clippings she'd morbidly kept of the crash and the coverage afterward. Why she'd kept them, she didn't know. Maybe she'd hoped one day she'd find something in them that might explain what had happened to Benji.

The small town of Cobra Creek wasn't big enough for a newspaper, but a reporter from Laredo had interviewed her and covered the investigation. At least, what little investigation Sheriff Gandt had instigated.

She noted the reporter's name on the story. Ashlynn Fontaine.

Hoping that the reporter might revive the story and the public's interest, now that Ron's body had been found and that his death was considered a homicide, she decided to call the paper the next morning and speak to Ashlynn.

DUGAN DROVE TO the bank the next day to speak with George Bates, the president. One woman sat at a desk to the left, and a teller was perched behind her station, at a computer.

He paused by the first woman and asked for Bates, and she escorted him to an office down a hallway. A tall, middle-aged man with wiry hair and a suit that looked ten years old shook his hand. "George Bates. You here to open an account?"

Dugan shook his head. "No, sir, I need to ask you some questions about Ron Lewis."

Bates's pudgy face broke into a scowl. "What about him? He's been dead for two years."

"True," Dugan said. "I don't know if you heard, but his body was discovered this morning at Cobra Creek. It turns out he didn't die in that car crash or fire. He was murdered."

Bates's eyes widened. "What?"

"Yes, he was shot."

Bates rolled his shoulders back in a defensive gesture. "You think I know something about that?"

"That's not what I meant to imply," Dugan said, using a low voice to calm the man. "But the fact that Ms.

Freeport's little boy wasn't with him raises questions about where he is. Ms. Freeport asked me to look into his disappearance. Learning who killed Lewis might lead us to that innocent little boy." Dugan paused. "You do want to help find that child, don't you?"

His comment seemed to steal the wind out of Bates's sails. "Well, yes, of course."

"Then tell me everything you can about Ron Lewis."

Bates tugged at his suit jacket, then motioned for Dugan to take a seat.

"Lewis came in here with all kinds of plans for the town," Bates said. "He had sketches of how he wanted to renovate the downtown area, parks that would be added, housing developments, a giant equestrian center and a dude ranch, along with an outlet mall and new storefronts for the downtown area."

"Did he have backing?" Dugan asked.

Bates scratched his chin. "Well, that was the sketchy part. At first he said he did. Then, when it got down to it, he approached me to invest. I think he may have hit on some others around town. Especially Lloyd Riley and Ken Canter. They own a lot of land in the prime spots for the equestrian center and dude ranch."

"He made them offers?"

"You'd have to talk to them about it," Bates said. "Neither one wanted to tell me any specifics. But I think Riley signed something with him and so did Canter."

So, what had happened to those deals?

"Were most of the people in town in favor of the project?"

"A few of the store owners thought it would be good for business. But some old-timers didn't want that dude ranch or the mall."

"When he asked you to invest, did you check out Lewis's financial background?"

Bates frowned. "I was going to, but then he had that crash and I figured there wasn't no need."

"Was he working with a partner? Another contact to deal with on the project?"

"If he was, he didn't tell me."

Probably because he was running a scam. Lewis had never had backing and was going to swindle the locals into investing, then run off with their money.

Had one of them discovered Lewis's plans to cheat him and killed Lewis because of it?

Chapter Five

Dugan stopped by his ranch before heading out to talk to the ranchers Lewis had approached.

He'd worked hard as a kid and teen on other spreads, doing odd jobs and then learning to ride and train horses, and had vowed years ago that he would one day own his own land.

Growing up on the reservation had been tough. His mother was Native American and had barely been able to put food on the table. Like little Benji's, his father had skipped out. He had no idea where the man was now and couldn't care less if he ever met him.

Any man who abandoned his family wasn't worth spit.

Then he'd lost his mother when he was five and had been tossed around for years afterward, in foster care, never really wanted by anyone, never belonging anywhere. It was the one reason he'd wanted his own land, his own place. A home.

He'd hired a young man, Hiram, to help him on the ranch in exchange for a place to live. Hiram was another orphan on the rez who needed a break. He also employed three other teens to help groom and exercise the horses and clean the stalls. Keeping the boys busy and teaching them the satisfaction of hard work would hopefully help them stay out of trouble. He'd also set up college scholarships if they decided to further their education.

Everything at the ranch looked in order, and he spotted Hiram at the stables. He showered and changed into a clean shirt and jeans, then retreated to his home office.

He booted up his computer and researched Trace Lanier. Seconds after he entered the man's name, dozens of articles appeared, all showcasing Lanier's rise in success in the rodeo. Other photos revealed a line of beautiful rodeo groupies on his arm. For the past two years, he'd been traveling the rodeo circuit, enjoying fame and success.

He had no motive for trying to get his son back. He had plenty of money. And now fame. And judging from the pictures of him at honky-tonks, parties and casinos, he enjoyed his single life.

At the time of Benji's disappearance, he was actually competing in Tucson.

Dugan struck Lanier off the suspect list, then phoned his buddy Jaxon and explained about finding Lewis's corpse and the phony identities.

"Sounds like a professional con artist," Jaxon said. "Send me a list of all his IDs and I'll run them."

Dugan typed in the list and emailed it to Jaxon. He could use all the help he could get.

"I'm plugging them in, along with his picture," Jaxon said. "Now, tell me what you know about this man."

"He came to Cobra Creek on the pretense of saving the town. Said he had a developer wanting to rebuild the downtown, and expand with an equestrian center, dude ranch, shopping mall and new storefronts. The banker in town said he approached him to invest and that he solicited locals to, as well. I'm going to question them next. But I'm anxious to learn more about his background. Does he have an arrest record?"

"Jeez. He was a pro."

"What did you find?"

"He stole the name Lewis from a dead man in Corpus Christi."

"A murder victim?"

"No, he was eighty and died of cancer."

"So he stole his identity because it was easy."

"Yeah, Lewis was an outstanding citizen, had no priors. His son died in Afghanistan."

"What else?"

"Three of the names—Joel Bremmer, Mike Martin and Seth Handleman—have rap sheets."

"What for?"

"Bremmer for theft, Martin for fraud and embezzlement and Handleman for similar charges."

"Did he do time for any of the crimes?"

"Not a day. Managed to avoid a trial by jumping bail."

"Then he took on a new identity," Dugan filled in.

"Like I said, he's a pro."

"Who bailed him out?"

"Hang on. Let me see if I can access those records."

"While you're at it, see if you can get a hold of Sheriff Gandt's police report on Lewis's car accident. I want to know if Lewis was shot before the accident or afterward."

"The sheriff doesn't know?"

"According to Gandt, he thought the man died in the car fire. Now we have a body, the M.E. pointed out the gunshot wound. When I asked Gandt if he saw a bullethole in the car, he sidestepped the question, and said the car was burned pretty badly. But all that tells me is that he didn't examine it."

"Shoddy work."

"You could say that."

Dugan drummed his fingers on the desk while he waited. Seconds later, Jaxon returned.

"Each time, a woman bailed him out. The first time, the lady claimed to be his wife. The second, his girlfriend."

"Their names?"

"Eloise Bremmer," Jaxon said. "After Bremmer disappeared, the police went to question her, but she was gone, too. Same thing with Martin's girlfriend, Carol Sue Tinsley."

"Hmm, wonder if they're one and the same."

"That's possible."

"How about the other names?"

"One more popped. Seth Handleman. He was charged with fraud, but the charges were dropped. Says here his wife, Maude, lives in Laredo."

"Give me that address," Dugan said. "Maybe she's still there."

She also might be the same woman who'd bailed out Bremmer and Martin.

SAGE RUBBED HER FINGER over the locket she wore as she parked at the coffee shop where Ashlynn Fontaine had agreed to meet her. After Benji had disappeared, she'd placed his picture inside the necklace and sworn she wouldn't take it off until she found her son.

It was a constant reminder that he was close to her

heart even if she had no idea if he was alive or…gone forever.

Clinging to hope, she hurried inside, ordered a latte and found a small corner table to wait. Five minutes later, Ashlynn entered, finding Sage and offering her a small smile. Ashlynn ordered coffee, then joined her, shook off her jacket and dropped a pad and pen on the table.

"Hi, Ms. Freeport. I'm glad you called."

"Call me Sage."

"All right, Sage. You said there's been a new development in the case."

Sage nodded. "I take it you haven't heard about Ron Lewis's body being found."

The reporter's eyes flickered with surprise. "No, but that is news. Who found him?"

"Dugan Graystone, a local tracker, was searching for some missing hikers and discovered his body at Cobra Creek."

"I see. And the sheriff was called?"

Sage nodded. "Sheriff Gandt said he would investigate, but he didn't do much the first go-around."

"How did Lewis die?" Ashlynn asked.

"He was shot."

"Murdered?" Another flicker of surprise. "So he didn't die from an accident?"

"No." Sage ran a hand through her hair. "He died of a gunshot wound. At this point it's unclear if he was shot before the accident, causing him to crash, or after it, when he tried to escape the burning vehicle."

"Interesting."

"The important thing is that they found Lewis's body but not my son's. So Benji might be alive."

Ashlynn gave her a sympathetic look. "Did they find any evidence that he survived?"

"No," Sage admitted. "But they also didn't find any proof that he didn't."

"Fair enough."

"Think about it," Sage said. "The shooter may have wanted to kill Ron. But maybe he didn't realize Ron had Benji with him. When he killed Ron and discovered Benji, he may have taken my son."

A tense heartbeat passed between them, fraught with questions.

"That's possible," Ashlynn said. "But it's also possible that he didn't."

Sage's stomach revolted. "You mean that he got rid of Benji."

"I'm sorry," Ashlynn said. "I don't want to believe that, but if he murdered Lewis, he might not have wanted any witnesses left behind."

Sage desperately clung to hope that Ron's killer hadn't been that inhumane. Killing a grown man for revenge, if that was the case, was a far cry from killing an innocent child.

Ashlynn traced a finger along the rim of her coffee cup. "I hate to suggest this, but did the police search the area for a grave, in case the killer buried your son?"

Sage's throat closed. She clutched her purse, ready to leave. "I didn't call you so you'd convince me that Benji is dead. I hoped you'd run another story, this time focus on the fact that Lewis's body was found but that Benji might still be out there."

She pulled a picture of her son from her shoulder bag. "Please print his picture and remind people that he's still missing. That I'm still looking for him." Desperation tinged her voice. "Maybe someone's seen him and will call in."

Ashlynn reached over and squeezed her hand. "Of course I can do that, Sage. I'll do whatever I can to help you get closure."

Sage heard the doubt in the reporter's voice. She didn't think Benji would be found.

But Sage didn't care what she thought. "I know you have your doubts about him being alive, but I'm his mother." Sage stroked the locket where it lay against her heart. "I can't give up until I know for sure."

Ashlynn nodded and took the picture. "Did Benji have any defining characteristics? A birthmark, scar or mole? Anything that might stand out?"

"As a matter of fact, he does," Sage said. "He was born with an extra piece of cartilage in his right ear. It's not very noticeable, but if you look closely, it almost looks like he has two eardrums."

"Do you have a photo where it's visible?"

Sage had actually avoided photographing it. But it was obvious in his first baby picture. She removed it from her wallet and showed it to Ashlynn.

"This might help," the reporter told her. "I'll enhance it for the news story. And I'll run the story today." Ashlynn finished her coffee. "As a matter of fact, I have a friend who works for the local TV station. I'll give her a heads-up and have her add it to their broadcast. The more people looking for Benji, the better."

Sage thanked her, although Ashlynn's comment about searching for a grave troubled her.

As much as she didn't want to face that possibility, she'd have to ask Dugan about it.

DUGAN ENTERED THE ADDRESS for Maude Handleman into the note section on his phone, then drove toward Lloyd Riley's farm, a few miles outside town.

He'd heard about the tough times some of the land-owners had fallen upon in the past few years. Weather affected farming and crops, the organic craze had caused some to rethink their methods and make costly changes, and the beef industry had suffered.

Farmers and ranchers had to be progressive and competitive. He noted the broken fencing along Riley's property, the parched pastures and the lack of crops in the fields.

He drove down the mile drive to the farmhouse, which was run-down, the porch rotting, the paint peeling. A tractor was abandoned in the field, the stables were empty and a battered black pickup truck was parked sideways by the house.

It certainly appeared as if Riley might have been in trouble.

Dugan parked and walked up the porch steps, then knocked. He waited a few minutes, then knocked again, and the sound of man's voice boomed, "Coming!"

Footsteps shuffled, then the door opened and a tall, rangy cowboy pushed the screen door open.

"Lloyd Riley?"

The man tipped his hat back on his head. "You're that Indian who found the hikers?"

"I was looking for them, but another rescue worker actually found them," Dugan said. He offered his hand and Riley shook it.

"Name's Dugan Graystone."

"What are you doing out here?" Riley asked.

Dugan chose his words carefully. Tough cowboys

were wary of admitting they had money problems. "I spoke with George Bates at the bank about that development Ron Lewis had planned around Cobra Creek."

Riley stiffened. "What about it?"

"Bates said he asked him to invest before he died. He also mentioned that he talked to some of the locals about investing, as well."

"So?" Riley folded his arms. "He held meetings with the town council and talked to most everyone in town about it. Didn't he approach you?"

Dugan shook his head. "No, he probably meant to, but he didn't get around to me before he died."

Riley pulled at his chin. "Yeah, too bad about that."

The man sounded less than sincere. And Bates had said that he thought Riley made a deal with Lewis. "I heard Lewis offered to buy up some of the property in the area and made offers to landowners. Did he want to buy your farm?"

Riley's eyes flickered with anger. "He offered, but I told him no. This land belonged to my daddy and his daddy. I'll be damned if I was going to let him turn it into some kind of shopping mall or dude ranch."

"So you refused his offer?"

"Yeah. Damn glad I did. Heard he cheated a couple of the old-timers."

"How so?"

"Offered them a loan to get them out of trouble, supposedly through the backer of this rich development. But fine print told a different story."

"What was in the fine print?"

"I don't know the details, but when it came time to pay up and the guys couldn't make the payments, he foreclosed and stole the property right out from under them."

Riley reached for the door, as if he realized he'd said too much. "Why'd you say you wanted to know about all this?"

"Just curious," Dugan said.

Riley shot him a look of disbelief, so he decided to offer a bone of information.

"Lewis was a con artist," Dugan said. "The day of his so-called accident, I suspect he was running away with the town's money."

Riley made a sound of disgust. "Sounds like it."

"Who was it he swindled?"

"Don't matter now. Lewis is dead."

"Why do you think that?"

"I figured the deal was void when he died. Haven't seen anyone else from that development come around."

That was true. But if they'd signed legal papers, the deal would still be in effect. Unless the paperwork hadn't been completed or whoever killed Lewis had him tear up the papers before Lewis died. "Can you give me a name or two so I can follow up?"

"Listen," Riley said. "These are proud men, Graystone. You know about being proud?"

His comment sounded like a challenge, a reminder that Riley knew where Dugan had come from and that he should be grateful he'd gotten as far as he had. "Yes, I do."

"Then, they don't want anyone to know they got gypped. Maybe that accident was a blessing."

"I guess it was for some people," Dugan said. "But, Riley, the body I found earlier was Ron Lewis's. He didn't die in an accident."

Riley's sharp angular face went stone-cold. "He didn't?"

"No, he was murdered." Dugan paused a second to let that statement sink in. "And odds are that someone Lewis cheated killed him." Anger hardened Riley's eyes as he realized the implication of Dugan's questions. "What about Ken Canter? Was he one of those Lewis cheated?"

"Canter didn't care about the money. He was just happy to unload his place. He wanted to move near his daughter and took off as soon as he signed with Lewis." Riley made a low sound in his throat. "We're done here."

Riley reached for the door to slam it, but Dugan caught it with the toe of his boot. "I know you want to protect your buddies, but Sage Freeport's three-year-old son disappeared the day Lewis was murdered." He hissed a breath. "Lewis was a con artist, there's no doubt about that. And I'm not particularly interested in catching the person who killed him, *except*—" he emphasized the last word "—except that person may know where Benji is. And if he's alive, Sage Freeport deserves to have her little boy back."

Chapter Six

Sage had slept, curled up with Benji's blanket the night before. Just the scent of him lingering on it gave her comfort.

But Ashlynn's comment about a grave haunted her.

After she arrived back at the B and B, she called Dugan. She explained about her visit with Ashlynn and her suggestion that the sheriff should have looked for a grave where the killer might have buried her son.

"According to the report my friend got for me, the sheriff arrived at the scene shortly after the explosion. I don't think the killer would have had time to dig a hole and bury Benji, but if it'll make you feel better, I'll check it out."

His words soothed her worries, but she couldn't leave any questions unanswered. "Thank you, Dugan. It *would* make me feel better."

"All right. I'll head over there now."

"I'll meet you at the crash site."

She hung up, poured a thermos of coffee to take with her, yanked her unruly hair into a ponytail, then rushed outside to her van.

By the time she arrived, Dugan was waiting. "You didn't have to come, Sage. I could handle this."

"This search should have been done a long time ago."

"Actually, the police report said that searchers did comb the area for Benji after the crash."

She studied Dugan. "Were you part of that team?"

He shook his head, the overly long strands of his dark hair brushing his collar. "I was out of town, working another case."

"I understand it's a long shot, and I hope there isn't a grave," Sage said, "but ever since that reporter suggested it, I can't get the idea out of my head."

"All right." He squeezed her hand, sending a tingle of warmth through her.

She followed him to the spot where the car had crashed and burned. He pulled a flashlight from his pocket and began scanning the ground near the site, looking for anything the police might have missed.

Sage followed behind him, the images of the fire taunting her. She'd imagined them finding Benji's burned body so many times that she felt sick inside.

But they hadn't found him, and that fact gave her the will to keep going.

The next two hours, she and Dugan walked the scene, searching shrubs and bushes, behind rocks, the woods by the creek and along the river and creek bank.

Finally, Dugan turned to her. "He's not here, Sage. If he was, we would have found something by now."

Relief surged through her. "What now?"

"Maybe the news story will trigger someone to call in."

She nodded, and they walked back to their vehicles. "I have a couple of leads to check out," Dugan said. "I found some information on the fake IDs and discovered that at least one of Lewis's aliases was married. I'm driving to Laredo to see if I can talk to the woman."

Sage's stomach lurched. So Ron had not only lied to her but proposed to her when he'd already had a wife.

DUGAN WAS RELIEVED when he didn't discover a grave. Knowing there had been a search team after the crash had suggested the area was clean, but Gandt had led the team and Dugan didn't trust him.

The sheriff had obviously taken the accident at face value and hadn't had forensics study the car, or he might have found a bullet hole and realized the accident wasn't an accident at all. Unless Lewis was shot after he left the burning vehicle…

"Let me go with you to see the woman," Sage said.

Dugan frowned. "If she's covering for her husband, she might not want to talk to us."

"You think she knew what he was doing? That he had other women?"

Dugan shrugged. "Who knows? If he's run the same scam in other cities, she might be his accomplice. Or… she could have been a victim like you were."

"Just a dumb target he used."

"You aren't dumb, Sage," Dugan said. "Judging from the number of aliases this man had, he was a professional, meaning he's fooled a lot of people."

"He also could have made a lot of enemies."

"That, too." More than one person definitely had motive to want him dead.

Sage's keys jangled in her hand. "Follow me back to the inn and then let me ride with you. If she was a victim, then she might talk to me more easily than you."

Dugan couldn't argue with that. "All right."

Ten minutes later, she parked and joined him in his SUV, and he drove toward Laredo. "How did you find out about her?" Sage asked.

"My buddy with the rangers plugged the aliases into the police databases. Lewis had a rap sheet for fraud, money laundering and embezzlement."

"He did time?"

"No. In each instance, a woman bailed him out. Then he disappeared under a new name."

"It sounds like a pattern."

"Yes, it does," Dugan agreed.

Sage leaned her head against her hand. "I still can't believe I was so gullible."

"Let it go, Sage," Dugan said gently.

"How can I? If I hadn't allowed Ron—or whatever his name was—into our lives, Benji wouldn't be gone." Her breath rattled out. "What kind of mother am I?"

Dugan's chest tightened, and he automatically reached for her hand and squeezed it. "You were— are—a wonderful mother. You loved your son and raised him on your own. And my guess is that you never once considered doing anything without thinking of him first."

Sage sighed. "But it wasn't enough. I let Ron get close to us, and he took Benji from me...."

Dugan reminded himself not to let emotions affect him, but he couldn't listen to her berate herself. "I promise you we'll find him, Sage."

Of course, he couldn't promise that Benji would be alive.

Tears glittered in Sage's eyes, but she averted her gaze and turned to stare out the window.

Dugan hated to see her suffering. Still, he gripped

the steering wheel and focused on the road, anything to keep himself from pulling over and dragging her up against him to comfort her.

SAGE LATCHED ON to Dugan's strong, confident voice and his promise. He seemed to be the kind of man who kept his word.

But she'd been wrong about men before. Her track record proved that. First Benji's father and then Ron.

No, she was obviously a terrible judge of character.

But this was different. Dugan was known for being honest and fair and good at what he did. Taking on her case was nothing personal, just a job to him.

She studied the signs and business fronts as they neared Laredo. Dugan veered onto a side street before they entered town and wound through a small modest neighborhood. He checked the GPS and turned right at a corner, then followed the road until it came to a dead end.

A small, wood house with green shutters faced the street. Weeds choked the yard, and a rusted sedan sat in the drive.

"This woman's name is Maude Handleman," Dugan said as they walked up to the front door. He knocked, and she studied the neighboring houses while they waited. If Ron had made money conning people, what had he done with it? He certainly hadn't spent it on this property.

Dugan knocked again, and footsteps pounded, then the sound of a latch turning. The door opened, revealing a short woman with muddy brown hair pulled back by a scarf.

"Mrs. Handleman?" Dugan said.

Her eyes narrowed as she scrutinized them through the screen. "If you're selling something, I don't want it."

"We aren't selling anything," Dugan said. "Please let us come in and we'll explain."

"Explain what?"

Sage offered her a smile. "Please, Maude. It's important. It's about your husband."

The woman's face paled, but she opened the door and let them in. "What has he done now?"

Sage followed Maude inside, with Dugan close behind her. The woman led them into a small den. Sage glanced around in search of family pictures, her pulse hammering when she spotted a photograph of Maude and the man she called Ron Lewis, sitting on the side table.

"All right," Maude said impatiently. "What's this about?"

Dugan glanced at her, and Sage began, "Your husband, what was his name?"

"Seth," Maude said. "Except I haven't seen him since I bailed his butt out of jail nearly four years ago."

"Mrs. Handleman, did you know that Seth has other names that he goes by?"

Surprise flickered in the woman's eyes. "Other names?"

"Yes." Dugan explained about finding the various drivers' licenses. "He has been arrested under at least three assumed names. That's how we found you."

She studied them for a minute. "Who are you—the police come to take him back to jail?"

Sage inhaled a deep breath. "Actually, no. Seth came to Cobra Creek where I live, but he told me and everyone in the town that his name was Ron Lewis."

Maude twisted a piece of hair around one finger.

"He posed as a real estate developer who had big plans for Cobra Creek," Sage continued.

"He did do some real estate work," Maude said.

"He was arrested for fraud and embezzlement," Dugan cut in. "And I believe he was trying to swindle landowners around Cobra Creek."

Maude crossed her arms, her look belligerent. "Look, you can accuse him all you want, but if you want me to pay back whatever he took from folks, I don't have any money." She gestured around the room. "Just look at this. He left me high and dry."

"We don't want your money," Dugan said.

"Then, what do you want?"

Sage sighed softly. "Maude, the day Ron Lewis left Cobra Creek, he took my three-year-old little boy with him."

"He kidnapped your son?" Shock flashed red on Maude's face. "He might have been a cheat, but I find that hard to believe."

Sage nodded. "It's true. He took him from my house. My son's name is Benji." She pulled a photo from her purse and handed it to the woman. "That was taken two years ago. I haven't seen him since."

Maude's alarmed gaze met hers. "I don't understand. Seth…he cheated people out of money, but he wasn't no kidnapper."

Sage's stomach knotted. "I don't know why he took Benji," she said. "But I know that he lied to me. He asked me to marry him, and he warmed up to Benji from the start. Did the two of you have children?"

She shook her head. "I had a miscarriage right after we got married. After that, I was scared to try again."

"Did he talk about children a lot? Did he want a family?"

Maude's lip curled into a scowl. "No."

"What about his own family?" Dugan asked. "Did he tell you anything about them? Did you ever meet his mother or father?"

"No, he said his parents were dead and he didn't have any brothers or sisters."

"When was the last time you saw or talked to him?"

"I told you, right after I bailed him out of jail about four years ago."

"Did he come home with you that night?" Dugan asked.

"Yeah. He spent the night, then said he was going to make things right, that he had to talk to someone about a job and that he'd be back when he got things worked out."

Sage lowered her voice. "Did you have any idea that he'd been arrested before?"

Maude shook her head no.

"How about that he used different names?"

"I told you I didn't know what he was up to."

"He didn't call you and tell you about being in Cobra Creek?" Sage asked.

"No. I… When I didn't hear from him, I was afraid something bad happened to him. That the law caught up with him and he was back in jail."

"So you didn't look for him?" Sage asked.

"I called his cell phone, but it was dead."

"You haven't heard the news, then?" Sage asked.

She crossed her arms, irritation tightening her face. "No, what the hell is going on?"

Sage glanced at Dugan, and he cleared his throat.

"I'm sorry to have to tell you, Mrs. Handleman, but Ron Lewis...aka Seth Handleman...was murdered."

Maude gasped and twisted the afghan between her fingers. "What? Who killed him?"

"That's the reason we're here," Dugan said. "I'm investigating his murder."

Sage studied Maude's reaction. She seemed sincerely shocked. And she'd given no indication that she'd killed him or that she wanted him dead.

"Please, Maude, if you can think of a place Seth would have gone or someone he would have contacted, tell me. I'm afraid that whoever killed him took my little boy, and that Benji's in danger."

MAUDE'S FACE PALED. "I...just can't see my Seth kidnapping your boy. If he did, someone must've forced him to."

Dugan had considered that. "But Ms. Freeport didn't receive a ransom note."

Maude threw her hands up. "I don't know what to say except I'm sorry, Ms. Freeport. But I don't know anything."

"Do you recognize the names Mike Martin or Joel Bremmer?" Dugan asked.

"No, should I?"

"They're two of Lewis's other aliases."

Maude dropped her face into her hands. "You think someone he conned killed him?"

"That's possible," Dugan said. "Or it could have been one of the other women in his life."

Maude made a strangled sound. "I shoulda known he wasn't faithful when he left me. Why do I always fall for the losers?"

Sage patted her back with compassion. "I know just how you feel, Maude."

He laid a business card on the table beside her. "Call us if you think of anything."

Sage sighed as they walked outside to the SUV and got inside. "What do we do now?"

"There were two other women on the list I want to question."

"Other wives?"

"One was a wife, one a girlfriend." He fastened his seat belt. "Maybe one of them can shed some light on Lewis. If he lied to Maude about having a family, one of them might know."

"You think if he had family, they might have Benji?"

"I don't know, but there might be some answers in his past that will tell us who killed him."

Chapter Seven

Sage laid her head against the back of the seat and dozed while Dugan drove to the address he had for Mike Martin. According to Jaxon, his girlfriend was named Carol Sue Tinsley. She volunteered at a local women's shelter.

The small town was south of Laredo and took him an hour to reach. Just as he neared the outskirts, Sage cried out, "No, please don't take him…."

Dugan gritted his teeth and realized she was in the throes of a nightmare. How many nights had she actually slept in the past two years without suffering from bad dreams?

"Please…" She choked on a sob.

Dugan gently reached over and pulled her hand into his. "Sage, shh, you're dreaming."

She jerked her eyes open with a start.

"It's okay," he said softly. "A nightmare?"

She blinked as if to focus and straightened as if to shake off the dream, although the remnants of fear and sorrow glittered in her green irises.

He turned into an apartment complex that had seen better days, checking the numbers on the buildings until he reached 10G, Martin's last known address.

A few cars and pickups filled the parking spaces,

although there were more empty spaces than those oc-cupied, indicating that the building wasn't filled to ca-pacity. The patios looked unkempt, and overlooked parched land, and the roof of the building needed repairs.

He parked and turned to Sage. "Do you want to wait here?"

"No, let's go."

Together they walked up to the building, then climbed the stairs to the second-floor unit. The cinder-block walls needed painting, and someone had painted graffiti on the doorway to the stairs.

"Ron liked money. He always wore designer suits and drove a nice car." Sage wrapped her arms around her waist. "I can't imagine him living in a place like this."

Dugan silently agreed. Although Mrs. Handleman's home hadn't been in great shape and her house wasn't filled with expensive furnishings, it was upscale com-pared to these apartments.

"Maybe he and Carol Sue were lying low until he made the big score." And his fancy suits and car were a show to make the ranchers believe he was big, impor-tant. That he could save them financially.

It was dark inside.

"No one is here," Sage said.

Dugan tried the door, but it was locked. He removed a small tool from his pocket and picked the lock. The door screeched open, revealing a deserted living area with stained carpet and faded gray walls.

"Stay behind me," Dugan said as he inched inside. He glanced left at the kitchen, then spotted a narrow hallway and paused to listen for sounds that someone was inside. Something skittered across the floor, and Sage clutched his arm. "It sounds like rats."

Dugan nodded, senses alert as he crept closer. There were two bedrooms, both empty. He stepped inside the first one, crossed the room and checked the closet. Nothing.

He and Sage moved to the next one, but when he opened the door, a bird flew across the room, banged into the window and then flew back.

"It's trapped," Sage said.

Dugan closed the distance to the window and opened it, giving the bird a way to escape.

"It looks like whoever lived here has been gone awhile."

Judging from the bird droppings and the musty odor, he agreed. "After I search the apartment, I want to speak to the landlord and find out if they left a forwarding address."

"I saw an office when we first drove in."

Dugan checked the closets, but they were empty. Then he led the way back to the living area. He stepped into the kitchen and searched the drawers and cabinets. "Nothing. And no sign of where she went."

They walked outside and Dugan locked the door. Then they drove to the rental office. Dugan carried a photo of Lewis inside, and a receptionist with big hair and turquoise glasses greeted them. "You folks looking for an apartment?"

If he was, he sure as hell wouldn't spend money at this dump. "No, just some information. Is the landlord here?"

She shook her head. "It's his day off."

Dugan checked her name tag—Rayanne—and faked a smile. "Then maybe you can help us, Rayanne."

She batted blue-shadowed eyes at him. "I'll sure try."

"How long have you worked here?"

She laughed, a flirty sound. "Feels like half my life."

He laid the picture of Ron Lewis on the desk. "Do you recognize this man? He lived in 10G."

She adjusted her glasses and studied the picture. "Well, that looks sort of like Mike Martin. Except he had sandy brown hair and a mustache."

Dugan glanced at Sage, then laid the phony license with Martin's picture on it. "This was him?"

"Yeah, that was Mike." She looked up at him with questioning eyes. "He was a real charmer, although that girlfriend of his was a piece of work."

"How so?" Dugan asked.

"She always ragged on him about this place. Didn't think it was good enough for her."

"Did you know them very well?"

"Naw, he was kind of a flirt. Kept telling me he was gonna make it big one day and then he'd show Carol Sue he was important. That she was wrong about him." She fiddled with her glasses again. "But they've been gone from here a long time. What's this about?"

"Did you know Mike was arrested?" Dugan asked.

Rayanne averted her gaze, a guilty look. "Why are you asking about that?"

"Because he tried to con the people in my town, and he conned me," Sage said. "He also ran off with my little boy and then he was murdered. I'm looking for my son now."

Rayanne's expression went flat. "Well, damn."

"What?" Dugan asked.

"I did hear he was arrested, but I didn't know what it was all about."

"Carol Sue bailed him out of jail after his arrest," Dugan said.

"Yeah," Rayanne muttered. "But the next day, both of them packed up and ran. Skipped out on the rent and left the place in a mess. Mr. Hinley had to hire someone to haul out all their junk."

"What did he do with it?" Dugan asked.

"Took it to that landfill," Rayanne said. "Wasn't anything worth keeping or selling."

Another dead end. "Did Mike ever mention anything about a family? His parents or a sibling?"

Rayanne shook her head.

"How about a friend he might have gone to when he needed a place to stay or hide out?"

Rayanne looked sheepish. "Well…"

"Give us a name," Dugan said.

"He had another woman on the side. Carol Sue didn't know about her, but she lived in 2D. Beverly Vance. She's a hairstylist down at Big Beautiful Hair."

"Does she still live in the complex?" Sage asked.

Rayanne nodded. "But I'd appreciate it if you didn't tell her that I sent you."

"Why not? Don't you two get along?"

Rayanne frowned. "Tarnation, that woman was as jealous as they come. She hated Carol Sue and told me to stay out of her way. Declared she was going to have Mike to herself, one way or the other."

Dugan grimaced. So, he could add Beverly Vance to the growing suspect list.

In fact, any one of the women Lewis had conned and scorned could have killed him.

SAGE SILENTLY PRAYED that Beverly Vance knew something about her son as they walked up to the wom-

an's apartment and knocked. "If Beverly killed Ron…
Mike…maybe she took Benji," Sage said.

"That's possible. But Rayanne didn't mention anything about a child living with her."

Sage's mind raced. "Maybe she dropped him at a
church or hospital, somewhere where he'd be safe."

"That's possible," Dugan said. "Although when the
story aired about Benji being taken by Lewis, if he had
been dropped off, someone would have probably noti-
fied the authorities."

"Maybe," Sage said. "But maybe not. Especially if
they took Benji to another state. And Gandt didn't issue
an Amber alert."

Dugan's dark look made Sage's stomach knot.

"Oh, God…what if whoever took him carried him to
Mexico?" Then she might never know what happened
to him or get him back.

"We can't jump to conclusions," Dugan said. "Let's
follow the pieces of the puzzle and see where they lead
us."

Sage just hoped they didn't lead to Mexico. Finding
Benji in the United States would be difficult enough,
but crossing into another country where the legal system was less than satisfactory would complicate matters more.

Dugan knocked again, but no answer, so they walked
back to his SUV and drove to the hair salon where Beverly worked.

Big Beautiful Hair was housed in a trailer on the
edge of the small town, across from a convenience store
called Gas & Go and a liquor store called Last Stop.
Several cars were parked out front, a sign painted in

neon pink-and-green advertising the big hair Texas women were famous for.

Sage hurried up the steps to the trailer, anxious to speak to Beverly. When she entered, the whir of hair dryers and blow-dryers filled the air, the scent of perm solution and hair dye nearly overwhelming.

There were three workstations, with patrons in various stages of coloring, cutting, highlighting and dying scattered through the long, narrow room. A half dozen bracelets jangled on the arm of the buxom brunette who approached her.

"Can I help you, miss?" She started to examine Sage's unruly hair, but Sage took a step back.

"I need to see Beverly."

The woman shrugged, then turned and called for Beverly. The platinum blonde at the second station glanced over, her sparkling eye shadow glittering beneath the lights. "Yeah?"

Sage crossed the distance to her, while Dugan hung back. On the ride over, they'd decided Beverly might open up to her before she would to someone investigating the man Beverly apparently loved. "Can we talk for a minute, Beverly?" Sage said in a low voice.

"You don't want a cut and color today?"

"No, I need to ask you some questions about Mike Martin."

Beverly dropped the curling iron she was using and hurried over to Sage. "Mike, good Lord... Now, there's a blast from the past."

"When was the last time you saw him?" Sage asked.

Beverly chewed her bottom lip for a moment before she answered, "About four and a half years ago."

"How was he?" Sage asked.

Beverly tapped one of her three-inch high heels. "Agitated."

"Did he tell you that he'd been arrested?"

Beverly coaxed Sage to the back by the hair dryers. "Yes, but that was a mistake. He said he was going to get it all worked out and then he'd come back for me."

Sage forced a calm to her voice when she wanted to scream at the woman that she'd been a fool to believe anything Mike Martin had said.

Just as *she'd* been a fool to believe Ron Lewis.

"So you knew he was leaving town?"

Beverly nodded. "He said he was due to make a small fortune and then the two of us would get married and buy a house. Maybe even a ranch of our own."

Disgust filled Sage. Ron certainly could be convincing. "Did he say where he was going to make this fortune?"

Beverly leaned in close. "Said he was into a real estate deal with this developer and he was buying up property left and right. He'd already picked out some land for us." She batted her eyes. "I always dreamed about having a big place in the country. Waking up to the sun."

Clearly Beverly had been snowed by Ron's charm. "Then what happened?"

An odd look glimmered in Beverly's eyes. "Then he just disappeared. I tried calling the phone number I had for him but got a recording, saying it was disconnected. I haven't heard from him since."

"What did you think happened to him?" Sage asked.

Tears moistened Beverly's big blue eyes. "I don't know, but I've been scared to death that something bad happened. That his old girlfriend Carol Sue found out our plans and did something crazy."

"What do you mean, crazy?"

Beverly's voice choked. "I mean, like kill him. She was always jealous of me."

"Did Carol Sue own a gun?"

Beverly nodded. "A .38. She was good at shooting, too. Mike said her daddy took her to the shooting range every week when she was a kid. That she won the skeet-shooting contest at the county fair three years in a row."

Sage dug her nails into the palms of her hands. They had to find Carol Sue. If she'd shot Lewis, maybe she knew where Benji was.

DUGAN SAW THE FRUSTRATION on Sage's face as they left Big Beautiful Hair and drove toward Cobra Creek. Beverly had been completely in love with Mike Martin, aka Ron Lewis.

Dammit, he needed the man's real name. Learning the truth about his upbringing might explain what had shaped him into a con artist. A man who not only swindled people out of their money, but charmed women into believing and trusting him when he told them nothing but lies.

Sage lapsed into silence until they neared the outskirts of Cobra Creek.

"I almost feel sorry for Beverly," Sage said. "She really thought he was coming back to her."

Dugan winced. "He fooled her like he did everyone else."

"Like he did me." Sage's tone reeked of self-disgust. "The minute I realized he took Benji with him, without asking me, I was done with the man. He knew how protective I was of my son. Even if he had simply gone shopping, like I thought at first, I would have been furious." Her voice gained momentum. "You just don't do that to a mother."

Dugan agreed.

"If Beverly was right about Carol Sue, and she shot Ron, what did she do with Benji?"

"I'm going to call Jaxon and ask him to search hospital and church records nationwide for any child who might have been abandoned or dropped off around that time."

"That should have been done two years ago."

"I agree," Dugan said, his opinion of the sheriff growing lower by the minute. Gandt should have explored every avenue to find Benji.

"But if Carol Sue dropped him off, surely Benji would have told someone his name."

A dozen different scenarios ran through Dugan's mind. Not if he was injured, confused, or traumatized. Or if she'd threatened him.

But he tempered his response so as not to panic Sage. "If Carol Sue did leave him, she might have given false information, signed him in using a different name."

"You're right," Sage said. "The woman could have claimed he was her child, given a fake name and said she was coming back for him."

Dugan nodded. "I'll call Jaxon now."

His phone buzzed just as he reached for it, but suddenly a car raced up behind them and a gunshot blasted the air, shattering the back window.

Sage screamed, and he swerved and pushed her head down, then checked his rearview mirror as the car sped up and slammed into their side.

Chapter Eight

Sage screamed as a bullet pinged off the back of the SUV. Dugan swerved sideways and sped up, but the car behind them roared up on their tail.

"Stay down!" Dugan shouted.

Sage ducked, clutching the seat edge as Dugan veered to the right on a side road. The SUV bounced over ruts in the asphalt, swaying as he accelerated. Suddenly he spun the car around in the opposite direction, tires squealing as he raced back onto the main road.

"What's happening?" Sage cried.

"I'm chasing the bastard now."

Sage lifted her head and spotted a black sedan peeling off and getting farther and farther way. "Who is it?"

"I didn't see his face." He pressed the gas to the floor and tried to catch the car, but they rounded a curve and the driver began to weave.

Dugan closed the distance, pulled his gun and shot at the sedan's tires. The car screeched to the right, skidded and spun, then flipped over and rolled. Metal scrunched and glass shattered as it skated into a boulder.

A second later, the car burst into flames.

Dugan yanked the wheel to the left to avoid crashing into it, then swung the SUV to the side of the road and threw it into Park.

Then he jumped out and ran toward the burning vehicle. Déjà vu struck Sage, images of flames shooting from Ron's car two years ago pummeling her.

That night she'd been terrified Benji had been inside the car.

Today...the driver had shot at them. Tried to kill them.

Why? Because she was asking questions about Benji?

She jerked herself from her immobilized state and climbed out. Dugan circled the car, peering in the window as if looking for a way to get the driver out. But the gas tank blew, another explosion sounded and flames engulfed the vehicle.

Sweat beaded on her forehead, the heat scalding her. She backed away, hugging the side of the SUV as she watched Dugan. He must have realized it was impossible to save the driver, because he strode back toward her, his expression grim.

"Did you see who it was?"

"A man. I didn't recognize him." Dugan punched a number into his phone. "Jaxon, it's Dugan. I want you to run a plate for me."

Dugan recited the license number, then ran a hand through his hair while he waited.

"Who?" A pause. "No, send a crime team. He's dead, but maybe they can find some evidence from the car."

When he hung up, Sage asked, "Who did the car belong to?"

"Registered to a man named Joel Bremmer."

"Bremmer?"

Dugan nodded. "One of Ron Lewis's aliases."

Sage gasped. "But Ron is dead, so he couldn't have been driving the car."

Questions darkened Dugan's eyes. "I know. The M.E. will work on ID once he gets him to the morgue."

Sage gritted her teeth. "Do you think he was working with Ron?"

"That's possible." Dugan traced his thumb under her chin. "Are you okay?"

She nodded, although she was trembling. Heat reddened his face, the scent of smoke and hot metal permeating him.

"Someone doesn't like us asking questions, Sage. But that means we might be on the right track to finding some answers."

Dugan's gruff voice wrapped around her just as his arms did, and for the first time in two years, she allowed herself to lean on another man.

DUGAN STROKED SAGE'S BACK, soothing her with soft, nonsensical words.

Whoever the bastard was driving the car—he had almost killed them. An inch or two to the right, and that bullet would have pierced Sage's skull.

Cold fear and rage made him burn as hot as the fire consuming the shooter's car.

If Sage had died...

No, she was fine. So was he. And he wasn't going to stop until he unearthed the truth. The fact that someone had shot at them meant he was on the right path. That someone was afraid he'd find Lewis's killer and Benji.

A siren wailed, and Dugan released Sage. "Are you all right now?"

She nodded and tucked a strand of hair behind her ear. "Yes, thanks, Dugan."

Blue lights twirled as the sheriff's car and a fire engine careened toward them. The fire truck screeched to a stop, three firemen jumping down along with a female firefighter who'd been driving.

They rushed to extinguish the blaze while Sheriff Gandt lumbered toward them. "What happened?"

Dugan explained, "The car ran up on us, and the driver shot at us." He pointed out the bullet hole in the back of his SUV. "I swerved to avoid him and he sped past. Then I turned around and tried to catch him, but he lost control and crashed."

Gandt scowled as he looked from Dugan to Sage. "He just come up and shot at you, out of the blue?"

Dugan choked back an obscenity. Gandt was the sheriff and he had to cooperate. If he didn't, the jerk would probably lock him up and then he couldn't find the truth. But he didn't like it. "Yes."

"You've been asking questions about Lewis?"

Dugan nodded. "Turns out Ron Lewis had a few other names he went by," he said. "Then again, I'm sure you already know that."

A cutting look deepened the sheriff's eyes. "Of course. I am the sheriff."

"Right. Have you made any progress on solving his murder?"

"I'm working on it," Sheriff Gandt said, "which means you need to stay out of my investigation."

Sage spoke up. "We're just trying to find my son."

"Right." This time Sheriff Gandt's tone was sarcastic.

A crime van rolled up, interrupting them, and Gandt's mouth twitched with irritation.

"You called them?"

Dugan nodded. "I figured I'd save you the time."

The van parked, and two CSIs exited the vehicle and approached them.

Gandt crossed his beefy arms. "If you know something, spit it out, Dugan. Because if I find out you're holding back, I'll haul your butt in for interfering with a homicide investigation."

Dugan gritted his teeth. The hell he would. "I've told you all I know." He gestured toward the charred remains of the sedan. "Tell me when you identify the driver. I'd like to know who tried to kill me."

Gandt's steely gaze met Dugan's, a challenge in his expression. "Sure thing. After all, I was elected to serve and protect."

Dugan bit back a surly remark, took Sage's arm and they walked back to his SUV. He had a feeling Gandt would have handed the shooter a gun if it meant getting Dugan out of his hair.

But he'd survived a rough childhood, taunts about being a half-breed, other taunts about being a bastard kid. And then the fights as a teenager, when he'd defended himself.

Gandt couldn't intimidate him into doing anything. In fact, his obstinacy only fueled Dugan's drive to get to the bottom of Ron Lewis's murder.

His phone buzzed, and he checked the number. George Bates at the bank.

Sage slipped into the passenger seat, her expression troubled as she watched the firefighters finishing up.

He took the call. "Dugan Graystone."

"Listen, Mr. Graystone, after you left the other day, I got to thinking about Lewis and that development and looked back into some foreclosures. Worst part of my job, but sometimes I don't have a choice."

"Go on."

"There were two that troubled me. Two ranchers I threatened foreclosure on, but they paid me off at the last minute. When I asked how they came up with the money, neither one wanted to tell me. They just said they'd had a streak of luck."

"How so?"

"In both cases, the ranchers were in bad trouble financially. I think they worked out some kind of deal with Lewis, that he offered to pay off their debt by loaning them money from his own company."

Money that he might have earned through another scam.

"What happened?"

"One of the men came to me complaining that when he got behind on the payments, Lewis took over his property. Said something about he hadn't read the fine print."

Dammit. That fit with what Lloyd Riley had told him. If Lewis had a large party interested in paying big bucks for the property once he took control of it, Lewis could have turned a big profit by picking it up at foreclosure prices and then reselling.

And Lewis would have given the men he'd conned motive for wanting him dead.

"When Lewis disappeared, the ranchers asked me to keep it quiet that they'd been cheated."

A strong motive to convince Bates not to go public, to void the deal. Although technically, they would have had to go through legal channels, fill out paperwork, and look at Lewis's will, if he had one.

"Which ranchers wanted the deal covered up?"

"I don't want my name mentioned," Bates said. "Bank transactions are supposed to be confidential. If folks think I talk about their private business, they'll quit coming to me."

"I understand. Just give me the names."

"Donnell Earnest," Bates said. "And the other man was Wilbur Rankins."

"Where are they now?"

"Both are still here. When Lewis died, they refused to move, said they had reason to believe the deals weren't legal. That they had a ninety day window that hadn't passed. And so far no one has come forward to uphold the contracts they signed."

Suspicious in itself. If Lewis had investors or a legitimate corporation, someone would follow up on the deals.

Dugan thanked Bates, then made a mental note to talk to both Earnest and Rankins.

He punched Jaxon's number as he started the engine and pulled back onto the road. He asked Jaxon to research children, specifically three-year-old boys, who were left at churches, orphanages, hospitals or women's shelters around the date Benji disappeared.

"Also find out everything you can on these names. Martin's girlfriend, Carol Sue Tinsley. Handleman's wife, Maude. And a woman named Beverly Vance. Any one of them could have killed Lewis."

Jaxon agreed to call him with whatever he learned and then Dugan headed toward Donnell Earnest's ranch outside Cobra Creek.

SAGE'S NERVES FLUTTERED. "You know, Carol Sue could have just run off with Benji. Or since she volunteered at a shelter, what if she faked spousal abuse to get help, then left Benji at one of those women's shelters. From there, they could have disappeared and we may never find them. Carol Sue could have changed their names a dozen times by now."

"Those groups do have underground organizations to help women escape abusive relationships," Dugan agreed. "But we have no real reason to suspect that Carol Sue took him. She may have just freaked out when Martin was arrested and decided to skip town in case she was collared as an accomplice."

"Or she could be dead, too," Sage suggested.

"Maybe. Hopefully Jaxon will find something on her."

Another frightening scenario hit Sage. "What if Benji was hurt or in shock? If he was in that crash or witnessed the shooting, he could have been too traumatized or terrified to talk." Or the shooter could have killed him so there would be no witness left behind.

God…

Dugan squeezed her hand. "I know it's hard not to imagine the worst that could happen, but Benji's age could have worked to his advantage. Toddlers and young children don't make reliable witnesses. And killing a child takes a certain brand of cold-bloodedness that most people don't possess."

"You sound like you have a trusting nature," Sage said wryly.

Dugan made a low sound in his throat. "Not hardly. But I think the fact that we haven't found Benji may be a good sign that he's alive."

Sage tried to mentally hang on to his words.

It was all she had. Besides, she wasn't ready to give up. She never would be.

DUGAN REFUSED TO SPECULATE with Sage, because all the scenarios she mentioned were possible and dwelling on them wouldn't do anything but frighten her more. God knows he'd seen his share of bad outcomes. He'd even met a couple of men he'd called sociopaths.

But intentionally taking the life of a toddler... That was a different breed. A sociopath, maybe.

He was banking on the fact that Lewis's killer wasn't one of them.

Sage's comment about Carol Sue triggered questions.

What if the woman had abducted Benji? If she was aware of Ron's various identities, she might have adopted another name and be living somewhere, raising Benji as her own son.

He phoned Jaxon and asked him to look into that angle and to talk to the people at the shelter where Carol Sue volunteered.

Meanwhile he wanted to check out some of Ron's aliases. Maybe he'd get lucky and find one of them was still active.

He reached the drive for Donnell Earnest's ranch, the Wagonwheel. Dugan turned the SUV down the dirt drive and drove past several barns and a horse stable. Donnell raised beef cattle, but Dugan saw very few cattle grazing in the pasture.

He parked in front of an ancient farmhouse. Live oaks spread across the dry lawn.

"What's his story?" Sage asked as they climbed out.

"Apparently Donnell Earnest was in trouble financially. Lewis offered the man a loan to help him pay off his bills, but when he fell behind, Lewis took ownership of his ranch. Bates said that no one has come forward from Lewis's company about the deal, and that there was a ninety day window that hadn't passed before Lewis died, so the ranchers think the deal wasn't legal." He paused. "Of course, with Lewis's phony ID, they would have had reason to question the legality anyway."

"*If* they'd discovered he was using an alias," Sage pointed out.

True.

A scrawny beagle greeted them by sniffing his boots and Sage's leg. She bent to pet him, and Dugan walked up the rickety stairs.

Before he could knock, a heavyset guy with a thick dark beard appeared at the screened door, a shotgun in his hand.

"Get off my property or I'll shoot!" Donnell shouted.

"The hit was botched. Graystone and the Freeport woman are still alive."

"Dammit to hell and back. That body washing up at the creek was a big mistake."

"You don't have to tell me that. But the guy deserved to die."

"That's not the point. The point is that I don't want to go to jail."

"Don't worry. They'll never know what happened that day."

"You swear. Because that Freeport woman is about the most persistent woman I've ever known."

"I told you not to sweat it." He'd take care of her if he had to.

They'd come too far to get caught now.

Chapter Nine

"Listen, Mr. Earnest," Dugan said. "I need to ask you some questions about the deal you made with Ron Lewis."

"That's none of your business," Earnest growled.

Dugan gently eased Sage behind him. "I know he cheated you and I don't care. I'm trying to help Ms. Freeport find her little boy. He disappeared the day Lewis did, and his mother misses him."

"I do." Sage stepped up beside Dugan. "I just want to find him, Mr. Earnest. He's probably scared, and he doesn't understand what happened to him."

Donnell waved the gun in front of the screen door. "What makes you think I know something about your kid?"

Sage started to walk forward, but Dugan caught her arm. "Careful. Stay back."

But Sage ignored him. "I know you don't have Benji," Sage said. "But I know Ron Lewis conned you out of your property."

"This land is mine!" Donnell bellowed.

"Yes, it is. Ron Lewis was not the man's real name," Dugan said. "He had several aliases and used them to swindle others besides you."

"You mean that deal was no good?"

"It's not legal," Dugan said, hoping to gain the man's trust. "The lawyers and bank will have to sort out the details."

The big man seemed to relax and lowered his gun. "That's good news, then."

"Except that Ron Lewis's body was found at Cobra Creek. He's dead. In fact, he died the same day of that car crash."

A moment of silence stretched between them. Then Earnest raised the gun again. "So you're here 'cause you think I killed Lewis?"

"I didn't say that. I'm talking to everyone who knew Lewis in hopes that someone Lewis knew or something Lewis said might lead us to Benji."

"I don't know anything and I didn't kill him," Donnell said. "But I'm not sorry the guy's dead."

Dugan started to speak, but Sage cut him off. "I understand, Mr. Earnest. All I want is to find my son. Did Ron mention someone he might meet up with once he left Cobra Creek? Or maybe he had a partner?"

The man lowered the gun, opened the screen and stepped onto the porch. "Naw. He talked about that developer that was going to make Cobra Creek big on the map."

"Was there a contact person or address on any of the papers you signed?"

Donnell scratched his head, sending hanks of hair askew. "Don't recall one." His voice cracked. "I can't believe I was such a damn fool. My mama always said if something was too good to be true, it probably was."

"He fooled a lot of us, Donnell," Sage said sympathetically.

A blush stained his cheeks. "Downright embarrassing to know I was stupid enough to let that jerk steal my land out from under me. Hell, if a man don't have land, he don't have anything."

"Did Ron ever talk about a family?" Dugan pressed. "Did he have parents?"

"Don't remember no folks." The big man rubbed the back of his neck. "Seems like he said he grew up near San Antonio. Or maybe it was Laredo. I think he mentioned a sister once."

"Did he mention her name?"

The dog nuzzled up to his leg, and Donnell scratched him behind the ears. "Janet or Janelle, something like that."

"Thanks," Dugan said. "That might be helpful."

In fact, he'd have Jaxon run the name through the system, along with all of his aliases. Maybe one of them would pop.

"Do you think Mr. Earnest killed Ron?" Sage asked as they left the ranch.

"It's too soon to say. He seems to be telling the truth, but he has motive."

"So do some of the other ranchers." Sage studied the withered grass in the empty pastures, and the stable that looked empty. "But he did seem surprised that Ron was murdered."

"People can fake reactions," Dugan said. "Maybe he was just surprised that we found the body. After two years, whoever killed Lewis had probably gotten complacent. Thought he'd gotten away with murder."

Sage fought despair. Two years a murderer had gone free.

Two years Benji had been gone.

Children changed every day. He would have lost any baby fat from his toddler shape, would have grown taller, more agile. Had the person who'd abducted him been good to him? Was he eating right?

Who tucked him in at night and chased the bogeyman away?

Benji had been afraid of the dark. She'd bought a cartoon-figure night-light and plugged it in before he went to bed. Still, he'd been scared of monsters, so they'd played a game where she checked under the bed and the closets in a big show that she'd chased them away before she kissed him good-night.

Tears pricked her eyes.

At five, he would have started kindergarten this year. She would have already taught him to recognize the letters of the alphabet, and he could count to twenty. Was he learning to read now? Could he write his name?

A dozen more questions nagged at her, but the idea of Benji being in school kept returning. "Dugan, Benji would be five now. He might be in school somewhere. In kindergarten."

Dugan slanted her a sideways look. "That would be risky for the person he's with."

"I suppose you're right. The kidnapper could be homeschooling him." Or locking him in a room and leaving him there alone and afraid.

"Then again, you made a good point. If the person who has Benji is working, he might need for him to be in day care or school." Dugan reached for his phone again. "And it's another place to check out."

He punched in a number and spoke to his friend Jaxon, then asked him to hunt for a Janet or Janelle who might be Lewis's sister. "Make sure the photo of

Benji Freeport is circulated to all the school systems in Texas and the surrounding states. Also try day cares."

Sage's heart pounded as Dugan hung up. "Thank you, Dugan."

"I haven't done anything yet," he said in a self-deprecating voice.

"Yes, you have." Sage swallowed the knot in her throat. "You're looking for him and exploring avenues the sheriff never did."

Dugan's gaze met hers, a guarded look in his eyes. "He should have done all this two years ago."

"I know. But he just assumed Benji was dead and told me to accept it and move on." She twisted her fingers in her lap. "But I couldn't do that, Dugan. Not without knowing for sure."

And maybe not even then. Because Benji had been her life. And if he was dead, it was her fault for getting involved with Ron Lewis.

An image of Benji writing his name flashed behind her eyes, and she battled another onslaught of despair as stories of other kidnappings on the news blared in her mind.

Stories where children had been brainwashed, told that their real parents didn't want them, that they'd given them away. Stories where a boy was forced to dress like a girl or vice versa. Stories where children were abducted at such a young age that they adapted to the kidnapper and accepted, even believed, that that person was their real parent.

She couldn't fight the reality that whoever had taken her son had most likely changed his name. That they weren't even calling him Benji anymore.

That the name he might be writing wasn't his own,

which would make it even more difficult for a teacher or caretaker to realize that he'd been abducted.

That even if someone asked Benji his name, he might not remember it.

He might not remember her, either, or that she'd once held him in her arms as a baby and rocked him to sleep. That she'd sung him lullabies and chased the bogeyman away and promised to protect him forever.

That she'd dreamed about what he'd become when he grew up.

God…she'd jeopardized her son's life by trusting Ron.

And now she might never see him again.

DUGAN DROVE TO Wilbur Rankins's ranch next. Both Rankins and Earnest had reasons to want Lewis dead.

And they were the only two that Dugan knew of at this point. There could be others. People he'd swindled, along with ex-wives and girlfriends.

The man had been a real class act.

Sage had lapsed into silence. No telling what she was imagining. He wished he could keep her mind from going to the dark places, but that was impossible.

He couldn't even keep his own mind from traveling down those roads.

Rankins's property was fifteen miles outside town and just as run-down as Donnell Earnest's. Both ranchers had probably been desperate and had fallen for Lewis's easy way out.

Dugan pulled up in front of the sprawling ranch house, bracing himself for another hostile encounter. "Stay here until I see if this guy is armed."

Sage nodded. "Okay, but I want to talk to him."

"Sure, once I make sure it's safe." He'd be foolish to let her go in without assessing the situation first. If Donnell had wanted, he could have blown their heads off before they'd even made it onto the porch.

He checked his weapon, then strode up the stone path to the front door. A rusted pickup sat to the left of the house, beneath a makeshift carport. He spotted a teenage boy out back, chopping wood.

Smoke curled from the chimney, and a Christmas tree stood in view, in the front window. He knocked, scanning the property and noting a few head of cattle in the west pasture. Maybe Rankins was getting back on top of his business.

He knocked again, and the door was finally opened. A man who looked to be mid-forties stood on the other side, his craggy face crunched into a frown. "Yeah?"

"Are you Wilbur Rankins?"

"Naw, that'd be my daddy. I'm Junior."

"Is your father here?"

"He's not feeling too good." The man crossed his arms, his tattered T-shirt stretching across his belly. "Who are you and what do you want with him?"

He heard the SUV door open and glanced back to see Sage emerge from the passenger side. He motioned that it was okay for her to join him.

"What's going on?"

Dugan explained who he was and introduced Sage.

"We know that Ron Lewis swindled you," Dugan said. "That you're not the only one."

"I heard he was murdered," Junior Rankins said. "But if you think I did it, think again. I didn't know he'd conned my daddy out of his ranch until after the creep had that car crash."

"Did you meet him yourself?" Sage asked.

Junior shook his head no. "My boy out there and I lived in Corpus Christi at the time. We came down a few months ago when my father took ill."

"I'm sorry," Sage said. "Is it serious?"

"Cancer. He's been fighting it about three years. That's when he started letting things go around here."

"And Lewis popped in to save the day," Dugan guessed.

A disgusted look darkened the man's eyes. "Yeah, damn vulture if you ask me."

Footsteps sounded behind the man, and Dugan saw an older man in a robe appear. *Must be the father.*

"What's going on?" the man bellowed.

Junior turned to his father. "Everything's under control, Dad."

"Mr. Rankins," Dugan said. "Can we talk for a minute?"

The old man shuffled up beside his son and motioned for them to come in. "What the hell's going on? A man can't get any rest."

"I'm sorry," Junior said. "I was trying to take care of it."

The older man looked hollow-eyed, pale, and he'd lost his hair. "Take care of what?"

Dugan cleared his throat and introduced himself and Sage again.

"Mr. Rankins," Sage interjected. "We know that Ron Lewis tried to con you out of your land. But the morning he was leaving town, he took my little boy with him. If you know anything about where he might have been going or who he was working with, please tell me. It might help me find my son."

"I don't know a damned thing." The man broke into a coughing spell. "But I'm glad that bastard's dead so he can't cheat anyone else."

"Where were you the morning he disappeared two years ago?" Dugan asked.

Junior stepped in front of his father. "You don't have to answer that, Dad." Junior shot daggers at Dugan with his eyes. "Now, I suggest you leave before I call the sheriff and tell him you're harassing us."

Dugan was about to make a retort, but his phone buzzed. Surprisingly, Sheriff Gandt's name flashed on his caller ID display. "Graystone speaking."

"Is Sage Freeport with you?"

Dugan said yes through gritted teeth. "Why?"

"Bring her to my office. I have something to show her."

"What?"

"Something that got overlooked after the crime scene workers searched the crash site."

"We'll be right there."

Dugan ended the call, an anxious feeling in his gut. Did Gandt have bad news about Benji?

SAGE'S HANDS FELT clammy as she and Dugan parked at the sheriff's office. Dugan said the sheriff was cryptic about the reason he'd asked them to stop by.

But it couldn't be good news or else he would have told Dugan over the phone.

She reminded herself that she had survived the past two years living in the dark, that she needed closure, no matter what the outcome was.

But she'd be lying if she didn't admit that finding Ron's body and not Benji's had rekindled her hope.

Dugan opened the door to the sheriff's office and gestured for her to enter first. She did, her insides trembling as the sheriff looked up at them from the front desk, his expression grim.

"Sheriff?" Dugan said as they approached.

Sheriff Gandt stood. "After we found Lewis's body, I decided to look back at the evidence box we collected two years ago after the original accident."

"You found something?" Sage asked, her voice a painful whisper.

He nodded. "This envelope was in the bottom of the box stuck under the flap." He opened it and removed a blue whistle.

Sage gasped. The whistle was Benji's.

And it had blood on it.

Chapter Ten

Sage sagged against the desk, then stumbled into a nearby chair. "That was my son's."

"Did you test the blood to see if it belonged to Benji?" Dugan asked.

"Not yet. I wanted to show it to Ms. Freeport first and see if she recognized it."

Sage struggled to pull herself together.

"Get it tested," Dugan said firmly. "It may be Benji's blood. But blood from the person who shot Lewis might also be on it."

"Did you find anything else?" Sage said in a choked voice.

"That's it," Gandt said.

"What about on the man who tried to shoot us?"

"M.E. has him at the morgue now." He gave Dugan a warning look. "Why don't you take Ms. Freeport home and let me do my job? I've got this investigation under control."

Sage bit her tongue to keep from lashing out and telling him that Dugan had already accomplished more in two days on the case than Gandt had in two years.

But arguing with the sheriff was pointless.

She gestured toward the whistle. "After you finish with that, I'd like to have it back."

"Of course."

"You'll let me know what you find?" Sage asked.

His eyes narrowed, but he offered her a saccharine smile. "Sure. And know this, Ms. Freeport, I'm doing everything I can to find Lewis's killer and your son."

"I appreciate that," Sage said, grateful her voice didn't crack. She wanted out of the room, away from Sheriff Gandt.

Away from that whistle with the blood on it, blood that might belong to her son.

DUGAN DROVE SAGE back to the B and B, well aware she'd hit an emotional wall that could crumble any second.

The big question was if she would be able to put herself back together again if she received bad news.

So far, she had held it together. Shown amazing strength and fortitude. But she also had held on to hope.

Damn. She was stubborn, beautiful and fragile and in need of something to turn the nightmare she'd been stuck in the past two years into a distant dream where her son emerged at the end, safe and back at home with her where he belonged.

Dugan walked her up to the door of the inn. "Sage, even if that whistle has Benji's blood on it, it doesn't mean that he's dead."

She winced, and he berated himself for being so blunt. But she had made him promise to be honest with her.

"I know. And I appreciate all you're doing." Her phone beeped that she had a text, and she pulled it from her purse.

"What is it?"

"I talked to that reporter, Ashlynn Fontaine. Not only is she running the story in the newspaper, but she said the story is airing on the news."

Dugan gritted his teeth. The media could be a double-edged sword.

"You think I shouldn't have contacted her?"

He hadn't realized his expression was so transparent. "I didn't say that."

"But?"

Dugan squeezed her arm, aching to do more. To pull her in his arms and promise her he'd fix all her problems and make her happy again.

But the only way to do that was to bring her son home.

"The more exposure Benji's story receives, the more chances are that someone might recognize him."

"That's what I thought."

Dugan lowered his voice. "But be prepared, Sage. It also may bring false leads. And letting everyone know the case has been reopened could be dangerous."

"Someone already shot at us," Sage said. "And just because it's dangerous doesn't mean I'll stop looking." She gripped his hands. "Dugan, I will never give up, not as long as I know there's a chance Benji's out there."

Dugan had heard of kidnapping cases and missing children that spanned decades. He honestly didn't know how the parents survived. They had to live hollow shells of their lives, going through each day on empty hope, like a car running on gas fumes.

"Call me if you hear from your contacts," Sage said. "I'm going inside now."

Dugan nodded, his chest constricting. He hated to leave her alone. But he had work to do.

He needed to track down that woman named Janet or Janelle, Lewis's alleged sister.

Perhaps Lewis had planned to make his fortune in Cobra Creek and then convince Sage to disappear with him. If so, he might have told a sibling about her.

And he might have asked her to watch Benji until he could clean up the mess and return for Sage.

It was a long shot, but Dugan couldn't dismiss any theory at this point.

SAGE WALKED THROUGH the empty B and B, hating the silence. The couple renting from her had gone home to be with their family for the holidays.

Just where they should be.

But the quiet only reminded her that she would spend another Christmas in this house by herself. When she first bought the place and renovated it, she'd imagined a constant barrage of people in and out, filling the rooms with laughter and chatter. She'd spend her days baking her specialty pastries and pies, with Benji helping her, stirring and measuring ingredients and licking icing from the bowl, his favorite part.

Ron must have picked up on that dream and played her. Although she'd wanted a houseful of people because she'd been without family for so long, he'd obviously thought she'd wanted the place to be a success so she could make money.

She glanced in the fridge and pulled out a platter of leftover turkey and made herself a sandwich. Although she had no appetite, she'd forced herself to eat at least one meal a day for the past two years, telling herself that she had to keep up her strength for when she brought her son home.

Would that ever happen?

She poured a glass of milk and took it and the sandwich to the table and turned on the TV to watch the news report.

An attractive blonde reporter, who identified herself as March Williams, introduced the story by showing a picture of Ron Lewis. She recapped the details of the accident two years ago.

"Police now know that Lewis was an alias, and that he was wanted on other charges across the state. They also know he was murdered and are searching for his killer." She paused for dramatic effect. "But another important question remains—where is little Benji Freeport?" A photograph of Benji appeared, making Sage's heart melt.

"Three-year-old Benji Freeport lived with his mother, Sage Freeport, who owns a bed and breakfast in Cobra Creek. The morning Lewis disappeared, he took Benji with him. Police have no leads at this time but are hopeful that Benji is safe and still alive. If you have any information regarding this case or the whereabouts of Benji Freeport, please call the tip line listed on the screen."

Sage glanced at the Christmas tree and Benji's present waiting for him. Each year she'd added another present. How big would the pile get before he came back to open them?

The treetop star lay in the box to the side, taunting her. She had opted not to hang the star, because that was Benji's job.

Battling tears, she folded her hands, closed her eyes

and said a prayer that someone would recognize Benji and call the police.

That this year he could hang the star for Christmas and they'd celebrate his homecoming together.

DUGAN STOPPED AT the diner and ordered the meat loaf special. He'd learned to cook on the open fire as a boy on the rez, but he'd never quite mastered the oven or grocery shopping.

Food was meant for sustenance, a necessity to give him the energy to tackle his job. Manning the ranch meant early mornings and manual labor, both of which he liked.It helped him pass the days and kept him busy enough not to think about being alone.

Not that being alone had ever bothered him before. But seeing Sage and the way she loved her son reminded him of the way his mother had loved him before she died.

And the way he'd felt when he was shuffled from foster home to foster home where no one really wanted him.

What had Lewis told Benji the day he abducted him? Where was he now?

He knew the questions Sage was asking herself, because they nagged at him.

Two old-timers loped in, grumbling about the weather and their crops. An elderly man and woman held hands as they slid into a booth.

Sheriff Gandt sat in a back booth, chowing down on a blood-red steak.

Donnell Earnest loped in, claimed a bar stool, removed his hat and ordered a beer.

Nadine, the waitress behind the counter, grinned at him. "Hey, Donnie, you all right?"

"Hell, no, that Indian guy was out asking questions about my business."

Nadine glanced at Dugan over Donnell's shoulder. "I heard he's looking for Sage Freeport's kid."

"Yeah, and Ron Lewis's killer. Son of a bitch deserved what he got."

"I hear you there," Nadine murmured.

Donnell rubbed a hand across his head. "Rankins called me, said Graystone was out there bothering him. That guy starts trying to pin Lewis's murder on one of us, we gotta teach him a lesson."

Dugan rolled his hands into fists to control his temper. The jerk was just venting. God knows, he'd heard worse.

Still, the names and prejudice stung.

The one woman he'd been involved with years ago had received the brunt of more than one attack on him by idiots and their prejudice. She'd broken it off, saying he wasn't worth it.

His daddy had obviously felt the same way.

He'd decided that day that his land and work were all that mattered.

A cell phone rang from the back. Then the sheriff jumped up from his booth and lumbered toward the door. "I'll be right there."

Anger flared on Gandt's face as he spotted Dugan. "What the hell were you doing out at the Rankins ranch?"

Dugan squared his shoulders. "I just asked him some questions."

"That's my job." Sheriff Gandt poked Dugan in the

belly. "Because of you nosing around, Wilbur Rankins just killed himself."

"What?"

"He shot himself, you bastard."

Dugan's mind raced. "Wilbur Rankins was dying of cancer. Why would he kill himself?" To end his pain?

"His son said he was upset about that news broadcast about Ron Lewis swindling folks in Cobra Creek. Said his daddy was too humiliated to live with people knowing he'd been foolish enough to lose his land."

Dugan silently cursed. The story hadn't revealed any names, though. "You going out there now?"

"Yeah, I'm meeting the M.E."

"I'll go with you."

"Hell, no," Gandt said. "You've done enough damage. You're the last person Junior Rankins wants to see."

Dugan held his tongue. But as Gandt strode from the diner, doubts set in. Had Rankins really killed himself?

Or had someone murdered him because he'd talked to Dugan? Because they thought Rankins knew more about Lewis's death than he'd told them?

SAGE CLEANED THE ROOM the couple had stayed in, needing to expend some energy before she tried to sleep.

That bloody whistle kept taunting her.

She stripped the bed, dusted the furniture and scrubbed the bathroom, then put fresh linens on the bed and carried the dirty sheets downstairs to the laundry room. Benji's room with the jungle theme and his stuffed animals and trains beckoned her. After she started the wash, she went back to his room and traced her finger lovingly over his bedding and the blanket he'd been so attached to.

She lay back on the bed and hugged it to her, then studied the ceiling where she'd glued stars that lit up in the dark. Benji had been fascinated with the night sky. She could still hear him singing, *Twinkle, twinkle, little star,* as he watched them glittering on his ceiling.

Did he dream about her, or did he have nightmares of that car crash? Had he felt safe with Ron or frightened?

A sob tore from her throat. Where was he, dammit?

She gave in to the tears for a few minutes, then cut herself off as she'd done the past two years.

She could not give up hope.

Taking a deep breath to calm herself, she tucked the bear beneath Benji's blanket, then whispered good-night. One day she would bring Benji back here and he'd know that she'd never forgotten him. That not a day had gone by that she hadn't thought of him, wanted to see him, loved him.

She turned off the light and closed the door, then walked to her room and slipped on her pajamas, latching on to the hope that the news report would trigger someone's memory, or a stranger would see Benji in a crowd or at school and call in.

Exhausted, she crawled into bed and turned off the lights. Dugan's face flashed behind her eyes, the memory of his comforting voice soothing. Dugan was working the case.

If anyone could find her son, he could.

Outside, the wind rattled the windowpanes, jarring her just as she was about to fall asleep. A noise sounded in the hall. Or was it downstairs?

She pushed the blanket away to go check, but suddenly the sound of someone breathing echoed in the room.

Fear seized her.

Someone was inside her bedroom.

She needed a weapon, but she didn't have a gun. If she could reach her phone…

She moved her hand to try to grab it off the night-stand, but suddenly the figure pounced on top of her, and a cold hard hand clamped down over her mouth.

"Lewis is dead. If you don't stop asking questions, you'll be next."

Chapter Eleven

A cold chill engulfed Sage.

"Did you do something to my son?" she whispered.

"Just let it go," he hissed against her ear.

The fear that seized Sage turned to anger. She would never let it go.

Determined to see the man's face, she shoved an elbow backward into his chest. He bellowed, slid his hands around her throat and squeezed her neck.

Sage tried to scream, but he pushed her face down into the pillow, crawled on top of her and jammed his knee into her back, using his weight to hold her down.

"I warned you."

Sage struggled against him and clawed at the bedding, but he squeezed her neck so hard that he was cutting off the oxygen. She gasped and fought, but she couldn't breathe, and the room spun into darkness.

DUGAN PLUGGED ALL the aliases Ron had used into the computer, then entered the name Janet to see if he could find a match.

The computer scrolled through all the names but didn't locate anyone named Janet associated with any of the aliases. The name Janelle popped, though.

Janelle Dougasville lived in a small town outside Crystal City, one of the addresses listed for Mike Martin. Dugan checked records and discovered she had a rap sheet for petty crimes and was currently on parole for drug charges. He jotted down the address. He'd pay her a visit first thing in the morning.

If she'd been in contact with Lewis around the time he'd disappeared, she might have known his plans and the reason he'd taken Benji with him.

If he'd known he was in trouble, why take a child with him? A child that would slow him down and bring more heat down on him?

It didn't make sense.

What if he'd left Benji with someone before the accident? Was it possible he'd dropped him off with an accomplice? Maybe with Janelle?

His phone buzzed, and he checked the number. Not one he recognized, but he pressed Answer. It might be a tip about Benji. "Dugan Graystone."

"Mr. Graystone, this is D. J. Rankins."

Dugan frowned. "D.J.?"

"Wilbur's grandson. I saw you at the house before, when you came and talked to my dad."

"Right. I'm sorry to hear about your grandfather."

A labored breath rattled over the line. "That's why I'm calling. You came asking him about his land, and he was real upset. He and Daddy got in a big fight after you and that lady left."

What was the boy trying to tell him? "What happened?"

"Daddy called Grandpa an old fool for falling for that Lewis man's scheme, and Grandpa yelled at Daddy to get out, accused Daddy of waitin' on Grandpa to kick the bucket so he could get his land. Then Daddy grabbed his rifle and stalked off."

"Was that when your grandfather killed himself?"

A tense minute passed. Then Dugan thought he heard a sniffle.

"D.J.?"

"Yeah, I'm here. I…probably ought not to be callin'. My dad is gonna be real mad."

But still the kid had called. "D.J., you called because you thought it was the right thing to do. Now, tell me what's on your mind."

Another sniffle. "I don't think Grandpa killed himself."

SAGE SLOWLY ROUSED back to consciousness. The room was dark, and she couldn't breathe. The musty odor of sweat and another smell…cigarette smoke? A cigar? Shoe polish?

Dizzy and disoriented, she rolled to her side and searched the room.

What had happened?

She gasped, her hand automatically going to her throat and rubbing her tender skin as the memory of the intruder surfaced. The man…big…heavy…on top of her, holding her down. Strangling her…

Those threatening words. "Lewis is dead. If you don't stop asking questions, you'll be next."

God… Was he still in the inn?

She froze, listening for his voice. His breathing?

But only the sound of the furnace rumbling echoed back.

The wind rattling the panes had woken her. He must have broken a window downstairs and snuck in.

Trembling, she slid from bed, grabbed the phone and punched Dugan's number. She hurried to look out the window, searching for her attacker outside, but clouds obscured the moon, painting the backyard a dismal gray.

The phone rang a second time as she hurried to her bedroom door and peered into the hallway. Downstairs seemed quiet, but what if he was still in the house?

The phone clicked. "Sage?"

"Dugan, someone broke into the inn. He...threatened me."

"Is he still there?"

"I don't think so," Sage said.

"Where are you?"

"In my bedroom."

"Lock yourself inside and don't come out. I'll call you when I arrive."

Sage stepped back inside the room, closed the door and locked it. She flipped on the light, then looked into the mirror above her vanity. Her hair looked wild, her eyes puffy, the imprint of a man's fingers embedded into her neck.

She tried to recall the details of her attack. How big her attacker was, how tall... Had she felt his beard stubble against her cheek when he'd whispered that threat in her ear?

Fear clouded her memory, but she heard his voice playing over and over in her head. A gruff, deep voice. Definitely male.

But who was he?

DUGAN SPED FROM his ranch toward Cobra Creek, his heart hammering. Sage had sounded shaken, but she was all right.

Unless the intruder was still there....

His tires squealed as he swerved down Main Street, then hung a right into the drive for the B and B. The drive was empty, but he spotted Sage's car in the detached garage. He scanned the street and property, searching for someone lurking around.

A dog roamed the street but took off running when his headlights startled him. A trash can lid rolled across the neighboring drive, clanging. Down the street, a truck rumbled, heading out of town.

Could it be the intruder's?

He hesitated, considered following it, but what if Sage's attacker was still in the house?

He flipped off his lights, parked and cut the engine. Pulling his weapon from the holster inside his jacket, he texted Sage that he was outside. Then he slowly approached the inn.

The front door was locked, and no one was around, so he eased his way to the fence, unlatched the gate and stepped inside, scanning the property. At least two miles of wooded land backed up to the creek. A walking trail wove through the woods, and park benches were situated by the water for guests to lounge and relax.

Sage didn't have enough land for horseback riding, but a ranch close by catered to guests craving the western experience. That ranch belonged to Helen Wiley, a middle-aged woman who loved kids and families and offered riding lessons to locals and tourists.

The silhouette of an animal combing the woods caught his eye, and he stepped nearer the woods to check it out. Deciding it was a deer, he turned and glanced at the back of the inn.

A rustic deck spanned the entire back side, with seat-ing areas for guests to relax and enjoy the scenery. The deck was empty now, although one of the windows was open, a curtain flapping in the wind.

The intruder must have broken in through the window.

He kept his gun trained as he climbed the steps to the deck, then he checked the open window. The glass was broken. He'd come back and look for prints.

Right now he wanted to see Sage, make sure she was safe.

His phone buzzed with a text, and he glanced at it. Sage wanted to know where he was.

He texted, Back door.

He turned the doorknob and it opened easily. The intruder had obviously snuck in through the window but exited the back door, leaving it unlocked.

Didn't Sage have a damn alarm?

He inched inside the kitchen, tensing at the sound of footsteps on the stairs. Keeping his gun braced at the ready, he crept through the kitchen to the hallway and waited.

Seconds later, Sage came running down the stairs. Pale and terrified, she threw herself into his arms.

SAGE HAD BEEN alone with her grief and fears and the terrifying questions in her head for so long that she couldn't drag herself away from Dugan.

How long had it been since someone had held her? Taken care of her?

Two years…but any affection Ron had had for her had been an act.

Dugan stroked her back, soothing her. "It's okay now, Sage."

She nodded against him, but she couldn't stop trembling. "He choked me until I passed out."

His big body went so still that she felt the anxiety coiled in his muscles. "God, Sage."

He pulled away just enough to tilt her face up so he could examine her. Rage darkened his eyes when he spotted the bruises.

"Did you get a look at him?" Dugan asked, his voice low. Lethal.

She shook her head, her heart fluttering with awareness as he traced a finger along her throat. "It was too dark. And he threw me facedown on the bed and shoved my head into the pillows."

"What else do you remember?"

"He smelled like sweat and something else—maybe cigarette smoke? He said Lewis was dead and that if I didn't stop asking questions, I'd be next."

"Damn," Dugan muttered.

Her gaze locked with his, the fierceness of a warrior in his eyes. Eyes the color of a Texas sunset.

Eyes full of dark emotion—anger, bitterness, maybe distrust.

And hunger. Hunger followed by a wariness that made her realize that he felt the sexual chemistry between them just as she did.

"Stay here. Let me search the rest of the inn."

She nodded and hugged the wall as he inched up the stairs to the second floor. His footsteps pounded above her as he moved from room to room. Seconds stretched into minutes, a moment of silence making her catch her breath in fear that her attacker had been hiding in one of the other rooms to ambush Dugan.

Finally, he appeared at the top of the staircase. "It's

clear." He tucked his gun back into his holster and strode down the steps.

Sage's heart was beating so frantically that she reached for him.

Emotions clogged her throat as he tilted her chin up again.

But this time instead of examining her bruises, he closed his mouth over hers.

Sage gave in to the moment and savored the feel of his passion. She parted her lips in invitation, relishing the way he played his tongue along her mouth and growled low in his throat.

Hunger emanated from him, in the way his hands stroked her back, and the way his body hardened and melded against hers.

A warmth spread through her, sparking arousal and titillating sensations, earth-shattering in their intensity. Dugan splayed his hands over her hips, drawing her closer, and she felt his thick erection press into her belly.

She wanted him.

Wanted to forget all the sadness and grief that had consumed her the past two years. Wanted to feel pleasure for a few brief moments before reality yanked her back to the ugly truth.

That her son was still missing.

Those very words made her pull away. What was wrong with her? Was she so weak that she'd fall into any man's arms?

She certainly had made that mistake with Ron.

She looked into Dugan's eyes and saw the same restless hunger that she felt. She also saw his turmoil.

He hadn't expected her to react like that to him.

It couldn't happen again.

DUGAN CURSED HIMSELF for his weakness. But one look into Sage's vulnerable eyes and he couldn't not kiss her.

Pain radiated from her in waves. For the first time, he'd forgotten about his resolve to keep his hands off her. She'd needed him.

And he'd needed to hold her and know that that bastard who'd tried to choke her hadn't succeeded.

Why had her attacker let her live? Did he really think he'd scare her so badly she'd stop looking for her son?

Chapter Twelve

Dugan adopted his professional mask, relieved she'd donned a robe over her long pajamas before he'd arrived. If he'd seen a sliver of her delicate skin, he might lose control, change his mind and take her to bed. "I'll check your room for prints."

"He wore gloves," Sage said. "Leather."

"Figures. Still, I'll look around in case he dropped something or left a stray hair."

She led the way, and he spent the next half hour searching her room. When he spotted the bed where she'd been sleeping when she was attacked, images of the man shoving her facedown assaulted him.

He was going to catch this jerk and made him suffer.

Sage excused herself to go to the bathroom while he searched the room. Grateful for the reprieve, he forced his mind on the task and checked the sheets. He ran his hands over the bedding but found nothing, so he stooped down to the floor and shone a small flashlight across the braided rug.

A piece of leather caught his attention. A strip, like part of a tassel to a boot or glove or jacket. Sage had said her attacker had worn gloves.

Hoping to find forensic evidence on it, he dragged on gloves and picked it up.

Sage emerged from the bathroom, her hair brushed, her robe cinched tight. "Did you find anything?"

He dangled the leather strip in front of her. "Do you recognize this?"

Sage shook her head no. "It's not mine."

"You struggled with the man?"

She shivered. "Yes."

"I'll bag this and send it to the lab." He strode toward the door. "Go back to bed, Sage. I'll stay downstairs and keep watch."

"I don't think I can sleep," Sage said, her voice as forlorn as the expression on her face.

Hell, he knew he wouldn't sleep. Not while worrying about Sage's attacker returning to make good on that threat.

And not while thinking about that damn kiss.

"Then just rest. I'm going to find something to fix that broken window."

She tugged at the top of her robe, pulling it together. "There's some plywood in the garage."

"That'll work." He forced his gaze away from her. "You need a security system."

"That's hard to do with guests."

"You can arrange a key system."

"Won't that be expensive?"

"It'll be worth it for you and your guests."

"I'll look into it," Sage agreed.

He turned to go down to the garage.

"Thank you for coming tonight, Dugan."

He paused, shoulders squared. "I'm going to catch this bastard and find Benji."

The soft whisper of her breath echoed between them. "I know you will."

Her confidence sent a warmth through him. Other than Jaxon, he'd never had anyone believe in him.

Especially a woman.

He didn't want to disappoint her.

Shaken by the thought, he rushed outside to the garage, found a toolbox and some plywood in the corner.

It took him less than ten minutes to cover the broken glass. When he'd finished, he walked around the other rooms, checking locks and windows and looking for other evidence the intruder might have left behind.

Then he made a pot of coffee and kept watch over the house until morning. But Sage's Christmas tree haunted him as the first strains of sunlight poured through the window.

More than anything, he wanted to bring Benji back to Sage for Christmas.

SAGE DIDN'T THINK she would sleep, but exhaustion, stress and worry had taken their toll, and she drifted off. She dreamed about Benji and the holidays and the attack. She felt the man's fingers closing around her neck, his knee jamming into her back, his weight on her. She was suffocating, couldn't breathe…

She jerked awake, disoriented for a moment. She scanned the room, searching the corners as reality returned. She was safe. The intruder was gone.

Knowing Dugan was downstairs watching out for her, she closed her eyes again. This time after she drifted off, she dreamed that Dugan was in bed with her, kissing her, stripping her clothes, making love to her…

When she stirred from sleep, her body felt achy and

languid, content yet yearning for something more. More of Dugan's touches.

But sleeping with him would be a mistake. She wasn't the kind of woman who could crawl in bed with a man and walk away. She was too old-fashioned. Making love meant more to her than just a warm body.

Still, she craved his arms and hands on her.

Frustrated, she jumped in the shower. One blast of the cold water and she woke to reality. She adjusted the nozzle to warm and washed her hair, letting the soothing spray of water pulse against her skin until she felt calmer.

Finally she dried off, dressed and hurried down the stairs. Dugan had cooked eggs and bacon, and poured her a cup of coffee as soon as she entered. With remnants of the dream still playing through her head, the scene seemed cozy. Intimate.

What in the world was she thinking?

She and men didn't work.

"Last night before you called, I looked for Lewis's sister."

Sage blew on her coffee to cool it. "You found her?"

"I discovered a woman named Janelle Dougasville who lived near one of the addresses for Mike Martin."

"Have you talked to her?"

"Not yet. I'm planning to pay her a visit after breakfast."

"Then let's go."

"Eat something first."

"Dugan—"

He gestured toward the plate. "Humor me. I need food in the morning."

She agreed only because he made himself an egg

sandwich using the toast he'd buttered, and wolfed it down. Her stomach growled, and she joined him at the table and devoured the meal.

"Thank you," she said. "I'm not accustomed to anyone cooking me breakfast. Usually that's my job."

Dugan shrugged. "Breakfast is the only meal I make."

She smiled, grateful for the small talk as they cleaned up the dishes.

"Where does this woman live?" Sage asked as they walked outside and settled in his SUV.

"Near Crystal City." He drove onto the main street. "I'll drop that leather strip at the lab on the way."

She glanced at the holiday decorations as they wove through town. Wreaths and bows adorned the storefronts. A special twelve-foot tree had been decorated and lit in the town square, and a life-size sleigh for families and children to pose for pictures sat at the entrance to the park where Santa visited twice a day.

Signs for a last-minute sale on toys covered the windows of the toy store. The bakery was running a special on fruit cakes and rum cakes, with no charge for shipping.

Soon Christmas would be here. Kids would be waking up to find the presents Santa had left under the tree. Families would be gathering to exchange gifts and share turkey and the trimmings.

The children's Christmas pageant at church was tonight.

Tears blurred her eyes. If Benji was here, they would go. But she couldn't bear it…not without him.

"I stopped by the diner for dinner after I left your place, and ran into Sheriff Gandt."

Thoughts of holiday celebrations and family vanished. "What did he have to say?"

"Wilbur Rankins killed himself last night after we left him."

Sage gasped. "Because of our questions?"

"His son claims he was ashamed over being swindled," Dugan said.

"Oh, my God." She twisted her hands together. "But the news story didn't name names."

"There's more," Dugan said. "D. J. Rankins, Wilbur's grandson, called me. He thinks his grandfather didn't commit suicide."

"What?"

"Apparently his father and grandfather argued after we left."

The implications in Dugan's voice disturbed her. "You think Junior Rankins killed his father?"

"I don't know," Dugan said. "But if he didn't, someone else might have."

Because they were asking questions. Because of the news story.

She'd been threatened, too.

Which meant she and Dugan were both in danger.

Two HOURS LATER, Dugan parked at the address he found for Janelle Dougasville. The woman lived in a small older home, with neighboring houses in similar disrepair.

According to the information he'd accessed, she didn't have a job. A sedan that had once been red but had turned a rusted orange sat in the drive.

"If Ron had made money on other scams, he certainly didn't share it with the other women in his life."

"True. And if one of those women discovered he was lying about who he was, that he had other women, or that he was hoarding his money for himself, it would be motive for murder."

That meant Carol Sue Tinsley and Maude Handleman were both viable suspects. So was Beverly Vance.

Dugan knocked, his gaze perusing the property. The cookie-cutter houses had probably looked nice when new, but age and weather had dulled the siding, and the yards desperately needed landscaping.

Inside, the house was dark, making him wonder if Janelle was home. He knocked again, and seconds later, a light flickered on.

Beside him, Sage fidgeted.

The sound of the lock turning echoed and then the door opened. A short woman with dirty blond hair stared up at them, her nose wrinkled.

"Yeah?"

"Ms. Dougasville," Dugan said. "We'd like to talk to you."

The woman snorted. "You the law?"

"No." Dugan started to explain, but Sage spoke up.

"We're looking for my little boy. His name is Benji Freeport. You may have seen the news story about him. He disappeared two years ago."

The woman hunched inside her terry-cloth robe, her eyes squinting. "What's that got to do with me?"

"Probably nothing," Dugan said. "But if you'll let us in, we'll explain."

"Please," Sage said softly.

A second passed, then the woman waved them into the entryway. Dugan noted the scent of booze on her breath, confirmed by the near-empty bottle of whiskey sitting on the coffee table in the den.

Janelle gestured toward the sofa, and he and Sage took seats while she poured herself another drink. Her hand shook as she turned up the glass. "All right. What do you want?"

Dugan explained about Ron Lewis, his scams and phony identities.

"I don't understand why Ron took my little boy with him that day," Sage said, "but I've been looking for him ever since."

Janelle lit a cigarette, took a drag and blew smoke through her nose. "I don't know anything about your kid."

Sage sagged with disappointment.

"What can you tell us about Ron Lewis? He was your brother?" Dugan asked.

Janelle sipped her whiskey. "Not by birth. We grew up in the foster system together."

"Do you know his real name?"

She snorted. "I'm not sure he knows it."

"What was he called as a boy?"

"Lewis was his first name."

"So that's why he chose it this last time," Sage said. Had he planned to keep it? "Tell us more about his childhood."

"He was a quiet kid. His folks beat him till he was black-and-blue. First time I got put in the same foster with him, he told me they were dirt poor. He was half-starved, had one of them bloated bellies like you see on the kids on those commercials."

"Go on," Dugan said when she paused to take another drag on the cigarette.

"We was about the same age, you know. My story was just about like his, except I never had a daddy, just a whore for a mama. So we connected, you know."

"When was the last time you saw him?"

She tapped ashes into a soda can on the table. "About three years ago. He showed up one day out of the blue, said he was on to something big and that he was finally going to make all those things we dreamed about come true." A melancholy look softened the harsh lines fanning from her eyes. "When we got sent to the second foster home together, we made a pact that one day we'd get out and make something of ourselves."

Judging from her situation, Dugan doubted Janelle had succeeded.

"We used to go down to the creek and skip rocks and dream about being rich. I used to dream about us getting married and having a real family."

"Did Ron… I mean, Lewis, share that dream?" Sage asked.

Janelle shrugged. "He said he wanted all that, but he also lied a lot. Every time we got moved to a new foster, he took on the people's names."

That fit with his ability to assume different identities. He'd learned early on to switch names and lives.

Dugan would have felt sorry for him if he hadn't destroyed lives and hurt Sage so much.

"Tell me more about his real parents," Sage said.

"His daddy blew all he made on the races, and his mama liked meth."

"Do you know what happened to them?"

"Last we talked, he said his mama died. Don't know about his old man. Seems like I heard he got killed, probably by one of the bookies he owed money to."

Sage sighed, a frustrated sound. "Was there anyone else he might go to if he was in trouble? Another girlfriend?"

Janelle stubbed out her cigarette and tossed down the rest of her whiskey. "There was one girl he had a thing for bad. A real thing, I mean, like he wasn't just using her. He was young when it happened, but they talked about getting married."

"What was her name?"

"Sandra Peyton," Janelle said bitterly. "He knocked her up, but she lost the baby, and things fell apart."

Dugan made a mental note of the woman's name. If Sandra was the love of Lewis's life and he thought he'd finally made the fortune he wanted, maybe he had been going to see her, to win her back again.

Another thought nagged at Dugan—what if he was taking Benji to replace the child they'd lost?

Chapter Thirteen

Dugan stopped for lunch at a barbecue place called The Pig Pit, but Sage's appetite had vanished. She kept replaying the story Janelle Dougasville had told her about Ron Lewis…rather Lewis, the foster kid.

His upbringing had definitely affected him, had motivated him to want more from life, especially material things. He was trying to make up for what he hadn't had as a child.

Being shuffled from one foster family to another had turned him into a chameleon. A man who could deftly switch names, lives and stories with no qualms or hesitation.

A man who had learned to manipulate people to get what he wanted.

One who played the part but remained detached, because getting attached to a family or person was painful when you were forced to leave that family or person behind.

That, Dugan could relate to.

"I almost feel sorry for him," Sage said, thinking out loud.

"Don't." Dugan finished his barbecue sandwich. "Sure, he had some hard knocks in life, but a lot of people have crappy childhoods and don't turn out to be liars and con artists."

"You're right. He could just as easily have turned that trauma into motivation for really making something of himself."

"You mean something respectful," Dugan clarified. "Because he was something. A liar and a master manipulator."

"Yes, he was." Sage sighed. "If he really loved this woman, Sandra Peyton, do you think he might have tried to reconnect with her?"

"Anything is possible."

Sage contemplated that scenario. If Sandra Peyton had Benji, at least she was probably taking care of him and he was safe.

But where was she?

DUGAN SNATCHED HIS PHONE and punched in a number as they left the restaurant and got in the car. "Jaxon, it's Dugan. Did you learn anything about that women's shelter where Carol Sue volunteered?"

"Women there are hush-hush," Jaxon said. "But when I explained that Benji might have been kidnapped they were cooperative. That said, no one saw him, and the lady who runs the house denied that Carol Sue brought Benji there."

A dead end.

"See if you can locate a woman named Sandra Peyton."

"Who is she?"

"Lewis's foster sister, Janelle Dougasville, claims that he was involved with Sandra Peyton years ago, so he might have reconnected with her."

"I'm on it."

Dugan's other line was buzzing, so he thanked Jaxon and answered the call. "Graystone."

"Mr. Graystone, this is Ashlynn Fontaine. I ran the story for Ms. Freeport about her son in the paper, and my friend covered it on the news."

"Yes."

"Ms. Freeport gave me your number to contact in case any leads came in regarding her son."

His pulse spiked. "You have something?"

"I received a call from an anonymous source who said that a woman and a little boy Benji's age moved in next to her about a month after Ms. Freeport's son went missing. She's not certain the child is Benji, but she said the woman was very secretive and kept to herself. Thought you might want to check it out."

"Text me her name and address."

A second later, the text came through. Dugan headed toward the address. It might be a false lead.

Then again, maybe they'd get lucky and this child might be Sage's missing son.

SAGE CLENCHED HER HANDS together as Dugan explained about the call.

"I hope this pans out, Sage," Dugan said. "But normally when a tip line is set up, it triggers a lot of false leads."

Sage nodded. She knew he was trying to prepare her for the possibility that this child might not be her son, but still, a seed of hope sprouted. Even if it wasn't Benji, maybe the tip line would work and someone would spot him.

Worry mounted inside her, though, as he drove. The

half hour drive felt like years, and by the time they arrived, she'd twisted the locket around her neck a hundred times. Her neck still felt sore from the attack, the bruises darkening to an ugly purple.

A stark reminder that someone wanted her dead.

The woman lived in a small ranch-style house with a giant blow-up Santa Claus in front and a Christmas tree with blinking, colored lights visible through the front window.

Sage's heart squeezed. If Benji was here, at least the woman was taking care of him and decorated for the holidays.

Although resentment followed. Those precious moments had been stolen from her.

Dugan parked on the curb a few feet down from the house. The front door opened and a woman wearing a black coat stepped out, one hand clutching a leash attached to a black Lab, the other hand holding a small child's.

Sage pressed her face against the glass to see the boy more clearly, but he wore a hooded navy jacket. He looked about five, which was the correct age, but she couldn't see his eyes.

Sorrow and fear clogged Sage's throat. Children changed in appearance every day. What if Benji had changed so much she didn't recognize him?

Sage started to reach for the door to get out of the SUV, but he laid his hand over hers. "Wait. Let's just watch for a few minutes. We don't want to spook her."

As much as Sage wanted to run to the boy, Dugan was right. If this woman had her son and knew Sage was searching for them, she might run.

Dugan pulled a pair of binoculars from beneath his seat and handed them to her, then retrieved a camera

from the back, adjusted the lens and snapped some photographs. She peered through the binoculars, focusing
on the little boy and the woman.

The woman kept a tight hold on the child's hand. A
natural, protective gesture? Or was she afraid he might
try to get away?

Stories of other kidnappings where the victims identified with their kidnapper nagged at her. Benji had been
only three when he was abducted.

Did he even remember her?

Or had he bonded with whoever had him? If it was
a woman, did he think she was his mother?

A pang shot through her. Did he call her Mom?

DUGAN SENSED THE TENSION radiating from Sage. Hell,
he couldn't blame her. She hadn't seen her son in two
years—she was probably wondering what he looked
like now. If he would even recognize her.

If he was alive and had been living with another
woman or a family, he might have developed Stock-
holm syndrome.

He studied the body language of the woman and
child as she spoke to the little boy. They seemed completely at ease with each other. The boy was saying
something, and she tilted her head toward him with a
smile. They swung hands as they rounded the corner,
then paused while the dog sniffed the grass in a neighboring yard.

"I can't really see his face," Sage said.

"I don't have a good shot of it, either," Dugan admitted. "When they reach the house, and he takes his coat
off, maybe we'll get a better look."

The dog nuzzled up to the little boy, and the kid

laughed. Then the woman looked up and scanned the streets, as if nervous. A second later, he swore her gaze latched with his.

Dugan lowered the camera to the seat. "I think she spotted us," Dugan said. "Drop the binoculars, Sage."

Dugan pulled a map from the side pocket of the car and pretended he was looking at it. But he continued to watch the woman and boy out of the corner of his eye.

"He looks happy and well taken care of," Sage said in a voice laced with a mixture of pain and relief.

Dugan gave her a sympathetic look. The woman suddenly turned and ushered the boy and dog back toward the house. This time, instead of walking leisurely, she picked up her pace and looked harried. Even frightened.

Sage sat up straighter. "She looks scared. Maybe we should go talk to her."

Dugan shook his head. "Wait. Let's watch and see what she does."

Sage's frustrated sigh echoed through the SUV. "What if she runs?"

"Then we'll follow her."

Panic streaked Sage's voice. "But if it's Benji, I don't want to lose him again."

Dugan wanted to promise her she wouldn't, but he bit back the words. They didn't know for certain that this was Benji.

When the woman reached the walkway to her house, she broke into a jog, half dragging the dog and the boy. She ushered them both inside, then shut the door.

But not before glancing over at them again. Fear had flashed in her eyes.

Dugan's pulse pounded.

What was she running from?

SAGE DUG HER FINGERNAILS into her palms to keep from opening the SUV door and bolting toward the house. She desperately wanted to see the little boy's face.

And the woman was definitely afraid.

Memories of Benji smiling up at her as a baby with his gap-toothed grin taunted her. His curly blond hair, the light in his green eyes, his chubby baby cheeks... Then he'd turned from a pudgy toddler to a three-year-old overnight.

More memories flooded her—his first words, the way he loved blueberries and called them BBs, his attachment to a pair of cartoon pajamas and the yellow rubber boots he'd worn to play in the rain.

The side door to the house opened, and the boy and dog spilled out. The dog barked and raced across the fenced-in yard, and the boy ran over to the swing set and climbed the jungle gym. She needed to see his ear, that piece of cartilage....

The hood to his jacket slipped down, and she stared at the mop of blond hair. Her breath caught, lungs straining for air.

Could it be her son?

Suddenly a siren wailed, and Dugan cursed. She looked over her shoulder and spotted the sheriff's car rolling up behind them.

"Damn. She must have called the law," Dugan said.

Sage bit her tongue. Would she have done that if she was hiding out with a child that the police were searching for?

Dugan shoved the camera to the floor, and she slid the binoculars into her purse. The sheriff's car door slammed, and then he hitched up his pants and strode toward them, a sour look pinching his face.

He tapped on the driver's window, and Dugan powered the window down. "Sheriff," Dugan muttered.

Sheriff Gandt leaned forward, pinning her and Dugan with his scowl. "What are you two doing here?"

Dugan indicated the map. "Just stopped, looking for directions."

"Don't lie to me," Sheriff Gandt growled. "Get out of the car."

Sage clenched the door handle. Was he going to arrest them?

Dugan opened the door, climbed out and leaned against the side of the SUV. She walked around the front of the vehicle and joined him.

Sheriff Gandt hooked a thumb toward the house. "The woman that lives inside there called, freaked out, said a couple was stalking her and her child."

Sage's stomach knotted. "We weren't stalking them."

"But you were watching them," Sheriff Gandt said, one bushy eyebrow raised.

Dugan cleared his throat. "We had a tip we were following up on."

"What kind of tip?"

"From the news story that aired about Benji," Sage explained. "Someone called with suspicions that the woman who lives here might have Benji."

Sheriff Gandt mumbled an ugly word. "Then you should have called me."

Why would she call him when he hadn't helped her before? When she didn't trust him?

DUGAN BARELY RESISTED slugging the imbecile. He should be following up on leads, searching for Benji, but so far he'd either been incompetent or just didn't care. "We assumed you were busy investigating Rankins's supposed suicide."

Gandt's eyebrows crinkled together. "What the hell does that mean?"

"Are you sure it was a suicide?" Dugan asked.

"Of course it was. His own son called me. Said he heard his daddy pull the trigger."

"Did you check Junior for gunshot residue?" Dugan asked.

Anger reddened Sheriff Gandt's cheeks. "Wasn't no need. His daddy was upset about your visit and he was dying of cancer and decided to end his misery. End of story." Gandt planted his fists on his hips. "Besides, I'm not the one breaking the law here. You are."

"We didn't break the law," Sage said.

"You scared that poor woman to death," Gandt said. "She thought you were child predators, here to steal her son."

Sage stiffened. Those words hit too close to home. "Maybe she's afraid because she's the one who stole Benji, and now that the story aired about him again, she's terrified someone will recognize Benji and call the police."

Which was exactly what had happened.

Gandt looked exasperated, but Dugan didn't intend to let him off the hook. If the kid inside was Benji, once they left, the woman would take him and run.

Then they might never find him again.

"There's one way we can settle this," Dugan said. "Let's go talk to her."

Sheriff Gandt huffed. "That could be considered harassment."

"Then go with us," Sage suggested. "You can explain

the circumstances. If she has nothing to hide, she'll talk to us. And if that little boy isn't Benji, then we'll go on our way and she won't ever see or hear from us again."

Gandt looked annoyed and frustrated, but he heaved a weary breath. "All right. But if she insists on pressing charges against you, I won't stop her."

Dugan nodded and pressed his hand to the small of Sage's back as they followed the sheriff up to the door.

He could feel Sage trembling beneath his touch as Gandt rang the doorbell.

Chapter Fourteen

Sage held her breath as they waited on the woman inside to open the door.

When she did, her wary look made Sage's heart pound.

"Ms. Walton," Sheriff Gandt said. "I came as soon as I got your call."

Dark hair framed an angular face that might have been pretty had it not been for the severe scowl pulling at her mouth and the jagged scar that ran down her left cheek. A scar Sage hadn't noticed from a distance because of the coat and scarf the woman had been wearing.

Ms. Walton glanced back and forth between Sage and Dugan, her eyes angry. "Why were you two watching me?"

"Can we please come in and explain?" Sage said, grateful her voice didn't quiver and betray her.

Ms. Walton looked at the sheriff, who rolled his shoulders. "They're not stalkers," he said, although his tone indicated they were barely a notch above it.

"I'm a private investigator," Dugan said. "And this woman is Sage Freeport. You may have seen the recent news story that aired about her missing son, Benji Freeport."

The woman clenched the door in a death grip as if she was ready to slam it in their faces and flee. "I don't see what that has to do with me."

"Maybe nothing," Sage said. "But we received an anonymous tip that you might know something about my little boy."

"Me?" Shock strained the woman's voice. "I don't know anything." She angled her head toward the sheriff. "Now, are you going to make them leave me alone?"

"Yes, ma'am, I'm sorry—"

"We're not leaving until you answer some questions," Dugan said.

Gandt shot him a warning look.

"I told you I don't know anything about your little boy, Ms. Freeport. But I am sorry about what happened to you, and I hope you find him."

Sage swallowed hard. The woman sounded sincere.

But if she was innocent, why was she so nervous?

DUGAN STUDIED MS. WALTON'S body language. She was definitely scared and hiding something.

But what?

"Did you know a man named Ron Lewis?"

"No." A noise sounded behind them, and Dugan realized it was the back door shutting. The little boy was coming back inside.

"How about Mike Martin or Seth Handleman or Joel Bremmer?"

"No, who are those people?"

"Aliases of Ron Lewis, the man who abducted Benji Freeport."

"I told you, I don't know any of them." She started to shut the door, but Sage caught it this time.

"How old is your little boy?" Sage asked.

A dark look crossed the woman's face. "He'll be six next week."

Sage's sigh fluttered in the tension-laden air. "What's his name?"

Ms. Walton's eyes widened with alarm, as if she realized the implications of Sage's question. A second later, anger sparked. "I named him Barry after my father." Her tone grew sharp. "He is not your son, Ms. Freeport."

"Then, you have his birth certificate?" Dugan asked.

Panic flared in her expression. "I don't have to prove anything to you."

Sheriff Gandt made a low sound in his throat. "No, you don't, Ms. Walton." Sage opened her mouth to argue, but Gandt continued. "But if you have it, please get it and we'll clear this matter up. Then these folks will be on their way and I'll make sure they never bother you again."

"I…actually I don't have it here," she said shrilly. "It's in a safe-deposit box at the bank."

Dugan cleared his throat. "Then you won't mind bringing the boy to the door so we can meet him." Not that they still wouldn't need DNA if Sage recognized the child.

The fear that had earlier pervaded Ms. Walton's eyes deepened, but she looked directly at Sage. "He's not your son. He's mine."

Dugan gritted his teeth. Was that her way of telling Sage the truth? Or could she be mentally and emotionally unstable?

If she'd wanted a child and had lost one or hadn't been able to have a baby, she might have taken Benji and now perceived him as her own.

SAGE FORCED HERSELF not to react to Ms. Walton's posses-
sive, defensive tone. Was she defensive because she was
an honest, loving mother who had to defend herself?

Or because she was a kidnapper, afraid of getting
caught?

"Just introduce us to the little boy," Dugan said.

Ms. Walton glanced at the sheriff, who managed a
grunt. "Do it, ma'am. Then we'll be out of your hair."

Ms. Walton shot Sage a wary look. But she turned
and yelled for Barry to come to her. A minute later,
the child ran to the front door and slipped up beside
his mother.

Sage soaked in his features. The wavy blond hair.
The cherub face. The wide eyes that looked distrust-
ful and full of fear.

Eyes that were brown, not green like her son's. And
his ears…no extra piece of cartilage.

Disappointment engulfed her, and she released a
pained breath. Dugan had warned her about getting up
her hopes, but still she had latched on to the possibility.

He looked at her for a response, and Sage shook her
head. She'd feared she wouldn't recognize her son, but
she immediately knew that this precious little boy was
not hers.

"Hi, Barry," Dugan said. "We saw you walking your
dog. He's pretty cool."

Sage tried to speak, but her voice refused to come
out.

"Well?" Sheriff Gandt said bluntly.

"No," Sage finally managed to say.

"I'm sorry we bothered you," Dugan said.

Relief softened the harsh lines of Ms. Walton's face,
and she stooped down and kissed Barry. "Honey, why

don't you get the spaghetti out of the pantry and we'll start dinner?"

Barry nodded eagerly and raced to the pantry. Ms. Walton squared her shoulders. "I'm sorry for you, Ms. Freeport. I didn't mean to overreact."

"But you were afraid," Sage said, still confused.

"I was. I am…" Her voice cracked. "My husband was abusive. He did this." She rubbed the scar along her cheek. "I had him arrested, but he keeps getting out of jail and looking for us. Barry and I went into a program and changed our names so he wouldn't find us."

"Why didn't you just tell us that when we first arrived?"

"I…when I saw you watching me, I was afraid he'd hired you to find us."

"You have a restraining order against him?" Sheriff Gandt asked.

"Yes," she said in a low voice, "but that didn't stop him before."

That explained the reason the caller said the woman stayed to herself and seemed nervous.

"I'm sorry," Sage said. "We honestly didn't mean to frighten you or your son." She reached inside her purse and handed the woman a card with her name and number. "I own the B and B in Cobra Creek. If you ever need anything, even just a friend to talk to, I'm there."

"I haven't made many friends 'cause I've been on the run. Thanks." Tears blurred the other woman's eyes as she gripped the card between her fingers. "I'll pray that you find your son."

Sage battled tears of her own. Tears for the woman whose little boy had to be afraid of his own father.

Tears for her child, who could be safe somewhere—
or in danger from whomever had stolen him.

COMPASSION FOR SAGE filled Dugan as they walked back
to his SUV. Gandt escorted them, his disapproval evident.

"You two need to go home and let me do my job. You
can't be scaring women and children like this."

"We didn't mean to frighten them," Sage said.

Gandt's nostrils flared. "But you did."

"Only because she had something to hide," Dugan
said, refusing to let Gandt intimidate him. If the man
had done his job as he should have, Dugan wouldn't
have jumped in to help Sage.

Gandt folded his beefy arms. "Hear me and hear me
good. If I receive another call like this one, I'll lock
both of you up just to get you off the street so that I
can do my job."

With a deep grunt, he turned and strode back to
his car.

Dugan slid behind the steering wheel, irritated that
Gandt waited until Sage climbed in his SUV and he
pulled away from the curb before he started his squad
car.

The sound of Sage's breathing rattled between them.

He turned onto the main road, then sped back toward
Cobra Creek, but his mind kept replaying that phone
call from Junior Rankins's son.

Had Rankins killed himself because of the cancer
or because he was embarrassed that he'd been duped
by Lewis?

Or had someone killed Rankins because he'd talked

to them? Because they feared he knew something that would lead them to Lewis's killer?

SAGE STRUGGLED TO hold herself together. If she fell apart, Dugan might drop her case.

But Benji's innocent face flashed in her mind, and she closed her eyes, vying for courage. A mother was supposed to protect her child. Keep him safe and guide him through life. Comfort him when he was scared, chase the monsters away and sacrifice everything to give him a good life.

She had failed at all of those.

She wrapped her arms around her middle, counting the minutes until they reached the B and B. Anxious to be alone and vent her emotions, she opened the SUV door as soon as Dugan parked.

The Christmas lights mocked her, twinkling along the street and the fence in front of the B and B. A blow-up Santa waved to her from across the street at the children's clothing shop, making her throat thick with unshed tears.

She wrestled with her keys, fumbling, then dropping them on the front porch. Dugan's footsteps pounded behind her. Then suddenly he was there, retrieving her keys and unlocking the door for her.

He caught her arm before she could rush inside. "Let me check the inn first."

God… She'd forgotten about the break-in and the attack.

He gestured for her to wait on the porch swing, and she sank onto it and knotted her hands together, looking out at the twinkling Christmas lights and the darkness as he pulled his gun and inched inside.

It felt like hours but was probably only minutes before he returned, holstering his gun as he approached. "It's clear."

She nodded, too upset to speak. If she lost it, he'd probably stop helping her and then she'd be all alone again, with no one looking for her son.

DUGAN KNEW HE should walk away. Leave Sage to deal with the fallout of the day.

Focus on the case.

He wanted to see the original file on the investigation into Benji's disappearance and Lewis's automobile accident.

But he'd made an enemy of Gandt, and the sheriff probably wouldn't hand over the file. So how could he get it?

Maybe the deputy? If he refused, he'd sneak in and steal it....

Sage looked up at him, her eyes luminous with unshed tears, then she stood and stepped toward the door.

"Thanks, Dugan."

Dammit, she was trying to be so strong. Holding herself together when he knew she was hurting inside.

He'd be a damn, cold-hearted bastard to walk away right now.

"I'm going to review the notes in the original file when Benji first disappeared," he said in a feeble attempt to soothe her.

She nodded, her back to him, clenching her purse strap with a white-knuckled grip. "You're not giving up?"

"No."

Hell, he wished he could. But he wanted answers now himself. Not just for her.

But for that innocent little boy out there who might be suffering God knows what. Who might not even know that his amazing mother missed him every day.

A mother who would sacrifice anything for her son.

Sage was strong and gutsy and tenderhearted and beautiful, both inside and out.

He stepped inside with her, so close he inhaled her scent. Some kind of floral fragrance that smelled natural, like a spring garden before the Texas summer heat robbed it of life.

She shivered, totally unaware of the effect she had on him.

Needing to touch her and reassure her that she wasn't alone, he rubbed her arms with his hands. "I made you a promise, and I intend to keep it. I won't stop until we know what happened to your son."

Sage turned toward him then, her face so angelic and tortured that it broke his heart. "No one keeps promises anymore," she whispered.

Dugan had let people down before. Hell, he'd let himself down.

But he would not let down this strong, loving woman who needed someone on her side.

"I do," he said simply.

But there was nothing simple about it. He just couldn't walk away.

Her gaze met his, and his heart clenched. A second later, he pulled her into his arms and kissed her, his lips telling her all the things that his heart couldn't say.

Chapter Fifteen

Sage felt as if she was unraveling from the inside out.

Dugan's arms around her gave her strength, and she leaned into him, grateful not to be alone.

His kiss set her on fire and aroused long-forgotten needs. Desperate for more, to be even closer to him, she parted her lips in invitation. Dugan made a low sound in his throat, a passionate sound that made her heart flutter.

He deepened the kiss, teasing her with his tongue as his hands raked down her back. Her nipples budded to hard peaks, aching for attention, and she threaded her fingers in his hair and moaned.

Titillating sensations tingled through her as he splayed his hands across her hips and pulled her closer. His thick length rubbed against her belly, stirring her passion.

He ended the kiss, then trailed his lips down her neck and teased the sensitive skin behind her ear. She moaned softly and unfastened the top button of his shirt. He lowered his head, his tongue dancing down her neck, and then he used his teeth to tug at the neckline of her sweater.

Sage wanted more.

She made quick work of his buttons, then pushed his shirt aside and kissed his neck and chest. His chest was rock solid, bronzed, muscles corded and hard. She traced his nipple with her tongue, then sucked it gently.

Dugan groaned, gripped her arms and pulled away. "We should stop."

"No," Sage said. "Please, Dugan. I don't want to be alone right now."

"And I don't want to take advantage of you," he said gruffly.

"You aren't." She raised her head and brushed her lips across his neck, a seductive maneuver that seemed to trigger his passion, then led him to her bedroom.

With a low groan, he tugged her sweater over her head. She lifted her arms, eager to be closer, for skin to touch skin. She pushed his shirt off and dropped it to the floor.

His dark gaze devoured her, his look hungry and appreciative. He gently eased her bra strap over her shoulder, then the other, and heat curled in her abdomen.

"You are beautiful," he said in a low, husky murmur.

Sage started to shake her head no. She didn't want words, didn't know if she believed them.

She simply wanted to feel tonight. To forget that he was with her only because she'd asked him to help her find Benji.

God… Benji…what was she doing?

Dugan must have realized her train of thought, because he tilted her chin up, forcing her to look into his eyes. The heat and hunger burning there sparked her own raw need.

"It's okay to feel, to take comfort," he said. "That doesn't mean you've forgotten your son. That you're a bad mother for needing someone."

Tears threatened, but his forgiving words soothed her nerves. The past two years, she had experienced guilt on a daily basis. Guilt for being alive when her little boy might not be.

"Shh, don't think," Dugan murmured against her ear.

She nodded and shut out the turmoil raging inside her as he kissed her again. He brushed his fingers across her nipples, teasing them again to stiff peaks, then he lowered his mouth and closed his lips over one nipple, sucking her gently and stirring sensations in her womb.

Sage reached for his belt buckle, her body burning with the need to have him inside her.

DUGAN CALLED HIMSELF all kinds of fool for letting things go as far as they had with Sage. But she'd looked too forlorn, defeated and disappointed for him to leave her alone tonight.

Her fingers skated over his chest, eliciting white-hot heat on his skin. Touched and honored that she wanted to be with him, he paused for a moment to drink in her beauty. Her breasts were high, round, firm.

One touch of his lips to her nipples and she clutched at him with a groan. He tugged the turgid peak between his teeth and suckled her, his own body on fire, with hunger for more.

The hiss of his zipper rasping on his jeans as she lowered it sounded erotic, and made him reach for hers, as well. He peeled them down her legs. A pair of the sheerest black lacy panties he'd ever seen accentuated her curves and hinted at the secrets that lay below.

His mouth watered.

She blushed at his perusal, and he threaded one hand into her hair while he trailed kisses along her neck and throat. She moaned and ran her hands down his chest, then over his hips, and his body jerked as sensations splintered through him.

She shoved his boxers down his thighs, and his sex sprang free, pulsing with need. Full, hard, thick. Then her hand closed around him, and he hissed between his teeth at the pure pleasure rippling through him.

But he had to slow things down. Tonight wasn't about him but about pleasing her. Giving her comfort. Reassuring her that it was okay for her to feel alive when she still had questions about her son.

Sometimes you had to feel that life in order to move past the darkness and survive.

He gently eased her down on the bed, his gaze raking in her feminine curves. She arched her back, like a contented cat, and he smiled, then tugged her lacy panties down over her hips. Cool air hardened her nipples again, making heat flood him as he rose above her and kissed her again.

Their tongues danced, mated, played a game of seduction, then he ripped his mouth from hers and trailed his tongue down her body again. He made love to her with his mouth, suckling each breast until she threw back her head and groaned. Then his tongue played down her torso, circled her belly button, and dipped lower to taste her sweet essence.

He eased her legs farther apart, lifted her hips and drove his mouth over her heat, tasting, teasing, devouring her as a starving man would his last meal.

Seconds later, her release trembled through her. He savored her sweetness as she cried out his name and gave herself to him.

SAGE SHIVERED WITH mindless pleasure. She closed her eyes, clawing at the covers as sensation after sensation rippled through her.

Dugan didn't pull away, though, as Ron had done. He consumed her with his mouth.

She groaned his name and reached for him, wanting more. Needing more.

Craving all of him.

The muscles in his arms bunched and flexed as he finally rose above her. He had an athlete's muscular body, broad shoulders, corded muscles. And hints of his Native American heritage in his slick dark chest.

The fierceness of a warrior in his dark, endlessly sexy, bedroom eyes touched her soul.

Eyes that had once seemed distant and unbending but now flickered with stark, raw passion.

She lowered her hand, cradled his thick length in her palm and stroked him. He threw back his head on a guttural moan, and feminine power raged through her.

"I want you, Sage," he said between clenched teeth.

She stroked him again, guiding him to her core. "I want you, too."

His breath rattled in the air as he left her for a moment, and she twisted, achy and missing him. He dug a condom from the pocket of his jeans on the floor, and started to roll it on.

She held out her hand and urged him to come to her. His eyes flared with unadulterated lust as she slipped the condom over his erection.

With one quick thrust, he entered her. Sage's body exploded with need and pleasure. He pulled out and thrust back inside her again, filling her to the depths of her soul with his rawness.

She gripped his hips, angling hers so he could reach deeper, and he rasped her name, his movements growing faster and harder as he plunged inside her. She wrapped her legs around his waist and clutched his back, their skin gliding together as they built a frantic rhythm and another orgasm began to spike.

A deep animal-like sound erupted from his throat, his release triggering her own, and together they rode the waves of pleasure.

Dugan's labored breathing echoed in the air as they lay entwined in the aftermath of their lovemaking. But he pulled away too quickly and strode to her bathroom.

A minute later, he returned. His expression looked troubled, his body tense.

Naked, he was so sexy and masculine that she reached for him again. The familiar guilt threatened, but she shut it out and pulled him back in bed with her.

He wrapped his arms around her, and she curled against him. "Sage?"

"Don't say anything," she said softly. She especially didn't want an apology or promises that he couldn't keep.

She trusted him to help her find her son, but she'd vowed never to chance losing her heart again.

All she wanted tonight was to have him comfort her and keep her warm and chase away the nightmares.

Those would be waiting in the morning, just as they had been for the past two years.

DUGAN WAITED UNTIL Sage fell asleep, then slid from beneath the covers and dressed. He walked downstairs and outside to the back deck overlooking the creek.

Dammit, he shouldn't have taken Sage to bed.

Normally he considered himself a love-'em-and-leave-'em kind of guy. Sex was sex. No attachments. No emotional ties.

He was not the kind of man to stick around or to belong to a family. Hell, he'd never been part of a real one and figured he'd screw it up just as his old man had.

The old man he'd never known.

Besides, letting emotions get in the way caused him to lose focus. And right now he needed to focus on finding Benji.

That one lead hadn't panned out, but the little boy's picture was all over the news, so hopefully if he was still alive, someone would spot him.

Yeah, right. If whoever had Benji had kept his identity a secret for two years, they certainly wouldn't want to be found now. Worse, the story might cause the person to panic and flee the state, even the country.

To take on another name, go into hiding somewhere completely off the grid.

He texted Jaxon and asked him to be sure to alert airports, train stations, bus stations and border patrols to look for Benji.

Somewhere in the woods, leaves rustled. The wind whipped them into a frenzy. An animal howled.

He stepped closer to the end of the porch, searching the darkness. Was that a shadow near the creek?

Senses on alert, he studied the trees and creek edge, hunting for a predator.

Another noise, and he spotted a figure slipping behind a boulder.

Dugan pulled his gun from his holster, descended the porch steps and crept through the woods. The figure moved again, tree branches crackling. Something darted across the dark…the figure running?

He hunkered low, using the trees as cover as he moved closer. A noise to the right startled him, and he glanced toward it. A flicker of a light. A thin stream of smoke.

Hadn't Sage mentioned that her attacker smelled like cigarette smoke?

Had he returned to make good on his threat?

"THEY'VE GOT HALF the country looking for that little boy. You have to do something. No one can ever know what we did."

"Dammit, I'm doing the best I can."

"Kill the woman if you have to. She's getting too close. She went to see Janelle Dougasville today."

"What did that woman tell them?"

"She told them about Sandra Peyton."

Hell. The Dougasville woman should have kept her trap shut.

Now Sandra Peyton had to die.

Chapter Sixteen

Dugan rounded the corner of the oak, his gun drawn. "Hold it or I'll shoot."

A shriek echoed in the air, and then the silhouette of a man filled his vision. A thin young man with his hands up in surrender. "Please, don't shoot, mister."

Dugan frowned, then pulled a penlight from his pocket and aimed it at the guy. Damn. He was a teenager. A big guy who looked as though he might play football.

And he was shielding the girl behind him, who was frantically rebuttoning her blouse.

"A little cold to be out here in the woods this time of night, don't you think?" Dugan asked.

The boy shrugged, his leather jacket straining his linebacker shoulders. "We weren't doing anything wrong."

The girl yanked on a jacket, then inched up behind the guy, her eyes wide with fear. "Please don't hurt us, mister."

"I'm not here to hurt anyone," Dugan said, irritated they'd drawn him away from Sage's. What if someone really was watching her house, and Dugan was chasing two randy teenagers and that person got to Sage?

"I thought you were stalking the inn, here to cause trouble for the owner."

The boy said a dirty word that Dugan didn't even use himself. "We came here 'cause Joy's mama won't let me come to the house."

"I can't say as I blame her," Dugan said, "considering you're mauling her daughter and cussing like a sailor."

"He wasn't mauling me," the girl said, her tone stronger now. "I'm seventeen. I make my own choices."

These teenagers weren't his problem. When he was the boy's age, he was probably doing the same thing.

Dugan tucked his gun back in his holster, then gestured for them to settle down. "Go on, get out of here." He gave the boy a warning look. "And don't come back to these woods again."

"No, sir, we won't." The boy grabbed the girl's hand, and they hurried back toward the wide part of the creek where they'd crossed in a small boat from the other side.

Something about seeing that boat nagged at Dugan. The creek ran wide and deep in certain areas and eventually emptied into the river that kayakers, rafters and boaters frequented. People could park in one area and boat to the other. In fact, rafters or boaters often parked cars in two areas, one where they put in and the other where they got out.

He remembered glancing at the report showing the location of Lewis's crash.

He wanted to see that report again. And he wanted to go back and walk the search grid, as well. Maybe the sheriff and his team had missed something.

THE NEXT MORNING Sage rolled over, sated and more rested than she had been in ages.

Memories of making love with Dugan the night before floated back in a euphoric haze.

But the bed beside her was empty. Not just empty but cold, as if Dugan hadn't slept there.

She'd been so deep in slumber that she hadn't even known when he'd left her bed.

Two years of exhausting, sleepless nights had finally caught up with her.

But morning sunlight poured through the window, slanting rays of light across the wood floors and reminding her that today was one more in a long list where Benji wasn't home.

One more day closer to another Christmas she would spend alone.

God, she was so tired of being alone.

Her heart clenched as if in a vise. What if she never found him? Could she go on day after day without knowing? Would the fear and anxiety eventually destroy her?

Throwing off the covers, she slid from bed. Muscles she hadn't used in forever ached, but with a sweet kind of throb that had eased the tension from her body and chased the nightmares away. At least for a little while.

She hurried into the shower, regretting the fact that the inn was empty of guests. At least having to cook breakfast for guests gave her something to do to start the day. Some sense of normalcy when nothing in her life for the past two years had been normal.

Dugan…was he still here?

She quickly showered and threw on some clothes, then dried her hair and pulled it back at the nape of her neck with a clip. Last night had sent them hunting down a false lead.

But today might provide another lead to pursue. She firmly tacked her mental resolve into place.

Rejuvenated by the night of mind-blowing sex, she pulled on boots and hurried to the kitchen. A pot of coffee was half-full and still warm. She poured herself a cup, then searched the living area for Dugan, but he wasn't inside.

Had he left? Why hadn't he told her?

She took her coffee to the back porch and found him there in one of the rocking chairs. He looked rumpled, his beard growth from the day before rough and thick, his eyes shadowed from lack of sleep.

"Have you been out here all night?"

"Off and on."

She sipped her coffee and sank onto the porch swing, using her feet to launch it into a gentle sway. "Why did you leave the bed?"

Silence, thick and filled with regret, stretched between them for a full minute before he spoke. "I offered to do a job, Sage. I shouldn't have slept with you."

True. But his words stung. Still, she sucked up her pride and lifted her chin. "So, what do we do today?"

"Last night I saw a shadow in the woods and came out to check it. Turned out it was a couple of teenagers necking in the woods."

Why was he telling her this? "So?"

"I ran them off, but it started me thinking about the day Lewis crashed."

"I don't get the connection."

"The teenagers tied a boat downstream. They took it back across the creek where they'd probably left a car."

Sage sipped her coffee again, the caffeine finally

kick-starting her brain and dragging her mind away from memories of bedding Dugan again.

That was obviously the last thing on his mind.

"Anyway, after the crash, no bodies were found in the fire or anywhere around the area. Which made me start thinking—if Benji is alive and he didn't die with Lewis, who we now know was murdered—how did the shooter escape? As far as I know, the police report didn't mention another car. No skid marks nearby or evidence anyone else had stopped until the accident was called in."

Slowly, Sage began to grasp where he was headed. "You're thinking that whoever killed Ron escaped on a boat across the creek?"

Dugan shrugged. "It's possible." He stood. "It's also possible that Lewis was meeting someone else. It's just a theory, but let's say that he had reconnected with his first love, Sandra Peyton."

"The woman who'd been pregnant and lost his child."

"Exactly." Dugan stood. "What if she was meeting him and he planned to take Benji to her so they could have the family they'd lost?"

Hope sprouted in Sage's head again.

They had to find Sandra Peyton. But if she had Benji, she probably didn't want to be found.

DUGAN WANTED TO look at that report again, and see the area for himself, so he drove to the sheriff's office.

Sage insisted on accompanying him. Luckily Gandt was out, but the deputy was in. Once Dugan explained that he was helping Sage look for her son, the deputy pulled the file, handed it over and allowed Dugan to make a copy while he returned some phone calls.

"Was there any mention of a boat?" Sage asked as she looked over his shoulder.

"I'm looking." Dugan skimmed the report. The accident had happened at approximately six-forty. A motorist had called it in when she saw the fire shooting up from the bushes.

Sheriff Gandt had arrived along with the fire department, but the car was already burned beyond saving. Once the fire had died down and the rescue workers found no evidence of anyone inside, Gandt organized a search party to comb the area.

During that two-hour interval, Lewis's shooter had escaped.

Dugan spread the photos of the area across the desk in the front office. Sage made a low, troubled sound as she studied the pictures. The land looked deserted. The weather had been cold that day, patches of dead brush and desolate-looking cacti.

"No boat," Sage said.

"The shooter could have been following Lewis. He caused the crash, then shot Lewis…or he shot him first, causing Lewis to crash."

"If he shot him first, why not let the fire take care of destroying evidence and his body?" Sage asked.

"Because finding the body proves Lewis was murdered, that he didn't die in an accident."

Sage shivered. "If the shooter dragged him out, he must have been bleeding. But I don't see blood in the pictures."

"You're right." Dugan analyzed each one, looking for signs that a body had been dragged from the car, but saw nothing.

He tried to piece together another possibility. What

if Lewis had planned to meet someone and fake his death with the car crash? Perhaps whoever it was he'd met had turned on him and shot him.

But why not leave Benji?

Maybe the shooter took Lewis and Benji at gunpoint, shot Lewis, then dumped his body? But again, why take Benji? Because he was a witness?

"Sage, I'd like to go back to the scene and walk the area."

"If you think it'll help."

"Sometimes I work with a dog named Gus. He's an expert tracker dog. Do you have something of Benji's that carries his scent, for Gus to follow?"

Another pained look twisted Sage's face. "Yes."

The deputy was still on the phone, so Dugan mouthed his thanks and they left. He drove to the inn, and Sage hurried inside to get something that had belonged to her son.

SAGE CLUTCHED BENJI'S BLANKET to her and inhaled his sweet scent. Even after two years, it still lingered. She hadn't washed it, and had held on to it for his return, the memory of him cuddling up to it so vivid that it still brought tears to her eyes.

She blinked them back, though, and carried the blanket to Dugan, who was waiting in his SUV.

"He slept with this all the time," Sage said. "I...don't know how he made it the past two years without it."

Dugan squeezed her hand as she laid it in her lap. "Hang in there, Sage."

That was the problem. She was hanging on to the hope of finding him alive and bringing him home.

As strong as she pretended to be on the surface, she didn't know if she could handle it if that hope was crushed.

Her mind traveled down that terrifying path that had opened up to her two years ago, to the possibility that he was dead and that they might find his body lying out in the wilderness somewhere. She'd seen the stories on the news and had no idea how parents survived something so horrible.

Dugan drove to his place, a ranch with horses running in the pasture and cattle grazing in the fields, and she forced herself to banish those terrifying images.

"I didn't know you had a working ranch."

Dugan shrugged. "I have a small herd, and I train quarter horses in my spare time."

"And you still have time to consult on cases?"

"Search-and-rescue missions mostly. I have a couple of hired hands, teens from the rez, who help out here."

They climbed out, and she noted the big ranch house. It was a sprawling, rustic log house with a front porch, a house that looked homey and inviting.

A large chocolate Lab raced up and rubbed up against Dugan's leg. He stooped down and scratched the dog behind his ears. "Hey, Gus. I've got a job for you."

The dog looked up at him as if he understood.

"Did you train him?" Sage asked.

Dugan nodded. "I need to grab a quick shower and change clothes."

Memories of the two of them making love the night before teased her mind, but she reminded herself that he'd stayed with her because someone had tried to kill them, not because he was in love with her.

"Gus, come." Dugan instructed the dog to stay at the front door when they entered, and she noted the Native American artifacts and paintings of nature and horses on the wall. Dark leather furniture, rich pine floors and a floor-to-ceiling stone fireplace made the den feel like a haven.

Dugan disappeared into a back room, and she heard the shower water kick on. She tried not to imagine him naked again, but she couldn't help herself.

Trace and Ron had been good-looking men, but more business types than the rugged, outdoorsy rancher Dugan was.

She spotted a collection of arrowheads on one wall and handwoven baskets on another. But there were no personal touches, no photographs of family or a woman in the house.

She couldn't imagine why a sexy, strong, virile man like Dugan didn't have a woman in his life.

He probably has dozens.

She dismissed the thought. She had to concentrate on finding Benji. When she brought him home, he would need time to acclimate. Like Humpty Dumpty, she'd have to put the pieces of her family back together again.

Dugan appeared, freshly shaven and wearing a clean shirt and jeans, and nearly took her breath away. Lord help her.

He attached his holster and gun, then settled his Stetson on his head and called for Gus. "Are you ready?" he asked.

She nodded and pushed images of Dugan's sexy body from her mind.

Finding Benji and rebuilding her family was all that mattered.

DUGAN PARKED AT the site of the crash, and they climbed out. He knelt and held Benji's blanket up to the dog to sniff. Gus was the best dog he'd ever had. He had personally trained him, and so far the dog had never let him down.

Although with two years having passed, it was doubtful he'd pick up Benji's scent.

Gus took a good sniff, then lowered his nose to the ground and started toward the creek. Dugan followed him, Sage trailing him as Gus sniffed behind bushes and trees and along the creek bank.

But Gus ran up and down the creek, then stopped as if he'd couldn't detect Benji's odor.

Dugan wasn't giving up. He began to comb the area, pushing aside bushes and bramble. Sage followed his cue.

Weeds choked the ground, the dirt dry and hard along the bank. Dugan leaned down to see something in the brush.

A second later, he pulled a tennis shoe from the weeds.

The devastation in Sage's eyes told him the shoe had belonged to her son.

Chapter Seventeen

"That's Benji's shoe." Sage stepped closer. "How did it get in the bushes?"

Dugan didn't want to frighten her with speculations, so he tried to put a positive spin on it. "He could have lost it near the car and an animal found it and carried it here."

Gus sniffed the ground again, and Dugan searched the bushes for the other shoe or any signs of Benji.

Grateful when he didn't find bones, he released a breath. Gus turned the opposite direction and sniffed again, then followed the creek, heading closer to the town and the inn. But again, the time and elements made it impossible to track.

However, they did find an area used for putting boats in and out.

Sage wrung her hands together as she looked across the creek. "Maybe Ron realized he was in trouble, that someone was on to his scam, and he planned to meet that woman Sandra here. Or Carol Sue, one of his other girlfriends or wives?"

Dugan knew she was grasping at straws, but he didn't stop her. "Sounds feasible."

"Maybe he handed Benji off to this woman before he was shot," Sage said.

Dugan shrugged. He doubted that was the case, but he'd be damned if he destroyed Sage's hopes without proof.

They spent another hour coaxing Gus with the blanket and shoe, but they turned up nothing, and Gus kept returning to the site where Dugan thought a boat had been.

The fact that they didn't find Benji's other shoe meant he could have still had it on or that it had floated downstream.

His phone buzzed, and he checked it. Jaxon.

He connected the call. "Yeah?"

"I have an address for Martin's girlfriend, Carol Sue."

"Text it to me."

They hung up and the text came through. Carol Sue lived about forty miles from Cobra Creek.

With no traffic, he could make it there in thirty minutes.

But as he and Sage and Gus headed back to his SUV, he spotted something shiny in the grass. He paused, bent down and brushed a few blades away, then plucked a bullet casing from the ground.

"What is it?" Sage asked.

He held it up to the light. "A bullet. I'll send it to the lab for analysis."

If it was the same one that had shot Lewis, identifying the bullet could lead them to the gun that had shot the man.

And to his killer.

SAGE FOLLOWED DUGAN into the lab, where he dropped off the bullet casing he'd found in the weeds by the creek. He introduced her to Jim Lionheart, who ran the lab.

"It's bent, but it looks like it's from a .38," Lionheart said. "I'll run it. Lots of .38s out there, though. If you bring me a specific gun, I can match it."

"I'm working on it," Dugan said. "Did you see the M.E.'s report on Wilbur Rankins's death?"

Lionheart shook his head no. "You want me to pull it up?"

"I'd appreciate it."

Dugan followed Lionheart to the computer. "Why are you interested in his autopsy?"

"Rankins's grandson called me and said he heard his father and grandfather arguing before he heard the shot."

"You mean his grandson thinks his own father killed his grandfather?" Sage asked.

"He was suspicious. Of course, Gandt didn't even question it."

Lionheart accessed the report, a scowl stretching across his face. "Hmm, odd. Rankins was shot with a handgun. But most of the ranchers around here use rifles or shotguns."

Sage saw the wheels turning in Dugan's head.

"Find out if the bullet I brought in is the same kind that killed Rankins."

"Will do."

"Didn't they do an autopsy?" Sage asked.

"It's standard in a shooting, but I don't think they've ordered one. Since Junior's daddy was dying of cancer anyway and was humiliated by the questions I was asking about the land deals, Junior figured his father just wanted to end the pain."

"I'll call you when I get something."

Dugan thanked him, and Sage walked with him back to his vehicle. "But why would Junior kill Wilbur?" Sage asked. "If he wanted his land, he'd eventually get it."

"Good question," Dugan said. "And one I intend to find the answer to."

QUESTIONS NAGGED AT DUGAN as he drove toward the address he had for Carol Sue. There were too many random pieces to the puzzle, but they had to fit somehow.

If Junior had killed his father, had he also killed Lewis? And why kill his old man if he was going to die and leave him his property, anyway?

The motive for Lewis's murder was clear. Someone—either a woman or a man Lewis had deceived—had gotten revenge by murdering him. If a female had shot him, she'd probably wanted to lash out against him for his lies and betrayal. She might have seen Benji and decided to take him as her own.

On the other hand, if one of the ranchers Lewis had swindled killed him, he wouldn't have wanted the kid. And he certainly couldn't have kept him in Cobra Creek.

There was always the possibility that someone from Lewis's past, another identity Dugan knew nothing about yet, had traced him to Cobra Creek under his new name and shot him.

A half hour later, he turned into a pricey condo development that featured its own stable, tennis courts and country club.

"Carol Sue lives here?" Sage asked.

"That's the address I have. Either she has her own money or Lewis did well when they were together and she benefited."

"Maybe she's just a hardworking woman Ron tried to con."

Dugan stopped at security and identified himself. The guard let him in, and Dugan checked the numbers for the buildings until he found Carol Sue's condo, an end unit at the rear of the complex.

Designated spots were marked for visitors, but each condo had a built-in garage. He parked, and he and Sage walked up to the door. Dugan punched the doorbell and glanced around, noting that the small lawns were well tended, each unit painted to create a unified feel.

When no one answered, he rang the doorbell again, then stepped to the side to peer in the front window. There was no furniture inside.

"Looks like she's moved out," Dugan said.

Sage sighed. "Are you sure?"

"There's no furniture in the living room. Let me check around back." He descended the brick steps, then walked around the side of the condo. A small fenced-in yard offered privacy, and when he checked the gate, it was unlocked.

Sage followed on his heels as he entered the backyard. The stone patio held no outdoor furniture. He crossed the lawn to the back but the door was locked.

Damn.

He removed a small tool from his pocket, picked the lock, then pushed the door open. The back opened to a narrow entryway with a laundry and mudroom to the left. Sage trailed him as he stepped into a modern kitchen with granite counters and stainless steel appliances.

"There's no table." Sage opened a few cabinet doors. "No food or dishes, either. You're right. She's gone."

A noise sounded upstairs. Footsteps?

Dugan pulled his weapon and motioned for Sage to move behind him. Then he crept through the hallway. He checked the living and dining area. Both empty.

The footsteps sounded again. Then a woman appeared on the stairs. She threw up her hands and screamed when she saw them.

She was dressed in heels and a dress and wasn't armed, so he lowered his gun.

"Sorry, ma'am. Are you Carol Sue?"

The woman fluttered her hand over her heart, visibly shaken. "No, I'm Tanya Willis, the real estate broker for the development. Who are you?"

Dugan identified himself and introduced Sage. "We're looking for Carol Sue."

"I have no idea where she is," the woman said. "Why do you want to see her?"

"We think she was connected to a man, Ron Lewis, whose body was recently found in Cobra Creek. Carol Sue knew him by another name, though, Mike Martin."

Tanya gasped and gripped the stair rail. "You said Mike was murdered?"

"Yes, ma'am," Dugan replied.

Sage stepped up beside him. "He also took my little boy, Benji, with him the day he was killed. You may have seen the story on the news."

"Oh, my God, yes." Tanya swept one hand over her

chest. "You think Carol Sue had something to do with that man's murder and your little boy's disappearance?"

"That's what we're trying to discern." Dugan paused. "Does Carol Sue own the condo?"

"Yes," Tanya said. "She was so excited when she first bought the place and moved in. Told me she'd never had a nice home before, and that her boyfriend had a windfall and they were planning to get married and live here together."

"When was that?"

"A little over three years ago," Tanya said. "I stopped to see her a couple of times after that, thought I'd meet her fiancé since he sounded so wonderful, but both times she said he was out of town."

"Her boyfriend's windfall was due to the fact that he was a con artist," Dugan said.

Again, the real estate broker looked shocked.

"When did Carol Sue move out?" Sage asked.

"Just a couple of days ago," Tanya said. "That was weird, too. She called me and said she had to relocate and wanted me to handle putting the unit on the market."

Dugan traded looks with Sage. Had the discovery of Lewis's body prompted her quick departure?

"Did she say why she had to relocate?" Sage asked.

Tanya shook her head, her lower lip trembling. "No, but she definitely sounded upset. Like she might be afraid of something."

Dugan considered that comment. Had Carol Sue been upset because she'd learned Lewis was dead and feared his killer might come after her? Or because she'd killed him and didn't want to get caught?

Or had the publicity about the murder and Benji's disappearance made her run because she had Sage's son?

SAGE TWISTED HER HANDS together as they left the condo complex. Dugan phoned his friend Jaxon, with the rangers, and relayed what they'd learned about Carol Sue.

Sage's cell phone buzzed, and she checked the number. An unknown.

Curious, she hit Answer. "Hello."

"You need to stop nosing around."

A chill swept up her spine. It was a woman's voice this time. "Who is this?"

"It doesn't matter who it is. If you don't stop, you're going to end up dead."

The phone clicked silent.

Sage's hand trembled as she lowered the phone to her lap.

"Who was that?" Dugan asked.

"I don't know," Sage said, shaken and angry at the same time. "A woman. She warned me to stop nosing around or I'd end up dead."

Dugan checked her phone. An unknown number. Probably a burner phone, but he called Jaxon to get a trace put on Sage's phone in case the caller phoned again.

When he hung up, he turned to Sage, trying to make sense of everything. "First, a man breaks in and threatens you. And now a woman calls with threats. They must be working together."

"Do you think it was Carol Sue?"

"Could be. Or it could have been Sandra Peyton."

"But if Sandra met up with Ron before he died and took Benji, who is the man?"

"I don't know," Dugan said. "As far as we know, Sandra had nothing to do with the land scams in Cobra Creek."

What if Sandra had reconnected with Ron and they'd planned to con the people in Cobra Creek, then disappear with the money?

If so, did she have Benji with her?

HE WAS CLOSE on Carol Sue's tail. The damn woman thought she'd get away, but she was wrong.

He had to tie up all loose ends.

He held back in his car, following her at a safe distance, careful not to tip her off. She'd been hiding out since Lewis disappeared.

But she'd tried to blackmail him first.

He didn't kowtow to blackmail from anyone.

Not that she had understood what was going on, but she knew enough.

Too much.

She swerved the little sedan into the motel, parked at the front and rushed inside, scanning the parking lot and checking over her shoulder as if she sensed she was being followed.

Stupid broad. She'd gotten greedy.

Now she would pay.

He parked to the side and waited until she rushed out with the key. She moved her car down the row of rooms to the last one at the end.

He grinned as she grabbed her bag and hurried inside the room.

Laughter bubbled in his chest.

Night was falling, but it wasn't dark enough to strike just yet. The motel backed up to a vacant warehouse parking lot. There he might stick out.

Better to blend in with the crowd, so he parked a few spaces down in front of a room with no lights on, indicating it was vacant. Satisfied she'd tucked in for the evening, he walked across the street to the bar/diner.

He slid into a back booth and ordered a burger and beer but kept a low profile as he enjoyed his meal. Night had descended by the time he finished, but he wanted to wait another half hour to give the bar time to fill up so no one would notice him leaving.

So he ordered a piece of apple pie and coffee and took his time.

His belly full, he paid the bill in cash, then stepped outside for a smoke. The first drag gave him a nicotine buzz, and he stayed in the shadows of the bar until he finished and tossed the cigarette butt to the ground. He stomped it in the dirt with his boot, then walked back across the street.

Still, he waited, watching her room until she flipped off the lights. He gave her time to get to sleep, then slid from his car and eased down the row of rooms until he reached hers.

He quickly picked the lock, then inched inside. The soles of his shoes barely made any noise as he walked toward the bed. She lay curled beneath the blanket on her side, one hand resting beneath her face.

He grabbed a pillow from the chair, then leaned over her. Her eyes popped open, and she started to scream when she saw him.

But he shoved the pillow over her face and held it down, pressing it over her nose and mouth. She struggled, kicked and clawed at him, but he was stronger and used his weight to smother the life out of her.

Even after her limbs went still and her body limp, he kept the pillow on her for another two minutes to make sure she was dead.

He didn't want her returning to haunt him and ruin all he'd done to get where he was.

In fact, he'd kill anyone who got in his way.

Including Sage Freeport and that damn Indian, who were asking questions all over Cobra Creek.

Chapter Eighteen

Dugan's phone buzzed as he drove back to Cobra Creek.

"Mr. Graystone," Donnell said, his voice hesitant.

"Yes. What can I do for you, Mr. Earnest?"

"I've been thinking about what you said that day, about my ranch and that Lewis jerk."

"Go on."

"I heard Wilbur Rankins is dead."

"That's true. The sheriff said he shot himself because of the truth about the scam coming out."

A tense moment passed. Earnest cleared his throat. "Listen to me, mister. I don't know what the hell's going on, but I do know Wilbur. That man was the most prideful man I've ever known. Sure, he would have hated being showed up by some bigwig stranger that duped him out of his land, but he would never kill himself. *Never.*"

"What makes you so sure?"

"First of all, he loved his grandson too damn much. He always said suicide was a coward's way out. His daddy took his own life, and Wilbur hated him for it."

Interesting. "What about his cancer? If he was in a lot of pain, maybe he committed suicide to keep his family from watching him suffer or to keep them from paying medical bills."

Earnest mumbled a crude remark. "He might have been worried about money and bills, but he just got a report saying he was doing better. He thought he was going to beat that cancer after all."

Dugan stifled a surprised response. That wasn't the impression he'd gotten. "Do you know who his doctor was?"

"Doc Moser sent him to some specialist oncologist in San Antonio."

"What is it you want me to do?" Dugan asked.

A long sigh echoed back. "Find out the truth. If Wilbur didn't kill himself, then someone murdered him. And if it has to do with the land, I'm worried they're gonna come after me."

Dugan scrubbed his hand over his neck. That was a possibility. "Thanks for calling, Mr. Earnest. I'll let you know what I find."

When he hung up, Sage was watching him, so he relayed the conversation. Then he turned the SUV in the direction of the doctor's office in Cobra Creek.

By the time they reached Cobra Creek, the doctor's office was closed.

"Do you know where he lives?" Dugan asked.

"Two houses down from the inn."

She pointed out Dr. Moser's house, and Dugan parked. "Do you know him?"

Sage nodded. "He's the only doctor around. He treated me and Benji."

Dr. Moser's house was a two story with flower boxes in front and a garden surrounded by a wrought-iron fence in back. His wife apparently spent hours tending her flowers.

Sage rang the bell while Dugan glanced up and down the street. A moment later, Mrs. Moser, graying hair and a kind smile, opened the door and greeted them.

Sage introduced Dugan and explained that he was helping her look for her son. "Can we come in?" Sage asked. "We need to talk to Dr. Moser."

The doctor appeared behind her, adjusting his bifocals. "Hello, Sage. Is something wrong?"

"Please let us come in and we'll explain," she said.

Mrs. Moser waved them in and offered coffee, but they declined. The doctor gestured toward the living room, and they seated themselves.

Dugan began. "I suppose you heard that Ron Lewis's body was found by the creek."

Dr. Moser nodded. "I did hear that. Saw Dr. Longmire yesterday, and he told me that Lewis was shot."

"Yes, he was," Dugan said.

Dr. Moser gave Sage a sympathetic look. "I'm sorry. I heard they still haven't found Benji."

Sage folded her hands and acknowledged his comment with a small nod.

"So what brought you here?" Dr. Moser asked.

Dugan explained about Lewis's scam. "I have reason to suspect that Wilbur Rankins might not have killed himself."

Dr. Moser pulled a hand down his chin. "I don't understand. I'm not the medical examiner."

"No, but you can answer one question. Sheriff Gandt said that Rankins shot himself because he was ashamed that he'd been duped by Lewis and because he was dying of cancer."

Dr. Moser looked back and forth between them. "He did have cancer. But you know the HIPAA law prevents me from discussing his medical condition."

"Dr. Moser," Dugan said bluntly. "The man is dead. In fact, he may have been murdered. All I need to know is if his condition was terminal or if he was going to get better."

Indecision warred in the doctor's eyes for a moment, then he leaned forward in his chair. "I do believe he'd just learned that the chemo was working."

Sage sucked in a sharp breath. If he'd just received a good prognosis, it didn't make sense that he'd take his own life.

DUGAN THANKED THE DOCTOR, Donnell Earnest's suspicions echoing in his head. Was Earnest right? Had someone murdered Rankins?

Someone who'd partnered with Lewis?

He drove toward the bank, wondering if Bates had any insight. "When Lewis was with you, did he ever mention a partner?"

Sage rubbed her temple. "Not that I remember."

"How about the name of the developer?"

She closed her eyes as if in thought. "It was something like Woodard or Woodfield. No, Woodsman. I remember thinking that it suited the business."

"We need to research it." Dugan parked at the bank, and he and Sage entered together.

"While you talk to Mr. Bates, I'm going to talk to Delores," Sage said. "She's the loan officer here. Maybe she knows something."

"Good idea." Dugan strode toward Bates's office while Sage veered to the right to speak to her friend.

When he knocked, Bates called for him to come in. The man looked slightly surprised to see him but gestured for him to sit down.

"What can I do for you today, Mr. Graystone?" Bates asked.

"Who was this developer working with Lewis?"

Bates tugged at his tie, nervous. "The company name was Woodsman."

"What about Junior? Does he know this?"

"Yes. Junior is irate. He was furious with his father for signing with Lewis in the first place."

So Junior might have killed his father...

Or someone from the company could have killed Rankins to keep him from challenging the legitimacy of the deal.

Dugan thanked him and phoned Jaxon as he left the man's office. He had to find the person behind Woodsman.

SAGE KNEW DELORES from the bank and church. In fact, Delores had helped her with her loan for the renovations with the inn when she first decided to buy and refurbish it. They had become friendly enough for an occasional lunch and social gathering.

Until Benji disappeared. Then she'd shut down and kept to herself.

Delores waved to her from her desk. "Hey, Sage. How are you?"

"Can we talk in private?" Sage asked.

Delores's eyebrows shot up, but she gestured toward the door to her office. Jingle bells tinkled on it as Sage closed it. She sank into one of the chairs opposite her friend's desk, noting a Christmas tin full of cookies and candy canes.

"What's going on?" Delores asked. "I heard that Dugan Graystone found Ron Lewis's body."

Sage knew some of the residents in town weren't as friendly to the people from the reservation as they should be, an archaic attitude that she had no tolerance for. Dugan seemed to travel between both worlds fairly well. Most of the single women in town were intrigued by his dark, sexy physique and those haunted bedroom eyes.

But the men were standoffish.

Normally she didn't listen to gossip, but occasionally, a grain of truth could be found beneath the murk. "What are they saying?"

"That he was murdered," Delores said in a low voice as if she thought someone might be listening.

"He was shot," Sage said.

"Do they know who did it?"

"No, but Dugan Graystone is investigating."

Delores thumbed her auburn hair over her shoulder. "That's why he's here?"

"Yes," Sage said. "He's also helping me look for Benji."

"Yes, that's what they said on the news." Delores sighed. "You don't think…?" She cut herself off as she realized the ugly implications. "I'm sorry, Sage. I know this must be horrible for you."

"It has been," Sade admitted. "That's why I want to talk to you. Ron Lewis wasn't really who he said he was. He was a fraud who conned people out of their land. Ron said that he worked for this developer by the name of Woodsman. Do you know anything about that company?"

Delores wrinkled her nose. "No. Although that name sounds familiar." She turned and tapped some keys on the computer, her frown deepening. "I shouldn't be telling you this, but that name does show up on an account here."

Sage leaned forward. "Do you have any more information about the person who opened the account?"

Delores tapped a few more keys, a look of frustration tightening the lines around her eyes. "Hmm."

"What is it?"

"Let me look into something."

Sage drummed her fingers on her leg as she waited while Delores worked her magic. Her friend had confided once that she was somewhat of a hacker.

Delores sighed, long and meaningful, into the silence. "Oh, this is interesting."

"What?"

"I think Woodsman might be a dummy corporation."

"One Ron Lewis set up so he could personally hide money he was stealing from landowners."

Delores nodded, although her face paled as she looked at Sage. "That's not all. There's one other person who has access to the money in that account."

Sage's mind raced. It had to be someone at the bank who'd figured out what was going on. "You mean Mr. Bates?"

Delores shook her head no. "Sheriff Gandt."

DUGAN'S PHONE BUZZED as he left Bates's office. "Graystone."

"It's Jaxon. Meet me at the motel outside Cobra Creek."

"What's going on?"

"The cleaning staff found a body in one of the rooms."

"I'll be there ASAP."

He waited outside Delores's office for Sage. Her complexion looked a pasty-gray as she exited the office.

"Sage?"

She motioned for him to walk with her, and they left the bank. She didn't speak until they'd settled into his SUV.

"What did your friend say?"

Sage heaved a wary breath. "Delores looked up the account for Woodsman."

"And?"

"There was another person attached to the account." She turned to him, her expression etched in turmoil. "You won't believe who it was."

Dugan's patience was stretched thin. "Who?"

"The sheriff."

Dugan muttered a curse. "So Gandt was working with Lewis?"

Sage shrugged. "It looks like that. I guess the question is whether or not Gandt knew Ron was running a con, and if he was in on it."

Chapter Nineteen

Dugan should have been shocked at the fact that Gandt's name was associated with the account, but he'd never liked the bastard, so shock wasn't a factor.

But he drove to the motel, furious at the idea that the man who was supposed to be protecting and taking care of the town might be dirty. And that he might have taken advantage of the very people who'd trusted him and voted him into office.

"Do you think the sheriff knew what Ron was up to?" Sage asked, almost as if she was struggling to face the fact that Gandt might have lied to her.

"That arrogant SOB thinks he owns this town. I wouldn't put it past him to join in on a scheme that would garner him a bigger part of the pie."

Dugan spotted Jaxon's car in front of the motel room at the far end, room eight, swung his SUV into the lot and parked.

"What are we doing here?"

"Jaxon called. A body was found here."

Sage's mouth twitched downward. "Oh, God. Who is it?"

"We'll find out." Dugan reached for the door and opened it, then walked around to Sage's door, but she was already out. He was amazed at the strength she emanated.

When they reached the motel room, a uniformed officer met them where he stood guard. Dugan identified himself, and Jaxon walked up.

"Wait outside, Sage," Dugan told her.

He followed Jaxon across the room where Sheriff Gandt stood by the body of a woman on the bed. The M.E. was stooped beside her, conducting an exam.

"Have you identified her?" Dugan asked Jaxon.

Jaxon nodded. "Found a wallet in her car outside, with her license. Her name is Carol Sue Tinsley. That's why I thought you'd be interested."

"Damn." He'd halfway hoped they would find her and Benji together.

Sheriff Gandt glared at him. "What are you doing here?"

"I phoned him," Jaxon said. "This woman had a prior relationship with the man you knew as Ron Lewis."

Gandt's thick eyebrows shot up. "How do you know that?"

"I'm a Texas Ranger," Jaxon said, a sharp bite to his tone. "It's my job to investigate murders and kidnappings."

Dugan almost grinned. He knew Jaxon well enough to understand the implied message, that it was his job to step in when incompetence reigned.

"What was cause of death?" Dugan asked.

The M.E. was conducting a liver temp test. "The petechial hemorrhaging in the eyes suggests asphyxiation." He used his fingers to lift her eyelids, one at a time.

Dugan glanced at the pillow on the floor by the bed. Probably the murder weapon.

No bullet this time.

Was she murdered by the same perp who'd shot Lewis? If so, why a different MO?

To throw off the police?

"Have you found any forensics evidence?" Dugan asked.

Gandt shook his head. "I searched the room, but no signs of who did this."

"Any sexual assault?" Dugan asked.

Dr. Longmire shook his head. "None." He pulled the sheet back to reveal that she was still clothed in flannel pajamas. "My guess is she was sleeping when she was attacked."

"Was anyone with her when she checked in?" Dugan asked.

"No." Jaxon rubbed his chin. "Her car was registered to the name on her driver's license. But at the registration desk, she signed in as Camilla Anthony."

"So she was hiding from someone."

"Or meeting a lover," Sheriff Gandt said.

Dugan scoffed. "Most women don't wear flannel pj's to a romantic rendezvous."

Jaxon murmured agreement. "I'm going to canvass the other rooms in case another guest saw something."

The M.E. lifted one of her hands, indicating a broken nail. "It looks like she put up a fight. I'll see if I can get DNA."

"Even a thread of her attacker's clothing could help," Dugan added.

The sheriff shifted, walked over and bent to study the body. "I still think she was probably running from an ex-boyfriend. Maybe he followed her here, waited till she went to bed, then slipped in and choked her."

"What about the lock?" Dugan asked.

"It was picked," Jaxon said. "So far, no prints."

"And her belongings?" Dugan asked.

"We found a suitcase," Jaxon said. "Clothing, shoes, toiletries. I searched her purse, but no indication where she was headed. No map or papers with any kind of address on it."

"Money?"

"She did have a stash of cash, nearly a thousand dollars," Jaxon said.

"So robbery was not a motive." Dugan chewed over that information, then turned to Gandt. "Did you know this woman, Sheriff?"

Gandt hitched up his pants. "No, why would I?"

Dugan studied the way the man's mouth twitched. "Because she was Lewis's girlfriend when he went by the name of Mike Martin."

"That so?"

"Yes," Dugan said. "He had a string of names he used for his other scams."

Gandt crossed his beefy arms. "What else have you found out about Lewis?"

"He has a rap sheet for arrests under three different names for fraud and embezzlement. And he conned some local ranchers in Cobra Creek." Dugan glanced at Jaxon. "Did you find a cell phone in her purse or car?"

Jaxon shook his head no. "If she had one, the killer must have taken it."

To cover his tracks.

Dugan turned and scrutinized the room. The neon lights of a dive bar flickered against the night sky. "While you sweep the room for forensics, I may take a walk over there." Dugan turned to the sheriff. "Like you said, if the killer was watching her, he might have gone inside to wait until he thought she was asleep."

The sheriff tugged at his pants. "I'll do that," he said in a tone that brooked no argument. "I'm the law around here, Graystone, and don't you forget it."

He was the law. But Dugan didn't trust him worth a damn, especially now that he knew Gandt's name was associated with the account related to the land deals.

Could Gandt have killed Lewis so he could gain access to the property and money for himself? So he really could own Cobra Creek?

And what about Carol Sue? Maybe she'd traced Lewis to Cobra Creek and come looking for Lewis or her share of whatever money she thought he owed her.

SAGE PACED OUTSIDE the motel room, anxious to know what was going on inside.

Finally Dugan stepped out with a tall muscular man in a Stetson wearing a Texas Ranger badge on his shirt. Dugan introduced him as his friend Jaxon, and Sage thanked him for his help.

"Who was the woman?" Sage asked.

"Carol Sue," Dugan said with an apologetic look.

Disappointment ripped through Sage. If Carol Sue had any information about Benji, she couldn't tell them now.

"She was smothered," Dugan continued. "She put up a fight, though, so hopefully the M.E. can extract DNA from underneath her fingernails."

"I'm going to talk to the other guests at the motel," Jaxon said. "Maybe we'll find a witness."

"Let's divide up and it'll go faster." Dugan touched Sage's elbow. "Will you be okay here?"

"Sure, go ahead."

Jaxon headed to the first unit while Dugan took the one next to the room where the woman lay dead.

Sheriff Gandt stepped outside. "Did you know the woman in there, Ms. Freeport?"

"No," Sage said. "Did you?"

The sheriff's eyebrows drew together, creating frown lines across his forehead. "No. She's not from Cobra Creek."

"What do you think she was doing here?" Sage asked.

Sheriff Gandt shrugged and made a noncommittal sound. "Looks like she was probably meeting a lover. They had a quarrel and he killed her."

"Still, it seems odd that she was in Cobra Creek," Sage countered. "Especially so soon after Ron Lewis's body was found."

"You think she came here looking for his killer?" Gandt asked in a skeptical tone. "Hell, it's been two years since he disappeared."

"She probably saw the news of his death and wanted to talk to you about it," Sage suggested.

The sheriff's mouth twitched. "I guess that's possible."

"You also had connections to the land deal Ron had put together."

Shock widened Gandt's eyes. "Who the hell told you that?"

"It doesn't matter who told me," Sage said curtly. "What matters is that you were in cahoots with Ron to buy up the land around Cobra Creek. You were swindling your own people."

A dark rage flashed in the sheriff's eyes. "You don't know what you're talking about, Ms. Freeport."

"I know that you never really tried to find my son." Sage was spitting mad. "And that your name is associated with the developer Ron was working with." She planted her hands on her hips. "And that you could have killed him so you'd get all the money and land yourself."

"I'd be really careful about making accusations, Ms. Freeport," he said with a growl. "I'd hate to see you end up like that woman in there."

Sage's heart hammered in her chest. Was he threatening her?

THE MOTEL HELD twelve rooms, but only half of them were occupied.

The first door Dugan knocked on held an elderly couple who claimed they hadn't seen or heard anything because they'd retreated to bed as soon as it got dark. Apparently they'd both grown up on a farm, and they rose with the roosters and went to bed with the sun.

He moved to the next room and knocked on the door. A minute later, a young man in jeans and a cowboy hat opened the door. He pulled off headphones from his ears. "Yeah?"

"I'm sorry to bother you, but there was a woman murdered in room eight. We're asking everyone in the motel if they saw or heard anything."

The guy gestured toward his guitar, which was propped against the bed. Two young guys in their twenties also sat in a circle with a banjo and fiddle, and a brunette was strumming chords on her own guitar.

"Afraid not. We were jamming, working on some new material."

"Are you guys from around here?"

"North Texas. We're on our way to Nashville for a gig."

Dugan gestured toward the others. "Did any of you see someone near room eight?"

A chorus of nos rumbled through the room. "I thought I heard some banging," the girl said. "But I figured it was someone getting it on."

This group was no help. Dugan didn't see any reason to collect their contact information, but he laid a card on the dresser. "Call me if you remember anything. Maybe a car or person lurking around."

He tried the door next to them, but a family with twin toddlers answered the door. "Sorry, we went to dinner and drove around to see the Christmas lights," the father said. "By the time we returned, the sheriff's car was already outside."

Dugan thanked them, then moved down the row of rooms. But it was futile. Barring the cars and trucks in the lot, which were all accounted for by guests, no one had witnessed anything.

His phone buzzed against his hip, and he checked the number. Unknown.

He quickly connected the call. "Dugan Graystone."

"I have some information about Ron Lewis."

Dugan clenched the phone and looked around the parking lot in case the caller was nearby. "Who is this?"

"Meet me at Hangman's Bridge. An hour."

The voice was blurred, low, hoarse. Disguised.

"I'll be there." He hung up and checked his watch for the time. It could be a setup.

But it could be the tip he needed to end the case and find Benji.

NERVES KNOTTED SAGE'S shoulders as she and Dugan walked across the street to the bar.

"The canvass of the motel turned up nothing."

Sage sighed. "The sheriff warned me not to go around making accusations against him."

Dugan's eyes flared with anger. "Bastard. He's in this. I just need to prove it."

Sage still couldn't believe it. She had turned to Sheriff Gandt two years ago and even trusted him at first. Sure, she'd been frustrated that he hadn't found Benji, but it had never occurred to her that he might have been involved in her son's disappearance.

Even if he had killed Ron, why would he do something to Benji? As sheriff, he could have covered up the murder, then returned Benji to her and looked like a hero.

The bar was dark and smoky as they entered. Dugan had snapped a picture of Carol Sue and showed it to the hostess. "Do you recognize this woman?"

She shook her head. "What's going on?"

Dugan relayed the fact that Carol Sue had been murdered in the room across the street. "Was she in here earlier?"

"I didn't see her," the hostess said. She waved the bartender over. "Lou, was this woman in here earlier tonight?"

Lou dried his hands on a towel. "Naw. She ain't been in."

Dugan explained about the murder. "It's possible that her killer came in," Dugan said. "Did you notice anyone suspicious? Maybe someone who seemed nervous? He might have watched the door or checked the time."

"All that's been in tonight is the regulars," Lou said.

"Well, 'cept for this group of young folks, said they was in a band."

"We talked to them." Dugan handed them each a card. "If you think of anything, no matter how small, please give me a call."

Sage and Dugan walked back outside to the SUV. An ambulance had arrived to transport Carol Sue's body back to the morgue for an autopsy. Sage looked up and saw Sheriff Gandt lift his head and pin her with his intimidating stare.

Dugan's expression was grim as he drove her back to the inn. Night had set in long ago and exhaustion pulled at her limbs. And it was another day closer to Christmas.

And still no Benji.

The memory of Dugan's arms around her taunted her, making her yearn to have him make love to her again. To comfort her and chase her nightmarish fears away for a few more hours.

But after he searched the inn, he paused at the door.

"An anonymous caller phoned that he has information about Lewis," Dugan said. "Lock the doors, Sage, and stay inside until I get back."

She nodded, then watched him leave. Too antsy to sleep, she combed the inn.

A knock sounded at the door, and she rushed to answer it. The sheriff stood on the other side.

"Sheriff?"

"Come with me, Ms. Freeport. I may have a lead on your son."

Sage's heart stuttered. After the visit at the bank, she didn't know whether or not to trust him.

"Let me call Dugan to go with us."

"That's not necessary," Sheriff Gandt said.

"But—"

Her words were cut off as he raised his gun and slammed it against her skull.

Pain ricocheted through her temple, and then the world went black.

Chapter Twenty

Dugan parked in the woods by Hangman's Bridge, his instincts on alert. The fact that the anonymous caller had chosen this area to meet aroused his suspicions.

It was called Hangman's Bridge for a reason—two teenagers had died in a suicide pact by hanging themselves from the old metal bridge.

He pulled his gun, surveying the trees and area surrounding the bridge, looking for movement. An animal howled from somewhere close by, and the sound of leaves crunching crackled in the air.

He spun to the right at the sharp sound of twigs snapping. Then a gunshot blasted. Dugan ducked and darted behind an oak to avoid being hit.

Another shot pinged off the tree, shattering bark. He opened fire in the direction from where the bullet had come from, searching the darkness.

The silhouette of a man lurked by the bridge, the shadow of his hat catching Dugan's eye. Dugan crept behind another tree, careful to keep his footfalls light so as not to alert the man that he'd spotted him.

Another shot flew toward him, and he darted beneath the rusted metal rungs of the bridge and returned fire. His bullet sailed into the bushes near the man, then leaves rustled as the gunman shifted to run.

Dugan raced from one hiding spot to another, quickly closing the distance, and snuck up behind the man just before he ran for his truck in a small clearing to the left.

Dugan tackled the guy from behind, slamming him down into the brush. The man struggled, but his gun slipped from his hand and fell into a patch of dried leaves and branches.

They wrestled on the ground as the bastard tried to retrieve it, and the man managed to knock Dugan off him for a second. Dugan scrambled back to his feet as the shooter jumped up to run. But Dugan lunged toward him, caught him around the shoulders and spun him around.

Lloyd Riley.

"Riley," Dugan said. "Give it up."

But Lloyd swung a fist toward Dugan and connected with his jaw. A hard right.

Dugan grunted and returned a blow, the two of them trading one after the other until Dugan kicked Riley in the kneecap and sent him collapsing to the ground with a bellow of pain.

Dugan kicked him again, this time a sharp foot to the solar plexus, rendering him helpless.

Riley curled into a ball, hugging his leg. "You broke my damn kneecap!"

"You're lucky you're alive." Dugan flipped the big man over, pressed one foot into Riley's lower back to hold him still while he jerked his arms behind him, yanked a piece of rope from his pocket and tied his wrists together.

Riley growled an obscenity into the dirt. Dugan rolled him over and shoved his gun into his face.

"Why the hell were you shooting at me?"

Riley's lips curled into a hiss. "I had to," he muttered.

Dugan gripped Riley's shirt collar, yanking it tightly to choke the man. "What does that mean?"

Blood trickled down Riley's forehead near his left eye, another line seeping from the corner of his mouth. Then Dugan noticed the leather tassel on Riley's gloves. One was missing.

"You damn bastard, you broke into Sage Freeport's bedroom and tried to strangle her."

"I'm not talking till I get a lawyer."

Dugan laughed, a bitter sound. "You will talk to me. I'm not the law, Riley." He shoved the gun deeper into the man's cheek. "Now, why were you trying to kill me?"

Riley's Adam's apple bobbed as he swallowed hard.

"Spit it out," Dugan snarled.

"Gandt told me to."

Dugan's stomach knotted. "What?"

"That Freeport broad found out he was in cahoots with Lewis, and he knew you were on to him."

"So it's true, Gandt and Lewis were working together?"

"Not at first," Riley said. "But Gandt figured out Lewis was a con man and wanted in."

"Then he got greedy and killed Lewis so he could have the land to himself."

Riley nodded. "He told me I could keep my ranch if I helped cover for him."

"If you killed me?" Dugan asked.

Riley spit blood from his mouth. "He said he'd frame

me for killing Lewis. Then I'd lose my ranch and go to jail."

"What about the driver of that car that ran me and Sage off the road?"

Riley's face twisted with pain. "He was one of my hired hands."

Dugan gripped the man's collar tighter. "Where is Gandt now?"

Riley averted his eyes, and Dugan cursed. "Where is he?"

"He went after the Freeport woman. Said if I took care of you, he'd take care of her."

Dugan went stone-cold still. He had to get to Sage.

SAGE STIRRED FROM unconsciousness, the world a dark blur. What had happened? Where was she?

Gandt... God, the sheriff had been in on the scam. And now he had her....

And he was going to kill her.

She had to find a way out, call Dugan. Make the sheriff confess what he'd done with Benji.

She blinked to clear her vision, then realized she was tied to a chair, her hands bound behind her back, her feet bound at the ankles. She struggled to untie the knot at her wrists as she searched the darkness.

The scent of hay and horses suffused the air. She must be in a barn. But whose?

The sheriff didn't own a ranch...did he?

Maybe it was one of the properties he'd confiscated through the phony land deals.

But which one? And where was he now?

The squeak of the barn door startled her, and she

whipped her head to the side and saw a shadowy figure in the doorway.

"What are you going to do, kill me, too?" Sage shouted.

His footsteps crushed the hay on the floor as he walked toward her. A sliver of moonlight seeped through the barn door where it was cracked, painting his face a murky gray.

"I warned you not to keep poking around," Gandt said in a menacing tone. "You should have listened."

Still struggling with the ropes behind her back, Sage clenched her teeth. "Where is my son?"

Gandt lumbered toward her, tugging at his pants. His gun glinted in the dark as he trained it on her. "I don't know."

Sage's heart raced. "What do you mean, you don't know?"

His scowl deepened, a muscle ticking in his jaw. "When I got to Lewis that night, he was alone."

Sage's head throbbed from where he'd slammed the butt of the gun against her temple, but she gritted her teeth at the nausea. "You're lying. We found Benji's shoe by the creek near the crash site."

Gandt waved the gun around. "I'm telling you the kid was already gone when I met up with Lewis."

Fear engulfed Sage. He had to be lying. "I don't believe you. Benji had to be with Ron."

Gandt cursed. "Listen, Ms. Freeport, I'm telling you, he wasn't. Lewis must have dropped him off before he came to meet me."

"You were going to meet him about the land?"

"Yeah," Gandt said with a smirk. "You think I'm not smart enough to figure out what he was doing?" He paced in front of her, his jowls jiggling. "Well, I am.

Once I talked to a couple of locals and they told me he'd offered to buy up their property, I started looking into him. Ain't nobody messin' with my town."

Sage almost had one end of the rope through the back loop. "So you blackmailed him for a cut of the money?"

"I wanted that land," Gandt said. "First off, he said no way, but I can be convincing."

"You killed him, didn't you?" Sage's stomach rolled. "Then you forged papers so you could take over the rancher's properties."

"Hell, they'd rather be beholden to me than let some stranger turn their ranches into shopping malls and those damn coffee shops."

He lit a cigarette, then lifted it and took a drag. The ashes sparkled against the dark.

"Then that Indian friend of yours had to find Lewis's body, and you started nosing around."

Panic seized Sage. "All I want is my son. Just tell me where he is, and I promise I won't tell anyone what you did to Ron."

A dark laugh rumbled from Gandt. "Sure you won't. You talked to people at the bank. You went to the stinking press."

Tears burned the backs of Sage's eyes. "Please, just tell me. Is Benji all right?"

Gandt blew smoke through his nostrils, smoke rings floating in the air between them. "I told you the truth. I don't know what happened to the boy."

Sage struggled to understand. Could he have been in the car when they crashed and ran when he saw Gandt? "What happened?"

"I set fire to the car to cover up the murder. And it

would have worked if you hadn't come along asking questions."

Sage's mind tried to piece together the facts. Had Ron left Benji with someone else when he went to meet the sheriff? Maybe one of the women from his past?

Not Carol Sue—she was dead.

Sandra Peyton…

Her conversation with Maude Handleman, then Janelle Dougasville echoed in her head. Sandra had lost Ron's baby, and so had Maude. And Janelle said he'd never had a real family.

Was that what Ron was chasing? The reason he'd chosen her in the first place, so he could take Benji and raise him with Sandra, his first love?

Frantically she worried with the ropes, but the sheriff inhaled another drag from his cigarette, then dropped it onto the floor of the barn. She gasped as the embers sparked and a blade of hay caught fire.

Gandt leered at her and backed toward the door, and fear paralyzed her. He was going to burn down the barn with her in it.

DUGAN CALLED SAGE, panicked that Gandt had hurt her. Her phone trilled and trilled, his heart hammering as he waited to hear her voice.

But on the fifth ring, it rolled to voice mail. "Sage, the sheriff is dirty. If he shows up, don't open the door. And call me so I know you're okay."

He ended the call, then punched her number again, but once more he got her machine.

Dugan jerked Riley up and hauled him to his SUV. "Where would Gandt take Sage?"

Riley's eyes bulged. "I don't know."

Dugan shook him hard. "Tell me, dammit. If he hurts her, you're going down for it, too."

"I told you I don't know," Riley bellowed. "He ordered me to take care of you and said he'd handle her."

Dugan wanted to kill him on the spot. But he had to find Sage.

He searched Riley for another weapon, but he was clean, so he shoved him into the backseat. For a brief moment, he considered calling the deputy, but the deputy might be in cahoots with Gandt.

Jaxon was the only one he trusted.

He reached for his phone and started to shut Riley's door, but Riley's phone buzzed from his pocket.

Maybe it was Gandt, checking in.

Riley frowned as Dugan retrieved the rancher's phone from his shirt pocket.

Dammit, not Gandt.

He flipped it around to show Riley the name on the caller ID display. Whalen.

"Who is that?" Dugan asked.

"The only ranch hand I have left," Riley said.

On the off chance that Gandt was at Riley's, Dugan punched Connect and held the phone up to Riley, tilting it so he could hear the conversation.

"Riley?"

"Yeah, what is it?"

"The barn on the south side of the property is on fire!"

"Good God," Riley shouted. "Call the fire department."

The man yelled that he would, and Dugan took the phone, fear riddling him.

He'd wondered where Gandt would take Sage....

What if he'd taken her to Riley's? He could have planned to kill her there, then frame Riley for her murder.

Heart hammering, Dugan jumped in the SUV and tore down the dirt road, slinging gravel and dust in his wake.

"Take me to my place," Riley yelled.

"That's where we're going," Dugan snapped. Although Riley would be going to jail when this was over. "I have a bad feeling Gandt is there with Sage, and that he's behind the fire."

A litany of four-letter words spewed from Riley's mouth. "He was going to set me up."

"Yeah, and probably frame you for it." Dugan couldn't help himself. He enjoyed the terror on Riley's face.

He pressed the pedal to the floor, speeding over the potholes and bumps in the road. The ten miles felt like an eternity, but finally he veered down the drive onto Riley's ranch.

"Turn left up there to go to the south barn," Riley said.

Dugan yanked the steering wheel to the left and careened down the dirt path. Pastureland and trees flew by. He passed a pond and saw flames shooting into the air in the distance.

"Holy hell," Riley said. "If that spreads, my pasture will be ruined."

Dugan didn't give a damn about the man's property.

He phoned the deputy to meet him at Riley's property to arrest the rancher as he zoomed down the narrow road. He wished the fire engine was here, but he'd beat them to it. An old beat-up pickup truck was parked by a shed, and he spotted an elderly man pacing by the fence.

His tires screeched as he slammed on the brakes and came to a stop. He jumped out and ran toward the burning building.

"Did you see anyone inside?" Dugan shouted.

"I didn't go in," the old man said with a puzzled look on his craggy face. "We didn't have any livestock in there."

But Sage…what about Sage?

The old man hadn't checked because he had no reason to think she'd be inside.

Panic streaked through Dugan. But he didn't hesitate.

"Don't bother to try and get away," he told Riley. He grabbed a blanket from the back of his SUV, wrapped it around himself and ran into the blaze.

Chapter Twenty-One

Sage struggled against the ropes as the fire began to eat the floor and rippled up the walls. The smoke was thick, curling through the air and clogging her lungs.

She was going to die.

And then she'd never know where her son was.

No…she couldn't leave him behind. He needed her.

She kicked the chair over, searching blindly for a sliver of wood to use as a knife. She managed to grab a rough piece that had splintered from one of the rails and clutched it between her fingers. Then she angled and twisted her wrists and hands to get a better stab at the ropes.

Heat seared her body and scalded her back, and she used her feet to push herself away from the burning floor to a clear patch. Her eyes stung from the smoke, and each breath took a mountain of effort. She curled her chin into her chest, breathing out through her mouth and focusing on sawing away at the ropes.

Wood crackled around her, the stall next to her collapsing. Sparks flew as the flames climbed the walls toward the ceiling. The building was so old, places were rotting, and it was going to be engulfed in seconds.

The sliver of wood jabbed her palm, and she winced

and dropped it. Panicked, she fumbled to retrieve it and felt heat burn her fingers.

Tears trickled down her cheeks as pain rippled through her, then a piece of the barn loft suddenly crackled and popped, debris flying down to the floor around her.

DUGAN RACED THROUGH the flames to the inside, where the fire blazed in patches across the barn. The raw scent of burning wood and leather swirled in an acrid haze around him. He scrutinized the interior, searching as best he could with the limited visibility.

Tack room to the left, completely engulfed in flames.

Three stalls to the right. Two were ablaze.

Flames inched toward the third.

Smoke clogged the air like a thick gray curtain, forcing him to cover his nose with a handkerchief.

"Sage! Sage, where are you?" Maybe he was wrong, and she wasn't here.

He hoped to hell he *was* wrong.

Wood splintered and crashed from the back. He dodged another patch as he ran toward the last stall. Fire sizzled and licked at the stall door.

"Sage!"

He touched the wooden latch. It was hot. Using the blanket to protect his hand, he pushed it open.

Sage was lying on the floor, her hands and feet tied to a chair. She wasn't moving.

Terror gripped him, and he beat at the flames creeping toward her, slapping out the fire nipping at his boots. His feet were growing hot, but he ripped his knife from his back pocket, sliced through the ropes, then quickly picked Sage up in his arms.

She was so still and limp that fear chased at his calm. But he had to get them out.

"Sage, baby, I've got you." She didn't make a sound, but he thought he detected a breath. Slow and shallow, but she was alive.

He wrapped the blanket around his shoulders, tucked her close to him and covered her with it, then darted from the stall. The front of the barn was sizzling and totally engulfed.

He scanned the interior, searching for a way out. An opening near the back door. Just enough to escape.

He clutched Sage to him, securing her head against his chest and tugging the blanket over her face as he ran through the patches of burning debris and out the back door. Flames crawled up his legs, but he continued running until he was a safe distance away. Then he dropped to the ground, still holding Sage as he beat the flames out with the blanket.

A siren wailed and lights twirled in the night sky as the fire engine raced down the dirt road toward them. They were too late to save the barn.

He hoped to hell they weren't too late to save the woman in his arms.

Sage stirred from unconsciousness, disoriented and choking for a breath.

"Here, miss, you need oxygen." A blurry-looking young woman pushed a mask over her face, and someone squeezed her hand.

"You're okay, Sage. Just relax."

Exhaustion and fatigue claimed her, and she closed her eyes, giving in to it. But her mind refused to shut down. Questions screamed in her head.

What had happened? Where was she? Where was Dugan?

Then reality seeped in, crashing against her, and she jerked and tried to sit up.

"Shh, it's okay, you're safe," Dugan murmured.

She rasped the sheriff's name, then looked through the haze and saw Dugan looking down at her, his forehead furrowed with worry.

"I called Jaxon. I'll find Gandt, Sage, I promise."

She wanted to believe him, to trust him, but Gandt had gotten away. And…he didn't know where Benji was.

Tears clogged her eyes. If that was true, finding the sheriff didn't matter. She still wouldn't have her son.

She clawed at Dugan's hand, silently begging him to move closer. A strangled sound came from her throat as she tried to say his name.

"Don't try to talk," Dugan whispered. "You need rest."

She shook her head, frantic that he hear her, then shoved at her mask.

The medic tried to adjust it, but she pushed her hand away.

"Dugan…"

Dugan finally realized she needed to tell him something and leaned closer. "What? Do you know where he went?"

She shook her head, her eyes tearing from emotions or smoke, she didn't know which. "Said… Benji…" She broke into a coughing spell.

Dugan clung to her hand. "Did he tell you where Benji is?"

She shook her head again, choking out the words between coughs. "Gandt killed Ron."

"I know, and he sent Lloyd Riley to kill me."

Sage's face paled even more. "Said Benji not with Ron…."

"What?" Dugan sighed deeply. "You're sure?"

She nodded, tears running down her cheeks, like a river.

He wiped them away and pressed a kiss to her lips. "Don't give up. I will find him, Sage, I promise."

Despair threatened to consume her, and she gave in to the fatigue and closed her eyes. She felt Dugan's hand closing around hers, heard his voice whispering to her to hang on, and the paramedics lifted her into the ambulance.

Dugan squeezed her arm. "I'll meet you at the hospital."

She nodded. At least she thought she did. But she was too tired to tell.

Then the ambulance jerked, a siren rent the air and she bounced as the driver raced off toward the hospital and away from the burning barn.

DUGAN HATED THE FEAR in Sage's eyes because it mirrored his own. If he'd been five minutes later, she would have died.

He shut out the thought. She hadn't died, and the medics would take care of her.

He had to find Gandt.

But if Benji wasn't with Lewis, and Gandt didn't know his whereabouts, where was he?

He'd already phoned Jaxon while waiting on the ambulance, and Jaxon agreed to put out a statewide hunt for Gandt.

What the hell should he do now?

Gandt was missing. Lewis dead. Rankins dead. Carol Sue dead.

Who had Benji? Sandra Peyton?

He jumped in his SUV and followed the deputy to the sheriff's office to make sure that he locked Riley up. He half expected Gandt to be cocky enough to be sitting in his office, with his feet propped up.

Did the sheriff know that Sage had survived? That Riley hadn't killed Dugan?

Did he think he'd gotten away?

Itching to know, Dugan decided to check the man's house. If he thought he'd gotten off scot-free, Gandt might be celebrating his good fortune. Or if he was afraid he was about to be caught, he might be packing to run.

Dugan knew where the man lived. Out on the river, by the gorge.

He whipped his SUV in that direction, eager to check it out.

Traffic was nonexistent on the country highway, the wilderness surrounding him as he veered off the main road and drove into the wooded property where Gandt lived.

The driveway was miles long, farm and ranch land sprawling for acres and acres.

Why Gandt was so greedy when he had all this, Dugan would never know.

When he neared the clearing for the house, he slowed and cut his lights.

He rolled up behind a tree and parked, pulled his gun and slipped through the bushes along the edge of the property. The sheriff's car was parked in front of the house, one car door open.

Dugan slowly approached it, bracing for an ambush. But as he crept near the car and looked inside, he saw it was empty.

Breathing out in relief, he ducked low and walked along the fence until he reached the side of the porch, which ran the length of the front of the house.

The door screeched opened, and Gandt appeared. Dugan ducked low and watched, surprised at the sight of Gandt pushing a gray-haired woman in a wheelchair out the door.

"I don't understand why I have to leave," the woman said shrilly.

"Because I'm going away for a few days and can't take care of you, Mother," Gandt said, his tone contrite.

"Can't you hire a nurse like you did before?"

"No, that costs a fortune. Gwen said you can come and stay with her."

The woman laid a hand on Gandt's arm. "But her husband doesn't like me."

"Mother," Gandt said, his patience wearing thin in his voice, "just please try to get along with them. When I straighten things out, I'll come back for you."

He pushed her down a ramp attached to the opposite side of the porch.

"What do you have to get straightened out?" she cried.

Dugan stepped from the shadows, his gun drawn. The woman gasped, and Gandt reached for his weapon.

"Don't," Dugan said. "I'd hate to have to shoot you in front of your mother."

The woman shrieked again. "Please don't hurt us." She clutched Gandt's arm. "Who is this man?"

"My name is Dugan Graystone," Dugan said. "I hate to tell you this, ma'am, but your son is not all you think he is."

Her sharp, angry eyes pierced Dugan like lasers. "You have no right talking to me about my son. What are you, some criminal on the loose?"

"Mother, be quiet," Gandt said through gritted teeth.

"I'm not the criminal here," Dugan said. "Mrs. Gandt, your son tried to have me killed, and he tied Sage Freeport—"

"Shut up," Gandt snarled.

"You don't want your mother to know what kind of man her son really is?"

"My son is a wonderful man. He takes care of this town."

"Mother—"

"He stole land from the ranchers and conned them. Then he shot Ron Lewis." Dugan paused. "Did you kill Wilbur Rankins, too?"

The woman turned shocked, troubled eyes toward Gandt. "Son, tell him that's not so…."

"It is true." Dugan waved his gun toward Gandt. "Now I want to know where Sage Freeport's little boy is."

Gandt walked toward Dugan, his eyes oozing steam as if he refused to admit to any wrongdoing. "You have a lot of nerve coming to my house, carrying a gun and making accusations." He handed his mother his phone. "Call my deputy and tell him to get over here right now."

Dugan stepped forward, unrelenting. Did Gandt really think he could get away with all this? "Fine, tell him to come, Mrs. Gandt. Also tell him he'll be arresting your son for murder."

The older woman gasped and clutched at her chest.

Dugan dug the gun barrel into Gandt's belly. "Now, where is Benji Freeport?"

Chapter Twenty-Two

A siren wailed, headlights lighting a path on the house as Jaxon roared up in his Texas Ranger truck.

Gandt cursed. "Let me take my mother back inside," he said to Dugan. "Then we'll talk."

Dugan felt sorry for the older woman, but he shook his head. No way did he intend to let Gandt out of his sight. Not even for a minute.

Mrs. Gandt curled her arthritic hands in her lap, around the phone, fear mingling with doubt in her expression now. Had she suspected her son was helping to swindle the town? Or that he was capable of murder?

Jaxon's car door slammed, and he strode toward them.

"Sheriff Gandt," Jaxon said. "You are under arrest for the murder of Ron Lewis and for the attempted murder of Sage Freeport." He read the sheriff his rights.

Gandt reared his head, shock on his face. He hadn't known Sage had survived. "You have no evidence of any crime I've committed. I'm the law around here."

"As a matter of fact, Sage Freeport is alive and she will testify that you tied her into the barn and set fire to it."

Gandt's mother gasped, her expression reeking of

shock. "No, no…tell them, son, you didn't do those awful things."

"Lloyd Riley also claims that you blackmailed him into helping and ordered him to kill me," Dugan added.

"And speaking of evidence," Jaxon said, "I just got confirmation from ballistics that the bullet that killed Wilbur Rankins is the same caliber you use, so add on another murder charge." Jaxon took handcuffs from inside his jacket. "Put your hands behind you, Gandt."

Gandt shifted to the balls of his feet, jerking his hands as Jaxon grabbed his arms. "Mother, call Sherman, my lawyer," he snarled.

"No one is going to get you off," Dugan said. "Because you're going to pay for what you've done to Sage and to the people in this town."

Jaxon snapped the handcuffs around Gandt's wrists, then spun him back around. "Do you know what happened to Benji Freeport? Did you kill him, too?"

Gandt shook his head. "I told that woman he wasn't with Lewis. I have no idea where he is."

Dugan ground his molars. Gandt was already facing murder and attempted murder charges, along with fraud charges.

Why wouldn't he tell them where the boy was?

Because he really didn't know. Which meant they might never find Benji.

SAGE WOKE IN the hospital to find Dugan sitting by her bed. He looked worn out, his face thick with beard stubble, his eyes blurry from lack of sleep, his expression grim.

She broke into another coughing spell, and Dugan

handed her a glass of water and held the straw for her to drink. "What time is it?"

"About four in the morning. You okay?"

Was she? She'd nearly died. And she still didn't have her son back. "I'll live," she said softly.

A pained smile twisted at his lips. "I got Gandt. He's in jail."

Sage sighed and took another sip of water.

"He blackmailed Lloyd Riley into helping him and ordered him to kill me."

Sage's eyes flared with shock. "Did he tell you where Benji is?"

A darkness fell over Dugan's face, making her stomach tighten with nerves. "Dugan?"

"He claims he has no idea, that Benji wasn't with Lewis when he killed him."

Sage closed her eyes, hating the despair overwhelming her. She'd thought for certain that finding Ron's killer would lead them to her son.

"I won't give up," Dugan said in a gruff voice.

"But Carol Sue, the woman we thought might have Benji, is dead."

"True, but Sandra Peyton is still unaccounted for."

"I know. Thanks, Dugan." Her earlier ordeal weighed her down. Or maybe it was defeat.

Sage closed her eyes, willing sleep to take her away from the memory of Gandt leaving her in that burning barn.

And the reality that she still had to face another Christmas without her little boy.

DUGAN SETTLED ONTO the recliner beside Sage and watched her sleep. Although the danger was over for her, he couldn't bear to leave her alone tonight.

Not with knowing he'd failed to find Benji.

And not with images of her lying in that blazing fire, nearly dead, tormenting him. He could have lost her tonight.

Lost her? He'd never had her....

The realization that he cared so damn much that it hurt made him stand and pace to the window. Cobra Creek was quiet tonight.

The deputy would temporarily take over for Sheriff Gandt. Once the red tape was handled, the ranchers who'd been duped would get their land back.

But Sage was right back where she was when he'd decided to help her.

Making matters worse, Christmas was almost here. The image of that pitiful little Christmas tree with the unopened package under it taunted him.

Sage should have a full-size tree with dozens of gifts beneath it, and her little boy should be home making cookies with her and opening presents Christmas morning.

He considered buying her a gift, but nothing he could buy would make up for the void in her life that losing Benji had left.

She stirred, restless, and made a mewling sound in her throat, then thrashed at the covers. He soothed her with soft words, gently stroking her hair with one hand, until she calmed.

More than anything, he wanted to bring Benji back to her.

He'd never felt this emotional attachment before. This intense drive to please someone.

God...he was falling for her. Maybe he had been

from the moment she'd looked up at him with those trusting, green eyes.

But what was he going to do about it?

He couldn't tell her or pressure her. Sage had already suffered too much. And she was vulnerable.

Besides, why would she want him when he'd failed her?

He finally fell asleep in the chair but woke a couple of hours later when the nurse returned to take Sage's vitals. He stepped out for coffee and to grab some breakfast while they helped her dress.

By the time he returned, the doctor was dismissing her.

"I'll drive you home, Sage."

She thanked him but remained silent as the nurse wheeled her to the exit and on the drive home. When they arrived at the inn, the Christmas lights mocked him.

"Thank you, Dugan. I have to go shower and get out of these clothes. They stink like smoke."

She was right. Worse, they were probably a reminder of her near-death experience. He climbed out and walked her to the door.

"I can stay with you for a while if you want."

Sage shook her head, fumbling with the key as she tried to unlock the door. "I need to be alone."

Dugan took the keys from her and unlocked the door, not ready to leave her. He needed to hold her, to know that she was still alive and safe. That there might be hope for the two of them.

But she stepped inside and blocked the doorway. "Good night, Dugan."

Dugan reached up to take her hand, but she pulled it away and clenched the door edge.

"I'm not giving up, I will find Benji," Dugan said earnestly. Sandra Peyton might be the key.

She gave a small nod of acceptance, yet the light he'd seen in her eyes had faded. Damn, she'd lost hope.

The hope that had helped her survive the past two years.

She closed the door in his face, and Dugan cursed.

Maybe she didn't return the feelings he'd developed for her. But he'd be damned if he'd let her give up on her son.

SAGE WAITED UNTIL Dugan left, then walked to the kitchen for a glass of water. The Christmas tree with Benji's present sat on the table, looking as bare and lonely as she felt.

Dugan said he wasn't giving up.

But she was smart enough to realize that they'd reached a dead end. If Gandt didn't know where Benji was, who did?

Sandra Peyton.

The woman could be anywhere by now. If she'd taken Benji knowing Ron abducted him, she had probably gone into hiding.

Angry and frustrated and full of despair, she took the water to her bedroom and jumped in the shower. The hot spray felt heavenly as it washed away the stench of the smoke.

But the memory of Gandt coldly leaving her to die couldn't be erased so easily.

The silence in the house echoed around her, eerie and

lonely, as she dried off, pulled on a pair of pajamas and collapsed onto her bed.

Dugan's scent lingered, teasing her senses and making her body ache for his comforting arms and touch.

But she couldn't allow herself to need him. She had to stand on her own.

The only thing she wanted right now was the little boy who'd stolen her heart the day he was born.

She had nothing to give to a man like Dugan. A man who deserved so much more than a broken woman like her.

Chapter Twenty-Three

Christmas Eve

Dugan had called Sage several times the past two days, but she had cut him off. Not that she hadn't been polite. She'd made it clear that if he learned anything new about her son, he should call her.

But she obviously didn't want a personal relationship with him.

Because he'd let her down. He'd promised to bring her son home and he hadn't, and she would never forgive him.

He let Hiram and his other two hands go early so they could spend Christmas Eve with their families.

Dugan would spend another one alone.

Normally the holidays meant nothing. Being alone didn't bother him. He loved his land and his work and his freedom.

He didn't know how to be part of a family.

So why did his chest have a sharp pain to it because he wasn't spending the night with Sage? Why couldn't he stop thinking about her, wondering what she was doing, if she was baking for Christmas dinner, if the inn smelled like cinnamon, if she was lighting a candle for her son, in hopes that it would bring him back to her?

Dammit.

He rode back to the stables, dismounted and brushed down his favorite horse, then stowed him in his stall. Just as he walked across the pasture toward his house, his cell phone buzzed.

Hoping it was Sage, he snatched it up, but Jaxon's voice echoed back.

"Dugan here."

"That reporter, Ashlynn Fontaine, called. Said she got another tip from that tip line."

Dugan's pulse jackknifed. "Tell me about it."

"This woman claims she thinks she's seen Benji, that she works with this waitress named Sandy Lewis, who has a little boy named Jordan. When she saw the news report, she realized Jordan was the spittin' image of Benji."

Sandy Lewis—Sandra Peyton Lewis? "What's the address?"

"I'm texting it to you now."

Dugan ended the call and referred to the text. He had to check this lead out. But the last time he'd taken Sage with him, it had been nearly devastating for her.

This time he'd go alone.

If Jordan turned out to be Benji and he recovered the little boy, he'd surprise her. If not, she would never know.

SAGE FORCED HERSELF out of bed each day, but the depression that seized her was nearly as paralyzing as it was the first few weeks after Benji disappeared.

She had to face the fact that she might never see her son again.

Could she bear to go on without him?

The women's group at church surprised her by stopping by with baked goods Christmas Eve morning. She had joined the group two months after Benji disappeared because she'd woken up one day with no desire to live.

It had scared her to think that she might do something crazy like take her own life. Worse, if she did and Benji was found, she wouldn't be around to take care of him.

That day had driven her to ask for help, and she'd gone to the church seeking solace and prayer. She had found it, both with the pastor and the women who'd embraced her and revitalized her spirit with their positive thinking and compassion.

Today she felt as if she'd regressed. They must have sensed it, because the coffee and goodies were simply a backdrop to let her talk.

She hugged them all goodbye and thanked them for coming, then waved as they hurried to their cars. Five women with five different backgrounds and lives. Families of all sorts. Troubles of their own.

But they had come to her when she needed emotional support the most.

Wiping at tears, she cleaned up the kitchen and stored the tins of cookies on the kitchen bar, setting them out as she would for Benji. The Christmas plate with reindeer on it awaited the cookies and milk they would have left for Santa.

The women had reminded her of the candlelight service at six, and she had promised she would attend. Determined to keep herself from spiraling downward, she spent the afternoon wrapping the presents she'd bought for the children's hospital and the women's shelter, then stacked them all in her car to carry to the church.

A group would disperse them in the morning to make sure that children in need had Christmas, like all the other kids in the world.

She had volunteered last year. Maybe she'd go this year, as well.

Anything to help her get through the long, lonely day.

Her mind turned to Dugan and the numerous calls he'd made. She wanted to see him, missed him in a way she'd never expected to.

And not just because he'd been helping her.

Because he'd stood by, solid and strong. He was handsome, sexy, protective, honorable. He owned and worked his own ranch, but he also worked search-and-rescue missions for strangers.

All qualities Ron and Trace had never possessed.

But Dugan deserved someone who could love and take care of him, not an empty shell of a woman who had to force herself to get out of bed to face the day.

DUGAN FOUND SANDY'S HOUSE fifty miles from Cobra Creek. It was a nondescript wooden house with a fenced yard, a swing set in the back and a gray minivan in the drive.

At first glance, it appeared to be homey. Christmas lights twinkled from the awnings, a handmade wreath garnished the front door and a tree complete with trimmings was visible through a picture window. A bike with training wheels sat in the front yard, and a soccer ball had been left in the driveway.

Was this woman simply a mother or a kidnapper?

He was just about to climb out when the front door

opened, and a woman stepped outside, pulling a rolling suitcase. She wore sunglasses and a scarf and seemed to be in a hurry. She glanced up and down the street, opened the back of the minivan and tossed her suitcase inside, then shut the door.

She rushed back to the house and seconds later, emerged with a little boy in tow, a jungle backpack slung over his shoulder. Dugan sat up straighter to get a better look. The kid was the right size, but he was wearing a baseball cap, and Dugan couldn't see his face.

She tugged the boy's hand, but he drew back, and she stooped down and appeared to be reprimanding him. The boy dropped his head, allowing her to lead him to the van.

Dugan almost interceded then. It looked as though Sandy was getting ready to take a trip. Had Gandt's arrest spooked her enough to run?

Deciding she might be meeting up with an accomplice, he waited until she backed from the drive, then followed her. He kept his distance, and maintained a steady speed so as not to alarm her.

A half hour later, she turned into the bus station. Dugan parked a couple of spaces from her and watched to see if she was meeting someone. She climbed out, looking over her shoulder and all around the parking lot as if she feared someone was after her.

Seemingly satisfied, she retrieved her suitcase, then pushed open the boy's door and helped him from the van. After kneeling to speak to him, she took his hand and ushered him toward the bus station.

Dugan didn't intend to let her get away.

He strode toward the entrance and caught up with her

just as she stepped up to the ticket counter. The boy kept his head down, and she had a death grip on his hand.

"I need one adult and one child's ticket to New Mexico." She fished out ID and a wad of cash.

"You're not going anywhere, Miss Peyton," Dugan said in a low voice near her ear. "Not until you answer some questions."

She gasped and turned around, wide-eyed. "Who are you?"

"A friend of Sage Freeport."

Her face paled, and she tried to tug her arm from his grip, but he held her firmly. "Now, unless you want me to pull my gun and make a scene here, do as I say."

She stilled, and he saw her glance at the boy in panic. The little guy made a frightened sound, which ripped at Dugan's heart.

"It's okay, son. I'm not here to hurt you." He hated to scare him, but if the child was Sage's son, he was saving the boy. He nudged the woman. "Walk back outside to your van."

She darted furtive looks around her as if she was debating whether or not to scream for help, but he opened his jacket enough to reveal his gun, and she sucked in a breath and headed toward the van. When they reached it, he ordered her up against the door.

"Please don't hurt my son," she cried.

"I'm not here to hurt him," Dugan said, intentionally lowering his voice to calm the kid, who looked as if he might bolt any second.

"Then what do you want? I have some cash—"

"This is not a robbery." Dugan gestured toward the boy, who had huddled up against her with his head buried in her stomach. "I'm here because of Benji."

Her eyes flared with panic, and the boy suddenly whipped his head around.

Dugan stooped down to his eye level and reached for the boy's hat. "Are you Benji Freeport?"

"His name is Jordan," the woman cried. "He's my son."

The hat slid off to reveal a head of choppy, blondish hair and eyes that looked familiar.

Sage's deep green eyes.

Remembering Sage said he had an extra piece of cartilage in his ear, he lifted the boy's hat. Yes. Just like the picture.

"You are Benji, aren't you, son?"

The boy fidgeted but didn't respond.

Dugan removed a photo that Sage had given him of the two of them from his pocket and showed it to him. "This woman, Sage, she's my friend. She wanted me to find you. She's your real mother, and she's been looking for you ever since you disappeared two years ago."

The boy's face crumpled. "Mama?"

"Yes," Dugan said softly. "Your mama loves you, and she misses you and wants you to come home."

Benji angled his head toward Sandra Peyton, his look sharp with accusations. "You said she didn't want me anymore."

Dugan's pulse hammered.

"She didn't, but I wanted you." Sandra's chin quivered, and she began to cry. "I love you, Jordan. I'm your mama now."

The boy looked confused, his gaze turning back to Dugan. "Sage is your mother," Dugan said. "And she never gave you up, never told this woman she could have you." He kept his voice gentle. "She loves you so much. She's kept your Christmas tree up with your presents under it, just waiting on you to come back and open them."

Benji's little face contorted with anguish.

"Do you remember what happened, Benji? A man named Ron Lewis took you one morning...."

Tears pooled in his eyes, but Benji nodded as if the memory was slowly returning.

A strangled sound came from Benji's throat. "He took me to the river and told me to go with her."

Dugan glared at Sandra. "You and Lewis were a couple. You planned the kidnapping together."

Sandra broke down in tears. "I loved Ron and he loved me. We hadn't seen each other since I had that miscarriage. But he called me one day and said he was about to make a big windfall, and that he wanted us to be a family." Her voice broke. "But I couldn't get pregnant again."

Disgust churned inside Dugan. "So Lewis cozied up to Sage so he could get to know Benji?"

She wiped at tears. "He didn't want Benji to be afraid when he left with him, so he got to know him. And it would have worked, too. We would have all been together if someone hadn't killed Ron."

Dugan punched Jaxon's number. "I have Sandra Peyton and Benji Freeport at the bus station. I need backup."

As soon as Jaxon arrested Sandra, he'd take Benji home to Sage, where he belonged.

SAGE LET HERSELF into the inn, grateful for her friends who'd convinced her to attend the service. Of course, when they'd lit candles, turned off the church lights and sung "Silent Night" in the candlelight, she remembered the joy on Benji's face as he'd held his candle up, and she nearly collapsed in tears.

The Christmas lights twinkled as she flipped on the light switch, and the scent of cinnamon and apples swirled toward her from her earlier baking.

Maybe she'd take the baked goods to the seniors' center in the morning. She couldn't stand the thought of eating cinnamon rolls by herself. She twisted the locket, her heart thumping. She thought she'd gotten accustomed to being alone, but tonight she ached for Benji.

Dugan's face flashed in her mind, and she wondered where he was tonight. He hadn't mentioned any family.

Was he still looking for Benji, or had he given up?

She dropped her keys in the ceramic pot on the table by the door, then decided to light the candles in the kitchen and living room.

She had just poured herself a glass of wine and started to play her collection of Christmas music when a knock sounded at the door. Probably someone else from church, checking on her.

She hurried to the front door, prepared to assure her visitor that she was fine, but Dugan stood on the other side.

He looked so utterly handsome that her knees nearly buckled.

"Sage, I had to see you."

The urgency in his tone sent a streak of panic through her. "Is something wrong?"

"No." A small smile tugged at his mouth, and his eyes were sparkling, making him look even more handsome. Come to think of it, she'd never seen him smile. "I have a present for you," he said gruffly.

Sage twisted the locket again. "You didn't need to get me anything."

"Yes, I did. I made you a promise, and I keep my

promises." Then he stepped to the side, and Sage's heart went wild as she saw the little boy beside him.

Emotions choked her. After two years, she'd been afraid she wouldn't recognize her son when she saw him again, but she instantly knew him.

Dugan had kept his promise. He had found Benji.

She dropped to her knees, soaking in the sight of him, desperate to pull him into her arms. But he looked hesitant, frightened, wary.

"Benji?"

She glanced up at Dugan, needing answers.

"Lewis took him to Sandra Peyton. He's been living with her for the past two years."

Sage wiped at the tears streaming down her face.

"She told him that you gave him up," Dugan said almost apologetically, "that you didn't want him anymore."

"Oh, God…" Pain rocked through Sage. Her poor little boy thought she'd abandoned him.

She took Benji's hands in hers and gave him a smile. She had to convince him she'd always loved him. "Benji, I never gave you up. I would never do that." She brushed at a tear. "One morning I got up, and Ron had taken you without telling me. I called the police, I called the news station, we put the story on TV, I did everything I could to find you."

He had grown taller and lost some of his chubby baby fat, but his eyes were just as bright and sweet. "I love you so much, Benji. I prayed every day that I'd find you."

He lifted his chin, big tears in his eyes. "Mommy?"

"Yes, sweet boy. I'm your mommy." She nearly sobbed at the feel of his tiny palm in hers. "Come on, I want to show you something."

She led him into the kitchen and showed him the tabletop tree, leaving Dugan in the foyer. "Remember when you used to decorate this for your room? It was your own tree."

His eyes widened as he stared at it. Then she pointed out the presents with his name on them. "This one in Santa paper was the gift I bought for you the year you disappeared. Do you remember it? You were only three, but you shook it every day and tried to guess what was in it."

He wrinkled his forehead as if he was trying to recall the memory.

"I bought this one in the snowman paper for you last year," she said as she gestured toward another package. "And this one wrapped in reindeer paper this year, because I was hoping I'd find you and you'd come home."

He looked torn as if he wanted to believe her but was still on the verge. She hated Sandra Peyton for what she'd done to him, for lying to him.

Then she had an idea. "Let me show you your room. I kept it just the way it was."

She led him up the stairs and to his bedroom, the room she hadn't changed since he left. Inside, she walked over to the bed and picked up the special blanket he'd slept with and held it out to him. "See, I saved your blankie. I knew one day that you'd come home."

His little chin wobbled as tears filled his eyes. "Mommy?"

"Yes, baby, I've missed you so much." She opened her arms, and he fell into them, his tears mingling with hers as they savored the reunion.

Chapter Twenty-Four

By the time, Sage and Benji came back downstairs, Dugan was gone. A pang of disappointment tugged at her. He obviously felt as if he'd done his job and had gone home.

But she missed him, anyway.

Still, her son was finally home. It was the day she'd been waiting for. And soothing Benji's fears and re-building his trust were the only things that mattered tonight.

They spent the evening making sugar cookies and talking about the past. At times they were both sad, but she tried to help him focus on the fact that they were together again, and he was safe.

Much to her relief, Benji indicated that Sandra had been good to him, had been patient and played with him and read him stories.

Of course, they'd moved around a lot. Sandra had probably known that one day the truth would catch up with her.

Sage fought against the bitterness eating at her. She was grateful Sandra had loved Benji, but the woman had stolen all that time and precious memories from her.

And Benji had suffered the trauma.

But focusing on the past they'd lost would only keep

her from enjoying the future, so she vowed to let go of the bitterness.

She read him Christmas stories and tucked him in, then watched him fall asleep, soaking in his features.

When she crawled in bed that night, she was happier than she'd been in ages. She and Benji were a family again.

But there was one thing missing.

Dugan.

She sat up, her heart stuttering. Oh, goodness.

While she'd been guarding her heart and looking for her son, she'd fallen in love with Dugan.

What was she going to do about it?

Did Dugan have feelings for her?

DUGAN MISSED SAGE like crazy. But she needed time to reunite with her son. Not pressure from him.

But when he rose Christmas morning and combed his ranch house, the deafening silence got to him. He couldn't help imagining Benji running down to find Santa's presents and Sage making breakfast for the two of them.

Work and the land had always been his first loves.

But his life felt empty now.

He suddenly felt antsy and had to get out. A ride across his ranch would do him good, help him clear his head, pass some time and take his mind off the woman who'd stolen a piece of his soul the past few days. And her kid, who'd won his heart the minute he laid eyes on him.

He combed the property, examining fences in case they needed mending, then checking livestock. Hiram and his other two hands had done a good job taking care of things while he worked the case. Now it was time for him to get back to it.

By the time he reached the farmhouse, his stomach

was growling. He had nothing in the house to cook, certainly no holiday dinner.

Maybe he'd drive into town for a burger. That is, if the diner was open. Most folks were home with family today.

He guided his horse up to the house, slowing when he saw Sage's car. What was she doing here?

His heart began to race. He steered the horse to the rail and dismounted, then saw Sage and Benji sitting in the porch swing. Sage had her arm slung around Benji, and he was leaning into her as they rocked the swing back and forth.

It was the most beautiful sight he'd ever seen.

His heart took a funny leap, his mind roaring down a dangerous path. What would it be like to have a family to come home to?

To have Benji and Sage in his life forever?

Sage looked up at him with a tentative smile, but Benji vaulted up and leaned over the porch rail. "Your horse is cool, Mr. Dugan."

Gone was the traumatized kid from the night before. One night at home with his mother had the boy smiling and at ease.

"Thanks. If your mama agrees, I'll take you riding sometime."

Sage stood, walked to the rail and leaned over it, then looked down at him. "Maybe you can take us both out?"

The subtle question in her eyes made him smile. Was she flirting with him?

"Maybe I will," he said with a wink.

She laughed softly in response, and he realized she *was* flirting.

One night with her son had erased the shadows and pain from her eyes.

Benji ran down the steps. "Can I pet him?"

"Sure." Dugan showed him how to gently rub the horse's mane.

"We brought dinner for you," Sage said. "That is, if you don't have plans."

Dugan met her gaze. "That was real nice of you."

She walked down the steps and rubbed a finger along his arm. "It wasn't nice. I missed you, Dugan."

He liked this side of her. He angled his head, heat sizzling between them. And something more. An attraction that went far beneath the surface. He admired her. Liked her.

Loved her.

"I missed you, too," he said in a gruff voice.

For a brief moment, his breath stalled as he waited on her to make the next move.

Finally she lifted a finger to his lips. "Did you?"

A grin split his face. She was fishing for a compliment? "Yes." He suddenly couldn't help himself. That big rambling farmhouse needed her and Benji in it.

He yanked her up against him. "I'm in love with you, Sage."

Her eyes sparkled as she looped her arms around his neck. "Good, 'cause I'm in love with you, too."

Then she rose on her tiptoes, closed her lips over his and kissed him. Dugan had never felt anything so sweet, so wonderful.

And suddenly he knew what being in a family was like. He would make one with Sage and Benji, and he would never let them go.

* * * * *

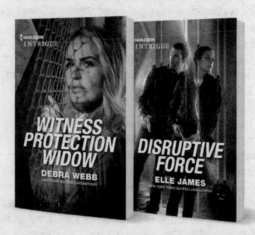

Chapter One

Maintaining a white-knuckle grip on the steering wheel while negotiating the treacherous curves up Prescott Mountain on his daily commute was typical for Ryland Beck. *Smiling* while he resolutely refused to look toward the steep drop on the other side of the road *wasn't* typical. Nothing, not even his phobia of heights, could dampen his enthusiasm this chilly October morning. Today he'd begin his investigation into a serial killer case that had gone cold over four years ago.

Bringing down the Smoky Mountain Slayer was the challenge of a lifetime. No suspects. No DNA. No viable behavioral profile. In spite of the lack of evidence, Ryland was determined to put the killer behind bars. He wanted to give the families of the five victims the answers and justice they deserved.

Unfortunately, what he couldn't give them was closure. Closure, as he well knew, was a fictional construct. The death of a loved one would always leave a gaping hole in the hearts and lives of those left behind. But knowing the victim's murderer had been caught and punished would go a long way toward making the excruciating grief more bearable.

He continued winding his way up the mountain toward UB headquarters as he considered the limited information he'd found on the internet about the killings. The Slayer's modus operandi was consistent: all of his victims were strangled, their bodies dumped in the woods in Monroe County. But aside from them being young women, the victimology was all over the place. Their educational and economic backgrounds varied, as did their ethnicity. Some were married, some weren't. Some had children, some didn't. All of that made it nearly impossible to build a useful profile to help figure out who'd murdered them.

The detectives from the Monroe County Sheriff's Office had deemed the case unsolvable. But here in Gatlinburg, Ryland had a unique advantage: an über-wealthy boss who knew firsthand the suffering a victim's family endured when a murder case went cold.

Seven years after his wife was killed and his infant daughter went missing, Grayson Prescott had given up on the stagnant police investigation. He decided to create a cold case company called Unfinished Business. Just a few months later, UB had solved the case. Now, the thirty-three counties of the East Tennessee region had formed a partnership with UB and were clamoring for them to work their cold cases.

Don't miss
Serial Slayer Cold Case *by Lena Diaz,*
available March 2022 wherever
Harlequin books and ebooks are sold.

Harlequin.com